Sexual Visuality from Literature to Film, 1850–1950

Palgrave Studies in Nineteenth-Century Writing and Culture

General Editor: **Joseph Bristow**, Professor of English, UCLA

Editorial Advisory Board: **Hilary Fraser**, Birkbeck College, University of London; **Josephine McDonagh**, Linacre College, University of Oxford; **Yopie Prins**, University of Michigan; **Lindsay Smith**, University of Sussex; **Margaret D. Stetz**, University of Delaware; **Jenny Bourne Taylor**, University of Sussex

Palgrave Studies in Nineteenth-Century Writing and Culture is a new monograph series that aims to represent the most innovative research on literary works that were produced in the English-speaking world from the time of the Napoleonic Wars to the *fin de siècle*. Attentive to the historical continuities between 'Romantic' and 'Victorian', the series will feature studies that help scholarship to reassess the meaning of these terms during a century marked by diverse cultural, literary, and political movements. The main aim of the series is to look at the increasing influence of types of historicism on our understanding of literary forms and genres. It reflects the shift from critical theory to cultural history that has affected not only the period 1800–1900 but also every field within the discipline of English literature. All titles in the series seek to offer fresh critical perspectives and challenging readings of both canonical and non-canonical writings of this era.

Titles include:

Dennis Denisoff
SEXUAL VISUALITY FROM LITERATURE TO FILM, 1850–1950

Laura E. Franey
VICTORIAN TRAVEL WRITING AND IMPERIAL VIOLENCE

Lawrence Frank
VICTORIAN DETECTIVE FICTION AND THE NATURE OF EVIDENCE
The Scientific Investigations of Poe, Dickens and Doyle

Sexual Visuality from Literature to Film, 1850–1950

Dennis Denisoff

First published 2004 by
PALGRAVE MACMILLAN
Houndmills, Basingstoke, Hampshire RG21 6XS and
175 Fifth Avenue, New York, N. Y. 10010
Companies and representatives throughout the world

PALGRAVE MACMILLAN is the global academic imprint of the Palgrave Macmillan division of St. Martin's Press, LLC and of Palgrave Macmillan Ltd. Macmillan® is a registered trademark in the United States, United Kingdom and other countries. Palgrave is a registered trademark in the European Union and other countries.

ISBN 1–4039–2163–6 hardback

This book is printed on paper suitable for recycling and made from fully managed and sustained forest sources.

A catalogue record for this book is available from the British Library.

Library of Congress Cataloging-in-Publication Data

Denisoff, Dennis, 1961–
    Sexual visuality from literature to film, 1850–1950/ Dennis Denisoff.
        p. cm. – (Palgrave studies in nineteenth-century writing and culture)
    Includes bibliographical references and index.
    ISBN 1–4039–2163–6
        1. English fiction–19th century–History and criticism. 2. Sex in literature. 3. Motion pictures–History. 4. Sex in motion pictures. I. Title.
II. Series.

PR878.S49D46 2004
791.43′6538–dc22   2003061327

10   9   8   7   6   5   4   3   2   1
13   12   11   10   09   08   07   06   05   04

Printed and bound in Great Britain by
Antony Rowe Ltd, Chippenham and Eastbourne

The pages of this book are warmed for me
by the love, affection, and support of Michael

Contents

List of Illustrations

The author and publishers have made every effort to trace the holders of copyright in the illustrations. If, inadvertently, any has been overlooked the publishers will be pleased to make the necessary arrangements at the first opportunity.

Acknowledgements

The research for this manuscript was funded extensively by a fellowship at Princeton University from the Social Sciences and Humanities Research Council of Canada, research grants from the SSHRCC and the Northeast Modern Languages Association, and research funding from the Department of English and the Faculty of Arts ˙at Ryerson University. I would like to express my gratitude to the staff at the Princeton University Rare Books Department, Robarts Library at the University of Toronto, the Ryerson University Library, the British Library, and the British National Portrait Gallery. I also wish to take this opportunity to thank the various people who discussed my work on this book with me, especially Henry Abelove, Joseph Bristow, Liz Constable, Holly Crumpton, Richard Dellamora, Diana Fuss, Jason Haslam, M. Morgan Holmes, Lilian Nayder, Liz Phillips, Matt Potolsky, Kathy Psomiades, Talia Schaffer, Elaine Showalter, Tony Spawforth, and my graduate students in visual culture and sexuality studies. I could not have asked for more helpful and patient editors than Paula Kennedy and Emily Rosser, and I would also like to thank the anonymous readers for Palgrave Macmillan.

Earlier versions of the first and second chapters appeared respectively in *Victorian Women Writers and the Woman Question* (ed. Nicola Diane Thompson, 1999) and *Reality's Dark Light: The Sensational Wilkie Collins* (eds Maria K. Bachman and Don Richard Cox, 2003). A version of the third chapter was first published in *Perennial Decay: On the Aesthetics and Politics of Decadence* (eds Liz Constable, Dennis Denisoff and Matthew Potolsky, 1999) and of the fourth chapter in *Women and British Aestheticism* (eds Talia Schaffer and Kathy Alexis Psomiades; Charlottesville, 1999).

Introduction: Unsightly Desires

Most people have an understanding of sexuality before they ever recognize experiencing it for themselves. Humans may have sexual experiences early in their lives, but they see sexualities and genders – that is, recognize them at a remove as opposed to as an uninvited sensation – only after learning languages of the body. Sex, in other words, is mediated and, even though our recognition of sex, sexuality, and gender at a distance may be seen as primarily visual, its manifestation is always the result of diverse discourses (visual, verbal, and so on) interacting and manipulating our ocular consumption of the body. Nicholas Mirzoeff refers to this system of signs in which depictions of the body occur as 'bodyscape'. 'In representation, the body appears not as itself', he explains, 'but as a sign. It cannot but represent both itself and a range of metaphorical meanings, which the artist cannot fully control, but only seeks to limit by the use of context, framing and style. ... At the same time, the corporal sign has very real effects upon the physical body, especially in regard to determining what is held to be "normal".'[1] In *Sexual Visuality*, I hope to clarify the way in which certain types of literature and film articulated notions of vision that impacted on possibilities of desire. The subject of my work, therefore, is not seeing *per se*, but more precisely visuality – a society's perceptions and representations, and the constructions of meaning arising in part from them.

When it comes to issues of sexuality, the visual artifacts that are most invested are those depicting humans, the predominant site of our desires. Portraiture has proven an especially illuminating genre in this regard because it is distinguished from the others by its central aim of rendering a *familiar* image of the human figure, an intent that enhances the emotional interaction between object and viewer.[2] Most scholars of Victorian visuality have noted general social tendencies to see visuality as rooted primarily in an essential morality or in scopic technologies. It is my contention, however, that a number of people wishing to contest traditional images of sex and gender did so by framing essentialist aspects of visuality through a verbal context. I have chosen to focus on texts in the Gothic and sensationalist traditions because they tend to emphasize the non-ocular elements of visuality; the texts' distortions of visual likenesses often destabilize fixed notions of gender and sexuality by bringing forward non-scopic media through which Western society has formed its sexual visuality. My interest is in the way in which individuals adapted especially familiar genres such as portraiture to encourage broader cultural visualizations of the new sex- and gender-based identities that arose from changes in taste, culture, and consumption. By demonstrating the presence of Victorian visuality in twentieth-century film, I also offer a revision to the dominant notions of innovation within the current sphere of visual culture studies.

Strategic visuality and the Victorians

The ubiquity and political complexity of nineteenth-century visuality is perhaps best reflected in the representations that had been hung on the walls of homes and institutions for centuries. To recognize the extension of portraiture's political rhetoric even into poor, rural communities, one need only look at William H. Snape's 1891 *The Cottage Home* (Fig. 1). The painting shows an elderly man reading at a table while a girl sits nearby. She may be listening, she may have nodded off, or she may have momentarily shut her eyes to enjoy the sunshine streaming through the window and past the geraniums on the cluttered window sill. Despite signs of financial straits, the over-all image is one of harmony and contentment. The walls of the cottage are covered with inexpensive visual reproductions, including a worn and tattered picture of Queen Victoria. Rather than implying a perfunctory attitude toward the matriarch, the shabbiness of the reproduction suggests a poignant devotion on the part of not only the country folk, but also the Queen herself, who gazes down benevolently on the domestic space.

Through the portrait of the cottagers, Snape allows the private individuals the privilege of visual space (however romanticized), while the scene also naturalizes what Michel Foucault has famously theorized as panoptic surveillance.[3] Snape's image of the Queen within *A Cottage*

Fig. 1 William H. Snape, *The Cottage Home* (1891)

Home – the watchful eye within such an innocuous, private space –
reinforces the omnipresence of national identity. By positioning her
likeness in the top center of the cottage's main wall, he implies a
harmony between the ruling order and rural society. The observing
monarch becomes a part of the other characters' identities, which
Snape has chosen to signify by the objects that surround them. The
ceiling of the humble abode consists of exposed boards and the floor is
covered in herbs, cats, and cleaning paraphernalia. With a realist attention to detail, Snape encourages the viewer to accept the veracity of the
scene, while he transmits a sustained aura of benevolence and control
on the monarch's part through the warm, honeyed tones that spread
over her subjects from the sunshine emanating from beneath her portrait. The spacial rhetoric of the visual artifact within Snape's painting
emphasizes the iconic power with which his audience would have
endowed the likeness. This everyday dynamic in which images entered

into relationships with people foreshadows our current popularized conceptualizations of cyberspace.[4] Moreover, through the portrait within his painting, the congenial context that Snape constructs for the viewer's visualization of Victoria's likeness offers a meta-textual display of the rhetoric of visuality. The text presents portraiture at a remove, inviting a reading not only of the Queen and her subjects but also of the politics of visualization as part of everyday life.

Snape's *Cottage Home* demonstrates the way in which the portrait, as a construct conventionally aimed at capturing a person's essence, is part of a media network that relies on harmonizing a belief in fundamental human traits with the essentialism underlying traditional notions of identity, selfhood, and perception. Portraiture is the intentional visual depiction of a likeness of a living or dead individual or group of individuals. Its main subjects are people for whom the intended audience had feelings. Due to this emotional interface, the genre has been especially subject to the moral burden of realism. Portraits have functioned in Western society as strangely 'living' authorities on human rights, obligations, and responsibilities. Like family members who eternally maintain the status quo and suggest that you do as well, they have operated as mediators of authority, crossing boundaries of class, gender, sex, privacy, health, and wealth. Seen as an aid in maintaining the dominant order, recognizable artistic representation helped reify inchoate identities and, in the process, naturalized seemingly ethical limits to desire and carnal pleasures.

Throughout the nineteenth century, most painters would have agreed that a realistic portrait is not the same thing as a scientific likeness. A principal aim of the artist was to bring the sitter's virtuous characteristics and values closer to the surface. As the Victorian photographer Julia Margaret Cameron declared, 'the portraitist had a moral obligation to reveal the inner spiritual qualities that ennobled mind and soul',[5] which could be done by 'combining the real and the ideal'.[6] The subterfuge, of course, had to remain most subtle, so portraiture took part in what Richard C. Sha, in his analysis of the sketch in British Romanticism, has called 'the artful rhetoric of denied rhetoricity' that makes a work more ideologically persuasive.[7] The aim was to encourage the viewer to read a likeness as a true representation of three things: the subject's physical image, the subject's virtues, and the moral conventions of the era in which the subject lived.

Portraitists also used the denied rhetoricity of the emotional interface, however, to fulfill sociopolitical aims. The politics are obscured by the strong interaction that the artefact mediates between subject and viewer. Mirzoeff articulates this blurring when he comments that the ancient and medieval world saw pictures 'not as presentations, artificial constructs seeking to imitate an object, but as being closely related, or even identical, to that object'.[8] As one of his own examples makes clear, the emotional morphing of a likeness into its subject continues to this day. He observes that recently a group of firefighters saw the Shroud of Turin as so empowered by Christ, whose image it is believed to bear, that they risked their lives to save it. It is probable that, throughout its history, portraiture has been recognized as having the power to evoke feelings from the viewer who senses some familiarity with the subject, whether it be a spiritual icon, a monarch, a political leader, a family member, or a lover. In Richard Brilliant's words, a portrait 'stimulates cognition with such force that the psychodynamics of perception interfere with the comprehension of the image as something different from the image of the actual person'.[9] This conflation is connected to what Hans-George Gadamer has called the 'occasionality' of a portrait – its function as an object referring to a human original as intended by the artist.[10] A likeness does not so much exist in the flux between image and original as it satisfies for the viewer some real need, desire, or habit that had previously been fulfilled by the actual subject. In the process, the genre defines a perceptual space where original and representation are indistinguishable. This virtual reality offered Victorians an effective context in which to reinforce the dominant image of their society as respectable, moral, and ordered.

During the nineteenth century, the increasing number of families with new wealth began to build private collections intended to signal their ownership of class and taste. Following a practice supported by the Queen, many had portraits done of themselves so as to intimate their exclusiveness and historical importance. When Great Britain's National Portrait Gallery was founded in 1856, the general public also gained access to hundreds of paintings that had formerly been the reserve of private collectors. Attending openings became a common middle-class outing, as suggested by George Bernard O'Neill's painting 'Public Opinion' (1863). The piece gently spoofs the experience by depicting a crush of viewers mobbing a single piece such that none of them have a decent view.[11] The interest of those less educated in the visual arts is more coarsely mocked in a number of cartoons in *Punch* magazine. Meanwhile, developments in popular journalism and reproductive techniques helped make portrait ownership common across most classes. The commercialization of photography, for example, spread the genre among the middle and working classes without infringing on a growing demand for oil paintings among the upwardly mobile. As with the wealthy, the middle class and those aspiring toward it used portraits as part of the symbolic system through which they formulated their identities. The interest in self-visualization is apparent in the fact that there were more portrait painters and miniaturists at this time than painters of landscapes, animals, or marine life, a pattern that was only enhanced by the arrival of photography.[12] The various forms of the genre – the intricate cameos and miniatures that the lovers of so many Victorian novels clutch to their chests; the family photos and inexpensive *cartes de visite*; the monumental depictions of Queen Victoria and other royalty that enforced the legitimacy of diverse social institutions – they all reflect the centrality of portraiture to the society's vision of its politics, industry, values, and desires.[13]

The increased importance of illustrations in newspapers and journals is matched in the influence of visual culture on everyday life only by the quick commercialization of photography. As Lynda Nead argues, in a summation of the influence of photography, print culture, and advertising on Victorian society, 'Culture had been revolutionised; it was public, visible and unavoidable, but was also powerful and potentially dangerous. For critics nostalgic for a slower and more containable world of high art, the commercial street culture of the 1850s and 1860s was an assault on the senses. Ugly images, poorly made, bombarded unsuspecting pedestrians from all directions.'[14] The dominant anxiety arising from the increased access to visual representations was that the producers of the material, in their attempt to attract buyers, were saturating the mainstream with a sensationalist excess that often transgressed into the obscene, while at the same time over-shadowing and gradually de-valuing the more ethical works produced within the higher cultural genres such as portraiture.

The impact of the democratization of portraiture itself through photography is effectively captured in *Punch* magazine's images of the *carte de visite*.[15] The *carte* was an inexpensive card that included the owner's image. It was a multi-purpose social tool used as a calling card, a business card, a love token, a gift, and even window advertising. Invented in the late 1850s by the French photographer André Disdéri and popularized in England by Queen Victoria, it was most common from roughly 1860 to 1880. According to Laurence Senelick, it became the pre-eminent form for portraiture by 1859, very soon after its invention, suggesting the speed with which fads of visual culture were able to spread at the time.[16] *Punch*'s spoofs of the *carte*, which make clear its familiarity across a broad demographic, also began soon after its introduction. These cartoons relied for their sources of humor primarily on vanity, ugliness, or heterosexual dalliance. While some wealthy consumers are portrayed in the cartoons, the vast majority of *Punch*'s illustrations depict the middle class. When the working class or poorer people are included, it is almost always to poke fun at the idea that individuals with such low status would desire to be represented at all.

This is the main joke, for example, in an anonymous and untitled piece published June 29, 1861. In the illustration, a street-side photographer, himself looking rather unkempt, tries to convince two scruffy workers to have their likenesses produced. A wall of samples can be seen in the background, signifying the crowd of individuals who has already made use of the service. Cramming shop windows with photographs, illustrations, and erotic or even obscene images had become common in London during the mid-Victorian period, offering a key source of suggestion for any passing citizen of the city. In 1858, an article in the *Daily Telegraph* condemned photographers whose 'doorjambs are hideous with frames filled with vilely-executed photographs of men and women, of squalid and repulsive appearance; the practitioners are ignorant, coarse, and clumsy in manipulation; and the result is a collection of faces and figures that reminds us of the Chambers of Horrors at Madame Tussaud's'.[17] The article goes on to criticize the sellers of these ugly wares as coarse, aggressive, and foul in their choice of language.

The butt of the joke in the *Punch* cartoon is not only the preposterous notion that the disheveled workers would want such a product, but also the class-blindness of the aggressive commercial entrepreneur who hawks his wares so indiscriminately. The aesthetic value of mechanical reproduction in the realm of portraiture had become a hotly contested issue. For both artistic painters and more commercial illustrators such as *Punch*'s own cartoonists, the cheap *carte de visite* photographer was seen to lack any real talent or skill, having not struggled sufficiently in learning his trade. While confirming that the *carte* was accessible to a broad class range, cartoons such as this one reflect the middle-class snobbishness that the magazine chose to reinforce. By the end of the 1880s, the *carte* had lost its popularity and was being produced primarily as a tacky source of entertainment at carnivals and sideshows. Once the genre had fallen out of favor, *Punch* no longer found any value in belittling it, and the cartoons eventually disappeared as well. The *carte de visite*'s quick saturation of the mass market and its diminishing cultural value confirms the effective systems of commodification active during the period.

A society's visual culture may, by definition, consist primarily of those producers, consumers, artefacts, and instruments distinctly concerned with sight, but it is also always making use of other media, senses, technologies, and epistemological frameworks.[18] Visuality is the physical and physiological process of seeing as it operates through these frameworks, what W.J.T. Mitchell calls a 'belief system'.[19] When Norman Bryson describes visuality as 'socially agreed description(s) of an intelligible world' or 'systems of visual discourse', he brings forward what visual culture studies has recognized as the sociopolitical production not just of objects but also of perception.[20] While this field of scholarship often addresses the impact of visuality on our understanding of the world in general, its main focus is on encoded artefacts such as portraits at which we are intended to look.

It is a common proposition in the field that developments in areas such as film, advertising, and computer technology have in the past hundred years endowed Western society with a self-reflexivity and hyper-awareness that has allowed for a more astutely politicized theorization of visuality. For this reason, visual culture studies has so far emphasized twentieth-century texts. As Snape's contextualizing painting of Queen Victoria's portrait demonstrates, however, nineteenth-century visuality was also characterized by self-awareness. But, while innovations do create ways of seeing, new perceptions are always first and immediately articulated through previous discourses, including non-visual ones. As Bryson has commented, 'when I learn to see socially, that is, when I begin to articulate my retinal experience with codes of recognition that come to me from my social milieu(s), I am inserted into systems of visual discourse that saw the world before I did'. The fact that recent theories of visuality are usually presented in application to recent texts and almost exclusively visual ones can be deleterious. In our eagerness to establish methods for understanding recent innovations, we risk obscuring the perceptual tools of past cultures.

Similarly, an exploration of visual culture from 1850 to 1950 such as mine must acknowledge its multimedia historical roots. Victorian society's method of understanding reality, for example, was too complex and required too broad a network of cultural reinforcement to have become a predominantly visual culture through the introduction of a single invention such as photography (which is usually described as the most important scopic invention of the era). Considering the impact of this technology specifically, Geoffrey Batchen argues that Western society's predominantly visual culture in fact arose from decades of innovations involved in trying to capture the unmediated image.[21] In *Fiction in the Art of Photography* (1999), Nancy Armstrong similarly describes mass visuality forming for more than a century before photography introduced realist imagery to society at large[22] and Kevin Z. Moore has pointed out that Victorian visuality is an extension of eighteenth-century developments such as engravings and etchings marked by 'entrepreneurial and scientific interest'.[23]

Visual culture studies for the past decade has been characterized by its promotion of the scholarly questioning of any hierarchization or developmental narrative including its own. Similarly, the field's use of theoretical approaches from various disciplines including cultural studies, discourse analysis, and rhetoric helps destabilize any claim to a separation between visual and other cultures. The field's recognition of such cross-influence is especially appropriate in light of the fact that a similar process takes place in the act of seeing itself. As Jennings, the hero of Sheridan Le Fanu's ghost story 'Green Tea' (1869), recognized over a century ago, 'They talk of the optic nerves, and of spectral illusions, as if the organ of sight was the only point assailable by the influences that have fastened upon me – I know better'.[24] While Jennings, being the Swedenborgian that he is, looks for a spiritual affect on his way of seeing, Le Fanu suggests that there are other crucial influences. In this regard, the author's views accord with current understandings of the impact of culture on the act of seeing. As numerous recent scholars have argued, when the light rays reflected from an object travel through the eyes, they encounter one's pre-established understanding of the outside world before one has a chance to make any sense of the data. John A. Walker and Sarah Chaplin explain that 'once signals have passed the retinas it no longer makes sense to speak of "the visual" in isolation. ... [I]nside the brain/mind visual information from the eyes merges with information arriving from the other senses, and with existing memories and knowledge, so that a synthesis occurs'.[25] Ella Shohat and Robert Stam have described the site of the encounter between light rays and knowledge as existing within a cultural framework. For them, the visual:

> never comes 'pure', it is always 'contaminated' by the work of other senses (hearing, touch, smell), touched by other texts and discourses, and imbricated in a whole series of apparatuses – the museum, the academy, the art world, the publishing industry, even the nation state – which govern the production, dissemination, and legitimation of artistic productions.[26]

Shohat and Stam's language accords with Mitchell's declaration in his 1994 study *Picture Theory* that, in painting, 'the notion of purity is invariably explicated as a purgation of the visual image from contamination by language and cognate or conventionally associated media. ... This sort of purity ... is both impossible and utopian, which isn't to dismiss it, but to identify it as an ideology, a complex of desire and fear, power and interest'.[27]

Armstrong has similarly argued for a historicized model of the rise of visuality's cultural authority that would see photography and realist fiction being mutually dependent in their development beginning in the 1850s: 'In order to be realistic, literary realism referenced a world of objects that either had been or could be photographed. ... Photography in turn offered up portions of this world to be seen by the same group of people whom novelists imagined as their readership.'[28] For Armstrong, 'the kind of visual description we associate with literary realism refers not to things, but to visual representations of things, representations that fiction helped to establish as identical to real things and people before readers actually began to look that way to one another and live within such stereotypes'.[29] The rise of realism in literature was not a result of an increased attention to the material world but a response to a proliferation of photographic images, 'a giddy expansion of referential possibilities'.[30] While the images were consumed as factual information, they in fact reflected a rhetoric that itself built on past discourses such as the conventions of landscape and portrait painting.

Jonathan Crary has made the argument most boldly, claiming that the common assertion of vision's centrality to twentieth-century culture 'no longer has much value or significance at all'.[31] In Crary's words, 'privileging the category of visuality runs the risk of ignoring the forces of specialization and separation that allowed such a notion to become the intellectually available concept that it is today. So much of what seems to constitute a domain of the visual is an *effect* of other kinds of forces and relations of power'. The visual cannot exist except as a combination of biological, mental, and cultural influences interacting to create coherent images. Thus Walker and Chaplin, as theorists of visual culture, recommend that visual and verbal signs be read in combination, because 'the dominant forms of communication are multimedia'.

If the visual is *always* more than simply rays, rods, and cones, what is it then that has lead a number of critics to conclude that Victorian culture is especially worthy of being defined as a mass visual culture?

During the nineteenth century, creations such as the diorama (1822); the stereoscope (1838) or – as Batchen defines it[32] – the first virtual reality machine; the heliograph, the first photographic process (1825);[33] the x-ray (1895); and film (1896) were all invented and became well known.[34] This bounty of ocular inventions alone, however, is not sufficient to demarcate Victorian culture as visual. Nor does the definition of this culture as visual necessarily mean that its members had ready access to most of these inventions, or that they looked at visual images more than read written text or relied on sound or another sense, or that they preferred or felt most entertained by visual images. Rather, to say that the Victorian era was defined by a visual culture is to say that the society developed a means of categorizing reality that relied primarily on visuality. As Martin Heidegger put it, the essence of the modern age arises as society developed 'a world picture', which 'does not mean a picture of the world but the world conceived and grasped as a picture'.[35] The growing dependence on sight for the dominant social structure also meant that people were looking more critically at the idea that it offered an unmediated sense of the essential ethical basis of humanity – a position underlying more than just the aesthetic theories of portraiture.

The desire for a direct correlation between sight and purity is rooted in a centuries-long tradition that endowed the sense with a spiritual even divine authority. John Ruskin argued that sight is 'absolutely spiritual',[36] and that talented artists have a unique sensibility arising from 'pure feelings of our moral nature' which is transferred into our 'physical perception of external objects'.[37] In this formulation, sight is inherently pure and moral, but it is tainted by the interpretations that individuals place upon it. Acknowledging the inevitable cultural contamination of perception, Ruskin argues that the greatest talent of painters is their ability to maximize the amount of unadulterated moral value that they transfer from external objects to canvas. The task is even greater than this because the artist must also encourage the viewers to allow their perception to be over-ridden by the artwork, with its maximization of unadulterated morality.

Ruskin accepted that photography may be utterly unburdened by mental interpretation, but this proved of little relevance because, for him, it did not have access to our moral nature in the first place. The truth captured by a camera is uselessly amoral because humans, as sentient beings, can never have the mechanical experience of a camera. According to Moore, however, many members of Ruskin's society did allow the conflation of visual and spiritual purity to transfer into the realism of mechanical representation as well:

> The Victorians saw themselves as moral people, and they related morality to accuracy of representation. There is nothing particularly moral about 'the spiritual in art'. Indeed, the spiritual in art often encourages the decadent in life. Yet there is always something morally telling about a photograph, even if only to say by picturing: 'Here are people like us; we share the common bond of a potential for non-being'. The point is that the Victorians were most moral, not in their various pontifications about morality, but in their commitment to realism as accuracy, the source of evidence, justice, and truth in any society wishing to establish itself as civil.[38]

Moore is in accord with Ruskin's formulation when he suggests that the spiritual dimension of sight is unattainable for most people. But, as Moore notes, the masses still required confirmation of their moral views and they found it in the realism supported by mechanical representation. The rise of realism during the Victorian era reflects a society 'captivated by "virtual reality" machines and accurate information gathering', one that 'embraced optical inventions and the more realist realities they could picture' and that 'desire[d] ... accuracy of representation and its corollary, precision of information transmitted precisely'.[39] In *Techniques of the Observer*, Crary points out that, during the nineteenth century, developments in science and technology combined with a growing reliance on these fields for a sense of social coherence, the result of which was a greater uncertainty that sight did offer an immediate, true transmission of the outside world. The age of realism was marked by an increasing skepticism of sight itself. Victorians' scrutiny of vision revealed its reliance on a biological, physiological, and cultural network that cast a strong shadow of doubt over the characterization of vision as pure and unmediated.

Moore describes Victorians as 'captivated by "virtual reality" machines'. They 'embraced optical inventions', he tells us, and 'desire[d] ... accuracy of representation'. With all this captivating, embracing, and desiring going on, it seems inevitable that some people would begin to feel smothered by the drive for one true value system; it follows that they would search for a means of escaping being put under the microscope. Which Victorians would have been made uncomfortable by this love affair with realist visuality and the rhetoric of morality that it reinforced? Which Victorians were unwilling – or felt themselves unable – to forego what Moore calls 'the decadent in life'? And how might they have effectively undermined the naturalized moral authority of visuality that impinged on their desires?

A recognition of vision's subjectivity is a first move toward understanding the way in which individuals attracted by such epistemological partiality might actually use this knowledge for personal or collective maneuverability around notions of sexuality and gender. Is it even possible for one to step to the side of the system of representation that conditions our perceptions in order to make the inconceivable visible? I am not interested in the possibility of an original catalyst for this process of enculturation but in gaining a clearer sense of literature and film's involvement in it. One of the questions in the background of the following chapters is whether the desire for change can manifest within one's culture what was previously not visible. To approach the issue from a different direction, if what is called 'the unsightly' is that which a society *refuses* to look at, then it already exists to be seen, but how did it attain visibility within such a hostile environment? In part, if the control that characterizes any dominant way of seeing fosters its own anxieties, then these anxieties themselves help fabricate the unsightly.[40] In this formulation, visualization arises through a desire *not* to see. This is also basically the logic behind the notion that the heteronormative relies on the articulation of marginalized genders and sexualities as the Other that establishes its own legitimacy and authority. The argument, however, also suggests that the unsightly would in turn have its own anxieties and foster its own counter-visualizations. Would it not also foster the alteration of epistemological models and visual discourses?

This notion is akin to Foucault's description of a reverse discourse, where homosexuality, in his example, 'began to speak in its own behalf, to demand that its legitimacy of "naturality" be acknowledged, often in the same vocabulary, using the same categories by which it was medically disqualified'.[41] There is no real distinction between 'the dominant' and 'the reverse' in this model, as Foucault notes; discourses can circulate 'without changing their form from one strategy to another, opposing strategy'.[42] What we have is 'a multiple and mobile field of force relations, wherein far-reaching, but never completely stable, effects of domination are produced'. Despite Foucault's acknowledgment of malleability, instability, and tactical maneuvering, his articulation implies that the marginalized sexuality is always reliant on the ability of the hegemony to put forward a new discourse in the first place. In response, theorists such as David Bergman, Judith Butler,

Marjorie Garber, and Eve Kosofsky Sedgwick have developed ways of understanding sexualities and gender configurations that do not necessarily arise in reaction against (and thus through a reliance on) the oppression or anxiety of a dominant model.[43] In *Aestheticism and Sexual Parody* (2001), I put forward such an argument with regard to critics and parodists' interface with the dandy-aesthetes and the Aesthetic Movement in general. As I argue there, the rhetoric of aesthetics as a philosophy for a way of life offered Victorians such as Vernon Lee, Walter Pater, and Oscar Wilde a relatively safe, established terminology for discussing desires that was not reliant on an institutionalized, demonizing discourse. Developments in visual culture during the nineteenth century similarly had a crucial impact on the formation of sexualities and genders through language that did not always assume a male, heteronormative omnipresence.

Constructed over centuries as honestly speaking the true moral character of their subjects, portraits offered a convincing grounding for the exploration of the unsightly. The conventional paintings of mainstream culture were met by the mutable counterparts that sprung forth from literature – sighing, sneering, leering, bleeding, aging, cross-dressing, or spontaneously combusting. The first of these in the Gothic tradition appears in Horace Walpole's *Castle of Otranto* (1767), where a picture of an ancient relative communicates his frustration with the actions of his living descendent Manfred. While Manfred frenetically concocts schemes of imprisonment and rape in order to ensure himself an heir, the painting – coming across as comically blasé – sighs heavily, shakes his head, and shuffles out of the room. It is as if the likeness finds it too easy to judge and discard the villain. Walpole's animate painting seems unimpressed with its own ability to use its significatory import to influence the actions and beliefs of humans. It also offers a beautifully concise image of portraiture's cultural powers – its ability to stand for the values of fixed traditions and inheritance, on one hand, and malleability, seduction, and deviance, on the other. The gallery of unlike likenesses that followed Walpole's image down the corridors of Gothic tradition helped popularize the idea that identities were not fixed but could be challenged and refashioned. That said, the amazingly different applications that writers and directors found for visual art make it all the more notable that they appear to have agreed that the sexual and gender dynamics of identity formation were inculcated in an especially effective manner through a visuality found in the genre of portraiture. Taking advantage of the oscillation between image and reality encouraged by the psychodynamics and occasionally of conventional portraiture, these authors defamiliarized the genre in order to frame their own notions of personal identity and to exhibit concerns over their displacement.

My study of the role of Gothic and sensationalist texts in the construction of sexual visuality begins by considering some of the issues that would have been on the minds of the producers themselves. The first two chapters therefore consider the relation of visuality to economics and the gender of the artist – first as a distinction between women and men, and then as one within the masculine gender. Addressing Geraldine Jewsbury's *The Half Sisters* (1848), Dinah Mulock Craik's *Olive* (1850), and Mary Elizabeth Braddon's *Lady Audley's Secret* (1862), the first chapter introduces the familiar view that men were better suited than women to artistic professions. It analyses the way in which this position led society to envision a woman who attempted to infiltrate the hegemony as a sexually deviant, masculine threat. As the chapter demonstrates, however, Jewsbury, Craik, and Braddon all tried to harmonize this image of women with that of artists through extended considerations of a woman-centered economy of art and attraction. In the following chapter, I consider Wilkie Collins's portrayal of ideal artists in *Hide and Seek* (1854), *The Woman in White* (1869), and *The Law and the Lady* (1873). Putting the conservative image of the hard-working, bourgeois, male painter on a pedestal seemed not to be enough for the author, who also worked to lower the image of other manly identities. He disputes the cultural and economic productivity of the art patron, while depicting the man whose physicality is most boldly scripted on the body as exposing an emasculating lack of self-control. A focus on Collins's descriptions of these categories of manliness demonstrates that he used visuality to relegate traditional signifiers of authority such as financial and physical strength to the sexually deviant margins and, in the process, accentuated and possibly even exacerbated the actual volatility of the mid-Victorian manly identities.

Having addressed novelists' sexualized visualizations of the artist, I turn in the central two chapters to an exploration of explicit depictions of deviance and portraits. While such images seem an obvious starting point for my project, I have found that their focus on the genre itself also offered the best opportunities for articulating some of the more nuanced elements of my argument. In Chapter 3, I address *The Picture of Dorian Gray* (1890, 1891), the most famous example of portraiture in literary visualizations of sexuality. Throughout the past decade, queer scholars explored the homoerotics filtered through the eponymous portrait of Oscar Wilde's novel. My discussion, however, moves the visuality of the literature into Wilde's social milieu. Opening with an analysis of two photographic portraits – one of Wilde and his boyfriend Bosie, the other of Bosie's litigious father and his bicycle – the chapter demonstrates the difficulty in distinguishing between Wilde's and Queensberry's everyday self-presentation, while also nevertheless revealing the aesthete's revisionary trace. Turning to Queensberry's poem *The Spirit of the Matterhorn* and the 1891 edition of Wilde's novel, the codes of portrait painting presented in the men's photographs are then used to shed light on the importance of visuality to the formation of decadent identities based on the interaction of sexuality, culture, and commerce.

The fourth chapter returns to the issue of a woman-centered economy with which *Sexual Visuality* opens, but the emphasis shifts toward the economy of desire. My claim is that Vernon Lee's ghost story 'Oke of Okehurst' (1892) and Virginia Woolf's equally supernatural novel *Orlando: A Biography* (1928) both imbue visual art with a feminist aesthetics that allowed them to take perceptual conventions that hindered self-expression and reconfigure them into tools of contestation for women who wished to articulate their unsanctioned emotional needs and desires. Indeed, as I demonstrate, the visual photographs interspersed through *Orlando* construct a counter-narrative to the verbal text. It is neither the verbal nor the visual but their interaction that produces a positive identity defined in part by same-sex female attraction.

The one question that loomed larger and larger over this project as it progressed was what would happen to Victorian sexual visuality once film overtook the novel as the dominant genre of popular culture. As the final two chapters suggest, the sexual visuality articulated through the novel changed but nevertheless maintained its potency into the twentieth century, with the mass visuality stimulated by the mainstreaming of cinema remaining heavily invested in the rhetoric and strategies found in Gothic and sensation fiction. My penultimate chapter analyzes a notion of masculinity related to but in large degree independent of sex and sexuality as it operates in Daphne du Maurier's novel *Rebecca* and Alfred Hitchcock's adaptation of the novel. My principal argument is that the visual culture that developed during the nineteenth century supports both a model of manliness defined by self-restraint and conservatism and another defined by boyish adventurousness. By disengaging the personae from a specific sex, the author reveals that the haunting found in so much portrait literature has been conceived as fantastic only because the spectral personae have been forced to cohere onto sex-based identities. As my consideration of gender ambiguity in du Maurier's *Rebecca* demonstrates, nineteenth-century visuality haunts twentieth-century literature and film as an inescapable inheritance.

The final chapter turns to film in order to consider more directly the way in which the ekphrastic strategies I have found in fiction play out in celluloid. Through three portrait-films within the genre of *film noir* – Otto Preminger's *Laura* (1944) and Fritz Lang's *Scarlet Street* (1945) and *Blue Gardenia* (1953) – the chapter notes the parallels between portraiture and Hollywood's roles as definers of both ideals and the possibilities of transgression. The films' are shown to use a meta-textual vantage point for exploring visuality's role in articulating both unattainable gender personae and unsanctioned sex- and gender-based desires. The films reveal that society recognized that portraiture offered an emotional space that sanctioned not just the visualization, but the vivification of the unsightly. It motivated readers – like the willing subjects of a portrait painter – to acquiesce to the destabilization of sexuality, economic privilege, and subjective identity. As the films make clear, nineteenth-century struggles over cultural authority resulted in the formation of a portraiture-based visuality that has circumscribed Western society's conception of sexuality and gender will into the twentieth century. The issue of spiritual essence and culturally inscribed perception explored in the aesthetic essays of Ruskin and others resurfaces in altered form in the Gothic melodrama of *film noir* where issues of mass production and 'star' commodification offer an indispensable lighting for the values that make up the big picture.

1
Lady in Green with Novel: Demonizing Artists and Female Authors

'"Pshaw – A woman make an artist! Ridiculous! ... Ha! take the rubbish away – don't come near my picture – the paint's wet. Get away!" ... And he stood, flourishing his mahl-stick and palette – looking very like a gigantic warrior, guarding the shrine of Art with shield and spear'.[1] Michael Vanbrugh's outburst in this passage from Dinah Mulock Craik's novel *Olive* (1850) demonstrates just what a dangerous threat some people saw women artists in nineteenth-century Britain to be. In this example, both the misogynist Vanbrugh and Craik's narrator, who is sympathetic to the difficulties facing women painters, suggest that something more than just a manly image is at risk. The intensity of the character's tirade has the situation come across as both comic and dangerously volatile. Not only Michael's hyper-protestation, but even his very suggestion that a defense of his authority is necessary exposes a doubt regarding the claim for men's inherent superiority in the field. In Anne Brontë's *The Tenant of Wildfell Hall* (1848), Helen Graham offers a provoking counter-image to that of Michael's war-like defense of his notion of the profession's gender. In Brontë's novel, we find the heroine using her palette knife not only to finance her liberation from an abusive marriage but also, in one scene, to protect herself physically from a male seducer. These images of combat suggest that the boundary marking whom can be allowed to produce Victorian society's visuality was under severe contestation.

By blurring the battle imagery's function as a metaphor and as an actual experience of physical abuse, Craik's and Brontë's representations capture the very real impact caused by the sexual and economic conflict that permeated Victorian conceptions of women's relation to the visual arts. The predominant conviction that men were both naturally and culturally better suited than women to artistic professions led

society to configure a woman who attempted to infiltrate the hegemony as a sexually deviant, masculine threat. Conversely, the circumvention of the hegemony through forms of affectionate female-female
interaction such as the gift-exchange of artworks was sanctioned only
because it was deemed relatively trivial. And yet, as Terry Castle has
argued, same-sex female attraction also contests men's philosophical,
economic, and sexual authority over women: 'It implies a whole
new social order, characterized – at the very least – by a profound
feminine indifference to masculine charisma.'[2] The Victorian correlation of women's socioeconomic concerns with visual art and its
commodity function is apparent from the numerous novels dealing
with the subject, including Mary Hays's *Victim of Prejudice* (1799), Mary
Brunton's *Self-Control* (1810), Jane Austen's *Pride and Prejudice* (1813),
Charlotte Brontë's *Jane Eyre* (1847) and *Villette* (1853), Geraldine
Jewsbury's *The Half Sisters* (1848), Anne Brontë's *The Tenant of Wildfell
Hall* (1848), Dina Mulock Craik's *Olive* (1850), and Mary Elizabeth
Braddon's *Lady Audley's Secret* (1862).

Joan Friedman, Jane Kromm, and Roszika Parker and Griselda
Pollock have all noted the sociopolitical maneuvering that encouraged
female artists to prefer the image of 'the lady amateur'.[3] Although there
was a cultural differentiation between women's proper amateur interests in the arts and improper professional participation, this distinction
did not constitute a complete separation. Respectable governesses, for
example, were expected to earn their income by teaching such things
as painting, sketching, and music. It is therefore more precise to say
that there existed a continuum that ranged from amateurs to instructors to professional artists, a spectrum imbued with an 'unnatural' sexuality that was deemed more threatening as the woman artist became
more involved in the public sphere, often as an active agent within the
circulation of cultural capital. In accord with this spectrum, women
performers, whose very creation of art occurs in public view, were
often associated with a sexual trasgressivity akin to prostitution.

In this chapter, I begin my exploration of sexual visuality by bringing forward some of the ways in which women writers worked to
unravel the tangled cultural metaphors that lead many people to see
professional or even confident women artists as, if not unsightly, then
as sexually deviant monsters. As Jewsbury's *The Half Sisters*, Braddon's
Lady Audley's Secret, and Craik's *Olive* demonstrate, female authors from
the mid-nineteenth century used the sexual fluidity that permeated the
culture of the arts not only to redirect against men the familiar accusation of sexual deviancy that was applied to professional women, but

also to empower their depiction of a woman-centered economy of the arts. Taking on the common practice of inscribing nonpassive females as visibly deviant, these authors ultimately propose that the aberrance resides not in the women but in the misogynistic visuality of their society.

Victorian women and the economics of painting

Consider portraiture – a popular, conservative, and potentially lucrative art form. While it was deemed acceptable for women of the Victorian era to dabble in the genre, they found it difficult to get any training or employment in the field.[4] At the same time, the conventions of the genre itself reinforced the image of 'woman' as framed and passive. Portraiture seemed to offer the possibility of women's creative and economic fulfilment and yet, in the same stroke, it also supported the status quo through socioeconomic and generic repression. The resulting tension turned portraiture into a semiotic lightning rod for the conflicts surrounding women's sexual, economic, and familial roles.

From the beginning of the nineteenth century, novelists such as Hays, Brunton, and Austen addressed the ways in which middle-class attitudes condoned women's participation in the arts while making it extremely difficult for them to reap any practical rewards for their endeavors. The visual discourses through which British society envisioned new identities were not simply the result of contemporary innovations but were also indebted to formulations of vision that preceded them, as Hays's novel *Victim of Prejudice* (1799) makes clear by focusing on a female artisan who takes up a long established trade. Hays herself struggled to make a living as a writer, finding some of her strongest sympathy from her close friend and fellow-feminist Mary Wollstonecraft. *Victim of Prejudice* echoes the author's efforts to succeed in a male-dominated profession, with the story intoning the conflict with a more tragic poignancy by entwining the work-based prejudice with sexual violence. The heroine's move toward artistic employment at a print shop is the direct result of her being raped. Her sexualization becomes visibly marked by her need to work. Hays challenges this demoralizing equation by having the heroine find pleasure in her work:

> I returned with my patterns to my humble lodging, with light spirits and a beating heart, anticipating the dignity of INDEPENDENCE. Stimulated by motives thus powerful, I surpassed the expectation of

my employer; a new creation, blooming and vivid, rose beneath my pencil: abandoning the models, and disdaining control, my fancy wantoned in luxurious varieties; every new effort brought an access of profit and of praise.[5]

The heroine's language – 'stimulated', 'blooming', 'wantoned', 'luxurious' – saturates her sense of financial independence and self-worth with an aura of invigorated sexuality. Mary's ability to profit by taking control of the artist's pencil such that she moves beyond the constrictions imposed by her employer comes across as a self-fulfilling erotic experience that makes men superfluous. The dangerous joy that the heroine describes in language suggestively masturbatory, however, remains open to being construed as wantonness by those, such as the heroine's employer, who cannot visualize a sexuality that does not invite male participation. The man uses this elision to warrant his own lechery, which eventually forces the woman to relinquish her source of livelihood. The novel ends with the death of Mary and her best friend, Mrs Neville, two women who were unable to offer each other economic support, but who fulfilled each other's emotional needs. In the passage cited above, the heroine chooses her language only to evoke her sense of freedom, but Hays would have been aware that the description also insinuates the riskiness of such forbidden pleasure. In this way, the author positively reinscribes the conflation of sex and artistic employment rooted in the cultural prejudice against rape victims, even as the tragic conclusion affirms the simultaneous dangers that the rhetoric of visuality held for women.

The sexualized language that was part of the image of self-determination was firmly grounded in economic concerns. The monetary basis for segregating female and male artists that is tragically rendered in *Victim of Prejudice* remains apparent throughout the century. Middle- and upper-class women were permitted to take lessons in painting and sketching, but their participation in the arts was expected to reflect domesticity and feminine charm, traits that were apparently sacrificed when they chose to become professionals. They were encouraged to dabble in watercolors and sketches rather than the more lucrative medium of oils, and to prefer picturesque works to dramatic pieces that dealt with historical or classical themes.[6] An 1868 engraving entitled 'Female School of Art' in the *Illustrated London News* depicts a class in the school, which was founded in 1843, that is indeed drawing from nude male statues, although the real thing was banned for most of the century.[7] The genitalia of the statues are conveniently obscured from our view by the women's easels but it is suggested that they are exposed. The students, however, all appear to be focusing their attention on the more respectable costumed, female model. The juxtaposition of the obscured and ignored male statues and the female model does raise the question of whether women should be allowed to objectify the human body, but ultimately the illustration implies that respectable women would not be interested in painting nudes even if they had the choice.

The narrator of Craik's novel *Olive* dismissively summarizes the products of the womanly genres as 'pretty, well-finished, young-ladyish sketches of tumbledown cottages, and trees whose species no botanist could ever define' and 'smooth chalk heads, with very tiny mouths, and very crooked noses'.[8] The essentialist assumptions behind the deprecation of women's art is more boldly advanced by the anonymous author of an 1857 article in the *Englishwoman's Review* who confidently pronounces that 'in the more heroic and epic works of art the hand of man is best fitted to excel; nevertheless there remain gentle scenes of home interest, and domestic care, delineations of refined feeling and subtle touches of tender emotion, with which the woman artist is eminently entitled to deal'.[9] The author of the article is willing to 'entitle' women to take on these seemingly more feminine subjects, but the wording of permission hints at the view that, even within this more appropriate realm, females are not guaranteed to make as good a job of it as males. Despite the rhetorical naturalization of men's superiority in the visual arts, many Victorians intentionally or inadvertently revealed the economic machinations motivating what was usually presented as an innate difference.

The arts were recognized as one of the few areas in which women might make a decent wage, but they were generally paid less than men for their work.[10] Moreover, they were not given the opportunities for training in those areas that offered the greatest financial reimbursement. As the American anthologist Elizabeth Ellet speculated, one of the main reasons why women artists neglected historical and allegorical subjects was because they did not have access to the time and education required to become experts in these areas. The painting of less respected genres, meanwhile, 'might be pursued in the strict seclusion of the home to which custom and public sentiment consigned the fair student. Nor were they inharmonious with the ties of friendship and love, to which her tender nature clung'.[11] Ellet recognizes that women could not specialize in the most lucrative of genres because they were not allowed to receive adequate training, being 'consigned' by society to a sort of house arrest. But then the imposition is justified through the suggestion that such confinement accords with a woman's nature. The argument is unconvincing, however, because the idealized image of emotional tenderness makes the system of disempowerment within the profession seem unnecessary. One is lead to conclude that, rather than arising from women's tender nature, the imposed career limitations and their alignment with the valuation of the genres is a result of the hegemony guarding not what Craik calls 'the shrine of Art', but that of Money.

George Du Maurier's 1874 *Punch* cartoon 'Female School of Art' (Fig. 2) encapsulates this correlation by acknowledging both the large number of women interested in the visual arts and the amateur status accorded to their efforts.[12] Other such caricatures can be found in various publications throughout the century, suggesting just how familiar a phenomenon the woman painter actually was. 'Female School of Art' depicts a male dandy surrounded by women painters. The cartoon implies that such fashion-conscious men, because of their frivolity and attention to self-image, belong in a female space, which is signified here both by the room crowded with women and by the man fulfilling what was seen as the passive role of object of the gaze. The illustration represents effeminacy and self-display as attractive in women but laughable in men, just as these qualities are promoted in women and yet depicted as unworthy of respect *in anybody*. In keeping with women's encouraged self-debasement, the illustrator crams a small space with eighteen awkwardly positioned artists (an extreme number even in light of the fact that studios were often crowded), thereby belittling any serious, career-based efforts by suggesting that the women choose to treat the role of artist as a hobby. The comic subject of their gaze and the mixing of young girls with mature women further enhances the amateurish quality of all of their endeavors. Notably, the object of their attention is dressed for the outdoors, complete with baggy trousers and a knee-length coat that almost entirely obscures his physique. Even the classical statue in the background, visible only from the waist down, wears an ankle-length robe. Despite the fact that painting the nude figure was often crucial to works with historical or classical themes, the artists in the cartoon show no apparent interest, reflecting the view that respectable women are asexual and pure of mind; their virtue over-rides their interest in being equitably rewarded for their work.

The gender distinction that Du Maurier aims to reinforce is that, while men might consciously choose to present themselves for

Fig. 2   George Du Maurier, *Female School af Art* (1874)

viewing, women inherently embody beauty. While the man in the cartoon is the main butt of the joke, the women artists – with their fluid poses, pretty faces, Pre-Raphaelite hair, and voluminous sleeves and skirts – draw the viewer's gaze away from the male poseur and suggest that 'true' beauty does not reside in the dandy at all but in the women whom Du Maurier has associated with idleness and ornamentation. It is this underlying conception of women as the objects rather than creators of beauty that women artists and writers found themselves constantly struggling to redress without re-visioning the more public or active members of their gender as oddities. In Craik's descriptive essay 'A Paris Atelier' (1887), the difficulties in such visualization are apparent:

> They did not look particularly tidy, having on their working clothes – an apron and sleeves grimed with chalk, charcoal, and paint – but all looked intelligent, busy, and happy. The room was as full of easels as it would hold; and in the centre was a rostrum, where the model, a picturesque old woman, sat placidly eating her morning bread and – I hope not garlic, but it looked only too like it.[13]

Craik confirms Du Maurier's suggestion that women artists worked in environments that were not the most conducive to serious development. However, while his drawing implies that the students did not really demand space for serious endeavor, Craik emphasizes the earnestness and pleasure that women experienced from the opportunity to learn. The author herself seems to take delight in their grimy work clothes and the untidiness of the space. The fact that the model is depicted as offering a carnal version of the picturesque rather than the beautiful also stands in contrast to Du Maurier's rendering of the women artists as stunners. The faux anxiety regarding the model's consumption of garlic, meanwhile, ensures readers that an artistic career would not foster a woman's fall from respectability and high moral standards.

And what of women's efforts to actually sell their work? The situation only became more perilous. The best known nineteenth-century painting of the economic struggles of the female artist is Emily Mary Osborn's 1857 *Nameless and Friendless* (Fig. 3), which deals directly with the envisioning of such women as having become as good as 'fallen' simply by entering a male-dominated milieu. Osborn herself had to put up with reviewers who claimed that her talents were not female.[14] This painting – which garnered a fair amount of attention when it was exhibited at the Royal Academy in 1857 – depicts a young, modestly dressed woman attempting to sell an artwork to a male proprietor. The store's windows are covered in visual works, suggesting the forceful hawking of art that, as Lynda Nead has noted, was recognized at the time as a source of degrading, sensationalist images for mass consumption. In 1873, the Vice Society 'brought a number of prosecutions against traders for selling indecent photographs... . The subjects of the prosecuted photographs ranged from portraits of actresses and ballet-girls in various states of dress and undress, to more sexually explicit images, which were generally sold inside the shop and were not displayed in the windows'.[15] Although the female artist in Osborn's painting appears to be trained, her bent head, troubled expression, and fidgety hands suggest that she has adopted the career out of necessity. The young boy at her side leads one to speculate on the reason for her namelessness, while the combination of a black dress and the lack of a wedding band suggests that she is an orphan. By depicting a second female dressed much like the central figure and leading another boy out of the store, Osborn establishes an echo that implies that the heroine's situation is not unique. Except for herself and the departing woman, all the people in the store are men who,

Fig. 3   Emily Mary Osborne, *Nameless and Friendless* (1857)

unlike the central character, appear relaxed and comfortable, giving the shop the distinct air of a private gentlemen's club. Two customers, having turned their gaze away from a print of a scantily clad female dancer (the only painting within Osborn's piece with a discernable subject), eye the painter with expressions of curiosity. Indeed, almost every man in the shop and even one outside on the street is attracted by the spectacle of a woman selling art. Ironically, the collective stare functions to demarcate the female producer not as something beautiful but as something repulsively attractive, something unsightly.

This composition offers a complex delineation between representations of women as individuals worthy of respect, on one hand, and as objects inviting sexualized derision, on the other. Osborn represents the central female in the painting as being in the former category, but also as having fallen into the latter category in the men's view. One man shields his eyes as he peers through the shop's window; another cranes his head around in order to take a long backward glance – the efforts to which these men go to stare at the woman are themselves performances intended to communicate their negative judgement to anybody who is watching the spectacle. They are, moreover, invitations for others to participate in the act of ostracization. Meanwhile, the male characters imply that the heroine, by entering the public art world, has invited their exploitation of what Laura Mulvey famously dubbed women's 'to-be-looked-at-ness'.[16] It is as if, by demonstrating agency, the character has proclaimed no need for the protective cover of bourgeois respectability, thereby demanding to be viewed as an 'unnatural' woman, a woman with masculine attributes of ambition, confidence, and self-determination. The facts of her history are less significant because she has turned to painting for a profession, a gesture to be read as proof of her 'nameless' status. As the hypocritical Conrad Percy comments in Geraldine Jewsbury's *Half Sisters*, 'A woman who makes her mind public, or exhibits herself in any way, no matter how it may be dignified by the title of art, seems to me little better than a woman of a nameless class.'[17] In Osborn's piece, the woman is seen to invite her sexualized objectification, even as she actually demonstrates gender and class confusion by displaying what were viewed as both male and female characteristics.

The main point that I wish to establish – one that echoes throughout the literary tradition of unsightly desires – is that the men are not actually attracted by what their society would describe as an image of womanly perfection. Their demand that women fulfill the apparently less interesting ideal arises not from their fascination with it but from a desire to have women function as a control mechanism for their own transgressive potential. Deborah Cherry has pointed out that Osborn's painting demonstrates the methods by which Victorian masculinity, couched in a discourse of protecting and aiding women, in fact functioned to exclude and to disempower them.[18] Rather than set up a contrast between the central figure and the semi-nude performer that the men are handling, the painting establishes a continuum which portrays women as constantly at risk of being pushed down toward the lower end of the scale of respectability, but never having the opportunity to push back.

Notwithstanding the fact that art institutions continued to limit or deny women access throughout the century, and that – as both Du Maurier's 'Female School of Art' and Osborn's *Nameless and Friendless* demonstrate – the objectifying male gaze was culturally sanctioned, the number of women who became professional artists increased during the Victorian era. By the end of the century, women had lobbied and maneuvered their way into institutions and galleries that had refused them access in the past, had established their own schools, and had set up publications such as the *English Women's Journal* which opened a new forum for the discussion and depiction of women and the visual arts. At the same time, one of their main artistic channels remained women-centered networks involving domestic training and same-sex gift exchange. This mode of transaction reinforced their amateur status but did not necessarily diminish the works' cultural value, even though it circumvented financial mediation through men. In *Surpassing the Love of Men*, Lillian Faderman establishes that, while sexological, juridical, and other institutional terminology from the nineteenth century did not reify what we now define as a lesbian identity, the very absence of such a controlling discourse meant that there existed 'a latitude of affectionate expression and demonstration that became more and more narrow with the growth of the general sophistication and pseudosophistication regarding sexual possibilities between women'.[19] In their novels, Jewsbury, Braddon, and Craik defend the position of female artists from the growing accusations of deviancy. They do so, however, by taking advantage of the conventional depiction of such people as a sexualized threat, using the image to empower the domestic same-sex female relationships that were commonly viewed as powerless and asexual.

Geraldine Jewsbury and the affections of the half dead

In *The Half Sisters* (1848), Geraldine Jewsbury propels two sisters on distinctly different paths – one as a housewife and the other as a performer – in order to compare the tribulations and sacrifices that the life narratives entail. Through a complex metaphor of vampirism, however, the author conflates the identities of the two characters to demonstrate that they are the result of a violent cultural logic that actually resides outside of the women themselves and within the hegemony. Throughout her adult life, Jewsbury was largely consistent in claiming that men were naturally intended to be in charge of society. She proved equally resolute in her critique of sensation novelists for their 'false, perverted taste', and immoral, unrealistic representation of women's agency and sexuality.[20] This conservatism makes it all the more interesting that her novel *The Half Sisters* actually correlates with sensation literature such as Braddon's not only in its exploration of the economic limitations suffered by women, but also in the strategies it uses to challenge them.

Over the decades, Jewsbury's attacks on sensation literature and her increasing conservatism have overshadowed the position on women's rights and freedoms that she had articulated earlier in her career and in her private letters. In an essay published a year before *The Half Sisters*, Jewsbury observes that 'men are afraid of women becoming less agreeable, less useful to them – lest they should become less relative in their existence, lead their own lives for their own soul's sake, and not with an eye to the pleasure and taste of men alone'.[21] The argument reveals an awareness of the potential for women to establish an economy that did not rely on being mediated and shepherded by men. The essay also alludes to a sexual bent in this enforced mediation, something that Jewsbury foregrounds in an erotically charged letter of frustration to Jane Carlyle in which she writes: 'I love you my darling, more than I can express, more than I am conscious of myself, and yet I can do nothing for you'.[22] Thomas Carlyle may have claimed that 'such mad, lover-like jealousy on the part of one woman towards another it had never entered into my heart to conceive',[23] but Jewsbury's essay suggests that most men did at some level recognize same-sex female bonds as a threat to their domestic and economic authority.

Jewsbury's sensitivity to the system of oppression impinging from both the private and public contexts is made clear in another letter that she wrote to Jane, in which she sympathetically describes a woman who found herself in a physically and emotionally abusive marriage. The woman's eventual escape is made possible only by her turning to the job of painting miniatures[24] – an artistic career, it is true, but one that still kept the woman out of the public eye. Nor was Jewsbury simply sensitive to the plight of others since, as her sister Maria recalled in *Letters to the Young*, it was difficult for:

> Geraldine to contain her energies and aspirations within the shrunken frame of woman's sphere. Her tendency was to expand and grow, to reach out perilously for a realm of action in which woman's place was at best ill-defined, at worst a glaring and unacceptable contraction; a realm in which, for a woman, the word 'fame' rhymed with 'shame'.[25]

Maria's description may conjure up a 'fictional Geraldine', as Norma Clarke observes.[26] However, it also reveals the rationale by which women within Jewsbury's social sphere calculated their opportunities, and the difficulties they faced in articulating motivations that took into account differences *among* women.

Such variance in women's opportunities is the central issue under analysis in *The Half Sisters*. Jewsbury's novel delves into the tension between women's potentials and their different cultural constraints by contrasting the Italian-English performer Bianca with her housewifely half-sister Alice, whose creative outlets are limited to 'the domestic arts'. The author's descriptions of the performer's experiences were grounded in her close friendship with the actress Charlotte Cushman, whom the press often described as notably masculine, who performed male roles, and who, as Lisa Merrill has demonstrated, had more than one female lover. According to Merrill, the character Bianca's life narrative echoes that of Cushman's in many ways, with Jewsbury's affections for the American actress finding a public site of articulation in the fictional context of the novel.[27] Jewsbury's female artist is forced into her public career when her father abandons the family. As with Hays's character, this narrative step absolves the heroine of the peculiarity of actually wanting non-domestic employment. While both novels see the shift into such a career resulting in the heroine's sense of liberty and fulfilment, however, in *The Half Sisters*, Bianca 'continued in it from choice'.[28] As she explains to Alice, 'I must realise myself in my own way, or not at all. I am already *flétrie* [stained] in the eyes of all the quiet, gentle, still-life people amongst whom you dwell',[29] words like '*flétrie*' and 'still-life' highlighting the art-based differentiation of the women's respectability.

Jewsbury's novel also follows Hays's in redirecting the signal of transgression away from anything the heroine might have done to the male-privileging act of visualization. The later author, however, shifts the accusation further onto men's shoulders by suggesting that the performer's threatening masculinity is unstoppable because the visualization of deviancy is in fact the result of male anxieties. In the eyes of the character Conrad, Bianca is a beast whose career:

> has unsexed her, made her neither a man nor a woman ... [Women in public life] may, and many of them no doubt do, keep virtuous in the broad sense of the term; but, in their dealings with men, they use their sex as a weapon; they play with the passions of men to some degree like courtesans ... she strides and stalks through life, neither one thing nor another; she has neither the softness of a woman, nor the firm, well-proportioned principle of a man... . She is a bat in the human species; when she loves, she loves like a man, and yet expects to be adored as a woman.[30]

This stalking vampire whose perceived gender transgression Conrad feebly attempts to reconstitute as an asexuality ultimately remains transgendered, in Conrad's eyes, because she is simultaneously sexually attractive and yet characterized by a desire to be economically independent. The combination is conceived of as monstrous greed because it is embodied by a woman; her ability to pass as a traditional, heteronormative female threatens to undermine the false essentialism and denied performances of individuals such as Conrad himself. For this reason, Conrad's image of Bianca does not focus on the notion of woman-as-artist, but constantly reverts to a consideration of the way in which her career undermines his own position.

Conrad's name-calling is a miniature of the dominant economic order's attempts to categorize independent women as dysfunctional. Such examples of attack, however, point to sites of inadequacy within the order itself. By gradually depicting Conrad himself as erratic, emotional and ultimately a predatory sexual transgressor, Jewsbury transposes the monstrous iconography onto the hegemony, with the housewifely Alice becoming one of the living dead who is allowed to do no more than reflect men's self-image back upon them. Threatened by the successful woman artist, Conrad concludes that in fact his preference is for a woman 'at anchor by her own fire-side, gentle, low-voiced, loving, confiding'.[31] To this vision of feminine domesticity his friend replies, 'Bravo, you paint well', a response that inadvertently brings attention to the idealistic artificiality of the image. Yet Bianca's half-sister Alice, when first described, does appear to fulfill this ideal:

> In an extremely neat sitting-room, without one particle of taste visible in the arrangement of the grave substantial furniture, sat the wife and daughter of the late Phillip Helmsby of Newcastle, engaged on a large piece of household needle-work. A bookcase, filled with books of uniform size and binding, stood in a recess by the fire-place; but none were lying about. An engraving of the Princess Charlotte, and another of her husband, hung against one of the walls.[32]

The woman is defined by the name of the dead patriarch, an echo of the family's self-definition through the more public, higher authority signified by the portraits. As Jewsbury and her English readers knew, Princess Charlotte, the only child of the man who was to become George IV, had died in 1817 after giving birth to a stillborn boy. The engraving demonstrates a system of abnegation which emphasizes the dependence of public order on women's private responsibilities. The portraits, like the untouched books, serve not as beauty or artistic inspiration but as signifiers of traditional order. Even the furniture echoes conformity, with all the chairs in their 'lawful' places and only the fire in the grate not being 'subdued down to the level of the presiding spirit of decorum'.[33] Completing the docile harmony, the Helmsby women turn their skills not to new creations but to mending. Alice, we are told, is taught to draw and play the piano, but her mother directs these talents as well toward marriage and domesticity; 'I do not object to your practising an hour a day – nor to keeping up your drawing', explains Mrs Helmsby, 'if you would only make it practical, and paint me some screens for my drawing-room, or a cabinet for the library, or a chess-table, or something that would be really useful'.[34] Elsewhere she scolds Alice for not turning her creative abilities toward making a dog collar!

The suffocation that the heroine feels within her domestic situation is echoed by broader cultural practices of confinement, a stable middle-class existence that leaves the woman feeling as if 'the life was almost choked out of her by the rank, over-fed, material prosperity which surrounded her'.[35] While the men of the community are off on business, the women 'fall into a fraternity of petty interests and trivial rivalries'.[36] As 'pretty, trifling, useless beings, waiting their turn to be married, and in the meanwhile, doing their worsted work, and their practising, and their visitings', they are precursors of the women in Ira Levin's novel *The Stepford Wives* (1972).[37] Not suprisingly, things fail to improve once Alice does marry, with her husband Bryant proving as practical as her mother in voicing 'a singular objection to meeting with authors, actors, artists, or professional people of any sort; except in the peculiar exercise of their vocation, which I am willing to pay for'.[38] In contrast to Bianca's fulfilling artistic career, the domestic arts in which Alice is driven to excel are depicted as forcing her to identify with, and remain reliant on, the 'still-life people' that have 'hemmed [her] in on all sides'.[39]

Alice, however, does not simply signify death by domesticity. Through the character, Jewsbury actually demonstrates the inevitable failure of these complex efforts to snuff out women's individuality and creative potential. Alice, like Bianca, has inherited her father's creative sense, 'a striving after some meaning she could not express',[40] 'the sensibility of genius',[41] while she lacked 'its creative power, ... [and] force enough to break through the rough husk of her actual life and assert her inner soul'.[42] And yet, even though the pragmatic widow sells the majority of her husband's art collection, one piece that remains proves enough to stimulate Alice's 'vague yearnings and dim aspirations', offering her 'an opening through which she escaped from the contact of the dull, harsh, common details by which she was hemmed in on all sides'.[43] The piece of art depicts a Spanish convent in a sublime, mountainous region during a twilight that gives 'a strange and weird-like stillness to the scene'. The Gothic escapism of the imagery functions within the narrative to sanction a visualization of a foreignness and exoticism which is attractive in its alterity, a realm of experience forbidden to women like Alice but to which her half-sister has greater access.

The visual manifestation of the forbidden is a symbol for not just Alice's attraction to unsanctioned pleasures but also, as Bianca's life demonstrates, for the real potential for personal fulfilment and economic independence. Unbearably constrained by her marriage to Bryant, Alice develops an interest in Conrad, even though he, after his difficulties with Bianca, visualizes the ideal womanly image as that from which Alice wishes to escape. Because of her marriage, the two avoid acknowledging their mutual attraction until Conrad, agitated by his own desires, breaks a lamp and Alice cuts herself while trying to pick up the pieces. Conrad reacts suddenly but strangely. Laying the woman on the sofa, he proceeds to suck her blood because 'it seemed to him like sacrilege to let any of the precious drops be lost'.[44] While it is Alice who has hurt herself, it is her lover who reacts most strongly: 'he seemed under the influence of violent emotion beyond his control, and the couch shook with the sobs that burst from his bosom'.[45] Alice is 'terrified at the expression of his countenance; his lips were still marked with blood, traces of tears were on his cheeks, and his eyes were pale and almost extinct'. Defining his love for Alice as the source of this transformation, the vampiric Conrad stands as 'pale as the handkerchief with which he had staunched the wound'. Contrary to convention, it is not the female lover who panics and acts erratically but the male. Conrad's hysteria arises from his inability to follow through on the couple's transgression and so, the sexual transgression is consummated with blood and the hero flees into the night.

His absence, however, could not be much shorter, but the man who returns is distinctly different from the emotional, distraught individual who had fled the house barely able to speak. When Conrad re-enters the house under the pretense of obtaining a drawing that Alice had promised him, his rhetoric is more effectively formulated. The gift is quickly subsumed by the man's restatement of his love, all couched in a discourse of purchase. The artwork is not so much forgotten as reconstituted as an attempt to buy her love and devotion: 'let me live as your slave... . [T]his last precious month ... would have been cheaply bought with an eternity of pain... . I will pay the penalty, if it be death or madness'.[46] Conrad undermines his own apparent desire for an exchange of affection via the drawing by using financial terminology – 'precious', 'cheaply bought', 'pay' – that highlights the economic assumptions that support his notion of love. But as it is Alice as embodiment of stability and control that Conrad admires and indeed requires, so too is it her control that allows her to banish him from her presence forever. Later Conrad, 'utterly transformed' by guilt over the woman's eventual demise,[47] decides to give up all his worldly possessions. 'The Conrad you knew', he tells Bianca, with some of his characteristic emotionalism, 'is dead. – The last day of my old life closed yesterday – to-day my new life has arisen'.[48] He kisses the performer with lips 'cold as death' and departs 'never [to reappear] in the world', although he does leave behind a miniature of himself.[49] By blaming his own ghastliness on Alice, Conrad shifts responsibility for his lack of control onto the object of his attention. The monstrously encoded exchange of affection is in fact a corporeal representation of the man's earlier attempts to blame his own weakness on Bianca's professionalism, an accusation that in both cases is part of an endeavor to drain the vitality of the women in order to justify their subordination. Jewsbury thereby has a single character, Conrad, enact the accusations of monstrosity against both Bianca – a woman who becomes a professional artist due to poverty – and Alice – a woman who's artistic aspirations are enhanced by the confinement of middle-class security. In doing so, the author makes it apparent that it is the man who is the means by which the desires are constituted as unsightly. At the same time, she demonstrates the effectiveness of the demonizing visualization by having it be readily applied to women of different financial positions.

Jewsbury also recognized that, in order to undermine the monopoly of male-centered relationships that her society encouraged, she needed to envision a fulfilling engagement between women. She comes closest to doing so through Alice and her half-sister. Upon recognizing a portrait of their father hanging over Alice's mantel-piece, Bianca realizes that, in addition to their artistic urges, the two women are also joined by blood. Although this discovery fills the performer with an 'ineffable yearning', the women's socioeconomic disparity make her determined 'to quell the mighty "hunger of her heart" for natural affection'.[50] At the same time, Jewsbury reinforces the fusion of artistic and emotional affinity by having Alice reciprocate the love even though she remains unaware of their family ties. In contrast to her apathy toward her husband Bryant, Alice tells Bianca: 'I cannot let you go so soon – I care for you, as I never cared for any one – you do me so much good'.[51] Bringing to mind Jewsbury's own dream of leading a same-sex domestic life,[52] Alice's declaration of love is followed by a scene of emotional harmony in which she briefly attains her marital aspirations by procuring Bianca a flat and fulfilling her 'labour of love' by furnishing the home, right down to the artworks that adorn the walls.[53] Within the limited economic realm of their society, the creative potential of both women meshes into a single attachment temporarily satisfying a hunger for affection. When Alice assures Bianca that she will visit often, the other woman replies 'As often as you are allowed, ... for you are not a free woman: but absent, or present, I shall love you equally.'[54] Bianca's necessarily pragmatic existence has made her keenly aware of the constraints against sustained relationships based on female-female emotional fulfilment, as well as the restraints placed on female mobility, desires, and independence once inside a conventional bourgeois marriage.

Echoing the contrasting perspectives in Osborn's painting, Jewsbury presents the professional artist as a hermaphroditic manifestation of Conrad's fear of his own potential transgressiveness; he finds Bianca sexually attractive as a woman but he also finds her repulsively manly as a female artist. Through Conrad's relation with both sisters, however, the author demonstrates that men's fears are aroused not simply by the threat of female transgression and their own disempowerment, but by men's recognition of their own potentiality for similar infractions. Conrad sees all women as his control mechanism. Just as Alice's nurtured docility and weakness allow him and other men to define their own self-worth and purpose in life, so too does the Britomart-like armor into which Alice is forced keep Conrad's own creative potentiality from unleashing itself in a sexual frenzy. Meanwhile, in contrast to his failed encounters with Alice and Bianca, the relationship between the two artistic women is emotionally fulfilling, although the harmonizing interests and affections fail to overwhelm the cultural teleology which encourages each woman to try to locate such fulfilment in a man.

Mary Elizabeth Braddon's secretions of artistry

The narrator of Jewsbury's *Half Sisters* describes Alice as a young middle-class woman having the life 'almost choked out of her by the rank, over-fed, material prosperity which surrounded her'.[55] Mary Elizabeth Braddon's *Lady Audley's Secret* (1862) likewise describes a woman who struggles against the visualization of women as little more than domestic automatons or the living dead. But while Jewsbury's heroines are depicted as virtuous women suffering for the insecurities of men such as Conrad, Braddon introduces us to the fabulously daring and aggressive Lady Audley. The author turns to scopic politics to help her readers visualize a heroine who does not simply struggle in private battles with a single man but who takes on and disrupts the hegemony. In *Lady Audley's Secret*, the heroine's agency impacts on institutions of power such as the legal and medical, which are forced to contort their own claims to logic in order to turn the unsightly female into the unseen.

Like Jewsbury, Braddon was sharply aware of the prejudices against female performers. Before attaining success and financial stability as a best-selling author of sensation novels, she had supported herself not only as a writer but also as an actress. The eponymous heroine of *Lady Audley's Secret*, who begins the novel as Helen Talboys, similarly finds herself struggling to attain financial security in a society that severely limits her options. Reflecting the standard gender-bias of the art world, she functions effectively as a governess skilled in art as well as music, and is able to paint from nature in the manner of the respected landscape artist Thomas Creswick,[56] but her financial situation remains tight. Moreover, the heroine who is now best known for her conniving dishonesty actually comes across, at the beginning of the novel, like one of the passive, humble female milksops created by Hays or Jewsbury. By having the woman struggle with the wealthy Sir Michael Audley's proposal of marriage because she is not sincerely drawn to him, Braddon develops sympathy for her plight. The heroine tells him outright not only that she does not love him, but that she '*cannot* be disinterested' in his wealth. But the man presses his suit until she accepts what he calls the 'bargain'.[57] The facade of affection is blatantly sacrificed to the monetary pragmatics that underlied most Victorian marriages.

Both Sir Michael and the heroine recognize the marriage as an economic transaction where the man pays for the ownership of her beauty and that which it signifies, but what exactly the value of this signification is remains unclear. Sir Michael never flaunts his purchase, preferring a relatively isolated life at the Manor. While he may objectify his new wife, he also shows her affection and sympathy. It seems then that the man does not only find the woman physically attractive, but is also fond of her character, so much so that he might indeed be in love with her. He might hope that she will grow fond of him as well, but he is not deluded into thinking that the woman has any strong affection for him despite accepting his proposal. So he carries 'the corpse of that hope' away from their discussion, while the heroine returns to her governess's room and sits down with an appropriately deathly pallor 'still and white as the draperies hanging round her'.[58] In this scene, the language of affection is interwoven with that of business and, as the narrator points out, the conflation is far from uncommon at the time, with many young, attractive women marrying older men in large part for financial reasons. What Braddon adds to this mixture of love and lucre, however, is the specter of the living dead. But while the corpse resides hidden at the man's 'heart', it is visualized in the paleness of the woman's flesh. Readers are discouraged to search for signs of duplicity in Michael, while they are lead to define sexual infidelity as written on the female body.

Lady Audley never turns to an artistic profession but, through strategies of bodily inscription, the novel connects her drive for self-determination to visual art, uncommon sexuality and monstrosity. The echo of this constellation of traits in Jewsbury's and Braddon's novels suggests the existence of what Judith Halberstam describes in *Skin Shows* as a technology of monstrosity that, in this case, coheres to women interested in greater self-determination. Such a technology is in operation when one of its attributes – such as a woman's desire for greater agency – seems to naturally encourage the association of the individual with the others – in this case traits such as artistry, duplicity, a loss of respectability, deviant sexuality, and monstrosity. Like Jewsbury's novel, however, *Lady Audley's Secret* ultimately suggests that this matrix of associations is not evident in women but that it is actually the projection of internalized patriarchal insecurities onto a demonized Other.

The narrative of the novel can be read as that of a woman struggling to avoid her own visualization, with Helen Talboys's physical image becoming a marker of her duplicity from the very moment of her decision to act in her own interests. When George Talboys leaves his wife and child to look for work in Australia, the heroine decides that she warrants another chance as well and one of the first thing she does is remove her portrait from its position beside that of her first husband.[59] The erasure of the painting must be followed by an erasure of the body, and so Helen fakes her own death and moves away with the intention of attaining security elsewhere. Braddon marks the inability of the woman to echo her husband's independent new life by dooming her to a visage of the living dead. She is repeatedly associated with the deathly pallor that she displays upon her engagement to Michael Audley. The chapter in which Lady Audley is condemned to an insane asylum carries the appropriately vampiric title 'Buried Alive'. Elsewhere, she is described as 'more pale than winter snow', like Lot's wife 'with every drop of blood congealing in her veins, in the terrible process that was to transform her from a woman into a statue'.[60] At one point, Michael notes his wife's 'poor white face' and 'the purple rims round [her] hollow eyes', and laments that he 'had almost a difficulty to recognise [his] little wife in that ghastly, terrified, ago-nised-looking creature... . Thank God for the morning sun'.[61] In yet another scene, when light falls on her through a window displaying the green and crimson Audley coat of arms, the woman's face remains a 'ghastly ashen grey'.[62] As this last example suggests, the familial iden-tity that she has procured for her own security ultimately fails to cover her deceit, which remains marked by the bloodlessness that first sur-faces when she makes a deal with the Lord of Audley Manor.

In support of her frequently deathly pallor, there also exists a series of artistic signifiers whose decay and bloodiness seemingly publicize her duplicity and unwillingness to remain framed by cultural regula-tions. These visual signs appear on objects other than the heroine herself. An engraving of some 'lovely ladies' is found 'yellow and spotted with mildew',[63] while other artworks in the estate grow a blue mold.[64] When Lady Audley, nervous about being discovered, drops a paintbrush onto her work, the paint blots out the subject's face 'under a widening circle of crimson lake'.[65] Likewise, when she has a new por-trait painted of herself, her complexion comes off as 'lurid', her eyes as 'strange' and 'sinister', and her 'pretty pouting mouth' as 'hard and almost wicked'.[66] Notably, the explanation that the narrator offers for this image of a 'beautiful fiend' is not the heroine's transgressiveness, but the possibility that the painter might have gone partially mad from copying 'mediæval monstrosities'.[67] The portrait – with its 'crimson dress, the sunshine on the face, the red gold gleaming in the yellow hair, [and] the ripe scarlet of the pouting lips' – is virtually dripping red, exposing the heroine's monstrous desires. Winifred Hughes has noted, however, that Lady Audley is never directed by sexual pas-sions;[68] it is her determination to gain control of her life that leads to her being constituted as sexually dissident. Appropriately, the scarlet sensuality seems not to adhere to the heroine herself. In the case of the Pre-Raphaelite portrait, the narrator suggests that the coloring that accords with a demonic visualization arises not from its subject, but from the perspective of the man who created the image. As with Jewsbury's novel, the bloodlessness of the heroine is contrasted with a sanguinary, sexualized symbolism connected to the woman but arising from a significatory system created without her input.

More than once, Braddon highlights the economic concerns behind the sexualization of Lady Audley's assertiveness, as in her depiction of the heroine's relationship with her maid Phoebe. Although female-female friendship was often sanctioned as a way of keeping women out of the public sphere, it was not viewed entirely as an innocent, idealist phenomenon. Victorian efforts to construct such bonds as impotent reflected a concern that relations between women threatened the core of order and decorum. In 'On the Treatment of Female Convicts' (1864), Mary Carpenter depicts the female criminal as a woman who moves from her domestic fate, 'the sphere which the Heavenly Father destined her to fill, ... her home and family' and who is then dragged by men to a police-station, and then to the institution of the courts 'where she has probably again disgraced herself by a shameless effrontery', and finally into the context of a public trial.[69] For Carpenter, there is a clear sense that a woman in public is an unattractive image not simply if she is criminal but even if she has simply left the private sphere of home and family. Indeed, moving from that context is the first step toward prison. Carpenter further demonizes the image of the shameless female by suggesting that convicts are akin to animals, foreigners, and the lower classes. At one point in her essay, she describes:

> various cases of wretched mothers being in prison, whose progeny had sprung up as much cut off from all Christian or civilized influences, as if they had been born in a heathen country. These poor women, these female convicts, will, we believe, usually be found to belong to a pariah class, which exists in our state as a something fearfully rotten and polluted, and which diffuses its poison around, undermining the very foundations of society.[70]

While deserving of sympathy, the female convict is also ultimately a network of evil significations conjoining gender with race, class, sexuality, atavism, and animalism.[71] A technology of monstrosity, the female offender is not just criminal; she is also polluted, diseased, corrupting, immoral, and so on – a collection of negative traits that together convert her into a monster.

The image of the female oddity, moreover, is something that all women should be concerned with becoming. As the nineteenth-century criminologists Cesare Lombroso and William Ferrero put it, in their 1894 study *Female Offender*, even 'the normal woman is deficient in moral sense, and possessed of slight criminal tendencies, such as vindictiveness, jealousy, envy, malignity, which are usually neutralised by less sensibility and less intensity of passion'.[72] 'Let a woman, normal in all else', they go on to claim, 'be slightly more excitable than usual, or let a perfectly normal woman be exposed to grave provocations, and these criminal tendencies which are physiologically latent will take the upper hand'. While not everybody would have agreed with the scientists' claims, the image of potential monstrosity in all women finds echoes in the more common sense that females were more likely than males to suffer from hysteria, insanity, and other uncontrollable conditions.

According to Lombroso and Ferrero, one of the main ways in which women become criminals is through an external influence such as a husband or female friend. In explanation of the latter, they note that women have a 'latent animosity' toward each other. Robert Audley, in Braddon's novel, similarly observes 'How pitiless these women are to each other… . She sniffs the coming trouble to her fellow female creature, and rejoices in it, and would take any pains to help me. What a world it is, and how these women take life out of our hands – all womankind from beginning to end.'[73] According to Lombroso and Ferrero, if a female friendship does develop, it is probably because one of the women is criminally 'stronger' than the other: 'criminals, being products of degeneration, develop variations which sometimes amount to monstrosities; consequently between any two of them there may be such a difference in character as lends itself easily to suggestion, the born criminal, that malignant semi-masculine creature, being able to influence the criminaloid, in whom bad instincts are latent'.[74] The criminologists' model makes no reference to affection, support, or protection. In fact, the trait of 'latent animosity' among women means that there can be no such thing as an acceptable female friendship unless it is clearly subordinated to heterosexual bonds. Just as Carpenter argues that criminal women fail to sustain a focus on a heteronormative, family model, Lombroso and Ferrero claim that same-sex female relations are structured around a masculine/feminine binary that is a reflection of an innate criminality.[75]

The cross-gender binary underlying the criminologists' model of female friendship demonstrates a heteronormative anxiety, but it does

not articulate a risk of lesbianism or even sexual deviancy. Such implications within the model are made more apparent, however, in
Braddon's portrayal of the relationship between Lady Audley and her
subordinate Phoebe. Foreshadowing Lombroso and Ferrero's hypothe-
sis, Braddon suggests a physiognomic basis to the two female characters' criminal potential. Phoebe looks so much like Lucy Audley that
'you might have easily mistaken her for my lady',[76] and even Lucy recognizes the maid as a pale version of herself: 'Why, with a bottle of
hair dye ... and a pot of rouge, you'd be as good-looking as I.'[77] The
visual echo supports their shared attraction to a luxury in discord with
traditional female domesticity. In the most erotic scene in the novel,
we find the heroine lounging about covered in satin and fur amidst the
opulence of her jewelry-strewn private bedroom. Phoebe, helping her
mistress prepare for bed, spends most of the time it seems combing the
other woman's profusion of golden blonde hair. Lady Audley, meanwhile, reciprocates by smoothing 'her maid's neutral-tinted hair with
her plump, white, and bejewelled hand'.[78] Through the gestures of
affection, the wealthier, more aggressive woman allows the maid to
participate in forms of pleasure that would usually have been closed off
to her due to class differences. Similarly, Lady Audley is described as
being guilty of putting new, strange ideas into her maid's head. She
does this, for example, by exposing the youth to 'yellow-paper-
covered' French novels.[79] Ironically, such literature was characterized
in Victorian society by risque and immoral scenes much like that
which Phoebe and Lady Audley themselves enact in the bedroom. It is
also at this point, moreover, that Lucy draws the maid into her economic machinations, passing on her criminal desires. The correlation
of sexual and economic transgression is most effectively encapsulated
in Lady Audley's boudoir, where the illegal business deal and mutual
petting are sealed with a kiss.[80]

The dominant cultural reading of this female-female relationship
would have it that the stronger woman has drawn the weaker into a
criminal perspective. A closer inspection of Phoebe's character reveals,
however, that she is not the innocent victim of another's treachery
but that she herself has been struggling against the oppression of her
spirit and the ghosting of her identity as a human being. Contrary to
Lombroso and Ferrero's model that suggests one female criminal's
contamination of her friend, Phoebe – it turns out – had already
found it necessary, on her own, to be as conniving as Lucy. Early in
the novel she stores away evidence with which to blackmail her boss
in the future. And later she subtly threatens to do just that when she

casually notes that she had been standing in a window with a clear view of the spot where the wealthy woman had thrown her first husband down a well. Ultimately, Phoebe lacks the daring and the breathtaking beauty of her friend and boss, and so decides to marry a laborer named Luke, despite his strong tendency to violence. As seems to be the pattern, this decision to legally subject herself to the man leads the newly-wed to appear as a Gothic specter: 'a superstitious stranger might have mistaken the bride for the ghost of some other bride, dead and buried in the vaults below the church'.[81] While the narrator of the story has strongly proposed that Phoebe's problems have arisen from the heroine's influence, Phoebe decided to marry *despite* Lucy's strong recommendation that the maid avoid the bond. And it is not the relationship with Lady Audley, but the marriage that turns Phoebe into an image of the living dead. The implication is that the potential for self-realization and independent agency is killed off not by the women's transgressions but by the fact that one of their few options for financial security is that of becoming a male-reliant domestic.

Braddon underscores the patriarchal impetus behind the depiction of the female character's criminality as sexual monstrosity through an extended showdown between the heroine and her step-nephew Robert – the most dogged supporter of the hegemonic order and (as a lawyer without any drive to work) the character in most need of its support. As with Conrad in Jewsbury's *Half Sisters*, Robert's sexual anxieties are most obvious in his misogynistic rants against women – 'bold, brazen abominable creatures, invented for the annoyance and destruction of their superiors'.[82] At the same time, he undermines his own claim for his gender's dominance as pre-ordained when he also criticizes women for making up 'the stronger sex, the noisier, the more persevering, the most self-assertive sex'. Meanwhile, Robert is himself consumed by a growing realization of the depth of his love for George Talboys, Lady Audley's first husband. Indeed, Michael, the heroine's second husband and the family patriarch, concludes that Robert is himself 'unnatural' because of his lack of heterosexual attraction and his obsession with George rather than Michael's daughter: 'because Alicia was a pretty girl and an amiable girl it was therefore extraordinary and unnatural in Robert Audley not to have duly fallen in love with her'.[83] As with Jewsbury's Conrad and Craik's Michael Vanbrugh, Robert's decision to visualize Lady Audley as an insane, monstrous threat is based less on the heroine's scheming than on anxieties regarding his own ability to fulfill society's gender-based expectations.

The title of *Lady Audley's Secret* appears on a first read of the novel to refer to the heroine's fear that she has inherited or will inherit her mother's insanity. It is Elaine Showalter who first argued that the issue at hand is rather an open secret – the fact that the heroine is not insane but, in order to maintain the status quo, must be constructed as such.[84] D.A. Miller has similarly demonstrated that Braddon effectively depicts the secret as both an individual, private phenomenon and, more broadly, as a cultural lie.[85] Lady Audley and Robert both try to convince Sir Michael that the other is mad, but that political maneuvering is hiding behind the accusations is made apparent by the fact that neither of the two ever secures any definitive proof. Robert does bring in a Dr Mosgrave to check the mistress' mental state, but he concludes that she suffers at most from an 'insanity which might never appear',[86] a condition sounding much like the latent criminality that Lombroso and Ferrero felt existed in all women. According to the sinisterly named Mosgrave, the heroine actually has a combination of cunning, prudence, and intelligence – traits one could easily interpret as valuable but which instead, in this woman, he deems dangerous. *Lady Audley's Secret*, it would seem, is less about what the heroine hides, than about what she, like some moldering portrait, secretes – what she threatens to expose regarding the deceit and essentialism of her society. As Pamela K. Gilbert has noted, Braddon's novel offers a 'subversive portrait of alienated patriarchy', in which so many of the male characters fail to fulfill their societal roles but escape punishment regardless.[87] The bloody, rotten artworks that seem to signify the heroine's sinister soul actually manifest the conflict, which the men and their institutions of law and medicine must deny, between a woman struggling for security and the patriarchal framework which demands that she conform to an image that disarms her. Although Robert sees the heroine as threatening to bleed the dominant hegemony dry, he cannot reveal her history without risking a seepage of social inequities. Therefore, rather than taking her to court, the family, under the auspices of benevolence, sends her off to a Belgian insane asylum. Braddon, however, makes sure that Lady Audley packs her art supplies,[88] signaling the possibility of her even now continuing to struggle to convert her cultural confines into a site of self-visualization.

Deformity, devotion, and *Olive* women

Dinah Mulock Craik's novel *Olive* (1850) accords for the most part with Braddon's text on the issue of women's rights to self-determination.

However, rather than embodying the conflict in sensational images of erotically vampiric females and decomposing artworks, Craik uses a hyper-virtuous heroine to argue that physical, emotional, and artistic anomalies do not reflect an immoral individual. Early in *Olive*, the narrator comments on the cultural correlation of beauty with virtue. Noting more than once that the heroine's mother is 'so pleasant to an artist's eye', the narrator naively voices a wish that 'the ideal of physical beauty might pass into the heart through the eyes, and bring with it the ideal of the soul's perfection, which our senses can only thus receive'.[89] In the next sentence, however, this idealist hope is reformulated with a sociopolitical bent: 'So great is this influence – so unconsciously do we associate the type of spiritual with material beauty, that perhaps the world might have been purer and better of its onward progress in what it calls civilization had it not so nearly destroyed the fair mold of symmetry and loveliness which tradition celebrates'. The naturalized conflation of physical beauty with virtue that is a central model of Victorian visuality and which the narrator so boldly articulates is, as it turns out, the principal assumption that the novel subverts. The beauty that inspires this particular declaration is that of a young mother who ultimately rejects her own baby upon discovering that the girl has a slight curvature of the spine. And it is this 'deformed' child, Olive, who proves to offer the purest embodiment of virtue.

Craik's correlation between a person's physical appearance, moral worth, and economic role (as implied by the narrator's reference to civilization's progress) is buttressed by a sustained sensitivity to visuality throughout the novel. The narrator refers to the description of scenery as 'verbal landscape painting'[90] and depicts the way in which Olive's mother stops idealizing her husband as an 'image, once painted there in such glittering coloring', beginning to fade.[91] The heroine's own admiration for her mother is described as a visual pleasure: 'no painter ever delighted to deck his model, more than Olive loved to adorn and to admire the still exquisite beauty of her mother'.[92] Upon seeing her first love, Olive 'thought she looked very picturesque – in fact, just like some of her own fantastic designs of "Norma of the Fitful Head", "Medora watching for Conrad", &c. &c.',[93] while another character is visualized as a figure from a painting of the 'Three Fates'.[94] Meanwhile, the narrator describes Reverend Harold Gwynne as a painting and a sketch,[95] and another character even has pets so beautiful that, if put before the artist Edwin Landseer, they would revolutionize the genre of animal portraiture.[96] When Olive's mother goes blind, the loss is minimized because the daughter 'paints' such 'vivid pictures' with words that they prove superior to the 'unregardful eyes' on which the mother had previously relied.[97] In *The Victorians and the Visual Imagination*, Kate Flint proposes that 'blindness offers up a central trope for examining the nature and limitations of visual experience. By forcibly reminding one of the fragility of sight ... it presents a challenge to those who assert the dominating nature of the gaze'.[98] The representation of blindness, Flint goes on to argue, can be used to accentuate the power dynamics between the spectator and the object of the gaze, in part by emphasizing the question of what the blind themselves envision. In reference to John Everett Millais's painting *The Blind Girl* (1854–56), Flint notes that 'the blind girl, in her sightlessness, may also be read as a vehicle which reminds the spectator of the importance of a higher, inward vision.... . Thus the dominance of the material and visible world is called into question'.[99] Prior to her physical blindness, Olive's narcissistic mother relished having all eyes on herself. It is only when she loses her sight that the woman is able to move out from under the subjugating force of her own beauty and to develop an indifference to her society's spectorial culture. The situation does foster a greater spiritual perceptiveness in the woman, but its greatest effect is to enhance her admiration for her daughter's character and skill. As with Millais's *Blind Girl*, the heroine's mother develops a handicap that functions to question the very notion of visual capabilities themselves. Craik thereby turns a skeptical eye on not only her society's hierarchization of biological sight over imagination or spiritual inner vision, but also its prioritization of physical beauty over subtler human traits such as compassion and fortitude.

In the introduction to this study, I noted Nancy Armstrong's discussion of nineteenth-century realism's roots in a visuality formulated through the rules and limitations of photography. In *Olive*, the characters' frequent perceptions and evaluations of each other through the values of painting demonstrate that Victorian's were themselves aware of the role that visuality plays in the formation of social values. Craik was especially sensitive to the politics of specularity. Having studied drawing at the Government School of Design at Somerset House in 1843, she was familiar with the contemporary arts scene, as suggested by works such as *Olive*, 'The Story of Elizabetta Sirani', and 'A Paris Atelier'. In the novel, the character Meliora Vanbrugh is aware of a number of women artists: 'Oh yes, plenty. There was Angelica Kauffman, and Properzia Rossi, and Elizabetta Sirani. In our day, there is Mrs. A— and Miss B—, and the two C—s. And if you read about the old Italian masters, you will find that many of them had wives, or daughters, or sisters, who helped them a great deal'.[100] While naming historical figures from previous centuries, Craik suggests the lack of recognition proffered on women artists in her time by erasing her contemporaries through the use of the ABCs. Notwithstanding the fact that the author believed that women should prefer employment as wives and mothers, she realized that, 'whether voluntarily or not, one-half of our women are obliged to take care of themselves – obliged to look solely to themselves for maintenance, position, occupation, amusement, reputation, life'.[101] For Craik, 'it is not necessary for every woman to be an accomplished musician, an art-student, a thoroughly educated Girton girl; but it is necessary that she should be a woman of business'.[102] While she felt that women met men 'on level ground' when it came to literature, she still believed that, for various reasons including 'the not unnatural repugnance that is felt to women's drawing from "the life"', women could not be men's equals as painters.[103] She then comments, however, that, if a woman did choose a profession in the arts, she could still be respectable because she need not leave the domestic sphere in order to succeed.[104] Craik's overarching conception of gender difference was patriarchal, with her main criticism not being that men had power but that some of them abused it.

Cora Kaplan has argued that Craik's depictions of men in her fiction reflect her own experiences, including her relationship with her father.[105] Sally Mitchell meanwhile has shown that Craik's views regarding women's rights can be found in *Olive* specifically.[106] Notwithstanding the fact that *Olive* reflects Craik's own patriarchal bias, the novel's most harmonious images are nevertheless of women's mutual reliance. The text depicts a strong admiration for female-centered relations that the author appears to have been less willing to articulate overtly in her nonfiction. However, echoing Craik's argument in her essays, the narrator of *Olive* observes that, even though a woman prefers to 'sit meekly by her own hearth, ... sometimes chance or circumstance or wrong, sealing up her woman's nature, converts her into a self-dependent human soul'.[107] The author offers her most complex and extended analysis of this type of unnatural woman in the eponymous heroine who, because of a deformation in her spine, albeit slight, ultimately concludes that marriage is an unlikely prospect. Her inability to attract the male gaze obviates her being seen as a viable woman, while also seeming almost to be the catalyst for a search for other discrepancies such as her having hands like her father's[108] and an 'almost masculine power of mind'.[109] Such deformity and gender ambiguity are then used to challenge the simplistic sexual division for artistic potential. Although Michael Vanbrugh claims that creative genius is of no sex, he still callously informs Olive that it 'does not exist in weak female nature, and even if it did, custom and education would certainly stunt its growth'.[110] Thus in the very breath that the man proposes an essentialist sexing of talent, he questions the paradigms feasability by turning to cultural restraints as the more reliable dividing force. His own body, moreover, undermines the biologist claim; while he stands out for being 'gigantic and ungainly in height',[111] his malformation proves not to be a visual correlative to his talent. Craik destabilizes the equation by emphasizing the man's mediocrity and his dependence on various women in order even to attempt to paint well. For Olive, conversely, visible difference functions as a liberating catalyst and 'that personal deformity which she thought excluded her from a woman's natural destiny, gave her freedom in her own'.[112] As with Bianca's poverty, the assumed unlikelihood of Olive entering into a respectable marriage sanctions her shift of attention away from heterosexual prospects and toward a career as a painter, a shift that threatens to constitute the heroine as a deformation of heteronormative signification.

While Bianca's differences – her confidence and her public art – make her more visible and more sexual, Olive's difference – her deformity – makes her less visible and leads to her being viewed as nonsexual. Olive's form of visible difference leads to a broad social disregard of her sexual potential that in fact fosters a greater freedom of emotional adventure beyond the strictures of moral surveillance. The general cultural de-sexualization of the deformed is in part why Olive's friend Marion need not be taken seriously when she confides to the heroine that, 'if I were a man, I should fall in love with you... . Aye, in spite of – of – ... any little imperfection which may make you fancy yourself different to other people'.[113] Nor do Olive's same-sex options end there. While her picture-perfect mother, 'a Venus de Medici transmuted from the stone',[114] poses for portraits painted by male artists, the daughter develops an interest in what she dubs 'my beauty next door', a young woman whom she finds so attractive upon first sight that she spends the entire evening drawing pictures of her from memory. The labor involved in artistic creation establishes such an act as one of the strongest sanctioned modes of communicating affection between women. In 'A Paris Atelier', Craik notes that the female art students have no adventures with men and yet, by the same token, there is nothing threatening about these women becoming same-sex couples. The students frequently paint pictures of each other and exchange them as gifts. A character describes two students who, foreshadowing a scenario in Radclyffe Hall's *The Well of Loneliness* (1928), 'for seven years ... have never been separated, and seem quite indispensable to each other. It is the clever one who is the most devoted, who carries the canvas, washes the brushes, arranges the easel, and, in short, does everything for her companion'.[115] If an art student should never find a man, concludes Craik, 'she learns to do without him, and will be all the happier and better woman for having put her life to useful account'.[116] Acknowledging her awareness of the fact that many saw an artistic career as a sexualized risk to a woman's respectability, Craik ensures her readers that 'these young students seem to go through the ordeal [of studying art in Paris] unscathed, and, so far as I could judge, without being unfeminized.[117] In Craik's view, careers in the visual arts repel heterosexual dalliance, while encouraging women to develop healthy bonds with each other and offering them access to greater socioeconomic liberty. Here then, in the description of two devoted female painters, is a mid-Victorian image of a female union that, through its masculine/feminine binary, proposes the potential replacement of cross-sexual bonding and foreshadows the butch/femme model of the twentieth century.

Lest readers should choose to brush aside Olive's own artistic signification of affection for the girl next door as nothing more than the desperate infatuation of an ostracized abnormality, Craik goes out of her way to establish the equivalency between this attraction and heterosexual desire. 'There is a deep beauty', she offers,

> – more so than the world will acknowledge – in this impassioned first friendship, most resembling first love, the foreshadowing of which it truly is. Who does not, even while smiling at its apparent folly, remember the sweetness of such a dream? ... How they used to pine for the daily greeting – the long walk, fraught with all sorts of innocent secrets. Or, in absence, the almost interminable letters – positive love-letters, full of 'dearests', and 'beloveds', and sealing-wax kisses. Then the delicious meetings – sad partings, also quite lover-like in the multiplicity of tears and embraces – embraces sweeter than those of all the world beside.[118]

Olive's narrator is not describing the passionate love between the seemingly less attractive female artist and another woman but, shifting into a philosophizing tone, appears to be reminiscing about her own experiences as she expounds on a type of relationship portrayed as familiar to all women. The narrator ultimately normalizes these affections by inserting them into an acceptable teleology of maturity. Craik offers a chain of significations that allows erotic transgression through the uncontrollable nuances of emotion. First, Olive's masculinizing deformities put her out of the loop of heterosexual relations. This marginalization ironically makes it safer for Craik to depict unconventional attractions because they are couched within a discourse of artistic creation and exchange. These bonds of art and friendship then seductively transform through the narrator's reminiscences into ideal affections which, we are informed, exclude men and which partially define the lives of all women, not just those who have been forcibly culled from the marital pool.

Like Jewsbury, Craik realized that the economy of women's amateur art, while existing within a constructed spectrum of deviant sexuality, nevertheless offered a context that sanctioned women's enjoyment of intense same-sex affection. Throughout *Olive*, the author reiterates that the heroine's physical deformity is far less relevant than her outstanding character and humanitarian spirit. In accord not only with the tradition of the Gothic and melodrama in which an innocent heroine's morality and faith are challenged and ultimately rewarded through the consummation of heteronormative ideals, Craik's heroine does eventually marry and discard her artistic career, having earlier concluded that, when she is not painting, she feels 'less of an artist, and more of a woman'.[119] While this conclusion concedes to generic closure, as Jewsbury's and Braddon's novels seem less jubilantly to do as well, it also complicates the demonization of women artists by presenting a person who spends part of her life as a professional painter and part of it as a traditional wife, while her respectable character remains unchanged.

Throughout Craik's novel, Olive struggles with a visual culture that directs women's participation as subjects and as creators of art toward enforcing a system that hinders their full creative and economic self-realization. Collectively, Craik, Jewsbury, and Braddon, through their depiction of distinctly different female artists, give some sense of the actual saturation and malleability of this system of oppression within the field. At the same time, however, they prove that diverse women could have used the visuality of the time to enhance their participation within the dominant economic model. *Olive* is the only novel of the three discussed that actually depicts a woman painter, and yet each of the authors uses the visual arts to address the hegemony's anxieties regarding women's circumvention of a male-centered system as they try to fulfill their own economic and emotional desires. Retaining the established equation of this challenge with unnatural sexuality, the authors redirect the accusation against anxious male characters such as Conrad Percy, Robert Audley, and Michael Vanbrugh. The constructions of gender, genius, and genre that these characters depend on ultimately collapse under the strain of their own contradictions. The efficacy of this strategy, on the authors' part, is registered most emphatically by the fact that they managed their revisions of the misogynistic conflation of economic self-determination, non-heteronormative pleasures, and art without disavowing women's rights to participate in all three.

2
Framed and Hung: The Economic Beauty of Wilkie Collins's Manly Artist

Bianca, the exotic actress; Alice, the repressed wife; Helen, the conniving beauty; Olive, the humble painter: in the novels discussed in the previous chapter, the variety of female characters with creative aspirations and talents counters the notion of a clear bi-gendered model of artistic capabilities. This very diversity, however, runs the risk of suggesting a process of divide-and-conquer by which creative women are separated into minority clusters that, individually, prove ineffectual against the monopoly of a unified patriarchy. But the female–female support found between Bianca and her half-sister Alice, Helen and her maid Phoebe, and Olive and virtually every woman she meets counters the sense of this diversity as divisive. Of equal importance, the patriarchy has never been unified, and a similar multiplicity can be found in male artists. Wilkie Collins's writing offers an extensive exploration into the ways in which this display of differences resulted in frictions within masculinity itself, and the resultant efforts to reify a single, stable ideal of the gender.

Despite its brevity, Collins's 'Terribly Strange Bed' (1852) and its depiction of a male portraitist at work encapsulates the complex issues entangled in the efforts to establish the professional artist as a manly authority. That which the artist wishes to communicate and that which the subject envisions are rarely the same thing and, as 'The Terribly Strange Bed' implies, the seemingly casual jockeying for control of visual meaning stands in for a broader economic competition. The narrator of Collins's story, a portraitist, finds himself with a subject whose awareness of the symbolism of his self-display results in a pose that the painter finds unnatural. In search of a strategy for distracting the man while he captures him on canvas, the artist asks his subject to tell a story. The latter complies by recollecting a time when, as a guest at an inn, he had been mesmerized by the painting of a sinister character 'looking intently upward – it might be at some tall gallows at which he was going to be hanged'.[1] The gallows humor lies in the fact that the character, as the subject of a portrait, will himself be hanged. The more sinister joke has broader implications. It turns out that, like a portrait, the guest's bed at the inn had been constructed to contain and control its subjects. The innkeeper, we discover, had converted the piece of furniture into a press that he was using to suffocate his patrons so that he could rob them. This particular guest obviously avoided such a fate, having not only lived to tell about his experience, but also remained wealthy enough to have his portrait painted. Or perhaps it would be more accurate to say that he has deferred such a fate, since he has escaped only to find himself entrapped by someone even more elusive and controlling – the portraitist to whom Collins gives final authority. While the story of 'The Terribly Strange Bed' may be the subject's, it is relayed by the man who has placed the subject off guard in order to paint a likeness according to his own rules of realism. It is the male commercial artist – and not the wealthy guest, the inn-keeper, or for that matter the old soldier or the inn's conspiratorial mistress – whom Collins presents as taking control by subjecting the others to his manipulation both on canvas and in words.

Notwithstanding Collins's depiction of his narrator as in full mental, aesthetic and economic control of his subjects, this image of the commanding artist did not dominate the landscape of nineteenth-century masculinity. A number of Victorians such as Mary Braddon, Vernon Lee, and Oscar Wilde have written texts that challenge the authority of the status quo by imbuing painting with a sexual dissidence that warns against generic and institutional entrapment. But Collins, not only in 'The Terribly Strange Bed' but also in a number of his novels, comes across as more sympathetic to the conservative image of the artist earnestly pursuing a mentally arduous regimen.[2] His investment in this compassionate image is made apparent by the fact that he not only works to enhance his readers' support for this persona, but also challenges popular alternatives. More specifically, he disputes the cultural and economic productivity of the aristocratic patron, while he depicts the man whose physicality is most boldly scripted on the body as exposing an emasculating lack of self-control. Despite Collins's use of sensational literature to relegate traditional models of authority such as wealth and physicality to the margins, the maneuvers reveal the actual volatility behind the contemporary claim of an inherently manly identity. Of equal interest, they expose his awareness that less common signifiers of masculinity held a notable importance for his own career as a writer. In Collins's prose, we find an author deeply invested in manipulating visuality so as to make apparent the manliness of a profession that lacked the demonstrative and decorated image of masculinity with which Victorians were most familiar. Through a complex manipulation of verbal and visual rhetoric, the author works toward establishing a symbiosis between masculinity and the artistic profession that gave professionalized, middle-class men privileged maneuverability within the changing career landscape.

Patronage, self-employment, and masculine artistry

The shift in British attitudes toward aesthetics and art during the first half of the nineteenth century reflected the rising power of the middle class, which was purchasing artworks in increasing numbers. According to John Ruskin, prior to the Victorian era, the fine arts were supported by the upper class and little attention was paid to the working masses; in their own age, without broad cultural support, the middle-class workmen would simply not be able to produce excellent art.[3] In his 1856 novel *A Rogue's Life*, Collins offers an extended derogation of the aristocrats who, rather than thinking for themselves, simply ignored modern artists and blindly venerated the old masters: 'It was as much a part of their education to put their faith in these on hearsay evidence, as to put their faith in King, Lords and Commons'.[4] The narrator happily points out, however, that the situation has finally begun to change:

> Traders and makers of all kinds of commodities have effected a revolution in the picture-world. ... The daring innovators started with the new notion of buying a picture which they themselves could admire and appreciate. ... From that time good modern pictures have risen in the scale. Even as articles of commerce and safe investments for money, they have now ... distanced the old pictures in the race.[5]

Even earlier, in 1843, Robert Vaughan noted that 'successful patronage of the fine arts depends less on the existence of noble families, than upon the existence of prosperous cities'.[6] Imbuing the arts with an economic vigor, Vaughan proposes that artistic quality is now the result of democracy and an admiration for the prosperity of the social state. As Paula Gillet has demonstrated, however, increased middle-class patronage did result in higher prices but it did not give artists greater freedom so much as demand the production of new genres. With minimal church or state patronage, the English painters now found themselves expected to satisfy the bourgeois taste for relatively small pieces evoking domestic life and local scenery.[7]

Despite the fact that there was no solid verification that this change in patron profile resulted in a greater artistic freedom, Collins, like many others, felt the artist's growing disconnection from aristocratic patrons meant an escape from impotent, blind convention. In accord with this attitude, the author is notably unkind in his own writings to characters who pride themselves on exclusive aesthetic values, suggesting that they generally lack knowledge in the field. In *Hide and Seek* (1854), for example, the unpleasantly rigid patriarch Mr Thorpe sees himself as superior to everybody around him, but not to his portraits of 'distinguished' and 'very sturdily-constructed' preachers 'with bristly hair, fronting the spectator interrogatively and holding thick books in their hands'.[8] As Collins implies, it is the sturdiness of the pose, the thickness of the books they happen to hold, and even the stiffness of their hair that constructs the preachers' social authority. It is, in other words, the artist who instructs us on how to read manliness. It is the artist who 'makes the man'. Emphasizing the blur between performing the rhetoric of authority and having its actual force, Collins even has the character Thorpe call on these visages to participate in his condescension toward other characters in the novel. Taking the conflation one step further, the man, in accord with his rigid lack of emotion, signals his own power by modeling himself on the artworks.

It was a familiar belief that the purpose of a man's portrait was to celebrate his masculinity. As Richard Brilliant observes, 'the formality and evident seriousness displayed by so many portraits as a significant mode of self-fashioning would seem to be not so much typical of the subjects as individuals as designed to conform to the expectations of society whenever its respectable members appear in public. In this sense, to be portrayed by an artist is to appear in public'.[9] In the character of Thorpe, we see the implications of this equation for social interaction; the man chooses to signify his own virtues by constructing his identity in line with the aesthetic conventions of an artistic genre. In this sense, portraits function as respected instructional diagrams of visible gender traits that establish the qualities one is to emulate in the molding of one's own image for public consumption and evaluation.

Collins's work shows more interest in this aesthetics of personae than in the aesthetics of art itself, although early in *Hide and Seek* he acknowledges that, for many in his society, the two were inseparable. Similarly, the novel's narrative circulates through the view that one's social value, like that of an art object, is determined as much by one's connections as by one's character or actions. To a notable degree, the worth of an art object is not determined through the image of the piece itself or the image of its creator but through the image of those who determine its value. In one scene in *Hide and Seek*, the narrator of the novel articulates a system of aesthetic valuation that ultimately subordinates the qualities of the artwork to those of its audience, demonstrating the emasculating disempowerment of the artist that this system entails. The visitors to a private exhibition are portrayed with a tone of condescension suggesting the superiority of the artist himself, even though he must hope for their favor:

> Thus, the aristocracy of race was usually impersonated, in his studio, by his one noble patron, the Dowager Countess of Brambledown; the aristocracy of art by two or three Royal Academicians; and the aristocracy of money by eight or ten highly respectable families, who came quite as much to look at the Dowager Countess as to look at the pictures. With these last, the select portion of the company might be said to terminate; and, after them, flowed in promiscuously the obscure majority of the visitors – a heterogeneous congregation of worshippers at the shrine of art, who were some of them of small importance, some of doubtful importance, some of no importance at all.[10]

The narrator describes here a form of social segregation inherent, he suggests, to artistic appreciation. Despite Collins's acknowledgment elsewhere that an artist inevitably has monetary concerns, the narrator's delineation of the three aristocracies of race, art, and money emphasizes the view that refined aesthetic appreciation is itself essentially anathema to financial rank. Collins's narrator brushes aside the 'obscure majority' with one hand, while the other takes a jab at patronage by having the aristocrats of money be more attracted to the countess than the paintings. Even the members of the Royal Academy are treated rather cursorily, reflecting Collins's sympathy for the growing number of young artists struggling to establish careers, such as his brother Charles and the Pre-Raphaelite painters with whom he was associated. Both Sophia Andres and

Ira B. Nadel have demonstrated Collins's close affiliations with the Pre-Raphaelites.[11] According to Simone Cooke, Collins felt the Pre-Raphaelites should see themselves as 'a generation of painters who were casting off their status as craftsmen for a moribund aristocracy and painting their pictures for the up and coming business class'.[12] The author was sensitive to their career difficulties and even helped them negotiate commissions not only because he was friends with members of the Pre-Raphaelite Brotherhood such as William Holman Hunt and John Everett Millais, but also because he would have recognized similarities between their chosen profession and his own. Reflecting this sympathy for the male artist, in the description of the private showing, the character of the painter is invisible during the interaction between art objects and viewers, and yet Collins succeeds in establishing him as admirably strong because he remains unscathed by the narrator's bitterness and undaunted by the other characters' callousness.

The image of the consumer-reliant artist became more familiar as the increased popularity of the visual arts was met by a concomitant increase in the number of men hoping to become professional painters. This also led to the strong possibility that many of them would have to settle either for being art instructors or for changing careers entirely. The very real economic difficulties experienced by this growing number of men also enhanced the importance of laborious commitment among the criteria by which the artist's social worth was evaluated. According to Dianne Sachko Macleod, their existed an unsubstantiated assumption among many Victorians that their successful artists started at the bottom and worked their way up to cultural and economic respectability.[13] Julie F. Codell has similarly shown that there was a strong tendency to construct Victorian artists as hard-working, persevering laborers.[14] In his 1859 study *Self-Help*, Samuel Smiles concludes that the major contribution of artists to the morale and character of their society was as exemplars of hard-working, unwavering laborers.[15] And one recalls Ruskin's attack on Whistler for basically not spending enough time in creating his art, regardless of its intrinsic merits.[16] The pragmatics of an artistic career meant that fewer and fewer men could consider fashioning themselves as individualists devoted to the Goddess Beauty. One therefore finds the Romantic persona giving up some of its cultural turf. In accord with the shift in the patron profile, the new 'musketeers of the brush' – as George Du Maurier glorifies them – were being seen as self-made men with commercial pragmatism.

It was this persona that Collins, like many other men involved in the arts, hoped to establish as inherently masculine and worthy of authority. Joseph A. Kestner has suggested that the volatility of gender categories was in part the product of the hegemony's efforts to erase or deny the constructed quality of manliness. Masculinity, he explains, is not a given but includes 'the codes of behaviour in culture, *including* those that construct male dominance in the process of constructing male subjectivity'.[17] Michael Roper and John Tosh similarly emphasize that 'Men's behaviour – and ultimately their social power – cannot be fathomed merely in terms of externally derived social roles, but requires that we explore how cultural representations become part of subjective identity.'[18]

With regard to Collins's manipulations, the site of interrogation is not just the construction of a masculinity, but the means by which it is inscribed with the signification of a naturalized authority. How, in other words, does Collins attempt to suggest the essential command of male artists even while acknowledging their reliance on so many other members of society? As the above description of the private gallery showing implies, the author relies in part on the suggestion that the subjugation of the artist is a shamefully unjust phenomenon of his society in general. The sense of embarrassment is then reinforced by sexual undertones that affirm the author's own vision of the manly ideal.

The previous chapter noted Dinah Mulock Craik's depiction of the character Michael Vanbrugh flailing his artistic tools as weapons against the encroachment of women. The usual image of the Victorian male painter at work on realist art, however, is more suggestive of passivity and impotence – involving as it does a slow pace, a private sphere, and a fastidiousness and attention to detail not in accord with the aggressive formation and defense of a stable social order. Moreover, this order was itself re-inscribed on the private level of family and home by a bi-gendered model that relied on a visible masculinity. In this 'technology of power and knowledge', as Foucault refers to the Victorian social system, the bourgeoisie deployed sexuality as a form of self-affirmation, 'a defense, a protection, a strengthening, and an exaltation that were eventually extended to others – at the cost of different transformations – as a means of social control and political subjugation'.[19] Wishing to reap the benefits of their gender, male artists had to affirm the virility of their careers, despite the 'feminine' traits of the practice and the association of artistic genius with the 'softer' qualities of sentimentalism, sympathy, and moral purity.

In *Modern Painters*, Ruskin articulates a common perception that 'Perfect taste is the faculty of receiving the greatest possible pleasure from those material sources which are attractive to our moral nature in its purity and perfection. He who receives little pleasure from these sources wants taste; he who receives pleasure from any other sources, has false or bad taste'.[20] This model is not uniquely Victorian, echoing as it does the Enlightenment valuation of moral and instructive art that Gothic literature challenged through its exploration of terror for terror's sake. In Dickens's famous article 'Old Lamps for New Ones' – which Nuel Pharr Davis describes as 'one of the most insulting and blatantly vulgar art criticisms ever printed'[21] – the novelist makes it clear that Victorian's were not concerned only with the immorality of rousing stimulation, but also with the subordination of beauty to money. Dickens voices a similar concern to Ruskin's that contemporary artists threatened to prioritize the fundamental rule that painting 'shall be informed with mind and sentiment' behind 'a narrow question of trade-juggling with a palette, palette-knife, and paint-box'.[22] According to Dickens, the sacrifice of wisdom and sensitivity to economics manifests itself most clearly in the works of the perverted and unhealthy Pre-Raphaelites, who depict 'the lowest depths of what is mean, odious, repulsive, and revolting'.[23] The language attains a sexualized tinge in a critique of a painting by John Everett Millais, one of Collins's friends. Dickens finds the image of Mary in 'Christ in the House of his Parents' so hideous as she kneels between two 'almost naked carpenters' that he feels she would be seen as a 'monster' even in 'the vilest cabaret in France'.[24] This language is part of a complex technology through which certain aesthetic, ethical, and economic views were welded together to create sexualized deformities – a sort of Frankensteinian creature condemned for a monstrosity that arose from the very animosity that instigated its construction. Any difficulties that Collins would have had with Dickens's 'Old Lamps for New Ones' would have been exacerbated by the fact that he respected both the novelist and the Pre-Raphaelites.

Dickens's rhetoric accords with the tendency among critics to define what they saw to be good art as masculine and what they saw to be bad art as feminine. In the anonymous 1849 piece 'Royal Academy: Portraiture', for example, certain portraitists are congratulated for their 'manly character' and 'good, honest, sterling style, without affectation'.[25] Meanwhile, another artist is criticized because 'his taste was not of high caste' and his works 'want masculine character in the men, purity in the women, and artlessness in infant life'. The painter's demasculinization of male subjects is part and parcel of what this reviewer dubs 'the degeneracy of portraiture' that has 'spread the evil till it became the epidemic which the walls of our Exhibition rooms now show'.[26] For the reviewer, portraiture, throughout its history, has been associated 'with the highest names and with the loftiest aim'; it has 'hand[ed] down to us the very presence, as it were, of the men who are yet morally with us by their influence on the condition of things amid which we live'.[27] These comments reveal an interesting political agenda. Portraits are not being valued here by aesthetic principles, but by their ability to sustain, through a sort of artistic cryogenics, the values of past influential men. Art becomes the holding house for the living dead and the genre is basically admired for how well it has maintained the sociopolitical hierarchy which ensures that it will continue to be valued in the same way. This leaves little room for inspiration, innovation, experimentation, or the participation of women or other people whose success in the field might challenge the hegemony.

The implications behind the feminization of certain types of men, as presented in this review, were especially volatile during the mid-century, when the biologized terminology of degeneracy correlated in Britain with the mainstreaming of a negative homosexual taxonomy. Although scientific and legal languages for discussing same-sex male desire were being articulated, a comparably overt aesthetic one was yet to surface. Aestheticism would not acquire a fully formulated example of its homoerotically coded discourse until Pater's 1873 *Studies in the History of the Renaissance* and even here the references are necessarily obscure. As Emmanuel Cooper has noted in his survey of homosexuality and art in nineteenth-century western Europe, the representation of male-male affection in the visual arts did not see any considerable increase at this time either.[28] Meanwhile, the rhetorical tendency to value most highly that art which signified masculine vitality basically discredited women's participation in the genre because the existence of artistic talent within women would signify deviancy. As the discussion in the previous chapter notes, Dinah Mulock Craik was sympathetic to women's economic difficulties, but she also believed that men were inherently superior to women in certain fields such as the visual arts. Even Marion Halcombe, presented by Collins as the smartest woman in *The Woman in White* (1869), confidently voices the opinion that 'Women can't draw – their minds are too flighty, and their eyes are too inattentive'.[29] Similarly, the creative mediocrity of Valentine Blyth, in Collins's *Hide and Seek*, is signaled by his inability to paint accurate likenesses of adults, although he is 'invariably victorious in the infant department', a genre seen to be one in which women excel.[30] The 1849 review 'Royal Academy: Portraiture' reflects the gendered essentialism underlying the disrespect for certain genres when the critic concludes that the best painter of both women and children, but not men, is a female artist – Margaret Geddes Carpenter.

Carpenter happens to have been Wilkie Collins's aunt. In fact, many of Collins's relatives made names for themselves in the art world and his own concerns regarding the demasculinization of the artist is rooted in part in this family history. The novelist was related to the Scottish painter Andrew Geddes through his mother, Harriet Geddes. Two of her sisters became portraitists and one of these, Carpenter, exhibited work at the Royal Academy and made an income from her art.[31] Collins's mother also could have supported herself as a painter, but her husband was against this. The author's paternal grandfather wrote *Memoirs of a Picture*, a biography of the painter George Morland. He also made his living as a picture dealer and cleaner, the latter job involving trips to the gentry to clean private collections. His insecure and often meager income led Wilkie Collins's own father to approach his career as a painter professionally, both by wooing wealthy patrons and by aiming to create broadly popular works. Lillian Nayder points out that William Collins adopted an aesthetic that white-washed the political instability of his time.[32] His landscapes reinforce an image of national order and coherence, while his paintings of rural life assuage their own dissident potential by implying that lower-class country life is saturated with bucolic bliss. Collins himself notes, in his *Memoirs of the Life of William Collins*, that among his father's paintings of rural life, 'No representations of the fierce miseries, or the coarse contentions which form the darker tragedy of humble life, occur. ... When his pencil was not occupied with light-hearted little cottagers, swinging on an old gate – as in "Happy as a King" – or shyly hospitable to the wayfarer at the house door – as in "Rustic Hospitality" – it reverted only to scenes of quiet pathos.'[33] The focus on popular themes and the support of an image of social harmony without any signs of disturbance eventually did lead to William Collins's success. He became a member of the Royal Academy and his work was commissioned and purchased by various highly positioned men, including the Prince Regent (later George IV) and Sir Robert Peel. But Macleod notes that – in accord with a general shift in the demographics of British art collectors – William Collins's patrons changed during his career from being primarily titled individuals to being untitled, middle-class buyers.[34] Macleod concludes that the man was less motivated to accommodate his purchasers than his artistic themes might suggest. However, middle-class patrons were in general becoming the main buyers of art, and their tastes did tend toward the paintings of domestic and local scenery in which he specialized.

Wilkie Collins's own career as a painter led to his exhibition of a landscape painting at the Royal Academy in 1849. But his novel *A Rogue's Life* leaves no doubt that he was put off by the traditional market system that reduced the artist to an 'accomplished parasite' who fawns upon his aristocratic patrons for money.[35] According to the narrator of the novel, in the business of portraiture, 'Everything is of no consequence, except catching a likeness and flattering your sitter.'[36] Echoing these views, Collins's memoirs of his father, as Tamar Heller effectively argues, enact a 'desire to construct a masculine artistic identity empowered by the father's example'.[37] Julie Codell has also shown that the memoirs mark a transition in Victorian artist biographies toward valuing professionalism and financial stability. They contain, for example, records of the pieces that William Collins painted each year, including the location of their exhibition, the people who eventually bought them, and the prices they paid.[38]

With regard to his own career as a writer, Collins claimed that he was free from 'the fetters of patronage' because of the growing mass market for both novels and the periodicals in which they were often first serialized.[39] But while he may not have been dependent on a few wealthy individuals, the success of his career was still dictated by the tastes of his consumers, which he was aware tended to favor sensational scenarios, Gothic terrors, and characters who were not especially self-restraining and who did not occupy their time with tedious, unacknowledged labor. Involved in various painters' lives, familiar with the sexualized rhetoric around the struggle for control of the standard definition of masculinity, and himself an artist sensitive to his audience's less-than-gentlemanly expectations, Collins was fully enmeshed in the mid-Victorian art world's contest among various personae for the title of the manly. His response was to try and naturalize an image of the professional painter as the masculine ideal while painting alternate masculinities as deviant.

Idealizing artists

Victorian men who identified with intellectual careers not characterized by physical labor found themselves struggling to establish a manly identity that would appear staunch and familiar. In his discussion of nineteenth-century French artists, Pierre Bourdieu refers to 'a new social personality, that of the great professional artist who combines, in a union as fragile as it is improbable, a sense of transgression and freedom from conformity with the rigor of an extremely strict discipline of living and of work, which presupposes bourgeois ease and celibacy'.[40] The difficulty that Collins explores is even greater, for the masculine ideal that he aimed to support did not even have the daring-do of the transgressive bohemian to add a tincture of sex-appeal. As James Eli Adams argues, in his study of the Victorian construction of masculinity, 'increasingly, middle-class professionals (including male writers) legitimated their masculinity by identifying it with that of the gentleman', who was rendered 'compatible with a masculinity understood as a strenuous psychic regimen, which could be affirmed outside the economic arena, but nonetheless would be embodied as a charismatic self-mastery akin to that of the daring yet disciplined entrepreneur'.[41] A man was to appear an intellectually rigorous artist whose gentlemanly qualities fit the positive contemporary image of the capitalist professional. 'Charismatic', 'daring' – it is this aspect of the persona that feels forced, when it is supposed to come across with an easy bravado.

Part of the problem lay in the fact that it was unlikely so many men were truly worthy of being accepted as intellectually rigorous. The term 'intellectual', when applied to the realm of art, was used to distinguish it from the 'decorative' arts, the former being seen as having no conventional utilitarian purpose beyond stimulating the mind and moral sentiment. This distinction favored the intellectual and was met with skepticism by, among others, William Morris, one of the period's strongest supporters of the decorative arts. In *Art and Society*, Morris argues that there are in fact two types of artists who find security under the umbrella of intellect:

> the first composed of men who would in any age of the world have held a high place in their craft; the second of men who hold their position of gentleman-artist either by the accident of their birth, or by their possessing industry, business habits, or such-like qualities, out of all proportion to their artistic gifts. The work which these latter produce seems to me of little value to the world, thought there is a thriving market for it, and their position is neither dignified nor wholesome. ... They are, in fact, good decorative workmen spoiled by a system which compels them to ambitious individualist effort.[42]

Such doubts about the performance of the intellectual, bourgeois artist exacerbated concerns regarding the artistic community as a site of manly perfection. In an effort to alleviate such uncertainty, Collins's novels turn to rhetorical steroids that pump up the gentlemanly artist's masculinity in an effort to make it appear both natural and self-evident.

Walter Hartright, the hero of *The Woman in White*, offers the standard image of the admirable, struggling artists. On first sight, the 28-year-old teacher of drawing strikes one as 'a modest and gentlemanlike young man'.[43] He himself ensures us that his deceased father left his dependants secure, 'having exerted himself in his own career as a drawing-master'.[44] But our hero, despite his efforts, continues to find himself unrewarded; 'I am an obscure, unnoticed man', he laments, 'without patron or friend to help me'. Ultimately, his hopes shift from a career in the 'high' arts to that of getting a permanent commercial position illustrating for a newspaper, although he still refuses to give up his intellectual aspirations. His character development is rooted in this perseverance, a virtue that, after many trials, is rewarded not with fame but with financial security and a traditional bourgeois family just like his father's.

Like Hartright, the hero of *Hide and Seek*, Valentine Blyth, is a combination of refinement and drive, and is portrayed 'as an artist, as a gentleman of refined tastes, and as the softest-hearted of male human beings'.[45] Despite his gentlemanly sensitivity, he is also characterized by strenuous mental labor. For him, 'Art wouldn't be the glorious thing it is, if it wasn't all difficulty from beginning to end; if it didn't force out all the fine points in a man's character as soon as he takes to it'.[46] The artist flourishes through the struggle, and it is his resultant effort that makes his masculinity visible – the intellectual exercise pumping up the muscles of his artistic identity until one can almost see them bulging beneath his gentlemanly garb. While Hartright's and Blythe's life narratives follow a familiar melodramatic story-line, it is useful to note that this model was also one toward which many Victorians themselves aspired. That Collins himself felt invested in the image of the artist as virile is supported by the fact that, as Nuel Pharr Davis has argued, the hero of Collins's novel *Hide and Seek* is in part autobiographical.[47]

The inevitable career failures that resulted from too many men trying to become financially secure through the visual arts required a reformulation of success itself. As Collins's narrator explains, in what seems a rather placating tone, 'it is not all misfortune and disappointment to the man who is mentally unworthy of a great intellectual vocation, so long as he is morally worthy of it; so long as he can pursue it honestly, patiently, and affectionately, for its own dear sake. Let him work, though ever so obscurely, in this spirit towards his labor, and he shall find the labor itself its own exceeding great reward'.[48] Now moral purity and patience reflect the strength of the man's conviction. What might have once been interpreted as rather passive acceptance is formulated here as a virile perseverance that insinuates a critique of men who turn too quickly to action, such as searching out an alternative career. Rather than being seen as solipsism, Valentine's own forbearance, buoyed by his wife's encouragement, allows him to avoid the 'danger of abandoning High Art and Classical Landscape altogether, for cheap portrait-painting, cheap copying, and cheap studies of Still Life'.[49] As a lesson in fortitude, Collins has the hero find it impossible to fulfill his financial goals without being treated as something less than a gentleman:

> No one but himself ever knew what he had sacrificed in labouring to gain these things. The heartless people whose portraits he had painted, and whose impertinences he had patiently submitted to; the mean bargainers who had treated him like a tradesman; the dastardly men of business who had disgraced their order by taking advantage of his simplicity – how hardly and cruelly such insect natures of this world had often dealt with that noble heart! how despicably they had planted their small gad-fly stings in the high soul which it was never permitted to them to subdue![50]

Affronted by the possibility of being dealt with as one of those 'good decorative workmen' to which Morris refers, Valentine is also repulsed by his patrons. In this scene, the hero's business naiveté becomes the virtue of directness and honesty abused by those who lack his qualities. While everybody from patrons to tradesmen transmogrify into insects, Valentine alone is marked by an admirable soul and a natural nobility.

The construction of persistence as a visible marker of manliness did not arise in the mid-Victorian era, although it definitely flourished at this time. Nevertheless, it could not in itself provide sufficient signification when positioned next to more immediate, physical signs. After all, Valentine's and Hartright's endurance would remain invisible to the stranger on the street. Having established the characters' innate gentlemanly virtues and even reinforced them among their familiars with the manly trait of stamina, Collins still found it necessary to mark their unique masculinity through a physicality that all could read. His efforts result in rather far-fetched depictions intended to prove that the men, despite their careers, can and do partake in physical labor. Of the two, it is the defense offered by the mediocre painter Valentine that is most unusual. In a state of drunkenness that it appears is intended to excuse the hero's egotism, he drops his composure in an overt defense of his masculinity specifically *as* an artist:

> When Michael Angelo's nose was broken do you think he minded it? Look in his Life, and see if he did – that's all! Ha! ha! My paint-ing-room is forty feet long (now this is an important proof). While I was painting Columbus and the Golden Age, one was at one end – north; and the other at the other – south. Very good. I walked back-wards and forwards between those two pictures incessantly; and never sat down all day long. ... Just feel my legs, Zack. Are they hard and muscular, or are they not?'[51]

This scene makes evident a central conundrum of the persona of the middle-class, masculine artist. In order to reveal the manliness of a hero who is not permitted to brag about or display his physicality, Collins must somehow sanction the man's loss of verbal and physical reserve. The author decides to do so by getting him drunk; indeed, the narrator tries to shift blame away from the hero by wondering whether the person who mixed the drinks had given Valentine more liquor than he knew. The end result is that the hero 'was not the genuine Valentine Blyth at all, – he was only a tipsy counterfeit of him'.[52] And through his fortuitous inebriation, the painter is given a window of opportunity in which to perform overtly the essential masculinity which is otherwise admirably and appropriately restrained.

Collins adopts a different strategy for demonstrating assertive manli-ness within *The Woman in White*, albeit one that is also extreme. In this novel, class difference keeps the lowly painter Walter from marry-ing the woman he loves and this failure results in a self-exile that for-tuitously forces the man to turn to physical self-defense. Downcast by his romantic failure, he goes off on an adventure to Central America: 'They were last seen entering a wild primeval forest, each man with his rifle on his shoulder and his baggage at his back. Since that time, civil-ization has lost all trace of them'.[53] After brushes with 'death by disease, death by the Indians, [and] death by drowning', which make Walter one of the few survivors of the trip, he returns confident that the experience has resulted in him being a stronger and worthier man: 'In the stern school of extremity and danger my will had learnt to be strong, my heart to be resolute, my mind to rely on itself. I had gone out to fly from my own future. I came back to face it, as a man should.'[54] The narrative of the lone man struggling against the elements had become a common representation of the initiation rite of masculinity, appearing frequently in the stories littered through the Penny Dreadfuls of the Victorian era. The primitivist retreat strips the hero of the effeminacies of civilization, allowing him to become one of Rousseau's noble savages who fortunately never loses his respect for a gentlemanly self-image.

While not permanently displaying the scars and muscle-development of a man who battled through hardship, Walter has been steeled by the ordeal in a way that has saturated his being throughout and forever. It is his having survived on his own skills and stamina that fosters the hero's new-found determination and self-reliance. Of greater importance, they allow him to erase his image of himself as patron-dependent, a conceptual shift that, Collins suggests, is necessary for a man's actual independence. His new-found manhood allows Walter finally to marry his beloved, the daughter of the feeble aristocrat Mr. Fairlie, thereby permitting the middle-class artist to get his foot into the door of a higher class. Meanwhile, his first-born son is described 'industriously sucking his coral',[55] demonstrating that the masculine rigor of his father has successfully permeated the child's identity, an infant who – because of his mother's lineage – is also an aristocrat, the Heir of Limmeridge. The novel's final flourish, the end result of Walter's 'long, happy labour',[56] is the hero and his self-fashioned identity as the masculine, gentlemanly artist usurping the title, authority, and wealth of the decadent upper classes not in spite of, but due to, his middle-class values and respect for healthy industry.

Monstrous masculinities

Collins's notion of masculine perception involves the coupling of aesthetic reverence with mental vigor and restrained physicality, an image that is rather unnoticeable and that fosters the creation of somewhat bland characters like Valentine and Walter. Aggrandizing rhetoric and an association of the heroes with innate artistic sensibilities do proffer an aura of masculinity upon the heroes but it appears brittle and tenuous in relation to the brute force of the working-class male or confidence and power of the wealthy upper classes. When Collins implies Walter's worth by simply grafting his family into an aristocratic line, he suggests the awkwardness in the image of the muscular artist that he saw for himself. In order to confront the key challengers to the manly title, therefore, the author juxtaposes the bourgeois ideal both with men who perform physicality at the expense of any intellectual or aesthetic exercise and with the aristocratic individuals whose power is based in old, inactive money. In Collins's novels, however, the strategy ultimately accentuates the rhetoric supporting an image of a virile artist that should need no support at all.

The problem with working-class masculinity – the middle class would have felt – is that it lacks maturity and responsibility, and thus threatens the stability of the nation and its progress and growth. In Collins's *Hide and Seek*, the character Zack Thorpe is a youth who the narrator and middle-class characters hope will attain masculine maturity by emulating a man like Valentine. But when the hero's drunken display of machismo ends in his entreating Zack to feel his muscles, the youth is attracted instead to the character of Matthew Grice – a bar-brawling, uneducated loner who had lost his scalp during adventures in the Americas. The man now roams the East End of London, getting beat up because of his skull cap.[57] In contrast to Valentine, Matthew stands for a physical excess that encourages a violently dissident misanthropy and social instability. The misdirected admiration on the young man's part demonstrates his – and all youths' – lack of judgement in the tendency to emulate the most obvious and immediate images of manliness.

Although physicality was the most readily available signifier of masculinity for young men, wealth was equally visible and more attractive, in part because the bourgeoisie itself admired financial security. The problem with old money, however, at least as far as the burgeoning middle class was concerned, was that it did not allow its stockpile of wealth to circulate and contribute to the overall welfare of the economy. The money-based image of masculinity finds its standard caricature in the Gothic persona of the wicked, immoral aristocrat, characters such as the Baronet Percival Glyde and Count Fosco in *The Woman in White*. Notably the female victim in the novel defines all men of rank and title as untrustworthy.[58] The fact that she has to ask Walter whether he himself is titled emphasizes the difficulty that the artist was having in controlling the signification of his gentlemanly image. Collins establishes the aristocratic and wealthy men's degeneracy through sexuality and gender ambiguity. Glyde is marked by delicate features explicitly defined as womanly,[59] while Count Fosco is portrayed as effeminately vain through his theatrical actions, facial expression, and extreme attention to sartorial detail. Mr. Fairlie, the wealthy man who decides to employ Walter, has, we are told, 'a frail, languidly-fretful, over-refined look – something singularly and unpleasantly delicate in its association with a man, and, at the same time, something which could by no possibility have looked natural and appropriate if it had been transferred to the personal appearance of a woman'.[60] When Mr. Fairlie complains that some pictures that he had purchased 'smelt of horrid dealers' and brokers' fingers', Walter seems barely able to withhold his contempt, as he comments that his own nerves 'were not delicate enough to detect the odour of plebeian fingers which had offended Mr. Fairlie's nostrils'.[61] Because Collins is working to establish a connection between the manly ideal and the middle-class artist, the excess of the aristocrat's refinement does not lead, as one might expect, to a privileged aesthetic sensibility but to a value system based on classist biases. 'We don't want genius in this country', comments Fairlie, 'unless it is accompanied by respectability'.[62] Fairlie's lack of taste reveals his claim to superiority to be unfounded. Ultimately *The Woman in White* encourages one to feel that old money results in impotent, immoral, effeminate men who do not want to work and could not if they had to. Their elitism, the novel implies, undermines economic development, which requires that society sustain a healthy, civilized exchange of goods and cultural currency across class- and money-based divisions.

Collins does not only vilify characters like Grice, Fosco, and Fairlie, but also rarely allows them to take the focus away from the heroes. It is when he does permit his readers to more fully visualize such characters, that the author's anxieties about his own manly ideals become apparent. From the author's pageant of deviant masculinities, it is the character envisioned through a fusion of both extremes who is ultimately the most memorable. I refer here to the Gothic artist Misserimus Dexter, from the novel *The Law and the Lady* (1875). Max Nordau, in his notorious 1892 study *Degeneration*, argues that a degenerate artist is characterized by, among other things, immodesty, egoism, impulsiveness, emotionalism, pessimism, and 'moral insanity' or a lack of moral sense.[63] A man with these traits, he explains, 'rejoices in his faculty of imagination, which he contrasts with the insipidity of the Philistine, and devotes himself with predilection to all sorts of unlicensed pursuits permitted by the unshackled vagabondage of his mind; while he cannot endure well-ordered civil occupations, requiring attention and constant heed to reality'.[64] Misserimus offers a textbook example of Nordau's degenerate artist. Although masculine, his energy is not coupled with cool, confident restraint. Speeding around his mansion, throwing tantrums, cruelly taunting his devoted female servant, shouting at all who come near him – Misserimus's force is uncontrollable. His hyper-virility comes across as grotesque, especially – the narrator claims – in light of the fact that he has no legs. Brawn and wealth – the two main threats to Collins's own vision of manliness – are overshadowed by this deformity.

Collins more than once juxtaposes this lack of limbs and Misserimus's physical beauty and impressive stature but rather than do so to establish a contrast, the blatant lack eventually comes across as part and parcel of the other traits. In an objectifying blazon more often reserved for mid-Victorian heroines, the narrator observes that, 'To make this deformity all the more striking and all the more terrible, the victim of it was – as to his face and his body – an unusually handsome and an unusually well-made man. His long silky hair, of a bright and beautiful chestnut colour, fell over shoulders that were the perfection of strength and grace. His face was bright with vivacity and intelligence'.[65] At this point, the narrator's intricate portrait takes a distinct turn: 'His large, clear blue eyes, and his long, delicate white hands, were like the eyes and hands of a beautiful woman. He would have looked effeminate, but for the manly proportions of his throat and chest: aided in their effect by his flowing beard and long moustache, of a lighter chestnut shade than the colour of his hair.' Although Misserimus's feminine features are defined as enhancing his attractiveness, this excessive beauty is described in a way that signals its potentially dangerous slip into effeminacy. The man of spectacular physicality, rather than standing as an ideal, signals an eccentricity and an absence of the self-control found in the intellectual gentlemen. His lack of legs symbolically counters the upward mobility toward which the middle class aspired while emphasizing his lack of restraint.

Through disability, the text encourages a visualization based in the portraiture conventions applied to women, while indirectly bringing attention to Misserimus's difficulties with mobility. As the narrator concludes, a painter would have reveled in him as a model.[66] This objectifying gesture functions as an aestheticization and symbolic disempowerment of the hyper-virile man by the artist. The same strategy occurs in *Hide and Seek* when Valentine (who, as we recall, is especially proud of his legs) is so impressed by Matthew Grice's muscles that he concludes he must capture the man on canvas. Through simply being an object of admiration, the physical man is read as soliciting objectification. It is precisely this nonverbal invitation to ocular consumption that allows Collins to join Misserimus's admirable physique to the persona of the effete aristocrat. As if to compensate for his handicap, Misserimus has become more proud of his physical attributes and has developed a strong inclination toward fine clothing. In a foreshadowing of twentieth-century strategic camp, he dons his wardrobe as a sexualized challenge to anybody wishing to abuse him for his differences. Physically handicapped, the man turns his image into an aggressive statement that he perceives as masculine both in its effrontery and in its sign of wealth.

Paying notable attention to one's appearance is of course contrary to Collins's male ideal. Masculine beauty resides in reserve, while display – as discussed in the previous chapter with regard to a cartoon by George Du Maurier – is a quality accepted as inherent to women. But Misserimus's self-awareness can be seen in his very wardrobe; in the scene that pays most attention to his clothing, we find him dressed in a jacket of pink quilted silk, while the 'coverlid which hid his deformity matched the jacket in pale sea-green satin; and, to complete these strange vagaries of costume, his wrists were actually adorned with massive bracelets of gold'.[67] Noticing the negative reaction that his clothing receives from the novel's heroine, Valeria Woodville, Misserimus explains that 'Except in this ignoble and material nineteenth century, men have always worn precious stuffs and beautiful colours as well as women'. Valeria, who herself challenges sexual convention as one of the first female detectives in literature,[68] remains unconvinced and shows minimal empathy for her partner in gender-bending. Misserimus's costume – as Collins describes it – connects the man with the normative Victorian woman. The coverlet which is intended to hide the absence of limbs is not just any blanket, but a part of his ensemble, a fashion statement signifying a decadent wealth that sanctions his appreciation of self-aestheticization over functionality. Through this makeshift skirt, his handicap is conflated with what was assumed to be the natural passivity of women, which is itself in part a sartorially imposed immobility.

Building on his image of the ideal man as invisible and restrained, Collins has Misserimus himself recognize that his dress contradicts contemporary standards of gentlemanly performance. His image, he boldly acknowledges, reflects an old-fashioned aesthetic and an aristocratic disrespect for hard-earned money: 'A hundred years ago, a gentleman in pink silk was a gentleman properly dressed ... I despise the brutish contempt for beauty and the mean dread of expense which degrade a gentleman's costume to black cloth.'[69] Despite Misserimus's meticulous justification of his attire as a sign of aristocratic confidence,

Collins quickly undermines the claim by having the man bring out his knitting basket and begin work on a strip of embroidery.[70] Misserimus offers another passing defense about the way in which needle-work allows him to compose his mind, but the reader is encouraged, through Valeria, not to buy it. A manly man, we are led to conclude, would remain composed without the need of such assistance.

A key discord in Collins's condemnation of the male poseur is the fact that such an attention to image generally signifies a notable degree of aesthetic awareness. But the author wished to venerate the image of the artist as somebody who, rather oddly, remained unaware of the possibility of himself being a subject of admiration; indeed, this artlessness made the man attractive. The establishing of this naive artist as an ideal of masculinity required a conception of the self-aware man as aesthetically deranged. Thus the way in which characters visualize Misserimus as aberrant is made to accord with the way in which he visualizes the world. 'I could see that there were pictures on the grim brown walls', Valeria reports with regard to the art collection in the man's ancient, dilapidated mansion, 'but the subjects represented were invisible in the obscure and shadowy light'.[71] Not only are the artworks paradoxically invisible, but Misserimus's slow-witted cousin at one point leaves through a side entrance hidden by one of the pictures, 'disappear[ing] like a ghost'.[72] The cousin's spectral shift into the artwork conjoins Misserimus's family to the paintings, obscuring both in the dark murkiness of a past era. The man's bonds with the past result in the subjects of his gaze being interpreted by the level-headed Valeria as apparitional if not utterly invisible to her.

At the time that Collins wrote the novel, the predominant rhetoric of visual art gave preference to what was perceived by many to be a masculine realistic style and equally masculine subjects such as renowned patriarchs and historical scenes. Misserimus's tastes, not surprisingly, are unrealistic and anti-industrial. His art collection includes portraits of people suffering from various forms of madness, plaster casts of famous, dead murderers, and the 'Skin of a French Marquis, tanned in the Revolution of Ninety-three'.[73] The works that he has painted himself focus on states of high emotion. The piece entitled 'Revenge', for example, depicts 'an infuriated man ... in fancy costume' with 'a horrid expression of delight' standing astride the dead body of a similarly attired man while blood drips 'slowly in a procession of big red drops down the broad blade of his weapon'.[74] The alliteration of Collins's description emphasizes the drawn out sadistic ecstasy of the image and its eroticization of male-male penetration. In a series of paintings on cruelty, Misserimus's subjects include a man disemboweling a horse with his spurs, a scientist gloating over his dissection of a live cat, and two pagans torturing saints – one by roasting and another by skinning. Needless to say, Misserimus's sadistic subjects did not fit the values and tastes preferred by mainstream art critics. Such topics as man's abuse of animals through sport and science in fact challenge the economic drive on which his society depended.

The choice of subject matter is interpreted as a reflection, more broadly, of the man's values and mental state. In spite of her admitted ignorance on the subject, the heroine of *The Law and the Lady* concludes that her host is an inadequate painter: 'Little as I knew critically of Art, I could see that Miserrimus Dexter knew still less of the rules of drawing, colour, and composition. His pictures were, in the strictest meaning of that expressive word, Daubs. The diseased and riotous delight of the painter in representing Horrors, was ... the one remarkable quality that I could discover in the series of his works'. But Valeria also grudgingly acknowledge that Misserimus does demonstrate 'signs of a powerful imagination, and even of a poetical feeling for the supernatural'.[75] The compliment is back-handed. Early in the century, art theorists such as Arthur Hallam associated the imagination with a necessary and valuable womanly component in the male artist.[76] This model lost ground as the traits of industriousness and perseverance became more central. By century's end, Nordau would be able to proclaim confidently that too much imagination was, simply put, a sign of degeneracy.[77] While the sensitivity to image displayed by the male poseur does reflect an attention to aesthetics, it is an aesthetics of excess rooted in the womanly sphere of the imagination and the supernatural rather than in the glorification of the self-image that the hegemony struggled to affirm through its advocation of classic themes and realist styles.

Collins makes it clear that the fundamental weakness in a man like Misserimus lies not in his inability to paint realistically but in his disinterest in even trying. The character seems even to be bourgeois-bating when he declares on an inscription near a display of his works in his own home that 'Persons who look for mere Nature in works of Art ... are persons to whom Mr Dexter does not address himself with the brush. He relies entirely on his imagination. Nature puts him out.'[78] 'My house', he informs some real estate speculators who want to buy the property, 'is a standing monument of the picturesque and beautiful, amid the mean, dishonest, and grovelling constructions of a mean, dishonest, and grovelling age.'[79] One might expect his devotion to the aesthetic and manly values of a past generation to be interpreted by the middle-class as an admirable sign of commitment and perseverance in the wake of change; this is not the case, however, because his values fail to accommodate the demands that industry, expansionism, and capitalism were placing on contemporary artists. One was not to glorify simply fortitude, but fortitude in support of a capitalist economic ethos. In order to establish turf for the new generation of painters, Misserimus's resilience is interpreted as an out-dated quality that has atrophied into elitism and numb inaction. As Collins argues in *A Rogue's Life*, those with money should be spending it not on antiques but on the purchase of new works by new men. And they should definitely not be painting the stuff themselves.

So what is an artist to do? In Collins's 'Terribly Strange Bed', the painter as narrator succeeds in containing what is depicted as the dissident potential of various other signifiers of masculinity – the man of wealth, the man of the criminal underworld, even the man of military reserve. The author's preference for the diligent, undemonstrative gentleman accorded with the values and aspirations of the growing middle class who wished to separate themselves from the self-display of the wealthy and the inevitable visibility of the laborer. Efforts to establish an image of the hard-working, gentlemanly artist as manly perfection were never fully successful, however, because the prize of cultural authority associated with the category of the masculine ideal was so great that the plethora of identities vying for the reward refused to accept defeat. The diverse masculinities continued to develop, change, and intermingle throughout the era. Participating in this complex cultural process, Collins attempted to make visual a persona whose manly restraint paradoxically encouraged invisibility. Life-threatening adventures in the Americas, drunken descriptions of aerobic painting – the author's efforts to establish the bourgeois, male artist as vital to the economic health of his society resulted in proofs that he himself implies are unconvincing or even comical.

Collins's depictions reflect in part his own conflicted position as a middle-class artist whose main product was sensation fiction. It is ironic that visual artists found themselves trying to establish their own visibility through a valorization of non-display. And it is doubly ironic that, on one hand, Collins tried to depict the artist persona with which he associated himself as self-determined while, on the other, he recognized that his success as a sensation author made him reliant on those that he wished to believe were socially and culturally unnecessary. For him, it was not simply a choice to include unconventional characters against which to highlight an ideal. Rather, he relied on the presence of uncommon individuals for his success. These deviants defined his genre. They ensured his popularity and paid his wage. Misserimus's awesome charisma, physicality, and imagination fulfilled a generic requirement. Just as Valeria displays shock on viewing the character's sadomasochistic art even as she lingers over its details, readers of sensation literature may have seen themselves as respectable and moral but they also expected authors such as Collins to use their dexterous imaginations to offer titillating characters and scenarios. Misserimus's private gallery of horrors proves distinctly more attractive than the glorified historical works that Walter and Valentine struggle to perfect. Family and friends made Collins sensitive to the growing number of men hoping to establish their masculinity by succeeding in artistic careers but, notwithstanding the similarities between their struggles and his own, the author's literary niche demanded that he supply his audience with imaginative visions of diverse gender- and sex-based identities. Not surprisingly, *The Law and the Lady*'s closing incarceration of Misserimus in an insane asylum is unconvincing in its suggestion that such characters can be easily excised from Victorian society. The story's turn to institutional authority ultimately proves too uninspired to contain the chestnut-haired, wheelchair-riding, hyper-creative, beautiful painter – a collection of significations so unusual, so sensational, and so characteristic of the popular tastes and interests of the time.

3
Posing a Threat: Wilde, the Marquess, and the Portrayal of Degeneracy

In 1875, Wilkie Collins's *The Law and the Lady* presented the elegant, emotional, wheel-chair riding character of Misserimus Dexter that was discussed in the previous chapter. It was only two years previous that Walter Pater's *Studies in the History of the Renaissance* introduced to the British populace the philosophical basis for an aestheticist lifestyle defined by a similarly uncommon combination of emotionalism and inaction. And it would not be long after Pater's and Collins's publications that Victorian society would be graced by the presence of the dandy-aesthete – the most famous cultural persona to be defined by a union of inaction, refinement, and emotionalism. It is also in the dandy-aesthete that the aberrantly feminine was eventually categorized as an aspect of the homosexual. As the story of John Sholto Douglas, the ninth Marquess of Queensberry makes apparent, however, in order to capture and categorize the sexual deviant, one had to see him first. While dandy-aesthetes had become almost as common as *cartes de visite* by the final decades of the century, their proclivities remained tantalizingly out of the picture. Queensberry's battle with Wilde and the reification of the homosexual identity turned not on the dandy-aesthete's artifice, but the cultural visualization of it as desire.

More was at stake for the Marquess than his son's reputation. Despite the unnuanced association of aestheticism with degeneracy and artifice, conscious self-fashioning was far from exclusively a trait of the dandy-aesthete. Indeed, even Max Nordau saw value in self-decoration, as long as 'the instinct of vanity' is ultimately 'a result of thought about others, of preoccupation with the race'.[1] But if the costume is purposely intended 'to cause irritation to others', to 'lend itself to ridicule', and to excite 'disapproval instead of approbation', then the 'predilection for strange costume is a pathological aberration of a racial instinct'. It was when one's performance was used to acknowledge the subterfuge through what were generally seen as, for example, exaggerated physical gestures or excesses in literary form that they were perceived as problematic. Nordau's effort to suture such cultural performance to a biological degeneracy would not have left the Marquess feeling absolved of responsibility. Queensberry's concern about his son's pose is only partially an issue of hereditary taint. His anxiety also reflects a growing social recognition that acknowledging the performative aspects of identities exacerbated the effects of conceptual shifts regarding such things as the nation, the family, class, and sex that already threatened the traditional hierarchies from which he drew his own authority – as a father, as a nobleman, as a heterosexual, as a man. A comparison of his and Wilde's writing and photographic portraits shows that what Queensberry hoped to curtail, as much as his son's sexual proclivities, was the exposure of the pervasive performance of identities and the radical reconceptualization of social authority that he felt such a revelation could induce.

Degeneracy and portraiture

On April Fool's Day, 1894, the Marquess of Queensberry sent off a letter to his son Alfred Douglas in which he complains about the young man's relationship with Oscar Wilde:

> I come to the more painful part of this letter – your intimacy with this man Wilde. It must either cease or I will disown you and stop all money supplies. I am not going to try and analyse this intimacy, and I make no charge; but to my mind to pose as a thing is as bad as to be it. With my own eyes I saw you both in the most loathsome and disgusting relationship as expressed by your manner and expression. Never in my experience have I ever seen such a sight as that in your horrible features. No wonder people are talking as they are. Also I now hear on good authority, but this may be false, that his wife is petitioning to divorce him for sodomy and other crimes. ... Your disgusted so-called father, Queensberry.[2]

The chain of associations in this accusation is extensive and convoluted but, through these links, the Marquess is able to convince himself that he can see Wilde's sodomy not only in his son's actions, but even in his features. Queensberry's reference to himself as the 'so-called' father suggests that the connection between a dandiacal image and what he saw as a degenerate 'thing' is so complete that it risks displacing Douglas's identity as his son.

Theories of degeneracy and decadence thrived during the *fin-de-siécle*. The term 'degeneracy' was used at the time primarily to suggest a biological process, while 'decadence' brought greater emphasis to cultural signs of inertia, immorality, and unhealthy excess. The two terms demonstrate considerable overlap, however, in part because of the rhetorical slippage that such mixing permitted. Barbara Spackman has noted, with regard to decadence in literature and the arts, that it does not sustain a binary model by celebrating that which is usually reviled, but reinscribes the on-going possibility of alterities, thereby destabilizing binary oppositions.[3] Rather than take a stance on one side of the binary divide, decadent literature and art (and, I would add, performance) more precisely takes a position against the notion of a divide itself. As Spackman puts it, the relation 'is one of contamination whereby the logic of diversity functions to contaminate and introduce an asymmetry into the logic of absolute difference'.[4] This process is pervasive both in decadent literature and scholarship. Through the metaphor of contamination, Spackman herself benefits from the biologizing rhetoric of degeneracy that infects decadence, just as I have just contributed to the same with the word 'infects'. The mutual infiltration of degeneracy and decadence offers an effective model for the analysis of decadent literature and art as a politics of the marginalized that does not use what Foucault called a 'reverse discourse' for undermining the universalism of dominant, institutional discourses. That said, it also offered those wishing to reinforce their advantageous position within a center/margin binary model a means of demonizing art and literature as a threat to the health of the nation, the family, and the body.

In Queensberry's case, the language of degeneracy added a medical and scientific authority to his attack against his son's dandy-aesthete image. The gesture of delegitimation in his reference to himself as the 'so-called' father is, of course, less a sign of actual doubt of biological generation then part of a broader financial threat. The first half of the letter combines a chastisement of Douglas for his poor performance at Oxford with a refusal to continue to give the young man an allowance: 'I will disown you and stop all money supplies'. Queensberry sees his son, like Wilkie Collins's character Misserimus, to be lacking in drive, choosing 'to loaf and loll about and do nothing'. At the same time, the young man (again like Misserimus) lacks emotional reserve, coming across as 'hysterical[ly] impertinent'. While *The Law and the Lady* was not the main catalyst for the development, it would seem that the sensationally Gothic peculiarity that Collins created in an attempt to demonize a spectrum of masculinities had, within the span of a couple of decades, come to populate a broad swathe of Victorian society. Once people realized what to look for, Misserimusi were popping up everywhere. The rhetorical cross-contamination of 'degeneracy' and 'decadence' begins to explain how such a seemingly far-fetched persona could be so fully construed as an actual menace.

Notwithstanding the fact that the Marquess's suggestions of illegitimacy appear primarily to be no more than puffery reinforcing his threat of financial punishment, the rhetoric reflects that he was deeply troubled by his belief that an off-spring's biological degeneracy reflected a weakness in the family line.[5] The situation was no better, as far as he was concerned, if his son was simply playing the role of a faddish dandy-aesthete, because people might still interpret the pose as reflecting inherited flaws. His only hope of absolving himself of any blame, therefore, was to persuade the public that Douglas's external signs of degeneracy were nothing more than childish artifice. Ironically, in order to do so, the oppressive, hot-headed patriarch had to convince the court of his own pose as the concerned and caring father. A glance at a couple of late-Victorian photographic portraits – one of Wilde and Douglas, the other of the Marquess – suggests the difficulty in distinguishing between Wilde's and Queensberry's everyday use of performance, while also nevertheless revealing the revisionary decadent trace.[6]

During the second half of the nineteenth century, portraiture was among the most lucrative artistic activities.[7] More often than not, the paintings, like most heirlooms, were expected to reinforce the view of genealogy as a fundamental measure of worth and to support established hierarchies. This correlation is even reflected by the financial stability suggested by simply owning painted portraits of one's blood-relations. As Bourdieu has argued, 'family heirlooms not only bear material witness to the age and continuity of the lineage and so consecrate its social identity, which is inseparable from performance over time; they also contribute in a practical way to its spiritual reproduction, that is, to transmitting the values, virtues and competences which are the basis of legitimate membership in bourgeois dynasties'.[8] Portraits helped defend the authority of the family against individualism and extra-familial communities. This model of authority, moreover, reverberated through society's approach to broader issues concerning culture and the nation.

The Victorian association of portraiture with concerns regarding economic and political growth extended through to the end of the century. Even during the Edwardian era, Kenneth McConkey notes, 'the disposition of the age was to monumental social realism, to landscape and to portraiture. This latter genre was born of the desire for confident self-projection associated with the exercise of power'.[9] The late-nineteenth century, however, was also a time of large-scale economic anxieties, and the portrait reflected concerns regarding the dissipation of both Britain's class system and its national vitality. The increased mixing of new and old money and the growing commodification of identities such as the male and female dandy-aesthetes brought about a destabilization of the wealth/heredity equation that turned the portrait into a signifier of riches without any immediate association with lineage, refinement, or dignity. The financial wealth signified by ownership of portraits was less readily seen as a reflection of hereditary values.[10] The tenuousness of the portrait's actual significance became disconcertingly apparent. Changes in the economic landscape impacted on how society at large valued portraits and the accuracy of their signification, while the new image of portraits themselves as lacking the clear delineation of identity that the genre once provided offered an uncomfortably accurate reflection of anxieties regarding traditional systems of identity formation and categorization.

What Heather McPherson calls portraiture's 'identity crisis'[11] was exacerbated by a growing community of photographers who frequently broke the rules of the genre while undermining its exclusivity by making the product available to a broader class range. During what Arthur Mayne describes as this 'decadent' period of portraiture,[12] portable photograph shops complete with comic costumes and props dotted towns and vacation spots throughout Britain. As mentioned in the introduction, *cartes de visite* and their photographic portraits had become so common that, by the end of the century, they had lost their caché almost entirely. At the same time, some photographers' intentions of having their work recognized as high art, combined with the growing interest among artists in general for expressing their personal sense of their subjects, resulted in portrait theory shifting attention further away from communicating a subject's public standing to the task of presenting an individual's 'essence', which was understood to be some moral or psychological dimension inherent to the sitter. The distilled essence was, of course, not actually captured but signified through elements such as color, form, fashion, posture, and facial expression. The confusion of external signifiers (uniforms, finery, props, and so on) with a moral or psychological essence, however, made portraiture a useful context for Wilde's analysis of surface and depth models of identity, and their relation to sexual politics.

During the nineteenth century, reserve and restraint were seen as the most appropriate posing attributes, with the subject encouraged to adopt physical signifiers of high social rank. The metaphoric affirmation of the individual's authority and self-assurance was more frequently rendered in male, rather than female, physiognomy and posture.[13] As Audrey Linkman notes, in posing for a portrait, men were allowed 'greater assurance and assertiveness. This was achieved by means of crossed legs, elbows out at angles, with canes and umbrellas projecting into the space around them'.[14] As Lisa Hamilton and others have noted, representations of Wilde often implied that effeminacy (and its implications of deviancy) were demarcated on the man's body.[15] Wilde's image in the photograph of him and Bosie at a country house (Fig. 4), however, would have made a satisfactory technical illustration of portrait conventions of masculinity; his facial expression is restrained, one of his feet is placed confidently forward, and one of his elbows juts boldly away from his body. The image is reflected even more precisely in the photographs of Wilde taken in 1897 and 1900 in Rome.[16] The exiled Wilde – famous at this time as much for his illegal sexual pleasures as for his writing – presents himself as the perfect model of his society's masculine ideal. His pose, suggesting no sense of parody or irony on his part, effectively demonstrates the constructed quality of late-Victorian masculinity as it participated in a sphere of issues involving sexuality, gender, class, age, and nationalism.

Since Wilde was aware that he was being photographed, the image in figure 4 cannot be seen as mimetically representative of his everyday public persona, the image with which Queensberry had taken offense. That said, as Joseph Bristow has demonstrated, 'for all his displays of unmanly behaviour, few of Wilde's contemporaries suspected that he harboured same-sex desires.'[17] Prior to the trials, any of Wilde's posturing that others might have deemed peculiar would not have easily been read as a reflection of same-sex desire. The picture of the two lovers was shot in the autumn of 1892, when they were staying alone at a country house in Norfolk. ('What about your country house, and the life that is led there?' Basil had asked Dorian a couple of years earlier, 'Dorian, you don't know what is said about you'.[18]) The fact that he and Douglas are not in a public space, however, combined with his awareness that he had some control over the image, means that

Fig. 4 Photograph of Oscar Wilde with Alfred Douglas (1892)

Wilde could more likely have chosen to include some signifier of his love for Douglas. Notwithstanding the facts that Wilde *is* touching Douglas, and that someone might read the men's white or light-colored clothing as an 'excessive' refinement of taste, there is nothing strongly suggesting what Queensberry claims to have recognized as sodomitical or degenerate characteristics. Indeed, it would not be difficult to read the image – if the subjects were unknown – as a father affectionately showing off (or possibly supporting) his son. The element of display derives from the placement of Wilde's right hand on the back of Douglas's left shoulder. Had Wilde draped his arm across Bosie's neck, the gesture would have been a blatant one of acceptable male camaraderie, as suggested by casual photographic portraits of the time. But Wilde is discrete and seemingly self-conscious in his display of affection. More than half-hidden, Wilde's hand implies that he wishes to signify something less accepted than conventional friendship. So gentle, so tentative, the fingers connote not only the caution in Wilde's effort to display same-sex erotic affection, but also the general fragility at this time of relations that undermined conventional family-based notions of love.

Compare this portrait to one of the Marquess, taken in 1896 for *The Cycling World Illustrated* (Fig. 5). The latter photograph is in many ways similar to the one of Wilde and Douglas. Both pictures have the subjects positioned outdoors against a bucolic background of foliage, and all three men nevertheless stand on solid ground. Wilde and Queensberry look to be about the same height, weight, and general shape, and hold almost the exact same pose. Each man appears on the right side of the photograph, his body angled to the camera and leaning slightly forward. Each has his left foot planted before him, and each has that 'masculine' angle in the left arm. The men are also dressed in similar hats and sharp suits. These correspondences of self-fashioning between Queensberry and Wilde as secure and supportive patriarchs signal the jockeying for position that was taking place with regard to the men's relations to Alfred Douglas.

Even Moisés Kaufman's play *Gross Indecency: The Three Trials of Oscar Wilde*, which opened in New York in 1997, offers a sartorial echo that accentuates the sociopolitical maneuvering of the two men. The play opens with nine actors forming two lines on a simple set colored red, white, and black. The pervading structural order accords with the sense of tragic inevitability which gradually permeates the performance, as characters offer mechanical banter and motions, stylized shifts in scenario, and precise, eloquent language, much of which is taken directly from the works and reminiscences of Wilde, Douglas, and others. The story of Wilde's adult life becomes a familiarly tragic scenario in which an individual's fall from fame appears in part encouraged by his own arrogance. Kaufman takes Wilde's cue that he stood in symbolic relation to his cultural era and refashions the person as a symbol of the

Fig. 5   Photograph of the Marquess of Queenberry with a bicycle (1896)

ostracized and persecuted, a relation reinforced by the costuming. As participants in a courtroom scene, the characters are dressed in dark, simple suits and basic ties of judicial colors. Against this structured and muted backdrop, one quickly notices Wilde's yellow boutonniere and loose, red cravat, despite their lack of excess. In fact, the latter is echoed by Queensberry's own black cravat. In *Gross Indecency*, the difference that Queensberry and Wilde for the most part successfully establish between themselves is called into question from the start by their similarly authoritative personae as defined by their sartorial distance from the rest of the actors. When, during the first trial, Wilde reminds the court that he is the prosecutor, the interchangeability of Wilde's and Queensberry's roles becomes uncomfortably clear. This performative echo only accentuates the anxious need that Queensberry felt for establishing his, and his son's, distance from the other man.

Likewise, in the two men's photographs, the similarities in their self-presentations function to accentuate notable differences. Wilde's light-colored wardrobe, for example, contrasts with the Marquess's darker outfit. Ironically, the sportsman's knee-socks, breeches, and white shirt under dark clothing echo the garb that Wilde wore for the dandiacal portraits taken during his 1882 lecture tour in the United States.[19] The main difference between the two photographs, however, is in the additional subjects. Wilde is shown displaying, supporting, caressing Douglas in a way that confuses the older man's pose as possibly that of lover or that of father. At the time the picture was taken, Wilde was finishing writing *A Woman of No Importance*, the message of which Ellmann summarizes as follows: 'We are not what we think we are or what other people think us, and our ties to them may be greater or less than we imagine.'[20] Lytton Strachey presents Wilde's challenge to conventional identity hierarchies more boldly, describing Lord Illingworth as:

> a wicked Lord, staying in a country house, who has made up his mind to bugger one of the other guests – a handsome young man of twenty. The handsome young man is delighted; when his mother enters, sees his Lordship and recognises him as having copulated with her twenty years before, the result of which was – the handsome young man. She appeals to Lord [Illingworth] not to bugger his own son. He replies that that is an additional reason for doing it (oh! he's a *very* wicked Lord!).[21]

Strachey had to take full advantage of any coded discourse that the play may have offered in order to attain this interpretation, but he was encouraged to do so because of the decadent persona already attached to Wilde. Strachey's reading of the play, with its dependence on a knowledge of Wilde's public image, reinforces the idea that the man's caress, in the portrait, was intended to communicate more than just display. Eve Kosofsky Sedgwick, in her analysis of *The Importance of Being Earnest*, asks us to 'Forget the Name of the Father'.[22] Wilde's own pose seems to demand that we forget old what's-his-name entirely. Meanwhile, in the portrait in *Cycling World Illustrated*, Queensberry – having won the legal right to a say regarding the people with whom Douglas maintains relations, having put all that sodomitical business behind him – now has the free time proudly to display, support, and caress his bicycle.

The heredity of the phantom son

> I say it is a pity and a disgrace that our laws are often such that to obey a social law we must disregard a natural one; and *vice versâ*, that in obeying a natural one we have to violate the social. I blame not the so-called offenders, but the wrong law for the present time.[23]

In the late-Victorian period in which it was written, this argument, vague as it is in its terms, could have been read as a criticism of the laws opposing sodomy. It is, however, a statement made by Queensberry in defence of what he called a 'plurality of marriage' and what others called polygamy. The Marquess goes on to argue that he and the other members of his society 'are now imperfect in both health and morals, and we require a social system adapted to men and women as they are'.[24] A society's official laws, he proposes, should accommodate its level of degeneracy. Queensberry hoped to prove that sodomy, however, did not warrant such an understanding approach because, at least when his sons were involved, it was not a sign of natural degeneracy but of decadent bourgeois-bating. The point to realize is that Queensberry felt he had more on the line than Douglas's public image; he saw his son's performance as partly constructing his own identity as well.

The Marquess strongly believed that he was fundamentally responsible for his children's behaviour, that he was, in Foucault's words, 'in a position of "biological responsibility" with regard to the species'.[25] In a speech entitled 'The Religion of Secularism and the Perfectibility of

Man', Queensberry argues that, because 'we reproduce our children bodily ... [and] the Soul is the effect of the body, then we certainly reproduce *their Souls as well*, and thus become directly responsible for what those Souls may be and are.'[26] His poem *The Spirit of the Matterhorn* brings out the parental anxieties associated with this responsibility:

> Dark flows the blood impure within their veins,
> To scourge their children with their fathers' sins
>
> - - - -
>
> 'Behold their sickly frames and stunted growth:
> Their pallid cheeks and eyes, that should be bright,
> Already show a weariness of life.
> Alas, that such a cruel wrong should be,
> Of sins upon the children visited! ...'[27]

Contrary to what it might initially seem, the depiction of a youth with 'pallid cheeks and eyes' and a 'weariness of life' is not a description of the Marquess's youngest son. Douglas was only ten when the poem was published and possibly not even born when it was written. The poem echoes such classic Gothic texts as Horace Walpole's *Castle of Otranto* (1764) not only in its imagery but also in the depiction of the sinful father's son being a sickly, pallid youth. In both texts, moreover, the narrative reflects an anxiety about maintaining a strong, family line of biological and material inheritance. The poem moreover voices the common Victorian notion – as Mary Cowling, Daniel Pick, and others have noted – that posture, physiognomy, and pathognomy (facial expression) signify a person's moral standing.[28] The equation of heredity and degeneracy remains obtuse unless written on the body or, more precisely, read into the body. One can do more than speculate whether, once Douglas had become a decadent aesthete, Queensberry recognized in his son the profile that his poem personifies as the sins of the father – his own verbal portrait of degeneracy somehow having come to life.

The Marquess's sense of potential personal inadequacy arose most prominently with regard to marital difficulties. Seven years after his first wife, Sybil Montgomery, divorced him for adultery, his second wife, Ethel Weedon, also began divorce proceedings by accusing her husband of impotence. Montgomery's accusation was not unbearable for Queensberry because, while he saw heterosexual monogamy as the familial ideal, he frequently spoke out in favor of a 'plurality of marriage' whereby a husband, in certain situations, would take more than one wife. Impotence, conversely, he probably would have interpreted as a sign of degenerate inadequacy. Queensberry's theory of hereditary responsibility, combined with his virtually undeniable marital inadequacy, would have strongly suggested to him that he was himself at fault for any degeneracy that he might detect in his children.

Unfortunately, in Queensberry's eyes, his children exhibited many such flaws. He was aware that his eldest son, Francis, had probably had a sexual relationship with Lord Rosebery, Gladstone's Foreign Minister. In addition, the secularist's second son, Percy, married the daughter of a Cornish clergyman. And now Alfred – through pose, telegram, and anything else he could get his hands on – was announcing his intimate relations with Wilde. Queensberry, according to his own notion of heredity, would either have to accept the blame for what he saw as his children's flaws or disown his progeny. And he was too proud to take the blame. In a letter to Douglas, he writes, 'If I catch you again with that man I will make a public scandal. ... I shall not be blamed for allowing such a state of things to go on.'[29] In another letter in which he chastises Douglas, Queensberry once again questions (one assumes rhetorically) whether his wives' children are legitimate, stating that 'in this christian country ... 'tis a wise father who knows his own child'.[30] He also frequently threatened to disinherit his children. At one point, he writes, 'Your intimacy with this man Wilde ... must either cease or I will disown you.'[31] And, in another letter regarding Douglas, this time written to Percy, the Marquess complains that 'this good-for-nothing, white-livered son of mine, *if he is so* ... refuses to receive or answer letters. ... [Y]ou will find the whole town has been reeking with this hideous scandal of Oscar Wilde. ... [H]e has almost ruined my *so-called* son' (emphasis added).[32] 'So-called' is right up there with 'white-livered' as one of the Marquess's favourite adjectives for his offspring.

Queensberry's self-depiction in court makes it apparent that a dexterous deployment of performance can be used not only, as Judith Butler argues, to displace the oppressive cultural and political orders supported by the more common essentialist views, but also to reinforce them.[33] Unlike Wilde's performance of the detached aesthete, the role of the innocent, concerned father posed no threat to public notions of social responsibility. While the ideal of Queensberry-as-father was a major factor in the *Wilde v. Queensberry* trials, however, the image of Douglas-as-son was significantly absent from the scene. Douglas's limited presence is especially peculiar since he is described as having been a major catalyst for many of the two men's actions.

The Marquess apparently stated in court that it was primarily 'to save his son' that he had left Wilde a card inscribed with the words 'Oscar Wilde / posing somdomite' at the Albemarle Club.[34] It was this card that lead Wilde to prosecute Queensberry for libel. Within hours of the first trial, in which Queensberry was found not guilty, Wilde wrote to the *Evening News* to state that 'it would have been impossible for me to have proved my case without putting Lord Alfred Douglas in the witness box against his father ... but I would not let [Douglas] do so'.[35] Shortly after the first trial, with his own conviction for gross indecency imminent, Wilde, in a sudden turn of mind, decided to disregard Bernard Shaw and Frank Harris's advice to leave the country; this change occurred immediately after Douglas had re-affirmed his allegiance to his friend.[36] Ultimately, Wilde implies in *De Profundis*, Douglas deserved much of the blame for the initial legal proceedings against Queensberry, the failure of the case, and his own subsequent prosecution.

Even after Wilde's death, Douglas would continue to argue that, had he been given the opportunity to testify regarding Queensberry's ill-treatment of his family, Wilde would probably have won the case. But Douglas was only allowed to appear as the phantom 'Exhibit No. 1' that validated Queensberry's accusations. The more he became the principal justification of the Marquess's actions – as a member of an ideal familial bond – the less he was allowed to be seen. A letter that could have been used to prove that the Marquess had threatened Douglas with delegitimation, for example, is read instead as demonstrating his sincere paternal concern for his son's reputation. 'From the beginning to end', the Marquess's lawyer would argue, 'Lord Queensberry in dealing with Mr Oscar Wilde has been influenced by one hope alone – that of saving his son.'[37] But saving his son from what exactly?

Well, from a homosexual lifestyle obviously. But Douglas's decision to give primacy to his relation with Wilde over that with his father was not just a disgrace but also a challenge to the authority from which Queensberry and the courts spoke. The gesture contested the very paradigm that allowed hierarchies such as father/son to define the main channels of identity fashioning. Claims such as Douglas's threatened to replace ostensibly substantive identities with context-dependent, positional ones: 'Immoral' in relation to whom?' 'Sodomitical' in relation to whom? 'A father, an athlete, a marquess' in relation to whom? Queensberry implicitly acknowledged the efficacy of this decadent move when he suggested that pose and artifice can be difficult to distinguish from fundamental modes of being: 'to pose as a thing is as bad as to be it'. It was only by saving his son from the repetitions of a pose that constructed and reinforced what he perceived to be a sodomitical identity that Queensberry could sustain his own heteronormative, paternal role. As much as he might have been trying to save his son, he was also trying to protect himself or, more precisely, protect his own identity (and the authority and power that it proffered him) from accusations of degeneracy.

A number of scholars have made the claim that Queensberry's behaviour toward his family was not relevant to the case. H. Montgomery Hyde, for instance, argues that 'the sole issue which the jury would have to decide was a simple one of fact. Did Oscar Wilde pose as a sodomite?'[38] Edward Marjoribanks and Brian Roberts make similar suggestions.[39] While I find the sodomitical pose a stickier concept than Hyde implies, my immediate point is that neither Queensberry nor Wilde wanted Douglas's private life to be exposed. Although it is true to say that the jury was specifically required to decide whether or not Wilde was posing as a sodomite (thus proving whether or not the Marquess's statement was libelous), the argument that Queensberry had acted solely out of concern for his son was also relevant to this first trial because it was this catalyst that was seen to justify his risk of libel in the first place. Certain bonds, such as the hereditary ones between father and son, were viewed as fundamental to the dominant cultural model and, in particular instances, allowed a person to act according to rules outside the law. After all, the law and the government were intended to uphold, not supersede, an apparently inherent moral order defined, in large part, by the conventional family. Or, as Queensberry put it, 'social law' must bend to accord with 'natural law'.

Unlike Wilde's views, which threatened to disempower the conventional family model, Queensberry's domestic problems were regarded as less hazardous to the Victorian sociopolitical order. The *Daily Telegraph* chose painfully ironic terms to describe the abusive Marquess, after his acquittal, as 'this sorely-provoked and cruelly-injured father'.[40] As Roberts observes, the crowd that responded to the acquittal with 'irrepressible cheering', according to the *Daily Telegraph*, was uninterested in Queensberry's actual family life: 'What did they care if he had tormented and betrayed his wife, hounded his sons and sent offensive letters to his daughter-in-law? Such behaviour was deplorable but at least it fell within the bounds of recognizable sexual conduct'.[41] The judicial context favored Queensberry's stance and therefore turned a blind eye when he took advantage of performance to brace his social position.

Wilde and the positional being

While the judicial system of the 1890s for the most part reinforced the values and power structures that Queensberry supported, the realm of art was a domain in which Wilde had greater authority. It was nevertheless perhaps unwise of the prosecution to turn to an aesthetic discourse model to defend Wilde's statements and actions, arguing that his language must be read from a different perspective than that used for writing associated with 'commercial correspondence ... or those ordinary things which the necessities of life force upon one every day.'[42] When Queensberry's defense questioned Wilde on a passage from *The Picture of Dorian Gray* (1890, 1891) in which Basil Hallward describes his feelings for Dorian, Wilde is quoted as stating, 'I think it is the most perfect description possible of what an artist would feel on meeting a beautiful personality that he felt in some way or other was necessary to his art and life.' 'You think that is a moral kind of feeling for one man to have toward another?' persisted the defense. 'I say', replied Wilde, 'it is the feeling of an artist toward a beautiful personality.'[43] When asked to explain the love letter/prose poem that he had written to Douglas 'apart from art' (that is, outside the aesthetic model and within a supposedly more objective model), Wilde replied that he was unable to do so.[44]

This aesthetic discourse model supported the persona for which Wilde was best known and appreciated. However, by 1895 when the trial was taking place, aestheticism was well into what is now often called its 'decadent' phase, and the image of the dandy-aesthete had become an object of widespread derision. The couching of affection in aestheticist terminology had already been parodied over a decade earlier in Gilbert and Sullivan's comic opera *Patience*, first produced in 1881. One of the opera's 'rapturous maidens', having learned all about romance from a dandy-aesthete, defines the experience of love as 'aesthetic transfiguration', 'a transcendentality of delirium – an acute accentuation of a supremest ecstasy – which the earthy might easily mistake for indigestion'.[45] A court of law may not have been the best place for defending transfigurations beyond the 'earthy' issues of familial politics, and the juridical system would have found an aestheticist defense indigestible. In contrast to Queensberry's claim to hereditary responsibility, what Wilde presented as the source of his identity lacked the frame of any conventional depth model. This situation, however, was not a liability within the artistic sphere, which Wilde held superior to any other.

In the 1891 edition of *The Picture of Dorian Gray*, the portraitist Basil – foreshadowing the Marquess's visualization of sodomy on his son – comments that 'sin is a thing that writes itself across a man's face. It cannot be concealed. People talk sometimes of secret vices. There are no such things. If a wretched man has a vice, it shows itself in the lines of his mouth, the droop of his eyelids, the moulding of his hands even'.[46] Immediately following this declaration, however, Wilde has Basil undermine the claim by using the wicked Dorian himself as an example of a physiognomy that signifies nothing but virtue. The author was aware of the role that many Victorian's saw heredity playing in degeneracy. Dorian is himself an earnest collector of miniatures,[47] so he probably did not need Basil to tell him about the conflation of morality and visuality encapsulated in painterly aesthetics; likewise, the young man has little difficulty in using the semiotics of portraiture to consider his own inheritance of degeneracy. Speculating on the character of an acquaintance, he comments 'with such blood as he has in his veins, how could his record be clean?'.[48] The accusation sounds as if Dorian was directing it at himself, coming as it does only a few pages after he has searched the family pictures hanging in the gallery of his country house for suggestions of his own evil:

> Here was Philip Herbert, described by Francis Osborne, in his *Memoires on the Reigns of Queen Elizabeth and King James*, as one who was 'caressed by the Court for his handsome face, which kept him not long company'. Was it young Herbert's life that he sometimes led? Had some strange poisonous germ crept from body to body till it had reached his own? ... Here, in gold-embroidered red doublet, jewelled surcoat, and gilt-edged ruff and wrist-bands, stood Sir Anthony Sherard, with his silver-and-black armour piled at his feet. What had this man's legacy been? Had the lover of Giovanna of Naples bequeathed him some inheritance of sin and shame? [W]ere his own actions merely the dreams that the dead man had not dared to realise? Here from the fading canvas, smiled Lady Elizabeth Devereux, in her gauze hood, pearl stomacher, and pink slashed sleeves. A flower was in her right hand, and her left clasped an enamelled collar of white and damask roses. On a table by her side lay a mandolin and an apple. There were large green rosettes upon

her little pointed shoes. He knew her life, and the strange stories
that were told about her lovers. Had he something of her temperament in him?[49]

The list goes on: George Willoughby, an eighteenth-century macaroni
with heavy-lidded eyes, sensual lips, delicate lace ruffles and a weight
of rings; the second Lord Beckenham, an organizer of orgies who
stands proud and handsome with his chestnut curls and insolent pose;
Beckenham's wife – pallid, thin-lipped, and dressed in black; Dorian's
own mother, with 'moist wine-dashed lips' laughing at him as she
posed with vine leaves in her hair. The portraits reflect a centuries-long
lineage of aristocrats whose self-fashioning and physical features
conflate cultural and biological signs of degeneracy that are, in Wilde's
text, strongly stained with sexual deviancy. Echoing the phlegmatic,
undirected lifestyles of Dorian's ancestors, the language itself offers an
excess of detail, adjectives, and lists that create a backwater in the flow
of the narrative. At the same time, Dorian seems to luxuriate in the
images, entering imaginatively into the lifestyles and values of the
characters through the decadent aesthetics of detail, intensity, and
excess. The hauteur of the subjects, the particularities of their portraits,
and Wilde's own writing style all accord with the inaction, amorality,
and indifference of Dorian himself. Indeed, as the passage is structured,
it is impossible to see the paintings except through the eyes of the
young man, whose imaginative submersion into their realm is echoed
back by his sense of the works as semi-animated – watching and laughing at him.

Just as Wilde undermines Basil's articulation of physiognomy as text
by having the artist fail to read evil in Dorian's face, the author also
enjoys the decadent stylistics of the gallery scene but ultimately uses
portraiture's function as a signifier of identity, inheritance, and affection in order to challenge the conventional primacy of biological
bonds. The scene of Dorian with the paintings of his ancestors strongly
echoes the opening paragraphs of Joris-Karl Huysmans's foundational
decadent novel *À Rebours* (1884), which describes the portraits of the
Des Esseintes family. Following the first few paintings of individuals –
'imprisoned in old picture-frames' – with broad shoulders, 'piercing'
eyes and 'bulging' chests, there is, the author tells us, a 'gap in the pic-
torial pedigree' before one reaches the hero of the novel, Duc Jean Des
Esseintes. The only piece bridging the rupture depicts a man who looks
much like the central character: 'It was a strange, sly face, with pale,
drawn features; the cheekbones were punctuated with cosmetic

commas of rouge, the hair was plastered down and bound with a string of pearls, and the thin, painted neck emerged from the starched pleats of a ruff'.[50] Huysmans's blend of make-up and paint appropriately accentuates Des Esseintes's aim of self-determination through artifice, while the breach in the hereditary chain accentuates the possibility of alternate lines of influence. This commingling of self-presentation and portraiture emphasizes a destabilizing slippage that, rather than undermining the essentializing aims of only the portrait genre, turns the same accusations against human identity itself.

Like Huysmans, Wilde challenges the notion that his main character's identity is solely the product of biological heredity. In *À Rebours*, Des Esseintes's parents both die while he is very young, his mother of 'nervous exhaustion' and his father of 'some obscure illness'.[51] A surprising number of Wilde's heroes are also in fact parentless. Dorian's father, 'a mere nobody', is campily written out of the narrative – 'the poor chap was killed in a duel at Spa, a few months after the marriage' – with his mother following quick on his heels: 'the girl died too; died within a year'.[52] Ernest, in the play whose title echoes his name, is free from a conventional family model until the end of the play, when his lineage is discovered in a book. Cyril Graham – described, in 'The Portrait of Mr. W. H.', as an 'effeminate' man who 'set an absurdly high value on personal appearance' – is also conveniently orphaned: 'I should tell you that Cyril's father and mother were both dead. They had been drowned in a horrible yachting accident off the Isle of Wight'.[53] But as Lord Henry points out, with regard to Dorian's orphanage, 'it was an interesting background. It posed the lad, made him more perfect as it were'.[54] In contrast to various tools such as governesses and boarding schools by which Victorian society absented children and allowed parents greater freedom without questioning their ultimate authority, Wilde absents the parents in order to leave his young character 'posed' and ready for alternative formative influences.

Dorian envisions the individual as 'a being with myriad lives and myriad sensations, a complex multiform creature that bore within itself strange legacies of thought and passion, and whose very flesh was tainted with the monstrous maladies of the dead'.[55] The to-die-for aesthete also believes, however, that 'one had ancestors in literature, as well as in one's own race, nearer perhaps in type and temperament, many of them, and certainly with an influence of which one was more absolutely conscious'.[56] Ed Cohen has insightfully argued that Basil's portrait of Dorian functions as an object of mediation for male-male desire.[57] In a related sense, this mediatory fulcrum also operates in

Dorian Gray to demonstrate the means by which individuals can inherit the attributes by which they identify themselves from texts and people other than blood relations.

The three central characters of Wilde's novel all note this mutual exchange of identities. Declaring that 'every portrait that is painted with feeling is a portrait of the artist, not of the sitter',[58] Basil claims that he has put too much of himself into the painting of his friend,[59] has in fact contributed 'the secret of his own soul'.[60] Soon after, however, he reverses the flow of influence, noting that Dorian's personality threatens to 'absorb [his] whole nature, [his] whole soul, [his] very art itself'.[61] Later he confesses to Dorian, 'your personality had the most extraordinary influence over me. I was dominated, soul, brain, and power by you'.[62] This would mean that, even if it is a portrait of Basil's own soul (as he claims), the painting is to some degree still a painting of Dorian, who has so influenced Basil's identity. Echoing Spackman's definition of decadence itself, the subject and artist contaminate each other such that a stable binary equation of influence proves inadequate. But Wilde's exploration of influence does not end there. During the crucial period of the painting's completion, Dorian is mentally usurped by a third man, Lord Henry, who finds 'something terribly enthralling in the exercise of influence. No other activity was like it. To project one's soul into some gracious form'.[63] Here as well the notion of mutual contamination is apparent, with Lord Henry having himself ultimately fallen under another's influence, as his highly specialized portrait collection suggests; 'I know you quite well by your photographs', Lady Henry tells Dorian, adding, with the driest of erotic innuendo, 'I think my husband has got seventeen of them.'[64]

Pointing to the complex cross-flow of influence through Basil's artwork, Wilde has Dorian overtly acknowledge the vital role of the painting – 'It is part of myself. I feel that'[65] – while Basil similarly concludes that Dorian 'is all my art to me now'.[66] In addition to being a mediator of affection, the portrait functions as an ontological nexus of Basil's, Dorian's, and Lord Henry's identities. The three men are neither just individuals attracted to and influenced by each other, nor aspects of one identity, but each is an individual combination of more than one history of identity formation that is not wholly contingent on conventional notions of biological heredity. The lines of influence energize the portrait so that it gains an identity in some ways as unique and valid as those of the three men. Not only does it possess an almost living force (signified by its protean visage), but its own transformative power destabilizes the other three individuals' control of their own identities, overwhelming their substantive façades with dynamic positionalities of varying critical effect. Basil, Dorian, and Lord Henry all recognize to differing degrees the flux of their own identities, an awareness that leads Dorian to revalue his identity as being no more fundamental than that of the portrait. Basil suggests his own awareness of the painting's independent energy when he replies, to Dorian's proclamation that the painting is part of him, with the affectionate joke, 'Well, as soon as you are dry, you shall be varnished, and framed, and sent home. Then you can do what you like with yourself'.[67] Kenneth McConkey argues that Wilde called the novel *The Picture* – rather than *The Portrait* – *of Dorian Gray* in order to emphasize the painting's partial self-control; 'picture' does not depend on the subject of the painting, while 'portrait' refers only to a representation of some other living thing.[68] The picture of Dorian, like any portrait, is the result of a range of personalities and of various lines of influence – including the hereditary, aesthetic, and emotional.

Once the painter has finished his work, however, the text remains open to competing rhetorics of visuality, just as viewers remain open to the influence of the art itself. In his novel, Wilde picks up on this active element of portraiture, a dynamism that Jeff Nunokawa has suggested in his discussion of 'the passion of the eye' in Wilde's work, a passion that acts in contrast to systems of homogenization and ossification such as those of science and commodity culture.[69] Dorian, unable to sever his relations with the painting, laments the existence of this force in the attic: 'there is something fatal about a portrait. It has a life of its own'.[70] Meanwhile, Basil finds that the absence of the object which he had helped bring into being fosters in him a new sense of freedom: 'after a few days the thing left my studio, and as soon as I had got rid of the intolerable fascination of its presence it seemed to me that I had been foolish in imagining that I had seen anything in it'.[71] The portraitist, however, has only suppressed his awareness of its influence on either his sight or identity. Ultimately, the 'thing' that he seems no longer to want to envision or name leads him to Dorian's dank and dusty confines. Here Dorian kills Basil and then blackmails an acquaintance into destroying the corpse, which Dorian now refers to as 'the thing, ... the dead thing',[72] perversely echoing Basil's term for the portrait (and eerily foreshadowing Queensberry's reference to his sodomitical son).

While the corpse is being destroyed, Dorian doodles miniatures of Basil's face, belittling the artist's affectionate painting of Dorian by himself propagating a plethora of portraits to replace the now dead man. The mass production of the victim's image can also be read as implying the murderer's sense of guilt, the presence of a conscience. The repetitive act is a pained reflection of the man's desire to bring his friend back to life. As portraits are shown to take part in the exchange of emotions to the extent where they themselves can be seen as participants in relationships, Dorian's doodles are, symbolically speaking, a conflicted attempt at resuscitation. The anxiety Dorian finally acknowledges by stabbing his own portrait reflects the fact that, despite his seemingly permanent beauty, his identity is not fixed. Nor is that of a portrait. The structure of the novel, moreover, ensures that, although those who see murder as less horrific than the destruction of an artwork are rare, the reader's emotions reach a climax not with Basil's death, but with the stabbing of the portrait. In accord with the importance that the novel places on pose and performance, Wilde shows the art object to have as great an influence as human beings on a person's identity. This is not to argue that the author saw art as having equal value to humans, but that he wished to emphasize art's impact on everyday visuality, identity, and human interaction.

Although artifice and pose have frequently been presented as decadent phenomena, Queensberry's and Wilde's performances in literature, photography, and the courtroom demonstrate that the actual distinction that categorizes something or someone as decadent is not between artifice and nature, but between the acknowledgment and denial of the role that self-display and performance play in identity formation. Wilde turned to portraiture as a volatile conflation of essentialist and constructed traits in order to demonstrate that sexuality can override familial affiliations as a principal influence on the fashioning of one's identity. Some queer activists and theorists have voiced a logical extension to this Wildean concern by questioning the motivations behind establishing a hierarchy of influence at all. This stance was apparent, for example, in the *mode de jour* at a recent Pride Day parade – a T-shirt with the bold and brazen phrase 'So what if it *is* a choice?' The question (which appropriately reads more like a declaration) is a response to the claim made by Queensberry and others that less common desires are learned and therefore can and should be unlearned or at least put aside. The slogan is also an attempt to move beyond the claim that whatever is viewed as fundamental or natural is unarguably ethical and justified. While some gays, lesbians, transsexuals, and transgendered individuals have defended their desires by stating that they had no choice, what this piece of casual wear points out is that the right to express one's desires should not be based on whether they are seen as inherent. This was also an aim behind Wilde's invigoration of the portrait genre. By empowering artistic representation with an identity that interacted with other human identities, he did not naturalize the pose or de-essentialize the body; rather, he destabilized the very binaries of essence and construct, degeneracy and decadence, identity and pose, on which cultural hierarchies – including those of artistic genres – base their authority.

Paradigms of degeneracy, disease, and infection have proven useful in theorizing decadent art, literature, and personae, and in discouraging a slip back into rigid binary models of haves and have-nots. The formulation is encouraged, moreover, by its echo of images that dominate the works of decadent authors themselves. A major difficulty with this language, however, is that it sustains the association of decadent authors, artists, and characters with the unconventional and damaged. Authors such as Huysmans and Wilde, however, have also put forward a more neutral model of nonbinary interaction that is characterized by a similar liquidity to that which is found in the 'infection paradigm' – the model of portraiture and visualization. As Queensberry and Wilde's interaction demonstrates, the rhetoric of visuality reflects both aesthetic and biological languages that were used to support differing notions of acceptable sexualities and desires. Victorians realized that sight was not purely objective, and the ambiguous language of perception sanctioned an ethical lee-way with regard to the exploration of sexualities without brazenly troubling the broader readership. Such an unthreatening language of desire would have proven especially useful for women, who were even less encouraged than men to discuss these issues. Two women who accessed this channel to sexual exploration were Vernon Lee and Virginia Woolf. In the next chapter, I with to turn to these authors and their use of the rhetoric of aesthetics and portraiture to undermine the broader values that such a conventional genre had supported for centuries.

4
The Forest Beyond the Frame: Women's Desires in Vernon Lee and Virginia Woolf

Portraiture and gender dissidence make for odd bed-fellows. Despite the supernatural calisthenics of portraits in Gothic and sensation literature, the conventions of the visual genre had throughout the nineteenth century remained for the most part ossified into reinforcements for the historical and biological claims of the status quo. They discouraged what could be conceived of as any destabilization by uncommon desires. By the turn of the century, the genre would have been seen as lacking the creative flexibility necessary to accommodate feminist and other gender-based interrogations of traditional depth models of identity. Some authors working within the aestheticist tradition, however, recognized that the brittleness of such a constricting genre actually offered a useful site of volatility, especially at the intersection of artistic and political value systems. The staid rules of portraiture actually helped foreground its spurious objective of fixity and allowed authors to turn this rigidity into a means of contesting the very ideals that the genre had conventionally enforced.

Scholars to date have not fully acknowledged portraiture's role in the on-going struggle to visualize a feminist aesthetic. In this chapter, I wish to bring forward the important impact of the author and intellectual Vernon Lee on later writers such as Virginia Woolf. Beginning with an articulation of Lee's feminist aestheticism, my aim in this chapter is to demonstrate that both Lee's 'Oke of Okehurst'(1892) and Woolf's *Orlando* (1928) use the malleable potential of visuality and aesthetics to break portraiture's characteristic inflexibility and, along with it, the fixed notions of gender and sexuality that it reinforces.

Despite my support in the first chapter for reading the presence of same-sex female desires in novels by Geraldine Jewsbury, Mary Elizabeth Braddon, and Dinah Mulock Craik, most efforts in Victorian literature to represent women whose main objects of attraction are other women had resulted in depictions of friends engaged in sanitized nonsexual relationships or silent spinsters cowering in the shadowy leaves of secondary narratives before withering away like the spindly branches of otherwise vibrant family trees.[1] Both Lee and Woolf, however, combined portraiture and aestheticism to offer a bolder vision of female-female passions. Doing so allowed them to take essentializing artistic conventions that hindered individual exploration and self-expression and to reconfigure them into tools of contestation for women who wished to articulate unsanctioned emotional needs and desires.

Aestheticism and Vernon Lee's undying empathy

It may be sticking one's neck out to argue that the opening description in Woolf's *Orlando* of the young hero playing at decapitation is a reference to Lee's own childhood participation in historical charades of the beheading of Mary Queen of Scots and the Earl of Essex,[2] even if one of the decapitations that Woolf refers to is Mary's.[3] Nevertheless, the author had read and even reviewed much of Lee's work. Christa Zorn has described Woolf as one of Lee's 'most outspoken critics', being especially critical of what she saw as the older woman's subjectivity and egocentrism.[4] This is a view with which Vineta Colby concurs,[5] although Colby points out that Woolf's reviews also include complements on Lee's ingenuity, passion, and extensive knowledge on the subject of aesthetics.[6] Woolfs's Hogarth Press had even published Lee's appropriately ekphrastic treatise *The Poet's Eye* in 1926, two years before *Orlando* hit the market. Woolf was also aware that their mutual acquaintance, Roger Fry, valued the older woman's views.[7] In fact, Fry's own highly influential aesthetic theory, which bases the experience of beauty in 'significant form' rather than in the things defined by forms, accords in a number of ways with the concepts of beauty and appreciation that Lee had begun articulating decades earlier.

Textual echoes of Lee's works are also scattered throughout Woolf's novel, from the arboreal titles of Lee's 'Oke of Okehurst' and the character Orlando's poem 'The Oak', to the sexually ambiguous Russian woman in both Lee's well-known 1884 novel *Miss Brown* and Woolf's *Orlando* (named Sacha and Sasha respectively), to the general setting of 'Oke of Okehurst' and *Orlando* in Kentish manor houses stuffed with history, mystery, and private galleries.[8] *Orlando* also follows *Miss Brown* in its abundance of portraits and lopped-off heads.[9] Meanwhile, the eponymous hero's time travel brings to mind not only 'Oke of Okehurst' but also Lee's first publication, *Les Aventures d'une pièce de monnaie* (1870), which depicts a coin (itself a type of portrait miniature) as it changes hands and experiences various adventures over hundreds of years. In addition to more intricate echoes, such as the representations of gender ambiguity, bisexuality, and female–female attraction, one of the most complex elements found in both Lee's texts and *Orlando* is the use of portraiture to critique the male-privileging, heterosexual conventions of aesthetics, inheritance, and affection.

Notwithstanding Lee's claim that aestheticism was dead in London as early as 1881,[10] her later discussions of beauty are aligned with the more popular theories of aestheticism – such as those of Walter Pater – in their attention to amorality and sensual pleasure. The only 'disciple' that Pater acknowledged as such,[11] Lee argues in her study *The Beautiful: An Introduction to Psychological Aesthetics* (1913) that beauty is amoral because it is the product of a person's psychological response not to an object but to its formal qualities. Despite the formalist slant of her argument, she refers to this experience of beauty as 'empathy' (from the German *Einfühlung*), the element of perception to which 'we probably owe the bulk of whatever satisfaction we connect with the word Beautiful'.[12] This empathy occurs when a person is stimulated to project sensations of movement onto the object whose form is being appreciated.[13] Each experience of beauty, moreover, operates in combination with a person's accumulated and averaged past experiences of movements of the same kind.[14] Beauty is therefore the product not of an isolated fleeting impression but of this impression in combination with one's memory (or some other mode of retention) of previous comparable experiences, as well as the cumulative history of such experiences. A transhistorical bond is reinforced by each experience of the beautiful because, regardless of its own transitoriness, it is part of an on-going empathy – a historical repetition of an emotional experience that knows no origin. Lee's notion that history is enlivened and made immediate through such an experience foreshadows Walter Benjamin's more encompassing image of the modern city as always existing as a combination of 'the new in connection with that which has always already been there'.[15] For Lee, however, the experience is inherently aesthetic; the sense of 'being companioned by the past, of being in a place warmed for our living by the lives of others',[16] arises whenever someone enjoys this form of pleasure, whether it be while viewing the Italian countryside, a Gothic arch, or the body of a human being.[17]

By having defined empathy as the appreciation of transhistorical beauty, Lee constructed a safer context for exploring in words her love and affection for other women such as Mary Robinson and Kit Anstruther-Thomson. The conceptual distance that most scholars at this time saw as necessary for aesthetic appreciation assumed a separation of the admirer from the object of admiration. The tendency would be to read erotically charged (albeit still covert) aesthetic discussions such as Lee's as disembodied and nonthreatening. Oscar Wilde made use of this sexual-aesthetic blurring in his courtroom defense of his love-letters to Bosie. Lee likewise reflects this perception, appearing to have no difficulty addressing sensuality if it is positioned historically. She readily compares 'this historic habit' to 'the capacity of deriving pleasure from nature, not merely through the eye, but through all the sense'.[18] The erotics of her notion of empathy are apparent from the sensuality of her descriptions of the experience, as well as from her focus on emotions, movement, and vitality. In *The Beautiful*, for example, she describes a landscape as being made up of 'keenly thrusting, delicately yielding lines, meeting as purposefully as if they had all been alive and executing *some* great, intricate dance'.[19] Elsewhere, she depicts her own experience of empathy as an indescribable 'kind of rapture ... compounded of many and various elements, its origin far down in mysterious depths of our nature; ... it arises overwhelmingly from many springs, filling us with the throb of vague passions welling from our most vital parts'. 'Swept along the dark and gleaming whirlpools of the past', Lee's empathy is nothing less than an orgasmic submersion into a flowing, throbbing rapture.[20]

In 'Oke of Okehurst', Lee uses portraits and their association with heredity to fuse the sensuality of her aestheticism with gender and sexual politics. Throughout Lee's life, portraiture reinforced the view of genealogy as an essential identificatory trait. Diane Gillespie has suggested that the genre fulfilled such a role for some of Woolf's characters as well by recalling 'family intimacy and identity, tradition and authority .... the paintings help to characterize their owners'.[21] Despite its strong connection to heredity and tradition, portraiture could not entirely alleviate contemporary concerns regarding the growing influence of the nouveau riche on class distinctions. The genre's confirmation of upper-class values had become increasingly tenuous not only through the influence of new money on consumer demographics but also by photography's role in the democratization of the genre by enhancing its accessibility. Kodak's 'Brownie' camera had appeared on the scene in the 1890s, making a portraitist out of virtually anybody with an urge to press the button.

In addition to challenging portraiture's elitism, photographers were adding pressure to the painter's claim of capturing the essence of a subject. For years, West European culture has seen the visual arts in general as accessing a source of expression unavailable to the written word. If a person's 'very essence' cannot be seized, laments the narrator of Lee's 'Oke of Okehurst', by 'the pencil and brush, imitating each line and tint, ... how is it possible to give even the vaguest notion with mere wretched words – words possessing only a wretched abstract meaning, an impotent conventional association?'[22] Woolf's great aunt, the photographer Julia Margaret Cameron, similarly concluded that, 'beyond the mere portrayal of external form and feature ... the portraitist had a moral obligation to reveal the inner spiritual qualities that ennobled mind and soul'.[23] She worked toward this end by 'combining the real and the ideal and sacrificing nothing of the Truth'.[24] In her photographs, Cameron used stilted poses and costuming; fictional and historical captions; and idealizing chiaroscuro that, as Natasha Aleksiuk has remarked, encourage a recognition of the constructedness of identity.[25] Nevertheless, in Cameron's view, the photographer's main aim in such artifice and idealization was to capture essential inner qualities of the sitter. Lee, however, contested the possibility of representing or defining such phantasmal phenomena. For her, the portrait was 'one of our most signal cravings after *the impossible*: an attempt to overcome space and baffle time; to imprison and use at pleasure *the most fleeting, intangible, and uncommunicable* of all mysterious essences, a human personality' (my emphasis).[26] In accord with this argument, 'Oke of Okehurst' depicts a portrait not entrapping a person's essence but allowing a person to breach temporal boundaries through empathy, a transgression that also challenges barriers to unconventional desires.[27]

'Oke of Okehurst' is the story of a woman who, with the imaginative aid of a portrait, develops an immense empathy for her ancestral namesake. The affiliation becomes so strong, that the heroine adopts the dead woman's attitude, clothing, and often androgynous appearance. As the male narrator of the story puts it, 'the Alice Oke of the year 1626 was the caprice, the mania, the pose, the whatever you may call it, of the Alice Oke of 1880'.[28] Left out of the heroine's emotional sphere, he criticizes her for being 'utterly incapable of understanding or sympathising with the feelings of other persons, [having] entered completely and passionately into the feelings of this woman'.[29] Alice's husband William, meanwhile, is a landed gentleman described as a perfect example of English masculinity – tall, strong, handsome, reticent, conservative, quiet, and moral. While the descriptions of the heroine are detailed and meticulous, Lee demarcates the patriarch's privileged social position through quick Impressionistic descriptions of him as daubs of pink and white. Like the story's portraitist, William is also disturbed by his wife's attachment to the dead Alice, primarily because the ancestor is rumored to have committed adultery. Nor are his anxieties alleviated by the added legend that the seventeenth-century Alice, while dressed as a man, had helped her husband kill the adulterer. The heroine now keeps hidden from William a miniature portrait believed to be of the murdered Cavalier poet. Despite this bit of secrecy, she takes every opportunity to nettle her husband with the possibility that the ghost of the Cavalier haunts their home. By aggravating her seemingly stolid, unimaginative husband with spectral possibilities, the heroine eventually forces him to reveal the superstitions and fabrications underlying his own façade of the rational, direct Englishman.

Because her affections are directed backward in time toward her namesake and the namesake's rumored lover, Alice is not bothered by the fact that she and her husband are childless, the end of a gnarled aristocratic family tree. For the same reason, she does not follow her ancestor in committing adultery. Nevertheless, William's doubts get the best of him, and in a state of delusion he visualizes the lover and then shoots his wife while thinking that he is shooting the Cavalier, an entity who has never in fact existed except centuries earlier. Although this anxious attack seals the Okes' hereditary fate, it does nothing to keep the overwhelming empathy between the Alices from being inherited by some future individual through the aesthetic admiration of what has by now, due to the heroine's adaptation of her ancestor's identity, become a painting of both women. While the Okes' chain of tradition and heredity is severed, a same-sex line of admiration and affection continues through portraiture, ironically the very genre whose main recognized purpose was to reinforce the normative lineage.

Zorn has recently demonstrated that Lee 'often connects sexual desires with places to create transcending subject positions beyond the boundaries of sex and gender'.[30] In 'Oke of Okehurst,' Lee's articulation of an alternate tradition of attraction attains a broader meaning through the narrator of this story – a man whom the Okes have hired to paint their likenesses. During his story he articulates principal elements of Lee's aestheticism. He brings to mind, for example, her sense of 'being in a place warmed for our living by the lives of others', when he comments that the 'impressions of the past' that he feels in Okehurst Manor 'seemed faded like the figures in the arras, but still warm like the embers in the fire-place, still sweet and subtle like the perfume of the dead rose-leaves and broken spices in the china bowls'.[31] In accord with the historic component of Lee's aestheticism, he also acknowledges that the essence always escapes the portrait because 'real beauty is as much a thing in time – a thing like music, a succession, a series – as in space'.[32] The temporality of identity is as important for the character as it was for both Alice and Lee. It is in their attitudes toward gender that the author and her male narrator diverge.

The painter's biases surface in his approach to the Okes both as subjects of his art and as members of society. He completes the likeness of William – the uninspiring embodiment of mainstream Victorian masculinity – without a hitch. The image of Alice, however, escapes him, remaining in the end 'merely blocked in, and seem[ing] quite mad'.[33] He cannot capture the woman's essence without understanding her desires, an experience that he claims is impeded by her mental instability but that actually comes across as being curtailed by his dependence on generic formulas. Lee contrasts the heroine's attraction to her ancestor with the painter's infatuation with the living Alice not as a person but as a collection of formal qualities, 'a combination of lines, a system of movements, an outline, a gesture'.[34] 'I never thought about her as a body – bones, flesh, that sort of thing', he observes, 'but merely as a wonderful series of lines, and a wonderful strangeness of personality'.[35] The portraitist ultimately decides that, regardless of the ramifications, he must paint the woman in the exact same clothes, stance, and setting as those in which the dead Alice appears in *her* portrait. What he fails to realize is that such a venture could at best only reproduce the painting that already exists or – looking at it from another direction – that the Victorian Alice is already the closest thing to the living form, the 'essence', of the portrait painted centuries ago, even as she is her own individual. The portraitist's unemotional aestheticization of the female body diverges from Lee's own theory of empathy, which we find embodied in Alice Oke, a woman whose beauty and affections transgress time.

The force of the same-sex bond in 'Oke of Okehurst' arises from the heroine's devotion to her namesake surpassing not only the portraitist's interest in the living Alice but also the dead Alice's dubious attachment to a lover who may have never existed and, if he did, who she then helped murder. The incommensurability of Alice's main attraction, on the one hand, and generic and cultural conventions, on the other, causes a disjuncture that established social and textual narratives appear unable to reconcile without killing off the heroine. More precisely, Alice's murder is the result of her society's inability or unwillingness to accept her attachment to this woman from the past. William kills his wife not for her interest in another man so much as for her undying devotion to another woman. The narrator, meanwhile, concludes that the heroine's empathy is a 'psychological peculiarity' that 'might be summed up in an exorbitant and absorbing interest in herself – a Narcissus attitude' combined with 'a perverse desire to surprise and shock'.[36] Despite his application of this rather thin coat of scientific discourse to reinforce his self-serving aestheticism, the ghost of the painter's own biases continues to show through.[37]

The portraitist's description of Alice as both self-absorbed and desperate for social confirmation strongly echoes the accusations that the eponymous heroine of Lee's 1884 *Miss Brown*, roughly a decade earlier, directs against a community of male artists. The novel's depiction of late-Victorian aesthetes is, as many readers of the time argued, an oversimplified caricature. Nevertheless, within the reality of the novel itself, the heroine's critique is warranted by the men's shallowness, elitism, and misogyny. The narrator of 'Oke of Okehurst', conversely, has a far flimsier basis for his medical prognosis, especially after he notes in passing his own mental instability. In one scene, he imagines that he sees the Cavalier poet and his dead horse in the middle of a room full of guests. He then quickly blames the hallucination on the other visitors and never mentions it again.

In a peculiar way, however, the male painter's delusion adds justification to the patriarch's mental instability. If the lunatics have taken over the asylum, then the norm must follow. The narrator himself becomes more and more interested in noting signs of William's illness, as if to justify his own difficulties. He mentions the man's recurring 'maniac-frown' and describes a number of occasions when the husband claims to see the Cavalier. The portraitist then goes out of his way to counter these signs of dementia by effusing over the man as a 'perfectly conscientious young Englishman',[38] 'a regular Kentish Tory',[39] a 'serious, conscientious, slow-brained representative of English simplicity and honesty and thoroughness'.[40] Recognizing that men like William are necessary to reinforce his society's current order, the painter shifts the responsibility for William's dementia (and his own) onto the woman. He describes Alice not only as deranged but also as forcing her husband to suffer mental abuse by encouraging him to envision the Cavalier's ghost. Reinforcing his essentializing discourses of portrait aesthetics and science, the painter makes Alice responsible for her own death by describing her as a conniving maniac lacking English simplicity.

The heroine meanwhile, through her attraction to her namesake, has made it apparent that the appreciation of beauty does not require the idealization and disembodiment that men frequently impose on their female subjects. Admiration may be a formalist quality for Lee, but it is also vital, dynamic, and empathic. The author's aestheticist challenge to dehumanizing notions of beauty are paralleled by the threat that Alice's affections pose to the power hierarchy by which traditional notions of family and nation are secured. It is this richness in portrait-ure's cultural role that Woolf, in *Orlando*, takes advantage of to inter-rogate the politics behind the interdependence of established notions of beauty, inheritance, gender, and desire.

The desiring narrative of *Orlando*'s portrait

Heads strung up by ropes, heads stuck on spears, heads tumbling through the streets – references to decapitation abound in Woolf's *Orlando*. The novel even opens with decapitation: 'He – for there could be no doubt of his sex, though the fashion of the time did something to disguise it – was in the act of slicing at the head of a Moor which swung from the rafters'.[41] This spill of heads is echoed by an equal pro-liferation of visual portraits whose figures, although conventionally intended to signify that the heads of the family and the nation remain securely in place, are often presented as severed by the picture frames, if not bodiless. Even the image of a privileged androgynous youth swinging a knife at a head hanging in an attic incorporates portraiture by bringing to mind the climactic scene of Wilde's *Picture of Dorian Gray* in which the hero slices at his own likeness.

Orlando and Dorian could have been brothers. Both of the knife-wielding men are wealthy, handsome, and sexually unconventional, and both maintain a youthfulness far beyond the powers of any skin care products of their time. The comic tone of Woolf's allusion to the earlier work suggests, however, that, although she may have appreci-ated Wilde's complex inquiry into the relations between pose and identity, she was also taking a jab at the aestheticist penchant for ideal-izing the human body, a practice that was anything but novel when directed at women. Although Woolf includes Pater among the humorously long list of friends whom she thanks in the preface to *Orlando*, she also felt that literature 'had grown a little sultry and scented with Oscar Wilde and Walter Pater'.[42] To see Woolf's ambivalence toward the views and styles of these men as a reaction to all that aestheticism had to offer, however, is to ignore her adaptation of Lee's research and writing on the relation of beauty and humanity.

One can detect Lee's aestheticism at various points in *Orlando*. Woolf's narrator questions the notion of a single identity, for example, by claiming that there are multiple 'selves of which we are built up, one on top of another, ... [with] attachments elsewhere, sympathies, little constitutions and rights of their own, call them what you will (and for many of these things there is no name), ... and some are too wildly ridiculous to be mentioned in print at all'.[43] This passage not only foregrounds nonnormative and often nameless 'attachments elsewhere' but also acknowledges that the printed text imposes limits on the iteration of such attachments. The layering of identity described by *Orlando*'s narrator brings to mind Lee's definition of beauty as a building up of experiences of empathy that transgress time. Prevented from fully addressing her needs and desires in the present, Lee describes 'being companioned by the past',[44] just as Orlando searches for signs of affection and empathy in ancestral portraits. In a note to herself Woolf wrote that *Orlando* was to be based on the theory that 'character goes on underground before we are born; and leaves something afterword [sic] also'.[45] Thus Orlando asks, 'how many different people are there not – Heaven help us – all having lodgment at one time or another in the human spirit?'.[46] Orlando eventually finds solace in an elusive entity from the past – 'something one trembles to pin through the body with a name and call beauty, for it has no body, is as a shadow without substance or quality of its own, yet has the power to change whatever it adds itself to'.[47] Like Alice Oke, Orlando is both a person who looks to the past for empathy and emotional fulfilment, and the omnitemporal embodiment that affirms that such a beautiful experience is possible.

Lee is of course not the sole influence on Woolf's interest in aesthetics, or even aestheticism. Woolf often tried to conceive of her writing visually. She even referred to some of her own works as portraits[48] and to her friends as 'a gallery of little bright portraits hanging against the wall of my mind'.[49] Invoking a central tenet of Cameron's portrait theory, Woolf experimented with styles of writing that might capture the character of her subject rather than simply offer a recognizable, physical blazon. In her biography of Fry, for example, she incorporated some of his own writings because, as she explained (turning to metaphors of visuality), she 'was certain he would shine by his own light better than through any painted shade of [hers]'.[50] In Woolf's words, 'in order that the light of personality may shine through, facts must be manipulated; some must be brightened; others shaded'.[51] The painter Lily Briscoe, in *To the Lighthouse* (1927), similarly voices the difficulty of capturing people's inner characters, of knowing 'one thing or another thing about people, sealed as they were'.[52] Gillespie, in an analysis of Woolf's representation of Lytton Strachey, has commented that the author turns to language suggestive of the visual arts in her effort to get at Strachey's 'essential character'.[53] These examples suggest something less coherent than Woolf's frustration with writing's limitations when it comes to capturing a human essence. In her discussion of the Fry biography, Woolf turns to painting as a metaphor for the *limits* of her insight, just as Lily has to struggle for much of *To the Lighthouse* before feeling that she has, as if by chance, captured a 'vision' on canvas. *Orlando* makes apparent that Woolf's interest in ekphrasis is not based on a preference for one art form over another, but reflects a more complex exploration into the politics behind her society's notions of essence.

Talia Schaffer has effectively argued that Woolf used marked differences between *Orlando*'s visual and verbal portraits to depict what Judith Butler has articulated as the performative element in identity formation.[54] The incorporation of visual portraits into *Orlando* also offered Woolf not simply a second medium for visualizing positive depictions of nonheterosexual emotions and desires, but also a new significatory system arising from the dynamics between the sister arts. The portraits incite an ekphrastic discord that accentuates differences between the life stories that are culturally proscribed for women and a broader range of narratives from which Woolf felt that they had a need and a right to choose.

The first published edition of *Orlando* is interspersed with painted and photographic portraits, most of which depict the eponymous character at different stages of life. The text opens with a full-length, painting titled *Orlando as a Boy* (Fig. 6) depicting a confident, aristocratic youth during the reign of Queen Elizabeth. Throughout the Victorian and Edwardian periods (as in the Renaissance), male subjects of portraits were encouraged to adopt qualities that reflected not just their high social standing but also their natural worthiness of the position, a combination intended to reflect a nation's strength and valor, as

Fig. 6   Orlando as a Boy (1928)

Audrey Linkman has noted.[55] Orlando's pose in Fig. 6 – the feet apart, the stern facial expression, the sharp bend in the elbow, the extended right hand – conforms perfectly to these conventions.

This portrait, which is the frontispiece to the novel, does not exactly accord with the opening description of the boy 'slicing at the head of a Moor which swung from the rafters'. The whimsy of the written text effectively highlights the constructed quality of masculinity by deflating the youth's awkward pose of grandeur in the portrait and suggesting the broader implications of the male inheritance of authority. 'Orlando's fathers', we are told, 'had struck many heads of many colours off many shoulders, and brought them back to hang from the rafters. So too would Orlando, he vowed'. This macabre little gallery is, like more conventional portrait galleries, both a national and a family heirloom: 'Orlando's father, or perhaps his grandfather, had struck [the head] from the shoulders of a vast Pagan who had started up under the moon in the barbarian fields of Africa; and now it swung, gently, perpetually, in the breeze which never ceased blowing through the attic rooms of the gigantic house of the lord who had slain him'.[56] In this passage, Orlando's amateurish performance of masculinity undermines the naturalized ideal of authority personified by the father and reinforced by a rhetoric of national, religious, and class-based superiority, as suggested by phrases such as 'barbarian fields', 'vast Pagan', and 'gigantic house of the lord'. The head hanging for perpetuity in Orlando's attic is that of a person who traditionally does not warrant such portraiture-like recognition, but the paradox is resolved for Orlando's family because the body part is abused by the rightful heir to power. Yet this image offers the reader the added paradox of the British elite coming across as barbarians. The African in the attic brings attention to the European's dependence on the Other for his conception of his own identity, resulting in a repeated yet awkwardly superfluous and childish act of aggression.

Woolf emphasizes the politicized identity that inheritance stamps onto the young hero by turning, immediately after this opening, to a description of the boy standing in the light passing through 'the stained glass of a vast coat of arms in the window', the symbol of Orlando's chivalric, 'noble' fathers. While the boy's body is 'decorated with various tints of heraldic light', his face is 'lit solely by the sun itself'.[57] He is both identified and physically painted by his lineage; as the narrator puts it (with cookie-cutter accuracy), Orlando is 'cut out precisely' for a career of glory.[58] Only his head hovers separate from this influence, leaving the image open to ambiguous readings of either decapitation or independent thought, or possibly genealogical decapitation in retaliation for independent thought.

Although the inheritance painted onto both Orlando's portrait and his body offer him an identity, the generic conventions fail to address his own interests and needs. The seemingly innumerable galleries scattered throughout the family home ensure that Orlando, the living embodiment of one extended lineage, remains as keenly aware of ancestry as Alice Oke does. Less fulfilled by such bonds than Alice, however, the heir spends an undefined period of despondency 'pacing the long galleries and ballrooms with a taper in his hand, looking at picture after picture as if he sought the likeness of somebody whom he could not find'.[59] The family portraits function only to sustain class and gendered privileges, without transferring any of the empathy and affection for which Orlando yearns. One gets a feeling of extreme isolation when the narrator describes the eponymous character wandering through the galleries while 'the dark visage of this Lord Keeper, that Lord Chamberlain, among her ancestors' 'loom down at her'.[60] Near the close of the novel Orlando sits at the end of a gallery that 'stretched far away to a point where the light almost failed. It was a tunnel bored deep into the past. As her eyes peered down it, she could see people laughing and talking'.[61] As she looks back at her centuries of existence, Orlando feels only a melancholy isolation. This sense of exclusion brings to mind Woolf's lover Vita Sackville-West's emotional loss of the family home of Knole when her father died and the estate was passed on to the closest male heir. Moreover, it suggests Woolf's own lack of emotional and sexual fulfilment, or the medium with which to celebrate it.

As scholars have noted, Woolf's depiction of lesbianism in *Orlando* is not explicit. The eponymous hero is portrayed as bisexual and the text does include acknowledgments of female-female desire. The narrator, for example, follows Mr T.R.'s claim that 'women are incapable of any feeling of affection for their own sex'[62] with the observation that Orlando 'enjoyed the love of both sexes equally'.[63] Despite such occasional directness, however, the playfulness of Woolf's novel does encourage a not wholly serious attitude toward identities based on nonnormative desire. On the verge of having sex with Nell, a female prostitute, Orlando reveals herself to be a woman, and then, and then ... Nell breaks out in laughter and invites Orlando to a cup of punch and a story.[64] Such sudden deflections occur more than once in the novel. Although one can argue that *Orlando* is often equally flippant regarding cross-sexual affection and that it incorporates extensive gender ambiguities, the novel offers far more depictions of hetero-sexual relationships, giving them a sense of primacy. Lillian Faderman has contended that the whimsy of the novel is used to obscure lesbian-ism specifically.[65] Adam Parke has shifted this argument in a somewhat different direction; giving the ambiguity a more positive spin, Parke has claimed that Woolf had intended *Orlando* not as a support of the dominant scientific and psychological defenses of lesbianism as purely innate, but as a fantasy that would force readers to question any nor-malizing notions of gender and sexuality.[66] Arguing that *Orlando* is the 'first positive, and still unsurpassed, sapphic portrait in literature', Sherron Knopp concluded that the allusiveness of the novel is not due simply to Woolf's concern about censorship and prosecution but a reflection of the absence of a language that allows a positive depiction of lesbianism.[67]

The language used by Knopp and Parke reflects the development over the past two decades of queer scholarship's attention to the polit-ical benefits of ambiguity. Merl Storr has noted a related approach in bisexual studies, where 'the overall thrust of bisexual epistemology has been opposed to categorization – particularly to binary division and dualistic thought'.[68] In accord with Storr's claim, Marjorie Garber argues that bisexuality is not 'just another sexual orientation but rather a sexuality that undoes sexual orientation as a category, a sexuality that threatens and challenges the easy binaries of straight and gay, queer and "het", and even, through its biological and physiological meanings, the gender categories of male and female'.[69] In Garber's description, bisexuality comes across as queerer than queer because the latter falls easily into one end of a polarity (a pattern that bisexuality avoids). There are considerable strategic benefits to a non-dialectic model and Garber is correct in arguing that bisexuality does disturb the binary tendencies of the major sex and gender categories. As R. Colker and others have put forward, however, perhaps the main problem with such a claim is that bisexuality is currently culturally subordinate to homo- and heterosexuality, and this means that reading bisexuality as predominantly a way of destabilizing other categories inadvertently retains a sense of these other categories' primacy.[70] In the case of *Orlando*, such a deconstructionist obfuscation of difference also risks dehistoricizing the author's own conception of sexual identity. As Storr points out, according to Havelock Ellis, by 1915 the term 'bisexual' was used predominantly to refer to an individual who felt desire for both sexes. Woolf would have been aware of this definition, although *Orlando*'s sexuality is not exclusively bisexual. The novel focuses on a character who, despite vacillations of gender, sex, and sexuality, remains uncategorizable as either bisexual or queer if the terms are historicized. Ekphrastic slippage offers a partial explanation for this lack of fit. The dissidence is also effectively exacerbated, however, by the text's historically specific elements of camp humor.

The magical gender shifting and amusingly flippant tone that permeate Woolf's novel encourage a sense of mischievousness that foreshadows the playfulness of many recent queer texts. It is the character of camp that is most precisely captured by this combination of a bravado of sexual exaggeration and a sense of silly inconsequentiality that offers protection for its subversiveness. This nuance of humor can be more sharply delineated through a consideration of responses to Sally Potter's 1993 cinematic adaptation of *Orlando*. Judith Halberstam has critiqued the film for refusing to capitalize on the queer potential of the narrative.[71] Meanwhile Marjorie Garber, acknowledging that Potter claimed that her work was only loosely based on the novel, argues that the film nevertheless guts Woolf's text of its comic strategies. For Garber, 'the high point of the film comes near its beginning, with the brilliant casting of the magnificent, flaming homosexual queen Quentin Crisp as Queen Elizabeth'.[72] Garber proposes that, in Potter's text, there is an absence of this humor which, for the sake of sexuo-historical sensitivity or what Halberstam calls 'perverse presentism',[73] is best distinguished as being camp rather than queer. Camp and queer humor both address sexual rights, but the former is more likely to pull back into ambiguity rather than sustain its political stance – a strategy of self-preservation rather than bold effrontery. Thus, for Garber, Potter's 'whole film, arguably, needs to be sent to Camp'.[74] Likewise, without this form of parody, Woolf's novel would itself offer a more diluted vision of the potential impact of gender- and sexuality-based destabilisation. In the process, the manipulation of portraiture would lose the teasing quality crucial to keep the audience invested in the sustained critique.

Orlando is a refreshingly open-minded character when it comes to alignments of sex and gender. Upon meeting someone of 'extraordinary seductiveness',[75] the hero gives the person the androgynous nickname Sasha but, in accord with the rules of portraiture, still reads the person's physical strength as male. Yet when he discovers Sasha to be a woman, the attraction of the masculine qualities does not wain. He is similarly unruffled when, later in the novel, he wakes to find that his biological sex has miraculously changed. Turning to portraiture, the narrator notes, 'The change of sex, though it altered their future, did nothing whatever to alter their identity. Their faces remained, as their portraits prove, practically the same'.[76] The alteration of Orlando's sex is also not immediately coupled with a shift in gender attributes. She maintains, for example, a masculine strength and self-determination, comically confirmed by her one-on-one combat during a life-threatening departure from Constantinople.

Orlando then falls into a rigorous life among a community of gypsies in which, the narrator makes a point of informing us, 'the gipsy women, except in one or two important particulars, differ very little from the gipsy men'.[77] In this section of the text the East appears to function for the hero as an orientalist liminal zone that permits gendered transfigurations that do not accord to mainstream British culture. In 'Vacation Cruises; or, The Homoerotics of Orientalism', Joseph Allen Boone has noted that Western authors have often turned to the East as a space that permits a broader range of sex- and gender-based experiences.[78] While Woolf does tap into this convention, *Orlando* also depicts such experiences as occurring in the West. In contrast to her brisk physical alteration, Orlando's passage through her own private Orient represents a gradual gender transition that disrupts the conflation of sex and gender. Qualities such as strength and stamina, which are traditionally defined as male in Woolf's society, are presented, among the gypsies, as traits defined by economic concerns; that is, in the gypsy culture's conception of physical power, a person's gender is secondary to his or her ability to meet the community's needs. By positioning Orlando's feminization within this context of non-Western values, Woolf is not merely using a fantastic exoticism to protect herself from accusations of deviancy but emphasizing the impact of cultural perspective on gender norms. This allows her, in the next section of the novel, to highlight the forced conflation of gender and sex in British society. Back in England, Orlando's own gender ambiguity persists throughout the centuries. When she and Shelmerdine meet, each is pleasantly surprised by the other's 'sympathy' and astonished 'that a woman could be as tolerant and free-spoken as a man, and a man as strange and subtle as a woman'.[79] It would appear that Orlando has finally found a kindred spirit, somebody who possesses a similar disposition and willingly ambiguous sexuality. Woolf, however, does not allow the narrative to sustain such escapism. The portraits of Orlando as a woman (actually photographs of Sackville-West) make it clear that such a blissful ambiguity is only part of the picture.

At one point in the novel, Orlando recollects that, when she was a man, she 'had insisted that women must be obedient, chaste, scented, and exquisitely apparelled'.[80] No doubt she had attained some of these expectations from her family galleries, since portraiture dictated that the main characteristics of women to be communicated were modesty, chastity, and passivity.[81] Nor were women allowed any boldness of action or gesture. In many works, the woman's neck and shoulders are exposed but, signifying her modesty and chastity, she is virtually never depicted as recognizing her erotic appeal and often does not even acknowledge the spectator. From the breasts down, the subject is frequently buried in a mass of folds, frills, and drapes, with this constriction of movement enhanced by the poses deemed appropriate for a woman to take. Unlike her male counterpart, a woman never poses with feet apart. Her hands, if they hold anything, do so in a feeble manner. More often, they just limply touch her cheek, chin, or cleavage. All else is smooth, rolling curves and turns that draw attention back to the woman's dignified, yet passive (if not semi-conscious) gaze.[82] In accord with these conventions, the narrator of Woolf's novel notes, in a comparison of portraits of Orlando as a man and a woman, 'The man has his hand free to seize his sword, the woman must use hers to keep the satins from slipping from her shoulders. The man looks the world full in the face, as if it were made for his uses and fashioned to his liking. The woman takes a sidelong glance at it, full of subtlety, even of suspicion'.[83] In the portrait 'Orlando on Her Return to England' (Fig. 7) we find a fine example of the conventional feminine pose, with soft lines in the body, exposed flesh, awkward clothing, and a gentle gaze. The confident stance of the young boy in the frontispiece has been replaced by a passivity that looks almost dysfunctional in comparison. The full-length portrait of the young heir is supplanted by the severed image of Sackville-West, the disinherited female.

Potter's film *Orlando* uses the cinematic gaze to foreground the issue of the subjugation of women. Like the novel, Potter's *Orlando* is full of surprises, even for somebody familiar with Woolf's text. Jimmy Somerville flies through the sky. Quentin Crisp performs a splendidly arch Queen Elizabeth. What perhaps grabs one's attention most is the frequent and potentially disconcerting scenes in which Orlando's gaze directly confronts the viewer. In part a postmodern expression of self-awareness, the gesture is also a signifier of authority that is a standard of male portraiture. The young aristocratic Orlando narrates events in his life and then, through his bold stare, dares us to question their veracity. But when Orlando becomes a woman and Woolf offers a more passive portrait of the character, Potter persists in these bold

Fig. 7   Orlando on Her Return to England (1928)

glances. When the film's heroine first finds herself wrapped in conventional women's garb, for example, the conflict between her situation and wishes turns the gaze into a question – if not accusation – of the viewer's complicity in the gendered narrative. 'Is this your idea of a joke?' she seems to be asking us. In Woolf's text, the interrogation of gender conventions comes across both through Orlando's queries and in the inter-artistic narrative.

Although Orlando sees marriage as 'the most desperate of remedies ... much against her natural temperament',[84] she eventually accepts the traditional female role and briskly marries and has a son. While her husband is still free to partake in adventures on the high seas, 'No longer could she stride through the garden with her dogs'.[85] But Woolf is heavy-handed in her mockery of marriage, with both the husband and child disappearing from the narrative as soon as they are identified. 'If one liked other people', asks the heroine, 'was it marriage?'[86] Heterosexual ritual does little for Orlando but stop an irritating itch. As the novel's last photograph implies, Orlando's life narrative remains anybody's guess. The final portrait in *Orlando* offers a more optimistic view than 'Oke of Okehurst' regarding the potential benefit of empathy for women's agency. A photograph of Sackville-West titled 'Orlando at the Present Time' (Fig. 8), the picture reflects a moment in the written text when Orlando, having stared back through the time tunnel of her portrait gallery, suddenly breaks from traditional influence and, accompanied by her dogs, walks determinedly into the garden.[87] A stroll in the yard is of course not as exciting as being an ambassador or living with gypsies. However, the photograph encourages a view of the gesture as a risky exploration into identities and affections that are either nameless or deemed unmentionable.

The aesthetic construction of the subject in the last portrait differs radically from that of 'Orlando on Her Return to England'. Gone is the noose of pearls around Orlando's neck, the exposed, vulnerable flesh, the soft facial expression. While in the penultimate portrait, 'Orlando About the Year 1840', the heroine displays the satirically gaudy ring adorning her wedding finger, the jewelry is not visible in the later 'Orlando at the Present Time'. Instead, we have a full-length shot of the bisexual Sackville-West confidently leaning against a fence out in the countryside, her two dogs vigorously scurrying about. Sackville's position can be read as enacting Maria Pramaggiore's recent coopting of the accusation thrown at bisexuality as a form of fence-sitting. Pramaggiore contends that such

Fig. 8   Orlando at the Present Time (1928)

ambivalence is a useful position to take in light of the on-going drive that she finds even in recent theories of sexuality and gender for identificatory fixity:

> Often precariously perched atop a structure that divides and demarcates, bisexual epistemologies have the capacity to reframe regimes and regions of desire by deframing and/or reframing in porous, nonexclusive ways. Fence-sitting – an epithet predicated on the presumption of the superiority of a temporally based single sexual partnership – is a practice that refuses the restrictive formulas that define gender according to binary categories, that associate one gender or one sexuality with a singularly gendered object choice, and that equate sexual practices with sexual identity.[88]

Such a theorization of bisexuality as a disruptive position refusing binary categorization can be seen to run the risk of conflating bisexuality with queerness. But, as Pramaggiore herself states, 'bisexual theorizing and activism are implicated in the fencing match already under way: bisexual theories have come of age in an environment of newly prominent queer movements of the 1980s and 1990s and might be unthinkable outside that context'.[89] The joining of the 'fence-sitting' image with that of fencing as a combative partnership enhances the image of bisexuality as having a dissident potency usually ascribed to queer identity politics. It also indicates the dynamism found in earlier texts like *Orlando*, which fittingly ends with a similar portrait.

The image of Orlando against a fence appropriately suggests neither fence-sitting nor being fenced in. The character's general pose and her angle to the viewer repeat those of Orlando as a boy in the frontispiece, as does the confident gaze, the parted legs, and the masculine crook in the right elbow. Her walking stick and the bend in her right leg both connote a boldness and conviction that actually surpass the boy's. The male youth, confident of his inheritance of power and authority, is depicted as secure if not exactly comfortable within the family manor while the outside world exists only as a partial blur behind a heavy curtain. In contrast, 'Orlando at the Present Time' actively explores this world beyond; she is in her element. In the picture, one gets a sense of comfortable fit between the outside space, the masculine pose, and the heroine. Echoing Lee's struggle for nonnormative sexual iterability, such images in Woolf's novel conjoin feminist aestheticism with a subversion of portraiture conventions in order to defend a diversity of desires, including those deemed illegitimate and, as the final photograph suggests, others not yet realized. We last see Orlando, having already experienced numerous sexual adventures, confidently poised to jump yet another fence and proceed into the forest beyond the frame.

5
Where the Boys Are: Daphne du Maurier and the Masculine Art of Unremarkability

It was not until the rise of cinema as common entertainment in the twentieth century that visual discourses clearly surpassed verbal ones as popular modes of representation. This shift in media did influence the efficacy of portraiture's symbolic function but, as my earlier discussion of Virginia Woolf's novel *Orlando* and Sally Potter's cinematic adaptation demonstrates, the genre nevertheless continued to play a role in the articulation of gender- and desire-based subjectivities in not only fiction, but now also film. The sexual visuality articulated through the Victorian novel changed but it maintained its potency, with the mass visuality stimulated by the mainstreaming of cinema remaining heavily invested in the rhetoric and strategies found in Gothic and sensation fiction. According to Patricia White, common nineteenth-century Victorian literary forms had a considerable effect on cinematic renditions of gender and sexuality. Referencing 'the familial and sentimental models' as particularly strong pre-cinematic contexts for lesbian itera-tion specifically, White argues that 'the inheritance of mid-century Hollywood films from nineteenth-century paradigms of women's culture and relationality represents an articulation of new identities with older forms of female homosociality'.[1] As White suggests, along with scholars such as Peter Brooks, Simon Shepherd and others, a major genre influencing this element of cinema was melodrama.[2] With regard to the cross-generic adaptations of portraiture, it is the Gothic and detective/crime genres that prove most enlightening, although there is a strong overlap between these genres and that of melodrama. Thus, in an essay on 'melodrama as a matter of seeing', Martin Meisel readily presents the *film noir Murder My Sweet* (1944) as his central text for analysis. For him, the work is a detective story, which he describes not only as 'the proper heir of the nineteenth-century evolution from

Gothic remoteness', but also as 'a form of modern melodrama'.[3] During the twentieth century, the psychodynamics of portraiture found in so much Gothic and sensationalist literature easily bled into popular cinema. Literary/visual ekphrastic inquiry had become so ingrained into the exploration and articulation of new sexual possibilities during the nineteenth century that cinema itself turned to the dynamics of the interaction for some of its own strategies of dislocation and subversion.

Alfred Hitchcock also recognized contemporary literature's continuation of the nineteenth-century use of portraiture to delve into sexual visuality, as his brisk cinematic adaptation of Daphne du Maurier's 1938 melodrama *Rebecca* suggests. The increased popularity of cinema and visual culture in general during the past century encourages the view offered by various scholars that Hitchcock's version of *Rebecca* has usurped the novel's cultural position as the primary text. The shift in cultural consumption fails to reveal the complete picture, however, because it does not take into account the fact that du Maurier's *Rebecca* itself uses visual signification. Nina Auerbach has argued that du Maurier's books presented Hitchcock with:

> a sensibility even more perverse than his own. In revenge, his three du Maurier films make the novels look sillier and soppier than they are. Those many potential readers who know du Maurier only through Hitchcock's films assume that the soppy parts come from du Maurier, while the sophisticated terror belongs to Hitchcock. So far he has won – unjustly – this battle of images.[4]

As Auerbach proposes, the director's indebtedness to du Maurier's works (including not only *Rebecca*, but also 'The Birds' and *Jamaica Inn*) suggests that he was attracted by the perversity, sensationalism, and suspense of the narratives. What scholars have yet to take into account is that he would have also been sensitive to the author's extensive reliance on Gothic visuality in her exploration of such things as unsanctioned desires and conflicts of masculinity. As du Maurier's text makes clear, to speak of nineteenth-century visuality is to speak of ways of seeing that continued beyond that century. *Rebecca* reveals, for example, the ongoing relevance of the sociopolitical matrix in which Victorian authors had entwined portraiture. More specifically, in her attempt to celebrate the genderless, ageless 'boy' with which she self-identified, we see du Maurier turn to a visual discourse of portraiture that remained less constricted by the moral sanctions that circumscribed the verbal and even in some cases the cinematic.

Gothic visuality and the instability of gender

A focus on visuality cannot diminish the important function fulfilled by of verbal texts within *Rebecca*'s storyline. It is impossible to ignore that the eponymous specter – with the help of her devoted servant Mrs Danvers or, as she fondly remembers Rebecca calling her, 'Danny' – had left her mark throughout Max de Winter's mansion in the form of notes, missives , and the large, scrolling '*R*'s emblazoned on linens, clothing, and so on. Her very initial, we are told, was 'alive' and 'full of force'.[5] A handkerchief – 'a scrap of a thing' the narrator makes note, twice – is marked by the initial's tendrils weaving through and ultimately 'dwarfing' the inherited 'de W'.[6] In retrospect, the narrator imagines the final exorcism of Rebecca's ghost as the visually dramatic erasure of this verbal signification: 'The letter R was the last to go, it twisted in the flame, it curled outwards for a moment, becoming larger than ever. Then it crumpled too; the flame destroyed it. It was not ashes even, it was feathery dust.'[7] The proliferation of these signifiers of the woman's presence, the consistency with which she brands her ownership on every bit of material, ultimately comes across as suggesting not Rebecca's unquestionable authority but her struggle to maintain agency and control. For this reason alone, an analysis of visuality in the novel requires that verbal significations not be ignored but be recognized as communicating as part of the visuality that problematizes a notion of the dead mistress as omnipresent. The letters contribute to the constellation of objects and events that articulate an interaction of masculinities, a constellation in which Gothic visuality functions as the most persistent force.

The struggle of the heroine to overpower the authority she feels is signified by Rebecca's letters cannot be charted as a visual/verbal juxtaposition reflecting a separation between the new mistress and the old, the virgin and the vamp, or the cinematic and the novelistic. After all, the verbal text itself is articulated not by a writer but by an amateur sketch artist, the heroine herself. Moreover, the narrator's interest in drawing and painting is often commingled with verbal communication. In one complex conflation of visual and verbal art, Max's sister Beatrice tries to explain to her deaf and blind grandmother that she had given the narrator books on art as a wedding gift because the young woman enjoyed drawing.[8] The older woman scoffs at the offering not only because there are no artists in the de Winter family, but also because the Manderley mansion is full of books, none of which she would ever bother to read. While visual artists are denigrated by the de Winter matriarch, so are writers, whose works ironically have been acquired not for their verbal text but, it would seem, for their visual signification of cultural authority. In this scene, the ability to sustain hereditary command so over-rides the sister arts' abilities to create beauty or to communicate that it blurs the two into a single functionary role. Similarly, the insignia-obsessed Rebecca is frequently associated with the visual, from Danny's bedroom memories, to the portrait of Caroline de Winter, to the crucial x-ray. By creating her artwork through a literary genre while relying on the visual as inspiration, catalyst, *and* source of resolution, du Maurier shows that the novel is not only invested in the visual but is to a degree a visual medium (even if it does not include actual illustrations or photographic images). Moreover, the author demonstrates that, at the time that she was writing, the literary Gothic had the ability to propose visualizations that optical technology was still unable to manifest and, in many cases, even simulate.

In *The Desire to Desire*, Mary Ann Doane offers an astute historicization of the Gothic's generic associations. As she notes, for roughly 10 years beginning with Hitchcock's *Rebecca* in 1940, the novel was replaced by film as the popular mode of presenting the female Gothic. At the end of the decade, preference shifted back to the novel in the form of paperbacks. Notwithstanding the fact that these films share many conventions with *film noir* and horror, 'in their articulation of the uncanniness of the domestic, and more especially in their sustained investigation of the woman's relation to the gaze, the Gothic films not only reside within the "genre" of the woman's film, but offer a metacommentary on it as well'.[9] Meanwhile Gothic literature, Doane explains, brings to cinema a nineteenth-century formula for exploring issues of women's identities and their struggles regarding sexuality and the domestic space. It also offers the device of the interior monologue, which assists in the analysis of such things as cultural authority and subjectivity. According to Doane, however, literature is limited by its inability to use visualization structurally: 'The novels, unlike the films, have only a mediated access to the auditory and the visual – the two most significant registers of paranoia.'[10] Because of its intense reliance on perception, film is more useful for exploiting 'the problematic wherein male violence is delineated as an effect of the voyeuristic gaze'.[11] Notwithstanding the fact that the 'axis of aggression' found in film is also explored in novels, the structural feature of cinema's relation to the visual register is, according to Doane, absent in verbal media and it is this feature that allows for the most intense metatextual exploration of the violence of the gaze.

Doane's distinctions between Gothic literature and film raise a number of important questions. Why, for example, would pulp fiction surpass film's popularity in the Gothic genre if the literature lacked satisfactory access to visuality, especially since the general social trend had, by the late 1940s, begun its shift away from books and toward movies? Doane also implies that the imaginatively visualized interpretation that occurs during the consumption of a novel is a mediated process distinctly inferior to the interpretation that takes place during the consumption of a film. While the systems of mediation are different, it is worth considering whàt would be the benefits and detriments of less mediated access to the violence of voyeurism, or visuality in general. Assuming that film's relation to visuality is closer than literature's, then cinema would have a stronger investment in a hierarchization of visuality above the written, an investment that could prove a deterrent to critique. The community that arises around film may find itself impelled to protect the privileged position implied by the notion of visual 'immediacy'. To approach the subject from another angle, the mediated relation that Doane sees between literature and the visual would in fact promote a distancing of visuality that more readily encourages a metacritical problematization of the gaze. Doane's look at 1940s cinema in relation to gender perception leads one to recognize that an understanding of cinema's gender politics requires an understanding of the role of visuality in the literature to which – as Doane and others have noted – cinematic discourse is heavily indebted. Moreover, as John A. Walker and Sarah Chaplin, Ella Shohat and Robert Stam, and others have argued, there is no such thing as visual immediacy; sight is always mediated through the multi-disciplinary, multimedia stew of cultural artifacts that makes up the context supporting our current model of perception.

Until recently, Hitchcock's *Rebecca* has received more scholarly attention than du Maurier's. Almost every study of the film makes some note of the director's innovativeness, although the claim has yet to be substantiated through a consideration of the way in which visuality functions in the novel from which the film arose. A number of analyses of the film have also explored the gaze as male in relation to the formation of nonnormative desires and genders in women. This topic also encourages an exploration of the relation of *the novel's* visuality to images of masculinity. By masculinity, I mean those characteristics that a society has enculturated itself to essentialize and often cultivate in men, while discouraging them in women. In western society, these traits have included bravery, adventurousness, aggression, athleticism, and an assumption of authority. Such an exploration is important not because masculinity is essentially male but because it was culturally conceived as such by many at the time, while masculinity in women was seen as a sign of sexually aberrancy.

One might speculate that the dearth of attention to the novel's visualist techniques and their relation to gender politics suggests that, by the 1940s, the inclusion of visual art in Gothic texts had lost its disturbing effect. Perhaps the portrait had become an expected and thus unremarkable prop of the genre. For many scholars, however, this unremarkability would bring to mind the actual centrality of invisibility and erasure to the study of marginalized identities. A number of works in the field of queer studies have demonstrated that less common subjectivities – and sex- and gender-based ones in particular – have for centuries been signified through images of erasure, ghosting, disembodiment, and elision.[12] The hegemony avoids remarking on the presence of the marginalized, the argument goes, because such acknowledgment would bestow power on the otherwise subordinated identities by marking them as worthy of articulation and categorization. My description of the familiarization of portraiture in the Gothic, however, accords more closely with what Ed Cohen has described as the process by which heterosexuality gains essentialist primacy in part due to the 'silent privilege of remaining unmarked'.[13] In this case, remarkability is avoided because it would imply that the established power relations are open to change. Through identification, the authoritative gender model is circumscribed, its limits are confirmed, and the artifice supporting its image of omnipresence is exposed. Portraiture as a genre within western culture has indeed become unremarkable through its familiar association with the status quo. However, the aberrant portraits to which I have been attending in this study also verge on unremarkability within the context of the Gothic and sensation genres because of their extremely long and successful run as markers of exciting threats to the dominant order. By the twentieth century, portraiture was a site of cultural contradiction in a way that did not exist before it became a Gothic cliché; the genre was now familiar as both a support and a threat to established models of gender, as well as sex, sexual orientation, class, and race.

Gothic literature enacts the anxiety arising from the contradiction of asserting authority by suggesting that there is no need to assert authority. William Patrick Day refers to this tense relation in the Gothic text as being 'defined by the struggle between the impulse to domination and the impulse to submission'.[14] The Gothic endows marginalized subjectivities – those usually inscribed as virtually nowhere – with an unsettling potential signified most distinctly by visualizing strategies such as the imaging of ghosts, the mutation of the body, and the animation of portraits. Meanwhile dominant gender models have to hide by being everywhere in order to avoid existing only somewhere. The main anxiety in the Gothic text is not that, through acts of visualization, less common genders and sexualities might stake out a part of the field of acceptable identities, but that normative identities would have to sacrifice their façade of manifest destiny and face their own limits. In her writing, du Maurier re-envisions this crisis scenario as a conflict between, on one hand, an established masculinity defined by inheritance and tradition and, on the other, a virile masculinity stimulated, if not made manifest, by the very threat of identificatory stability.

Visualizing masculinities in du Maurier's world

Much of the basis for du Maurier's interest in the subject of masculinity's relation to visuality can be found in her own history. In *Forever England: Femininity, Literature and Conservatism Between the Wars*, Alison Light locates the root of du Maurier's exploration of gender in the novelist's sense of nostalgia for the pre-war culture of her childhood.[15] Visual art had been interwoven throughout her life, and is especially apparent in her ongoing admiration and affection for the men in her family. She had consumed the visual and verbal works of her grandfather, George Du Maurier, an aspect of whose own exploration of visuality I discussed briefly in my introduction. Nina Auerbach observes that the man's characters 'crop up again and again in her fiction'.[16] In 1951, the novelist wrote a loving tribute with which to introduce her edition *Young George du Maurier*, a selection of letters that he wrote while studying painting at Charles Gleyre's atelier in Paris in the 1850s. His most successful work, the 1894 novel *Trilby*, focuses on this same community of painters. Relationships among art, gender, and sexuality circulate heavily throughout the novel, in which the painter Little Billee and the musician Svengali ultimately objectify the eponymous heroine to death. George Du Maurier's own career as a painter was cut short when he became blind in one eye, but his interest in the visual arts did not wane and he eventually became a famous illustrator and cartoonist for *Punch* magazine. His vision of London society – with its wasp-waisted beauties; direct, manly 'swells'; effete dandy-aesthetes; and soft, simple servants – circumscribed mainstream perceptions of the era. In his granddaughter's words, his drawings 'became the fashion, the latest thing, the usual light topic of conversation in society drawing-rooms'.[17] By the time of his death, she writes, much of London society 'had come to know him through his drawings and his novels, and [they] felt, although they had never met him, that here was an artist and a writer who had expressed for many years all of the graces of the world they knew'.[18] In his granddaughter's eyes, the man's cartoons and self-illustrated novels did nothing less than visualize the characters of mainstream society for the late-nineteenth century. Noting the impact of his most successful novel, *Trilby*, on a veritable sub-genre of films in which female performers are possessed by their mentors, Auerbach writes that 'George Du Maurier's material is so inherently spectacular that it radiates throughout film history'.[19] Notably, his granddaughter's writing would have an equally forceful impact on the industry.

The adaptability of du Maurier's prose into film is also in part due to her attachment to her father Gerald, who was an actor in the theater. In 1934, the year of his death, she published her biography of the man, for which she chose the visual title *Gerald: A Portrait*. Other references to the visual surface throughout the book. Gerald's father's art studio is portrayed as the center of the family home, with the 'five children tumbling over [George's] feet as he worked'.[20] On evenings, Gerald's parents would entertain the who's-who of the late-nineteenth-century art world: painters, poets, and members of the theater such as Edward Burne-Jones, Frederic Leighton, John Everett Millais, Val Prinsep, James Whistler, William Morris, Algernon Swinburne, and Arthur Sullivan. Her father's greatest admirer, du Maurier's descriptions of the private Gerald reveal some of the gender politics of visualization that persisted throughout her career. In *Gerald: A Portrait*, she describes him as 'feminine but not effeminate', by which she means that his femininity was more a part of his personality than his image. She notes that he had 'a woman's eager curiosity about other people's private lives, a woman's tortuous and roundabout methods of getting to a certain point, a woman's appreciation of gossip, a woman's love of intrigue and drama, a woman's delight and absorption in little mysterious flirtations that last a day'.[21] At the same time, she saw in her father the image of a boy's mind and heart crammed into the role of a responsible patriarch. She would have felt an affinity with her father on this point because of a shared difficulty with the contradictions that arise between the gender conventions one was expected to perform, on one hand, and one's personal perspectives and interests, on the other.

Du Maurier's novels reflect the tensions of gender that she felt within her own identity, what Alison Light has described as a 'desire to be differently female'.[22] One gains fresh insight on the situation, however, by considering it as being as much a desire to be differently male. From an early age, du Maurier sympathized with a form of boyish masculinity whose repressed presence she continued to discern within not only her father but also herself. 'Why wasn't I born a boy?' she laments, 'They do all the brave things.'[23] As a teenager, she created the persona of the athletic and brave Eric Avon. 'Yet why did I pick on Eric Avon as an alter ego, and not an imaginary Peggy Avon', she asked herself, 'Whatever the reason, he remained in my unconscious, to emerge in later years – though in quite a different guise – as the narrator of the five novels I was to write, at long intervals, in the first person singular, masculine gender'.[24] Despite the heroic image of the young man, the author depicts the mature Eric-collective in more ambivalent terms, describing him as 'undeveloped, inadequate. ... Each of my five male narrators depended, for reassurance, on a male friend older than himself'.[25]

Alison Light has proposed that du Maurier's novels with male narrators signify the author's difficulties with female sexuality. Avril Horner and Sue Zlosnik, meanwhile, have argued that these narrators reflect du Maurier's perception of her own authorial identity as masculine.[26] It is also the novels with male narrators, rather than the three that have women as narrators, that Auerbach finds most nuanced and subtly realistic. For her, du Maurier's 'finest and most characteristic novels appear indifferent to female, feminine, or even feminist fantasies or realities'.[27] In the male-centered novels:

> du Maurier provides no ideal of heroic masculinity from which the characters degenerate. Their doting passivity, their drunkenness and dependency, do not mark them as failed men but simply as men. It is this irreverent empathy with powerful males – not her supposed romantic sensibility – that makes Daphne du Maurier so consummate a woman writer.[28]

The men's passivity, dependency, and other traits traditionally associated with the feminine are, for Auerbach, not constructed as inadequacies; rather, they are part of the combination of qualities that make du Maurier's men effective and original. The author herself would have found these traits familiar, most obviously in her father Gerald but, of greater importance, also in herself.

Du Maurier did not only empathize with a masculine subjectivity under the strain of contemporary social expectations, but also envisioned herself as a male dependent on or invested in an older man. Describing the origins of the character Philip Ashley in her novel *My Cousin Rachel*, she writes 'I was identifying myself with my boyish love for my father, and my boyish affection for old Nelson Doubleday [her publisher], and suddenly was overwhelmed with an obsessional passion for the last of Daddy's actress loves – Gertrude – and the wife of Nelson, Ellen'.[29] This complex string of human connections does not make sense if it is read as a convoluted attempt to appease personal anxieties about same-sex desire. If this were the case, then she would surely not try to explain away lesbianism by redefining it as incestuous male–male love. Her attachment to older males is based in part on a sense of herself – even when an adult – as a boy, that is as a child given a freedom associated with youthful masculinity to explore one's imagination, creativity, and adventurousness. This is the masculinity that du Maurier most admired and lamented having to give up. Her perspective as a masculine youth is heavily invested in an empathy toward people such as her father whose boyishness had been bullied into hiding by social expectations. As an adult, du Maurier herself would have experienced these forces to conform.

In *Female Masculinity*, Judith Halberstam theorizes the concept of tomboyism – an understandable desire in young females 'for the great freedoms and mobilities enjoyed by boys'.[30] The phenomenon is socially sanctioned when read as a sign of a girl's 'independence and self-motivation', but becomes punishable when it appears to be 'the sign of extreme male identification (taking a boy's name or refusing girl clothing of any type)', a concern that becomes drastically heightened when a tomboy reaches puberty. In *Rebecca*, du Maurier offers a useful male correlative to this attitude toward children's cross-gendered interests. The character Colonel Julyan comments that his daughter is such an avid golfer that she 'ought to have been the boy', adding that his son's preference for poetry over sports, while not admired, does not bother him too much because he is sure that the youngster will 'grow out of it'.[31] Du Maurier undermines the father's façade of confidence, however, in the next bit of dialogue; in response to Julyan's claim that his son's interests will eventually align with the gender norms of his society, the character Frank offers:

> 'Oh, rather ... I used to write poetry myself when I was his age. Awful nonsense, too. I never write any now'.
> 'Good heavens, I should hope not', said Maxim.

'I don't know where my boy gets it from', said Colonel Julyan, 'certainly not from his mother or from me'.

There was another long silence. Colonel Julyan had a second dip into the casserole.[32]

In complement to Halberstam's discussion of tomboyism, du Maurier depicts here what can be called 'sissyism', a young male's preference for things seen to be feminine or acceptable in girls (in this case, a poetic inclination), a preference that is tolerable during the immaturity of youth but which is, as Maxim forcefully asserts, utterly unacceptable in adult males. Du Maurier's depiction of the scene, however, mocks the men's concerns regarding a sexual deviancy implied by the boy's interest in poetry; their defensiveness belies an anxiety about exposing some weakness or even just suggesting the possibility of a weakness. The passage also belittles the heteronormative aggression of the colonel, who would rather imply his wife's infidelity than have anybody speculate that he himself passed on a hereditary taint of male femininity or, in his daughter's case, female masculinity. The pregnant silence followed by the colonel's diminutive 'dip into the casserole' reinforce the emasculated image against which the colonel has attempted to defend himself. Du Maurier's own desire to be a boy and her adoption of the personae of Eric Avon would with time have also positioned her in the punishable category of gender deviance and her work frequently addresses this point of conflict. The author's main area of exploration, however, is not limited to the subject of tomboyism or sissyism. As the example of Max and the Colonel already suggests, it does not even really limit itself to portraying a tomboy/sissy binary model. Rather, the subject that du Maurier most thoroughly investigates in *Rebecca* and a number of her other works is the punishment endured by any person regardless of sex who retains an identification with boyishness to the detriment of adult gendering and a traditional heterosexual life narrative.

The information we have on du Maurier's gender associations and erotic attractions during her life support the notion that she saw masculinities as traits that did not necessarily adhere to one specific sex, to any person permanently, or to the exclusion of femininities or other gender alignments. Just as the author herself sometimes self-identified as a boy, and sometimes as 'neither girl nor boy but disembodied spirit',[33] she also referred to herself as a girl and as a woman. Similarly, her boyish masculinity and its trait of male-male mentoring did not eliminate the possibility of cross-sex attraction on her part, just as it did not efface her lesbianism. Du Maurier had been lovers with the actress Gertrude Lawrence[34] and had acknowledged her own love from Ellen Doubleday, the wife of her American publisher. Meanwhile, she also threatened to 'tear [the] guts out' of anyone who referred to her same-sex affections by 'that unattractive word that begins with "L"',[35] suggesting that people had been making just such references or that du Maurier had considered the possibilities herself. Notably, in the love letter to Doubleday just quoted, she seems to be averting accusations of lesbianism by defining herself as a boy, and yet she describes herself as being of the not-so-boyish age of 18. Doubleday's lover is thus old enough to experience and understand her sexual desires, but she rhetorically promotes the visualization of her identity as more safely within the pre-sexual persona of a child. By self-identifying here and elsewhere as a male youth, du Maurier permits herself not only to elide the negative image associated with same-sex desire, but also to move her sexual interests into the irresponsible realm of pre-pubescence. Like a tomboy, the naive and carefree Eric Avon could love whom he pleased because he would not be expected to know the broader implications of the attraction; it was all part of a carefree masculine adventure.

The tomboy's painful shift into puberty is demarcated in du Maurier's model through a character that she referred to, in a fantasy story, as 'the boy in the box'. This young male, she writes, lived a carefree existence until he realized that it was time to grow up, at which point he turned into a girl, 'and not an unattractive one at that, and the boy was locked in a box forever'.[36] The concept of a boy whose responsible adult self is gendered female suggests du Maurier's own split adult self-image as one who fulfills adult responsibilities culturally constructed as female while maintaining a more authentic, creative identity that she associates with a masculinity that was permitted its greatest freedom during childhood.

Notably, when du Maurier sat down to write a biography of somebody outside her family, she chose the unsuccessful writer and artist Branwell Brontë, a man whose life was defined by the conflict between a creativity sanctioned by acceptable boyish irresponsibility and then, as she describes it, suffocated by the demands of age. Foregrounding connotations of visuality, the preface of the book opens with praise for Elizabeth Gaskell's earlier biography of Charlotte Brontë and the fact that she 'painted so vivid a picture' of the family's life at Haworth parsonage.[37] Soon after, du Maurier quotes a letter that Branwell's father wrote to Gaskell, after her biography was published, in which he notes that 'the picture of my brilliant and unhappy son is a masterpiece'.[38] Du Maurier begged to differ, arguing that both Gaskell and Brontë failed to recognize that Branwell's brilliance 'existed to a great extent in his own imagination', and was caused by 'his inability to distinguish truth from fiction, reality from fantasy'. Brontë was, for du Maurier, a misunderstood artist. His father arranged to send the young man to the Royal Academy for Artists in London to study and we know that the journey to the city was made but, for whatever reason, the young man never took up classes. Du Maurier notes some of the speculations as to why his career as a visual artist ended so early: a failure to be accepted into the school, a lack of finances, an epileptic attack. Through her sympathetic depiction of the man, however, she suggests that the real cause was the fact that the vibrancy of his imagination would simply not allow itself to be boxed in by the aesthetic and bureaucratic conventions of the academy. It would not be long after Branwell's misadventures that a number of young artists would collectively challenge the authority of the Royal Academy. The best known group of dissenters was the Pre-Raphaelite Brotherhood, most of whose members would become friends with Daphne du Maurier's grandparents.

While discussing the subject of artists and visual art in her nonfiction, du Maurier turned to fiction to explore the relation of visual art to sex- and gender-based conflict. More often than not, in works such as *Rebecca*, *The King's General*, *September Tide*, 'The Alibi', 'A Border-Line Case', 'The Little Photographer', and 'Not after Midnight', the men's subjectivities are under equal if not greater scrutiny than those of the women. In *The King's General*, the effeminate Dick recites his father's comments on his son's choice of a career as an artist: 'Painting was womanish, a pastime fit for foreigners. My friends were womanish too, and would degrade me. If I wished to live, if I hoped to have a penny to my name, I must follow him, do his bidding, ape his ways, grow like my Grenvile cousins'.[39] Like the Colonel in *Rebecca*, the older man never offers the younger any support for his creative passions, and ultimately Dick dies after being physically boxed in by either his own hands or his father's in a small, secret room in the family home.

Du Maurier takes a different approach to masculine anxiety in her short story 'Not after Midnight'. The narrator is an art teacher at a boys' school who resigns from his position because of a 'bug'. With an eloquence suggestive of Wilde in the witness box, the narrator states:

My complaint is universal, and has been so through the ages, an excuse for jest and hilarious laughter from earliest times, until one of us oversteps the mark and becomes a menace to society. Then we are given the boot. The passer-by averts his gaze, and we are left to crawl out of the ditch alone, or stay there and die. ... Fellow-sufferers of my complaint can plead pre-disposition, poor heredity, family trouble, excess of the good life.[40]

The implication is that the 'bug' is some unaccepted form of sexuality, although the narrator also imbues the dilemma with a sentimentalism for the lost joys of his boyhood. For the painting teacher, the illness becomes unbearable only when the students figure it out and begin snickering at him.

That the character's feeling of crisis arises not from simply his actions but from his own sense of his desires is apparent from the fact that it continues even after he departs to do some painting. On his vacation, he is given a mysterious drink by a crass, slovenly neighbor named Mr Stoll, at which point the narrator becomes erotically charged by what he had once seen to be a repulsive piece of art pottery: 'I felt the scalloped ears, the rounded nose, the full soft lips of the tutor Silenos upon the jar, the eyes no longer protruding but questioning, appealing, and even the naked horsemen on the top had grown in grace. It seemed to me now they were not strutting in conceit but dancing with linked hands, filled with a gay abandon, a pleasing, wanton joy'.[41] Soon after, he discovers Stoll murdered by his wife and pinned to the ocean floor with an anchor while his limbs 'swayed backwards and forwards at the bidding of the current'. The image of the swaying corpse parodies the gay dancing satyrs and the narrator's first reaction is to cast into the ocean the object which he now sees as 'Not innocuous but evil, stifling conscience, dulling intellect, the hell-brew of the smiling god Dionysus, which turned his followers into drunken sots ... The eyes in the swollen face stared up at me, and they were not only those of Silenos the satyr tutor, and of the drowned Stoll, but my own as well'.[42] Dionysus, the god of irresponsible play, signifies not only the boyish creativity that the narrator sentimentalizes and that du Maurier admired but also a sexualized debauchery marked by the drunken 'sots'. For du Maurier, such revelry is a non-threatening privilege of the young that becomes coded as dangerous when in the hands of an adult. The 'satyr tutor' and his followers live in a realm of art and beauty distanced from the moral strictures of contemporary society; as such, they bring to mind the Hellenic model of *paederastia*, in which an older man attracted to the beauty of a youth instructs the eager acolyte in aesthetic appreciation. Du Maurier establishes a parallel between this model of male–male attraction and the influence of the art instructor on his own students. At the end of the story, the narrator is left repulsed by the potential of his own creative pleasures (signified by the art object he has cast into the ocean) and yet lamenting the loss of his gay revelry.

The *paederastic* trope of 'Not After Midnight' brings to mind du Maurier's appreciation for her own subjectivity as a boy whose creativity and adventurousness was rooted in the artistic talents of older men that she loved and admired. Auerbach has commented that the author's most effective works are the male-centered novels because they make us 'believe in and live with her terrified, violent non-heroes'.[43] These writings also enact the crisis between creative adventure and traditional responsibility faced by the narrator in the conclusion of 'Not After Midnight'. The complexity of the subject is made apparent, however, when one realizes that this age-based segregation of masculinities is not exclusive to her male-centered novels. Considering du Maurier's own protean self-identification with more than one gender, an association of masculinity with only men and the male turns a blind eye to other possibilities explored not only in the descriptions of her own boyish subjectivity but also in her use of visuality in *Rebecca*, a female-centered novel with a female narrator.

Old boys

Of the various masculinities that du Maurier depicts in her work, her greatest sympathy is for the adventurous boy forced to grow old – the image of 'the boy in the box' that she saw reflected in her father and grandfather. In *Rebecca*, this masculinity is problematically alluded to in the 42-year-old Max de Winter, who himself voices regret that he is not as young as the heroine.[44] The idiosyncrasies that arise due to the contradiction between his muted youthful traits and actual age are fondly tolerated by people such as his sister Beatrice, who brushes his immature quirks aside for the heroine's benefit with a playful 'Funny old boy'.[45] Even this phrasing captures the contradiction of being both aged and youthful, as well as the peculiarity of people who found themselves in this position. While the heroine coopts her sister-in-law's terminology, she uses the diminutive 'old boy' to refer not to her husband but to the irresponsible family dog, Jasper.[46] The pet is less fettered than Max in following the whims of his interests, his attention being as easily absorbed by a feather blown by the wind as by the simple-minded man who hangs about a dilapidated, old boathouse muttering libelous secrets about Rebecca. The dog is more than an innocent catalyst in the heroine's growing concerns regarding her husband's past attempts at heterosexual conformity. He is also a metaphor for the minds of funny old boys like du Maurier herself, both acting out the innocent playfulness that the author admired, but also demonstrating the dangers that unleashed interests posed to the hegemony.

Jasper is not only a metaphor for Max but also for the heroine, who self-identifies as the youthful counterpart to the funny old boy. Max himself cultivates his bride-to-be in this male role and laments to the woman: 'It's a pity you have to grow up'.[47] Similarly, in her affection for the man, she feels most comfortable envisioning her role in relation to the older man as that of 'the schoolboy ... who carries his hero's sweater and ties it about his throat choking with pride'.[48] Even when, much later in the narrative, she acknowledges that they, like Max and Rebecca, will never form a conventional loving couple, the heroine doggedly persists in her hopes for the school-boy model: 'I don't want you to love me. I won't ask impossible things. I'll be your friend and your companion, a sort of boy.'[49] The language comes across as desperate and one feels it unlikely that the heroine's homosocial ideal will ever be given a chance.

Even if the heroine's language did not suggest doubt about their marital success, readers would still have sensed that Max's personal conflicts predestined him to relationships collared by crisis. The hero's very name echoes the structure of his conflicted masculinity, with the puppyish energy implied by the name 'Max' being held back by the seasoned maturity of 'de Winter'. The whiff of aristocracy in the name adds the additional burden of inherited responsibility that, as Vernon Lee and others have argued, was reinforced by portraiture. Lee's aestheticist notion of empathy and inheritance accords with du Maurier's own sense of the inherited responsibilities that keep one from sustaining a boy's masculinity. As discussed in the previous chapter, Lee defined beauty as amoral because she felt it arose through an uncontrolled psychological response to an object's formal qualities. She called the experience 'empathy' because it was an emotional reaction formulated in large part both by one's past experiences and by a cumulation of others' similar experiences throughout history. Through this process, a past existence remains alive emotionally even after a person has died, creating what Lee describes as a sense of 'being companioned by the past, of being in a place warmed for our living by the lives of others'. Du Maurier similarly articulates her sense of the dead existing among the living. Turning like Lee to the domestic space as a metaphor for the sensation, she asks in the biography of her father, 'Who can ever affirm, or deny that the houses which have sheltered us as children, or as adults, and our predecessors too, do not have embedded within their walls, one with the dust and cobwebs, one with the overlay of fresh wallpaper and paint, the imprint of what-has-been, the suffering, the joy?'[50] 'We are none of us isolated in time', she goes on to state, 'but are part of what we were once, and of what we are yet to become, so that these varied personalities merge and become one in creative thought'.[51] Du Maurier's description of communion with the dead as rooted in the creativity of the imagination echoes Lee's notion of the experience as being based on aesthetic appreciation. That said, du Maurier's conception comes across as more anxious in its suggestion that, regardless of whether one searches for the experience of transhistorical empathy, one is nevertheless destined to feel the weight of past joy *and* suffering. In this sense, the responsibility of inheritance that burdens Max and which is most blatantly manifested by Manderley itself is not just an issue of contemporary social pressure, public image, or pride, but one of maintaining a coherent identity inherently derived from a collocation of past personalities. One is born into past subjectivities even as cultural pressures force an individual to develop a new one. Such a burden of heredity is not something that even du Maurier's creatively irresponsible boy can easily ignore.

The weight that cultural signification places upon even those pre-destined to benefit from the regime of specularity is brought across with astounding nuance in *Rebecca*'s heroine. Presented early on in the novel as little more than the unnamed paid companion to a brash, insensitive American called Mrs Van Hopper, we are encouraged to forget that she is also the first-person narrator of the text. Despite the string of people who have critiqued du Maurier's heroine for her insipid incompetence, it is she – as narrator – who has chosen to portray herself as anonymous and disempowered, erasing the fact that she controls much of the story. It is also she who chooses to hold back the image of Max de Winter, building the reader's desire to visualize him much as one might hold back a ballroom beauty's grand entrance down the spiral staircase. Within the rhetoric of visual culture, the heroine emasculates the hero before he even has a chance to perform his own self-image. The character is born into a subjectivity pre-fabricated by the heroine's cultural conception of a manly idea. In fact, the heroine chooses to conjoin her first mention of Max's name not to his image but to the tag 'the man who owns Manderley',[52] the aural repetition emphasizing that whatever defines the hero as 'man' is inseparable from the popular image of the famous house and its history. She ends the chapter with this reference to him as home-owner. In part a cliff-hanger, the deferral of visualization also emphasizes how foundational the house and its history are to Max's masculine subjectivity and, of equal importance, to the way in which the heroine sees it.

The gradual unveiling of the hero of the novel enhances the allure of the man as subject of the gaze. In the first scene in which she and Max are actually together, we are given nothing but a Cheshire-cat-like reference to 'a provocative glance, and a gleam of teeth'.[53] When the narrator finally begins her description of the man's physicality, moreover, it is first contextualized within a culture of visuality that emphasizes surface image over any sort of depth model of identity. This context is established through a boring monologue that Mrs Van Hopper directs at the owner of Manderley about some 'snaps' of her nephew and his new wife honeymooning at Palm Beach. The new money suggested by Palm Beach, the image of crass American's (common to du Maurier's work), and the relatively recent casual attitude toward visual technology itself combine to establish the older woman as lacking in sensitivity, depth, or culture. It is against this shallow backdrop of surface imagery that the narrator finally focuses in on Max:

> His face was arresting, sensitive, medieval in some strange inexplicable way, and I was reminded of a portrait seen in a gallery I had forgotten where, of a certain Gentleman Unknown. Could one but rob him of his English tweeds, and put him in black, with lace at his throat and wrists, he would stare down at us in our new world from a long distant past – a past where men walked cloaked at night, and stood in the shadow of old doorways, a past of narrow stairways and dim dungeons, a past of whispers in the dark, of shimmering rapier blades, of silent, exquisite courtesy.[54]

The narrator constructs him as a portrait, a genre that invites her analytical gaze even as its Gothic ambiguities challenge her attempts at perceptual control. Bringing to mind du Maurier's notion of the past embodying a subjectivity in the present, this description has the man virtually subsumed by the exoticism of a former era. Meanwhile the man's unremarkability – the obscure origins of his visage, the ambiguously articulated lineage, the chiaroscuro of the very setting – evokes an inheritance that affects authority. The subject 'stares down at us in our new world', his hereditary privilege being so forceful that the portrait virtually robs the spectator of the gaze.

Tellingly, the heroine's attention is drawn back to Mrs Van Hopper's monologue when the topic shifts to Manderley with its minstrel gallery and 'very valuable portraits'.[55] At this early stage in her encounters with the master of the mansion, the heroine constructs his identity as inseparable from that of his house and its history. When she next sees the man, a quick glance is enough for her to confirm the unremarkability that justifies the authority implied by his position within a historical, conventional portrait rather than an over-exposed Palm Beach snap. Through a juxtaposition of shadow and light demarcated by a contrast between traditional oil portraits and contemporary photography, du Maurier establishes the superiority embodied by Max over the brashness and aggressiveness embodied by Mrs Van Hopper. While the American struggles to attain favor by reminding the man of whom she is, Max retains the privilege of the unremarkable, finally using it to snub the woman and her mousy companion.

Although a male subject's masculine authority can give him agency to remove himself from observation, the severance is never complete because the image of the individual remains in memory, although now risking the influence of cultural clichés to take the place of individual traits. Soon after Max's brusk departure, the heroine makes use of this space of re-visualization by sketching 'in fancy with an absent mind a profile, pale and aquiline. A somber eye, a high-bridged nose, a scornful upper lip. And I added a pointed beard and lace at the throat, as the painter had done, long ago in a different time'.[56] Drawn by the authority connoted by Max's ambiguity, heredity, and sense of superiority (marked by the 'scornful upper lip' in her sketch), the heroine finds herself reverting to fantastic signifiers of a past age. The subject's very absence works as a catalyst and opportunity for the heroine to use her own sense of lineage to warp Max into a cliché. It is only when he sends her an apology that the distortion instigated by his desire for control shifts into her sense of him as a feeling human being. Despite her growing delineation between ideal and reality, the two visions are never fully separated and their mutual dependency and conflict circumscribe the man's masculinity. As his signs of emotion become more pronounced, the heroine reworks her initial portrait of him; in her eyes, 'he seemed less fettered than he had been before, more modern, more human, he was not hemmed in by shadows'.[57] While the emotional individual that the heroine admires exists simultaneously with the respectable, reserved subject position into which Max

was born, the man responsible for Manderley's current image is struggling to hide his sexual secrets behind a false image of composure.
When the heroine first mentions Manderley and Rebecca to the man,
he is left immobilized and 'looking more than ever like someone
medieval who lived within a frame. He did not belong to the bright
landscape, he should be standing on the steps of a gaunt cathedral, his
cloak flung back, while a beggar at his feet scrambled for gold coins'.
'The friend had gone', she proclaims, 'with his kindliness and his easy
camaraderie, and the brother too, who had mocked me for nibbling at
my nails. This man was a stranger.'[58] Max explains his reaction as the
result of something that makes him want to forget his past entirely. As
du Maurier's notion of the living dead implies, 'the past' here refers to
the individual's responsibility to the spirits of the dead. In Max's case,
this means his responsibilities both to Rebecca and to the ancestral
lineage of Manderley, all of which lead to any desire for boyish comradery being restrained by the mature masculinity framed by the
Gothic painting.

Portraiture functions here not as the signifier of a singular identity
trait but as the site in which different masculinities battle for control.
Du Maurier suggests that masculinity – existing as it does within an
always protean subjectivity – must itself be defined by perpetual struggle. The greatest conflict for Max is between the old values that
bestowed masculine authority upon him from birth and the new more
democratic method of bestowing authority upon those who can prove
they deserve it according to current standards; it is a distinction captured in the difference between a costly portrait done in oils and one
taken as a snap, which indeed is the last portrait of the man that the
heroine offers – 'an awful blurred photograph of Maxim that must
have been taken at least fifteen years ago'.[59] The reproduction appears
in a newspaper article written after Rebecca's bones have been discovered under suspicious circumstances on the ocean floor. 'It was
dreadful', grieves the narrator:

> seeing it there on the front page staring at me. And the little line
> about myself at the bottom, saying who Maxim had married as his
> second wife, and how he had just given the fancy dress ball at
> Manderley. It sounded so crude and callous, in the dark print of the
> newspaper. ... It was true of course, though sprinkled with little
> inaccuracies that added to the story, making it strong meat for the
> hundreds of readers who wanted value for their pennies. Maxim
> sounded vile in it, a sort of satyr.[60]

Words like 'crude' and 'callous' affiliate the newspaper article with the crass virility embodied by Mrs Van Hopper. It is not the photograph of the roughly 27-year-old Max that bothers the heroine, but the subordination of both his hereditary privilege and his boyish peculiarities to the aggression of contemporary systems of public exposure. The authority of Mr and Mrs de Winter is submerged and made monstrous when offered up as a commodity for the gawking public. Democratic legal procedures impinge upon the usually protected, albeit archaic, value system of the aristocracy. That the narrator sees herself as equally disempowered by the move is confirmed by her anxiety about the photograph of Max 'staring at me', bringing back the first, Gothic portrait of the man, which she felt 'stared down at us in our new world from a long distant past'. Unfortunately for her, his is not the only portrait at the mansion.

Danny boys

Through Max, du Maurier demonstrates a complex tangle of masculinities within which even a privileged male of the early-twentieth century was forced to struggle. The most polymorphous sexuality in du Maurier's novel, however, is that of a dead, masculine woman whose influence is appropriated and misrepresented by various members of the living. The ambiguity of Rebecca's desires was reinforced, if not exacerbated, in the film version in part because of the industry's conscious efforts not to make any of them explicit. Hollywood Production Codes at the time when Hitchcock was filming discouraged strong inferences of what was seen as sexual perversion. The head of the Production Code Administration, Joseph Breen, even explicitly told David O. Selznick, *Rebecca*'s producer, that:

> it will be essential that there be no suggestion whatever of a perverted relationship between Mrs. Danvers and Rebecca. If any possible hint of this creeps into this scene, we will of course not be able to approve the picture. Specifically, we have in mind Mrs. Danvers' description of Rebecca's physical attributes, her handling of the various garments, particularly the night gown.[61]

Despite industry attempts to erase the lesbianism in the film, same-sex female desire does have a presence in Hitchcock's text. In large part this is because, as Patricia White has argued, industry censorship fostered sexual encoding that 'can be reconstructed to reveal occluded possibilities that underlie the politically and libidinally invested process of decoding'.[62] Such censorship also encouraged audiences to become subtler reader's of a text as they searched for hints of the risqué; part of the titillation of a film was its implication of sexual differences that conjured up alternate narratives than those proposed by the main storyline. The system of decoding, however, is necessarily ambiguous. The strong lesbian subtext of *Rebecca*, for example, is constructed from hints and insinuations that over time became such clichés that they could now be misread as overt acknowledgments of same-sex desire. But because of their vagueness, which would have been greater at the moment of publication, the suggestions of nonconformity could also have been used to weave other unsettling narratives. Indeed, the momentum of both the novel and film is sustained in large part because du Maurier coaxes her audience to speculate on the nature of Rebecca's desires or, more precisely, the disparate desires that so many characters – including Danny, Max, the narrator, Favell, and Mrs Van Hopper – imagine the woman embodying. When Rhona J. Berenstein states that reviewers 'shied away from enumerating exactly what kind of threat [Rebecca] (dis)embodied',[63] this was not only because they did not want to mark lesbianism or bisexuality overtly, but also because Rebecca held the promise of satiating a range of appetites.

In an earlier 1995 article on Hitchcock's *Rebecca*, Berenstein herself complicates a single reading of the eponymous character's desires, describing her poly-sexuality as being characterized by queerness – 'the breaking of boundaries, by an incision into the ontological justification and valorization of heterosexuality'.[64] Noting the importance of same-sex desire to queerness, Berenstein goes on to clarify that, in her article, the term 'queer' refers both 'to the text's circulation of lesbian desires and to its movements between same-sex and other-sex desires'.[65] This definition emphasizes the protean quality of desire, while undermining any attempt to adopt the concept as a pat means of categorization. *Rebecca* itself accords somewhat more closely to the camp qualities to be found in Woolf's *Orlando*, as discussed in the previous chapter; rather than put forward a politicized claim for sexual equality, du Maurier's and Hitchcock's texts proceed more coyly. In part, this reticence falls in line with the legal strictures imposed on art in the first half of the century. At the same time, it reflects the degree to which the intended audience was prepared to acknowledge their pleasure in envisioning less common sexualities. In this sense, camp is a signal of cultural limits. When Danny does not only lovingly show the heroine Rebecca's underwear, but explains that it was sewn by the nuns of the Convent of St Claire, the excess of detail is a camp invitation to laughter that also allows those sympathetic to the camp reading to continue to enjoy a rare display of same-sex female love. While du Maurier's and Hitchcock's texts both use camp to promote audience awareness of sexual equivocation, they do not necessarily reinforce a politically queer reading. And yet, when one considers Max's unremarkable manly qualities and his wife's desire for a boyish comradery in relation to Rebecca's and Danny's gendering, it becomes apparent that the intricacy of du Maurier's representations of masculinity is part of a complex defense of adult boyishness in men and women.

Pat Califia's exploration of transgenderism offers an explanation of why an individual such as that suggested by the character Rebecca might be able to sustain such an ambiguous subjectivity indefinitely. In *Sex Changes: The Politics of Transgenderism*, Califia proposes that 'to be differently-gendered is to live within a discourse where other people are always investigating you, describing you, speaking for you; and putting as much distance as possible between the expert speaker and the deviant and therefore deficient subject'.[66] Although not transgendered in the biological sense to which Califia is referring, du Maurier's Rebecca arises from within a discursive constellation much like the one that she proposes. The theorist's suggestion of the passivity of the differently-gendered person being articulated by the discourse of others in fact effectively foregrounds what, for Rebecca, is the individual's source of strength. In the novel, characters' attempts to categorize Rebecca within personally framed paradigms of desire continuously fail to reach consummation. Because she is simultaneously invisible and required by the characters to be under intense inspection from many different standpoints, she comes closest to representing all, but never representing any, of the imagined models. What Califia's 'experts' would refer to as a deficiency manifests itself in the novel as sustained potentiality – that which becomes most attractive precisely because it refuses to fulfill any established expectations.

In du Maurier's terms, Rebecca would not be best defined as either a man or a woman, because her strongest defining trait, even as an adult, was her boyishness. As Danny puts it, 'She had all the courage and the spirit of a boy, had my Mrs. de Winter. She ought to have been a boy.'[67] The language repeats Colonel Julyan's description of his daughter, the golfer, suggesting that du Maurier wanted her readers to recognize this not as a singular anomaly but, more broadly, as a type of woman or a persona. Seemingly taken over by fond memories of the feisty youth, Danny's eulogy goes on:

> She did what she liked, she lived as she liked. She had the strength of a little lion too. I remember her at sixteen getting up on one of her father's horses, a big brute of an animal too, that the groom said was too hot for her to ride. ... I can see her now, with her hair flying out behind her, slashing at him, drawing blood, digging the spurs into his side, and when she got off his back he was trembling all over full of froth and blood. "That will teach him, won't it, Danny?" And that's how she went at life, when she grew up.[68]

Ending her revery with a lament for Rebecca's demise, Danny poetically asserts: 'it wasn't a man, it wasn't a woman. The sea got her'. The maid's description of her mistress as a high-spirited youth heroizes the boyishness that du Maurier recognized in herself. Meanwhile, Rebecca's turn to the older maid for affirmation not only foregrounds female-female empathy, but also echoes the *paederastic* trope that appears elsewhere in du Maurier's writings. The image suggests less a butch-femme relationship than a female line of masculinity defined in part by affectionate instructions in ways of maintaining agency despite the male-privileging hegemony.

The struggle for sustaining boyishness is depicted in the above passage as gendered, with Rebecca's actions defying the patriarchal forces contained within the image of her father, her cousin Favell, the groom, and even the stallion. While the gender of the groom is unspecified, it is unlikely that du Maurier envisioned a female groom not only because the image would have been nontraditional and thus would have encouraged textual acknowledgment, but also because the term 'groom' itself effectively points to the woman's unbridled defiance of her (as yet unestablished) husband. Nevertheless, du Maurier makes the gender-based symbolism of this passage accord with her notion of boyishness as non-gender-specific by having Danny ultimately portray Rebecca as an individual who would not tolerate the constraints of anybody, man or woman. While not suggesting futility, the maid's melancholy rhetoric – 'that's how she went at life. ... The sea got her' – leaves one with a sense that Rebecca's fight to retain the privilege of masculinity continued throughout her life and that Danny herself recognizes the likelihood that it never would have ceased should her mistress have lived longer.

Danny's passionate recollection of her acolyte reinforces a defense of the younger woman's independence as an adult. Turning to visual art, Danny describes Rebecca's critical shift into puberty as already fostering the objectification that would motivate her self-identification as a conforming woman: 'She was lovely then ... Lovely as a picture, men turning to stare at her when she passed, and she not twelve years old. She knew then, she used to wink at me like the little devil she was. "I'm going to be a beauty, aren't I, Danny?" ... She had all the knowledge then of a grown person, she'd enter into conversation with men and women as clever and full of tricks as someone of eighteen.'[69] Having passed into the age at which tomboyism becomes punishable, Rebecca was still turning to her instructor for affirmation of her cultural readings. As Danny points out, however, she had also already developed the skills that she would need if she was to continue to succeed in sidestepping the heterosexual conventions of her society. Due to her exceptional training at gender maneuvering, Rebecca was able to carry the bravery and adventurousness that defined her youth into her role as a woman.

Recognizing early on that women were encouraged to define being 'lovely as a picture' as a source of agency, Rebecca uses that power to defy social expectations. The association of the woman with visual art attains particular poignancy when du Maurier uses portraiture to capture a permanent image of the young Rebecca's masculinity, an image that the subject – as a painting – would never 'grow out of'. A likeness had been done depicting Rebecca, appropriately, on horseback. Now, even if the mistress of the house should change to conform to social expectations of womanly conduct, her vibrant masculinity would remain forever on display. According to the maid, the portrait was such a success that it hung in the Royal Academy. The celebration of the woman's bravery and adventurousness within not only a conventional genre but also a conventional institution reinforced Rebecca's own success at infiltrating the bastion of authority on which Max de Winter had always relied for confirmation of his own identity. If female masculinity is celebrated by an institution and genre characterized by their support for convention, then what was a man to turn to for support of his own less aggressive, less visible manliness? Finding no solution to this conundrum, Max is limited to maintaining a semblance of authority within the confines of his home, where he refuses to allow the work to be hung. Unfortunately for Max, the portrait of the boy he married resurfaces every time he envisions Rebecca. Even when confessing to his second wife that he is a murderer, the image that he presents of his victim is a cross between a painting and a beautiful youth: 'She looked very pale, very thin. She began walking up and down the room, her hands in the pockets of her trousers. She looked like a boy in her sailing kit, a boy with a face like a Botticelli angel.'[70] The scene encapsulates the conflict between Max's traditional, unremarkable masculinity and Rebecca's own vigor and bravery, something which is supposed to have been temporary but which in her case – like a portrait – continuously asserts itself.

The only source of authority left to Max is that derived as his birthright, but du Maurier demonstrates that this too can be culturally displaced when Rebecca tells Max that she is pregnant with the heir to Manderlay. 'You would like an heir, wouldn't you, for your beloved Manderley?' she taunts, '... It would give you the biggest thrill of your life, wouldn't it, Max, to watch my son grow bigger day by day, and to know that when you died, all this would be his?'[71] The man does want a son. Not only would the child maintain the de Winter line, but he would also proffer upon Max the youthful virility that, in the present state, only his wife possesses. He knows, however, that the child that Rebecca carries is not his own and – more obviously in the film than the book – the result of this knowledge is the patriarch's utter emasculation. As Auerbach notes in her discussion of Hitchcock's direction, Laurence Olivier's 'Max' appears most feeble in those scenes in which the hero must address Rebecca's death. Hitchcock directs Olivier:

> to give a performance so passive and effete that whatever the script tells him to do, this Maxim seems incapable of killing Rebecca or even of hurting a fly. ... In the big confession scene, in which he blurts out that he hated Rebecca, he puts his hands in his pockets as he reads the line. Through most of the scene, he sits weakly, swathed in an unbuttoned coat that seems too big for him and smoking needily as if the cigarette is a maternal breast. Olivier has been derided for his uncharacteristically limp performance, but Hitchcock surely put the big coat on him and told him to sit during the scene.[72]

The scene on the boat represents the moment at which Rebecca threatens to usurp a masculinity that Max has always had the privilege of characterizing as essentially, inherently his. While his murder of Rebecca was not permitted in the film version, in the novel it allows du Maurier to demonstrate the way in which even the most direct of actions intended to enforce Max's conventionally masculine image turns out to undermine itself. Having learnt that she is dying of cancer, Rebecca now finds it in herself to taunt Max until he murders her, thereby ensnaring him in a debilitating guilt. Perhaps the coldest element in their relationship is the fact that the progeny that signifies the couple's battle for the control of the Manderley line is not simply outside the realm of sight; the unborn heir does not seem even to exist for the couple except as a handy site for conflict.

Echoing Max's difficulties in defeating Rebecca's masculinity, the heroine's attempts to take on the mantle of Manderlay's mistress are similarly depicted as a struggle of visualization. The woman may claim that 'as we wandered about the rooms downstairs, and looked at the pictures, and Maxim put his arm round my shoulder, I began to feel more like the self I wanted to become, the self I had pictured in my dreams'[73] but, as her husband eventually admits, 'The beauty of Manderley that you see to-day, the Manderley that people talk about and photograph and paint, it's all due to her, to Rebecca'.[74] The narrator is bothered, many would say obsessed, by the absent image of this influential predecessor. While still in Monte Carlo, the first moment that she has alone in Max's hotel room, she searches for pictures of Rebecca: 'No photographs. No snapshots. Nothing like that. Instinctively I had looked for them, thinking there would be one photograph at least beside his bed, or in the middle of the mantelpiece. One large one, in a leather frame.'[75] The listing of possible portraits, the tactility of the frustratingly empty frame emphasizes the earnestness with which the narrator already, even prior to a marriage proposal, competes with Max's past wife. Early in her relationship with the man, she laments this lack of visual containment.[76] The ability to visualize Rebecca would be a step toward usurping her power. The source of Danny's authority, in the heroine's view, is the maid's privileged vision of Rebecca: 'Mrs. Danvers knew the colour of her eyes, her smile, the texture of her hair. I knew none of these things, had never asked about them, but sometimes I felt Rebecca was as real to me as she was to Mrs. Danvers.'[77] The reality to which the narrator refers is the omnipresence that the maid herself has made manifest by converting the de Winter mansion into a shrine to the dead woman.

Danny's advantage of visualization is the greatest hurdles in the heroine's efforts to attain jurisdiction of the estate. The maid had been blindly devoted to her charge during both Rebecca's childhood and her reign as mistress. In her unrelenting efforts to sustain the image of Manderley's hereditary authority as embodied in Rebecca, Danny also takes on the responsibility of communicating this female masculinity to the heroine. Immediately upon arriving at the house, the young woman is confronted with a portrait gallery of judgmental faces:

> I can see the great stone hall, the wide doors open to the library, the Peter Lelys and the Vandykes on the walls, the exquisite staircase leading to the minstrels' gallery, and there, ranged one behind the other in the hall, over-flowing to the stone passages beyond, and to the dining-room, a sea of faces, open-mouthed and curious, gazing at me as though they were the watching crowd about the block, and I the victim with my hands behind my back. Someone advanced from the sea of faces, someone tall and gaunt, dressed in deep black, whose prominent cheek-bones and great, hollow eyes gave her a skull's face, parchment-white, set on a skeleton's frame.[78]

In a veritable explosion of Gothic supernaturalism, the portraits it would seem have taken over Manderley and visual maneuvering has become the prime source of meaning. The first things to meet the new bride are traditional portraits from a distant era, signifiers alien to her own history and alienating within her new home. The narrator's lack of control is marked by the way in which her vision is dragged from works by specific artists up the staircase to the gallery and then rushed along past the faces overflowing the hallway and into the passages and rooms beyond. Before she can calculate her position in relation to the other members of Manderley, the heroine finds herself drowning in a sea of gaping maws. Rather than envisioning herself as the head of the household, she sees herself as decapitated by the authority of the masses. And the leader of the waves of faces, we soon discover, is Danny, whose skeletal visage emerges with 'scorn upon her lips'.[79] The derisive gesture usurps the 'scornful upper lip' that the heroine had drawn in an early sketch of her then unfamiliar husband, marking her shift of the classist attitude from Max to the maid. In the drawing, the gesture functioned as a sign of the breeding that the heroine assumes defines the patriarch's authority. Danny, however, offers the gesture as the first of many signs that this authority had been taken over by Rebecca.

Danny's facial code demonstrates the ability of masculine cultural values to transfer from individual to individual not through biology or inheritance but through empathy. Only when Max informs his new wife that he hated Rebecca, does the heroine begin to feel she has the backing required to challenge Danny's worship of the adventurous boy: 'The jig-saw pieces came together piece by piece, and the real

Rebecca took shape and form before me, stepping from her shadow world like a living figure from a picture frame. Rebecca slashing at her horse; Rebecca seizing life with her two hands; Rebecca, triumphant, leaning down from the minstrels' gallery with a smile on her lips.'[80] But here again we see the empathic transference of authority from Rebecca to Danny when the first wife's visage takes shape as a portrait come to life, the same process by which the heroine saw Danny introduce herself. For the narrator, the threat of authority takes on the body of Danny who, while sharing Rebecca's masculine force, lacks her aesthetic charm. As Max's brother-in-law so succinctly puts it, Danny is 'no oil painting'.[81] A twentieth-century Gothic icon of uncommon gendering, it is also she who most effectively demonstrates the cultural demonization of female masculinity. Metaphorically speaking, the maid appears as a distillation of the rebellious evil buried within the alluring *femme fatale*, the rotting portrait to Rebecca's Dorian-like boyish beauty.

In the earlier chapter on Wilkie Collins, I suggested that masculine authority relies for its success in large part on the benefits of being recognized as an object worthy of the gaze. In Collins's work, male middle-class artists are shown struggling to make visible a masculinity characterized by restraint. In *Rebecca*, however, du Maurier depicts the power of beauty as it impacts on female masculinity. This function is apparent in the contrast between Rebecca's triumphant reign and Danny's less glorious efforts to sustain the previous mistress's authority at Manderlay. The culmination of the heroine's attempt to usurp Rebecca's power is similarly mediated through a Raeburn portrait of the 'famous London beauty' Caroline de Winter.[82] An image of a stunner in golden curls and flouncy white gown, Caroline's portrait sustains the family's hereditary power while her feminine allure affirms her role as an object encouraging perusal. It is this invitation to objectification that the narrator had so desperately sought as a means of containing her predecessor. According to Teresa de Lauretis, Caroline's picture marks 'not only the place of the object of the male's desire, but also and more importantly, the place and object of a female active desire (Mrs. Danvers's)'.[83] While it was Danny who first planted the idea in the heroine's mind to dress up as the portrait of Caroline, the narrator is herself drawn to a portrait of one of the de Winter women as a means of taking over the dead woman's identity. In costume, she comments: 'I felt different already, no longer hampered by my appearance. My own dull personality was submerged at last.' 'I did not recognize the face that stared at me in the glass', she elaborates euphorically, 'I watched this self that was not me at all and then smiled; a new, slow smile.'[84] But unbeknownst to the narrator, Rebecca had already taken over the portrait's significatory potency, having presented herself as the image in the painting at a previous costume ball. As Max's sister Beatrice comments, the sight of the heroine in costume did not evoke Caroline but Rebecca. With the privilege of actual history, Danny had convinced the mistress of Manderley to enter into a competition with Max's first wife that leads the man to repel his new bride as a mocking reminder of his own emasculation.

The passages of *Rebecca* that I have discussed – the fake pregnancy, the gallery of servants, the costume ball fiasco – all present the novel as a study in misperception. The portraits scattered throughout the text – and I have mentioned but some of them – mark moments in characters' struggles to have others acknowledge their masculinity as dominant, if not permanent. At the same time, however, du Maurier problematizes such visual fixity through the introduction of new tools of specularity. Never leaving her hotel, Mrs. Van Hopper's comically contradictory declaration that any young woman would 'give her eyes' for a chance to see Monte Carlo encapsulates the short-sightedness that allows people to mistake preconceptions for actual visions of reality. Similarly, the final dissolution of Rebecca's specter is made possible not by verbal evidence but by x-rays that allow those involved to see deeper into the long dead individual than her husband ever had. Such technological developments in visualization have proven not so much to foster an epistemological denaturalization of assumptions about truth being rooted in the ocular, as to be taken as presenting new visual foundations of truth. The x-rays are read as revealing not only Rebecca's cancer, but also the fact that she knew she was dying, had lied about being pregnant, and thus had intended her harassment of Max to lead him to kill her.

The x-ray, albeit a nineteenth-century invention, would have suggested to du Maurier's readers a cutting-edge optical potential that surpasses that of something like the common camera. The state-of-the-art machinery proves more effective than snaps in de-mythologizing the woman for the other characters and for du Maurier's readers. A mode of perception that arises at the last minute and that was previously not considered is taken as the one that allows us to see what previously could not be seen and thereby changes our perception of much of what the narrative meant to that point. Hitchcock is more overt in questioning the false security of this reliance on new specular reinforcements of hegemonic authority. The film version of *Rebecca* does not closely follow du Maurier's use of portraiture to problematize the masculinity of inheritance. He undermines the rule of specularity itself, however, through the introduction of an entirely new scene in which the couple watches home movies of their honeymoon. In yet another attempt to attract Max's gaze, the heroine arrives to view the movies dressed up in imitation of a model in a fashion magazine. The cosmopolitan dress, the string of pearls, the long corsage creeping down toward her waist – the entire outfit pleads to be admired. The huge, low-hanging collection of blossoms brings attention to the woman's stomach and Max's concerns regarding having an heir. Enjoying the home video, he emotes 'Won't our grandchildren be delighted when they see how lovely you were?' However, the awkwardness with which the heroine wears the virgin white flowers and the way she clutches at both them and her stomach when Max critiques her outfit foreshadows Rebecca's conflation of a de Winter pregnancy with a cancerous growth promising no family lineage at all.

The painful contrast between the woman's attempt at glamor and the honeymoon image of her frolicking with naive joy is obvious to her and Hitchcock's audience. Meanwhile, the man's double-image offers the inverse – with Max coming across in the private footage as uncomfortable in the role of the fresh-faced lover as he playfully but still awkwardly sticks his tongue out at the camera. He prefers his current position as one unseen in the dark handling his equipment. This desire to be the man in control behind the scenes accords with his own shocked reaction when his wife speculates aloud as to whether Max had married her to stop local gossip. Upon the suggestion, he steps angrily between the woman and the screen, creating a chiaroscuro image of his face suggestive of the portraits that the novel's heroine imagined early on. By stepping in front of the home movie, Max substitutes himself for the screen and, according to Mary Ann Doane:

> activates an aggressive look back at the spectator, turning [the heroine's] gaze against itself. The absolute terror incited by this violent reorganization of the cinematic relay of the look is evident in her eyes, the only part of her face lit by the reflected beam of the project. ... All these aggressions and threats are condensed in the penultimate shot of the sequence which constitutes the most explicit delineation of projection as an assault against the woman. The project light reflected from the screen fragments and obscures [the heroine's] face ..., contrasting it with the clarity, coherence, and homogeneity proffered by the home movie image of the next shot.[85]

The perception of the hero as a controlling authoritarian, however, does not take into consideration the masculinist anxieties that surround Max's character throughout both the novel and the film. Hitchcock's back-and-forth of shots between the faces of the two de Winters during their heated conversation over gossip sets up an equation between the discomfort signaled by the heroine's half-lit face and Max's own fragmented visage. The couple pick up on and reflect each other's sense of inadequacy. Surrounded by darkness, the right side of Max's face is hit by the harsh light of the film projector, exaggerating his features into those of a classic, Gothic villain. As with the heroine, the focus is on his eyes, metaphorically emphasizing not only both characters' inadequate control of their position in the specular power relation, but also their lack of insight into the relationship. Against the backdrop of their artificially pastoral honeymoon, Max and his wife are presented as groping in the dark for some understanding of each other and their wounded relationship. In accord with the novel, Hitchcock avoids offering such fulfilment and instead laces their need with irony. After chastising his wife for raising the specter of gossip, Max continues to glare at the woman but steps to one side such that we can see the honeymoon footage again. The image that appears in the private film is one of the relatively sprightly groom looking through binoculars at something off screen. Thanks to Hitchcock's arrangement of the shot, however, the newlywed also appears to us to be staring out of his private picture frame and at the more earnest Max's own head as the latter, turned away from the action on the home screen, talks at his frightened wife. The juxtaposition offers a peculiar double image of the hero – one of him as an awkward newlywed and another as the defensive master of Manderley – a comparison that correlates with the boyish and the unremarkable masculinities that battle throughout du Maurier's novel. While Max may have, for a moment, physically blocked the heroine's and our objectification of him, the home movie itself mocks his attempt at maintaining this authority. Busy bringing his wife in line, he is unaware that his own diminutive double is staring puckishly at the side of his head. The romantic sunshine and foliage of the honeymoon footage similarly pierce the brooding darkness in which Max is now struggling to maintain control. While he lashes out against the questioning of his authority, his frightful visage is undermined by the alternate image of self-scrutiny that highlights the man's doubts about his position of privilege.

As this cinematic addition to du Maurier's plot suggests, the man is panicked even by the idea of others remarking on him. The fact that his authority has been placed under scrutiny, that he is no longer unre-markable, only emphasizes his inability to perform the boyish dynamism that both he and his wife desire. If one superimposes this model of maturity and youth upon the relationship between nine-teenth-century fiction and later film, one recognizes that the strategies developed by the older medium are also something on which the younger relies for the privileges of irresponsibility, adventure, and innovation. Hitchcock's addition to du Maurier's metaphors of mas-culinity can be read as a metaphor for the novelty and adventurous-ness of cinema usurping the control of the established medium of fiction. In the next chapter, I wish to explore this gendered power dynamic of specular technology further, focusing on its manifestation in *film noir*.

6
The Face in the Crowd: *Film Noir*'s Common Excess

When a portrait takes the spotlight in a nineteenth-century novel, it is generally to signify a constricting tradition or an individual's subversive potential to break free from such confinement. Similarly, both of the twentieth-century novels that I have discussed so far, by Virginia Woolf and Daphne du Maurier, adapted this Victorian visual symbolism to represent forms of stifling authority from their own eras, whether it be defined by race, class, age, gender, sexuality, or something else. Moreover, they continued to use the rhetoric of portraiture to challenge that authority. Through a Gothic ekphrasis, a melodramatic excess that often spills into camp, and an interrogation of visuality's own cultural biases, the authors invite readers to envision and sympathize with less common sex- and gender-based identities such as those of the bisexual and the adult, female boy. As Potter's and Hitchcock's adaptations make apparent, the use of these techniques also translated into cinema. During the first half of the twentieth century, the popularity of Gothic and sensational literature was all but usurped by that of the related genre of *noir* and it is here that one finds some of the richest cinematic applications of the techniques I have been discussing. Despite the new media for visualization, directors of *films noir* appear to have been loath to scuttle the old portraits off to collect dust in the attic of popular culture. Instead they used the artworks' established signification of dissidence to develop and interrogate the new personae of their own medium and its mass production of sexual visions. Meanwhile, the shift from a literary/visual translation to one more in line with two types of visual art highlighted a self-referentiality that raised fresh doubts about authenticity, tradition, and essence, while simultaneously proposing new methods of exploring identity formation. Building on the stimulating dissidence of Gothic and sensation literature, *noir* texts invitingly taunt their audience with the unsightly. They draw the viewer to imagine that which has been previously constructed as repulsive (repulsive in part because it threatens to undermine the privileged position of the consumer's own unremarkability).

Early Hollywood itself can be seen as having enacted one of the main conundrums that nineteenth-century literature used portraiture to explore. On the one hand, its star system maintained a cultural architecture of idealism and exclusiveness which echoed the elitism and rigid social boundaries reinforced by traditional portraits. On the other hand, it encouraged a sense of inclusiveness by having the star's persona embody an idealized or fringe sexuality that evokes audience sympathy even as it affirms its own impracticality. Not surprisingly, the.most explored subjects in the academic study of *film noir* have been gender and sexuality. Addressing female aggression, the masculine gaze, men's sexual anxieties, and other topics, scholars such as Florence Jacobowitz, E. Ann Kaplan, and Deborah Thomas have demonstrated the genre's emphasis on the conflict and mutual reliance of genders within specific historical eras.[1] One issue that scholars have yet to adequately accommodate, however, and one that inflects much of the previous scholarship, is the fact that *noir* texts frequently encourage sympathy for the anti-social misfits who fail to be accurately represented by the standard binary sex model of women and men. While the normative model cannot be ignored when it comes to *noir*, it is possible at least to decenter it for the sake of shedding some light on other sexual personae that tend to be lost in the shadows. As canonical films like Otto Preminger's *Laura* (1944) and Fritz Lang's *Blue Gardenia* (1953) and *Scarlet Street* (1942) reveal, *noir* texts use portraiture to depict various paradigms of sexuality that we are encouraged to desire despite their false idealization. This seemingly dehumanizing gesture is maintained through a camp melodrama that offers sympathetic support for marginalized sexual and gendered identities. In accord with this form of artifice and excess, the portraits that participate within the cinematic picture signify outside of its circumscribed reality and this meta-textual visuality does not only stand as a challenge to normative sex and gender paradigms but, within the context of cinematic culture, successfully critiques their commodification.

Noir portraiture as meta-textual commentary

Film noir's adaptation of Victorian fiction's dissident portraiture is not as surprising in light of the fact that a principal source for *film noir* in general was popular literature. In his book on *film noir*, Frank Krutnik notes that Hollywood film has 'relied to a significant degree upon adaptations of novels and short stories which have already proven themselves popular'.[2] Every film that Nino Frank included under his 1946 rubric of '*film noir*' was adapted from a literary text, and the majority of scholars argue that *film noir* as a genre is most directly indebted to the hard-boiled detective fiction of the 1930s. One does not have to look much further back in the annals of popular literature to recognize that *film noir* and hard-boiled novels both strongly echo the Gothic and sensation literature which first turned the consumption of crime, detection, and fatal seduction into a popular pastime. Meanwhile, the melodrama popularized in nineteenth-century fiction, drama, and painting offered the emotional excess that would find complements in *noir* chiaroscuro, heightened emotionalism, and caustic dialogue. Detective fiction gained momentum in large part through the narrative conventions popularized by authors such as Mary Braddon and Wilkie Collins. Fritz Lang associated his own films with sensation literature, including Collins's works. And as far as the influence of the Gothic goes, Michael Walker has already discussed the distinctly 'gothic strand' in *film noir*,[3] while Krutnik defined an entire subcategory of *film noir* as the 'gothic suspense thriller'.[4] He includes *Rebecca* (1940) and *Gaslight* (1944) in this subgenre and I would add *The Picture of Dorian Gray* (1945), although elements of Gothic suspense are arguably present in all *films noir*.

Even the most basic core of the *film noir* canon has strong literary origins. *The Maltese Falcon* (1941), *Murder, My Sweet* (1944), *Double Indemnity* (1944), *Laura* (1944), and *The Woman in the Window* (1944): these are the American movies released in Paris in 1946 that lead Nino Frank to coin the descriptor '*film noir*'. The roots of his term are in the novel, echoing the phrase '*série noire*' that was used in France at the time to describe crime fiction in which the hero finds himself an invested member of the urban, unlawful society that he is expected to control. Although one might expect that the growing popularity of such an intensely scopic medium as film undermined the destabilizing signification that the visual arts had fulfilled in literature up to that time, all five films that Frank had in mind make use of art objects to some degree. Two of them – *Laura* and *The Woman in the Window* – even give portrait painting a central position in the narrative. Many other *films noir* also used portraits not only as narrative catalysts, but also as part of their visual discourse. Some texts continue the Gothic tradition of the protean portrait, with an obvious example being

The Picture of Dorian Gray. Others, meanwhile, emphasize individual and social instability or inadequacy through an ironic play on the sense of fixity and coherence that the artworks conventionally implied.

Whether applied to literature or film, the word '*noir*' generally refers to a mood of disenchantment and isolation communicated through a combination of stylistic, structural, and thematic traits. These characteristics include dialogue littered with wise-cracks and urban, world-wise slang; story-lines dealing with sexuality, suspense, and spectacular crimes; and distinct character types such as the *femme fatale*, the hard-boiled detective, and the unfeeling newspaper writer or photographer. *Noir* visual stylistics are often exaggerated and unrealistic, consisting of such things as chiaroscuro, a disturbingly empty urban environment, and shots with extreme angles. The Gothic lighting, sexually loaded banter, and urban setting – none of these elements in itself is necessary for a text to be defined as *noir*. It is their distinctive combination that fosters a sense of tension regarding the hostile environment and a sense of sympathy for its isolated, struggling denizens.[5] Together, they also reinforce the artifice of the campy, melodramatic performances and encourage a reading of *noir* texts as a critique of Western society's bourgeois values. In accord with the characters in the parlor-room dramas made most famous by Wilde, *noir* characters often appear two-dimensional, even cartoonish, combining arch dialogue and exaggerated expressions with stiff or splashy acting. The lack of realism motivates a reading of the gestures as reflecting internal emotions, while also promoting a view of the characters not as individuals but as symbolic personae going through the motions of a deterministic narrative.[6] On this scale, the camp melodrama emphasizes the frustrating unattainability of the apparently common heteronormative lifestyles that the texts use as their backdrop.

The excessive theatricality of early Hollywood cinema most obviously echoes the popular melodramas of the nineteenth century. This influence is apparent in numerous films including *films noir*, especially those like *Laura* and *Blue Gardenia* that have a strong traditional love narrative. According to Marcia Landy, the 'familiar terrain' of melodrama covers 'Seduction, betrayal, abandonment, extortion, murder, suicide, revenge, jealously [sic], incurable illness, obsession, and compulsion', and it can be found in various genres including 'romances, narratives of crime and espionage, thrillers, and historical narratives', as well as 'women's novel', soap opera, and the western.[7] The diverse genres and range of emotions and violence that Landy mentions point to the notoriously broad coverage of the phenomenon – itself a type of excess that threatens to wash over other categories including those of the Gothic, sensation literature, and *film noir*.

This is not the first time that the tendency to extremes has caused difficulty for melodrama. In *The Melodramatic Imagination*, Peter Brooks argued that the theatrical form of melodrama has suffered from critical disrespect precisely because of the exaggeration and artifice of its dialogue. The excess of language, Brooks argues, is itself a signal of the inadequacy of words, which melodramatic works therefore buttress with visual rhetoric such as the tableau, what he describes as a 'stage picture' demanding the audience's recognition of the significant meaning of its composition.[8] Jacky Bratton has argued, however, that early melodramas themselves 'easily accommodated the comic response, without embarrassment; it was, indeed, vital to the genre, as it should be to our understanding of it'.[9] The verbal excess of melodrama was not simply a weakness requiring visual assistance but a comic element that carried part of the emotional meaning. Of equal importance, it directed the audience to a second reading of the visual messages as well.

Comic excess as it relates to the politics of gender and sexuality has received greatest theoretical analysis when considered as camp. Although the term 'camp' had been used for centuries, the first English definition was not published until 1909 when J. Redding Ware's dictionary *Passing English of the Victorian Era* described it as 'actions and gestures of exaggerated emphasis. Probably from the French. Used chiefly by persons of exceptional want of character.'[10] Camp can be distinguished from melodrama because of its more overtly sexual and often self-aware display of excess, a trait that can also be found in both the verbal and visual components of *film noir*. Camp in this sense is a form of parody whose most constant threads are excess, artifice, the evocation of sympathy and, in David Bergman's words, 'a self-conscious eroticism that throws into question the naturalization of desire'.[11] In earlier chapters, I argued for a historicized sensitivity regarding camp that would keep it from being too briskly celebrated as a queer gesture. My concern is that a queer theorization risks erasing camp's potential at different times in history. The theorization of camp must remain sensitive, for example, to the possibility that people and personae defined as camp may themselves not base their sex or gender on a binary model of heterosexuality and homosexuality or male and female. As Cynthia Morrill contends:

> bringing queer subcultural discourses into debates constructed within an economy informed by heterosexual investment in sexual

difference serves to untie these discourses from their homosexual contexts by subjecting them to an un-queer ontology that characterizes itself as inevitable and natural. Indeed, the appropriation of Camp as a theoretical strategy for the interests of postmodern and/or feminist deconstruction follows a troublesome critical tradition of refashioning queer subculture into dominant culture's discursive metaphors.[12]

Morrill's main argument is that camp is not itself a heteronormative cultural phenomenon; it is the interpretation of camp as dependent on a heterosexual paradigm that risks the co-opting of the strategy. One possible way of avoiding this pitfall is by reading camp not as an attribution of gender- or sex-based identity but, more broadly, as a sympathetic recognition of an individual's marginalized position within a society only capable of visualizing an inadequately limited spectrum of identities. This is not to argue that camp with a specifically gay or queer politicization does not exist, but that camp prior to the 1950s, for example, usually maintained a level of coyness and ambiguity that reflected the sexual climate of the times. Such reticence meant that the sexual parody blurred more fully into a sphere of allusion and titillation that allowed for mainstream tolerance and even enjoyment. A theoretical reading of such innuendo requires a historicized awareness of other subtler hints of dissidence.

Camp's façade of confidence, its tenuous bravado, has often made it attractive to people such as gay men who recognized in the phenomenon a reflection of themselves persevering despite the vulnerability they have felt due to discrimination or the sense of futility in efforts to fulfill their sexual desires. Eve Kosofsky Sedgwick refers to this sympathetic bonding as 'camp-recognition', which occurs when one sees one's own marginalized, if not isolated, sensibility in somebody else.[13] According to Sedgwick, camp-recognition involves 'projective fantasy (projective though not infrequently true) about the spaces and practices of cultural production'. 'Generous because it acknowledges (unlike kitsch) that its perceptions are necessarily also creations', she adds, 'it's little wonder that camp can encompass effects of great delicacy and power in our highly sentimental–attributive culture.' Jack Babuscio appropriately emphasizes that camp, rather than being a person or object, is most effectively viewed as a relationship. According to him, it is an interaction between 'activities, individuals, situations, *and* gayness'.[14] While he implies at one point that 'gay' and 'homosexual' *are* synonymous,[15] he also defines 'gay sensibility' more broadly as 'a creative energy reflecting a consciousness that is different from the mainstream; a heightened awareness of certain human complications of feeling that spring from the fact of social oppression; in short, a perception of the world which is colored, shaped, directed, and defined by the fact of one's gayness'.[16] Babuscio's definition of gay sensibility may not use the term 'homosexual' in part because it constitutes an attempt to encompass what Pamela Robertson refers to as a camp sensibility.[17] Robertson describes this sensibility as something that does not reside in an individual but that is interactive, relying on a person's sense of empathy toward another's taste, attitude, or view. Sedgwick's, Babuscio's, and Robertson's language reflects the ambiguities of desire that camp supports. Not only is it not an exclusively gay male phenomenon but being read as camp does not mean that everybody involved in the experience is necessarily complicit.

While studies have defined the conscious use of camp as a political strategy deployed by individuals against sex- gender-, or desire-based oppression, not all individuals involved in a camp encounter need be conscious participants.[18] While some *noir* writers, actors, and directors would have recognized the sexual humor and insinuations of unconventionality, for example, camp performance within *film noir* may also often be inadvertent. A gumshoe detective's exaggerated machismo and wise-cracking heartlessness can appear comically over-the-top, even while it effectively undermines the cocky posturing with a sense of awkwardness that invites sympathy. The performance might not be purposefully camp, but it can nevertheless be read as such through its context of exaggeration and artifice and an audience's identification with the sense of insecurity beneath the performance of bravado. While not all melodrama is camp, its quality of emotionalism fosters a camp tendency that – with the aid of its themes of sympathy and isolation – easily slips into camp or, more indeterminately, supports such a visualization. Regardless of whether one can establish that a *noir* text was intended as camp by any individual contributors to its creation, its combination of wit, artifice, excess, sexuality, melodrama, and sense of living out of the mainstream supports the creation of a camp sympathy instigated by the viewer's or reader's own sex- or gender-based sense of incompatibility and isolation. As a closer consideration of *Laura, Blue Gardenia*, and *Scarlet Street* demonstrates, the artifice and self-referential visuality of *noir* texts function as a camp stylization that – in concord with the performances – encourages sympathy for those burdened by a sense of misfit alienation.

Laura and the death of the pictures

Walter Benjamin famously depicted mechanical reproduction as a threat to authenticity and society's valuing of the individual. The concern displays a more human face when one recognizes the parallels between this issue and the most common accusation around the cultural construction of identity – its visualization of women as objects of desire, an immensely popular topic in *films noir* as well. As Otto Preminger's *Laura* (1944) demonstrates, however, *film noir* has used camp to decenter falsely naturalized gender categories that risk such objectification. A barrage of camp dialogue mixing sexual innuendo with gallows humor permeates the film, thereby maintaining a distance in relation to the acts of objectification. In Vera Caspary's novel version of *Laura* (1942), for example, a female reporter who is trying to gain the attention of the handsome male detective quips 'I shouldn't mind being murdered half so much, Mr McPherson, if you were the detective seeking clues to my private life'.[19] The woman's clunky metaphor is fine black comedy, but her contrived exaggeration and failure at seduction make us feel sympathy for her as well. But notice that our interpretation of the joke and our emotional response would be notably different if a man had made the same comment to a woman. For example, in the movie version of *Laura*, the detective (Dana Andrews), when asked why the murder victim had to be photographed, responds 'When a dame gets killed, she doesn't worry about how she looks'. The individual victim is replaced here by the generalizing image of any woman – 'a dame' – while one person's unease about the callousness of recording the gruesome image is subverted into a derogation of women's concerns about their ability to attract the gaze. Notably, the connotations of image-consciousness are themselves first suggested by the taking of the photographic portrait of the victim, such that the objectification referenced in the dialogue is literalized by the woman no longer being seen as a human but as a corpse.

The murder victims in *noir* texts offer many opportunities for black humor that accentuates the dehumanizing objectification and cold-hearted attitude that defines the predominant *noir* mood. The living characters' lack of compassion generally comes across as unrealistic, but this only works to emphasize their callousness and draws sympathy for the victims who are treated so inhumanely. It is often *noir*'s camp dialogue that prompts a correlation between the disrespect for the dead and that directed at the living. In one scene, the detective Mark McPherson is asked if he has ever loved a woman, to which he grunts 'A doll in Washington Heights got a fox fur out of me'.[20] Here, love does not receive the glorification usually found in standard melodrama; instead it is smothered in issues of monetary exchange and the quest for beauty marked both by the woman's preference for expensive clothing and the man's reference to her as a doll. Detective McPherson, the columnist Waldo Lydecker (Clifton Webb), Laura's aunt Ann (Judith Anderson) – they all partake in the hard-hearted banter, with only the comparatively uninspired heroine Laura Hunt (Gene Tierney) contributing little as she functions instead as the moral ruler against which the other characters are measured. With this onslaught of camp quips, it is only a matter of time before almost every statement begins to seem affected, every action calculated, every stance posed. In *noir* texts, one begins to discern, sincerity walks a lonely street.

The calculating, hard-nosed personae that the individuals adopt seem to signal a disdain for idealized human emotions, but one eventually gets a sense in *Laura* that the icy façade more precisely reflects each person's sense of isolation and vulnerability. When the especially witty Waldo Lydecker is actually passionate, his lines reveal a strained lack of control that makes them even more humorous. In an apparent earnestness that results in pure image overload, he challenges Laura's manly ideal as that of someone 'in the garments of Romeo, Superman, and Jupiter disguised as a bull'.[21] When the heroine denies her love for Mark, Waldo absurdly exclaims, 'Don't lie, woman. I've got the eye of a fluoroscope',[22] a fluoroscope being an x-ray device that allows one to see inside a person on the spot. Although older, more frail, and dressed more fastidiously than the dapper detective, Waldo is anxious to be seen as a masculine ideal. While he struggles to endow himself with the super-human vision of fluoroscopy, he hopes to ridicule Mark through an excess of masculinity by associating him with – among others – a super hero whose talents over the years have come to include microscopic vision, photographic vision, telescopic vision, flouroscopy, and even telescopic fluoroscopy (which allows him to see through distant objects). Since the first Superman comic did not appear until 1938 and the hero's diverse powers of vision arose over the decades, it cannot be said that the novelist was overtly addressing his technologies of human perception. What I find important in Caspary's reference to such things as fluoroscopy and Superman is the notion of visualizing talents as a sign of strength within a detective, a person whom one would expect to be especially perceptive.

Waldo hopes to portray the detective's visible masculinity as a lack of restraint, a weakness that shifts the man into the position of the object being desired. But when the detective's image of perfection is undermined, his masculinity becomes even more dangerous a lure. Waldo's simultaneous jealousy of and attraction to the detective attains full camp sympathy when he learns that Mark's slight limp was caused by a gunshot wound:

> [Mark's] remarking upon my preference for men who are less than hundred per cent exposed his own sensitivity. Reared in a world that honors only hundred per cents, he has learned in maturity what I knew as a miserable, obese adolescent, that the lame, the halt, and the blind have more malice in their souls, therefore more acumen. ... My own failings, obesity, astigmatism, the softness of pale flesh, can find no such heroic apology. But a silver shinbone, the legacy of a dying desperado! There is romance in the very anatomy of the man.[23]

The detective's metal tibia signifies both a super-human physicality and a humanizing weakness. Waldo's admiration, meanwhile, becomes comic in the melodramatic excess of his recollections of his teenage years, and the idealizing hyperbole of phrases such as 'the legacy of a dying desperado'. When complemented for his bravery, the detective comments: 'I'm as gun-shy as a traveling salesman that's known too many farmers' daughters'.[24] Even as Mark deflects the flattery by suggesting his actual vulnerability, his humor affirms the sexual virility that Waldo has already inscribed on the detective's lean, hard (indeed, metallic) body. The disproportion between, on the one hand, Mark's lukewarm fame and daring and, on the other, Waldo's admiration is then reinforced by the reader's kind understanding of the columnist who, despite his pretensions to taste and exclusivity, cannot help but be awestruck by the hunk of man who has come to visit him. Regardless of his performance of cultured superiority, Waldo (like Mark) exposes a personal sense of inadequacy.

The question then becomes one of how to envision this form of male–male attraction, rooted as it is in a combination of admiration and sympathy. Notwithstanding the fact that the men's relationship arises from their desire for the same woman, the urbane columnist's crush on the hard-boiled detective encourages a reading of the attraction as homoerotic. The eponymous heroine, in this sense, appears to be what Sedgwick has described in *Between Men* as a site of mediation for unsanctioned male-male desire.[25] One must be cautious, however, to avoid slipping into a binary model that erases other currents of emotional magnetism. It should be noted, for example, that early depictions of Waldo's attraction to Mark, such as the one just discussed, take place before Laura enters the plot. It is while they admire the woman's portrait that their affections first surface, suggesting that it is a complicity in objectifying aggrandizement that brings the men together. It is the portrait that leads Waldo to ask Mark if he has ever been in love. And while both men do eventually confirm loving Laura, their attractions to the woman are markedly different.

The visuality of the film – which is more constant than that of the novel – encourages a construction of the hero-worship as a polymorphous eroticism coded through an aesthetic discourse. Throughout the movie, the strongest sexual draw remains that of a supreme male body. Meanwhile, through the levity of excess, the objectification and eventual commodification of the manly physique is kept from being seen as a serious threat to the normative model of masculine authority. The sympathy both encourages and sanctions the audience's participation in visually codifying an uncommon erotics that is seen as based on a desire for affiliation. The positioning of the attractions found in *Laura* within a binary model would not only have erased those rooted in a sense of mutual understanding or dependence, but would also have derailed camp recognition and its extension beyond the text to include relationships among characters, artists, and audience. The self-scrutiny and ekphrastic commentary would exist as a bloodless exercise of skill rather than an exploration of the construction of identities and desires.

The textual self-referentiality of *Laura* emphasizes the different conceptions of masculinity that Waldo and Mark defend. Waldo is far more comfortable with a sense of gender as a construct. Laura refers to an encounter with him as 'unreal, ... a scene from a Victorian novel',[26] and, while Waldo comments that 'Mark's future unrolls as upon a screen', Laura notes that it is 'Waldo's plump hand [that] unrolled the future'.[27] Waldo, preparing to write his part of the narrative, complains, 'I have never stooped to the narration of a mystery story. ... I still consider the conventional mystery story an excess of sound and fury, signifying, far worse than nothing, a barbaric need for violence and revenge in that timid horde known as the reading public'.[28] At one point, the columnist even addresses his audience directly: 'Surely the reader must, by this time, be questioning the impertinence of a reporter who records unseen actions as nonchalantly as if he had been hiding in Mark's office behind a framed photograph of the New York Police Department Baseball Team, 1912.'[29] While Waldo readily acknowledges the fabrications of his identity, the detective, who has more to lose in the acknowledgment of his façade, fights the fiction-based image that others construct of him: 'I'm a workingman, I've got hours like everyone else. And if you expect me to work over-time on this third-class mystery, you're thinking of a couple of other fellows.'[30] Mark struggles against the pulp wave of gumshoe detectives that he feels are taking the spotlight away from the workingman iden-tity that he wants everybody to envision as more natural and sincere. He comes across as fighting a losing battle in which his sense of indi-viduality is wallpapered by a mass production of like detectives, a process encouraged in part by the success of his own idealization.

Mark and Waldo constitute two masculine identities struggling for authority – the first deriving its power from the essentialist traditions exploited by realism and the latter attaining its force through a hyper-awareness of the formative status of all gendered identities. The strug-gle between the two characters is driven by their unacknowledged desire to be viewed as the most desirable in the eyes of a woman who might as well be dead, her function being primarily schematic. It is for this reason that, despite his sensitivity to the cultural influence on a person's image, Waldo easily contributes to the mechanical reproduc-tion of Laura's death as commodity. At one point, he describes the media's depiction of her murder as pulp entertainment:

> Scarlet-minded headline artists had named her tragedy THE BACHELOR GIRL MURDER and one example of Sunday edition belles-lettres was tantalizingly titled SEEK ROMEO IN EAST SIDE LOVE-KILLING. By the necromancy of modern journalism, a gra-cious young woman had been transformed into a dangerous siren who practiced her wiles in that fascinating neighborhood where Park Avenue meets Bohemia. Her generous way of life had become an uninterrupted orgy of drunkenness, lust, and deceit, as titivating to the masses as it was profitable to the publishers.[31]

Despite his attack on the papers, the man fails to recognize that his own columns and dialogue rely on the same flamboyance that he belit-tles in the scandal sheets. The above passage – with its alliteration and adjectival excess – is itself a spoof of pulp sensationalism. The gestures of self-referentiality might signal the audience to pay attention to the subterfuge of artifice and performance, but on another level, characters like Waldo demonstrate that the individuals themselves – despite their attack against a system of mass reproduction – fall victim to the shal-lowness of their own constructions. They are shown vehemently defending themselves against detectives who are no more than pulp-fiction gumshoes or, even more poignantly, contributing to the murder of the very people whom they love.

The complicity of characters like Mark and Waldo in the objectification of humans that they also vehemently criticize is positioned, in *Laura*, against a backdrop of mass commodification. Photographers hound the characters in the *film noir* from beginning to end. When we first arrive at Laura's apartment after the murder, the building is swarming with photographers and members of the public in search of visual confirmation of the story. A newspaper boy takes advantage of the smell of blood to hawk his wares, bleating 'Extra Extra, Read All About It! Girl Victim in Brutal Slaying!' While the paperboy offers a verbal compendium to the theatricals of the murder-site, the photographers gather the visual data seen as verifying the exaggerated narrative itself. The verbal and visual constructions reinforce not the veracity of the events (which they actually get wrong) but of each other.

Such brazen, even inhumane efforts to dominate mass visuality are then positioned alongside other portraits such as family photographs, romantic likenesses, and self-portraits. Through this juxtaposition of alternate forms of visual identification, the *noir* text does not only participate in the modernist deconstruction of photographic realism but also problematizes narratives of desire that encourage the sexualized reverence of the individual. In the process, it leads its audience to question the false essentialism of the marriage paradigm that has assumed the position of the ultimate goal of the narrative. Throughout Preminger's *Laura*, the eponymous portrait slips from the grasp of naturalized notions of heterosexual love. In the very opening of the film, we encounter the title superimposed not over the heroine but over a painting, immediately establishing a connection between the name on everybody's lips and the painted image. Reinforcing this enlivening of the painting as an individual, Waldo instructs the detective, when he first enters the apartment, to look at 'her', rather than 'it'. 'Not bad', says Mark, his reticence reflecting the fact that his brisk appraisal is based on a valuation of the painting 'Laura''s effect on his desires rather than his aesthetic taste. Waldo then offers a monologue on his view of the portrait, its painter, and desire: 'Jacoby was in love with her when he painted it. But he never captured her vibrance, her warmth'. What Waldo puts forward here is the view that effective portraiture exudes the emotional relationship between subject and artist. Therefore, it is Jacoby's lack of talent that has resulted in a construction of 'Laura' as spiritless and cold. The movie audience is unaware at this point that the columnist is the murderer who has left Laura herself equally spiritless.

If we accept the saturation of western culture by commodity-based systems of identity valuation, the most grisly potential of its constant slippage into the commodification of humans is that of objects attaining greater value than people. This is basically what occurs when Waldo murders Laura because of his love for the image of the woman that he feels he has constructed. Immediately after his critique of Jacoby's portrait, Waldo does not, as one might expect, turn to an elaboration on his own love for Laura or even 'Laura', but chooses instead to discuss his relationship to Jacoby:

> 'I'd never liked the man. He was so obviously conscious of looking more like an athlete than an artist. I sat up the rest of the night writing a column about him. I demolished his affectations, exposed his camouflaged imitations of better painters, ridiculed his theories. I did it for her, knowing Jacoby was unworthy of her. It was a masterpiece because it was a labor of love'.

What Waldo describes as his devotion to Laura manifests itself not in a celebration of her beauty or other qualities that he might admire, but in a verbal attack on the athletic men that she prefers. Despite his own penchant for affectation and self-display (complete with Van Dyke goatee and walking stick), he chooses to undermine Jacoby by revealing the artificiality of his gestures, talents, and views, much as he later challenges Mark's masculinity as bizarre excess. By defining his published rant against the painter as a 'masterpiece', the columnist proposes an authenticity for his own text that allows him to value it above the derivative works of both the portrait 'Laura' and the person Jacoby.

Similarly, Waldo envisions the detective's infatuation with 'Laura' as necrophylia:'You'd better watch out McPherson or you'll end up in a psychiatric ward. I don't think they've ever had a patient who fell in love with a corpse'. Because Laura is understood to be dead, Waldo's attack on Mark cannot be read as romantic sparring. The competition is over something less carnal, with Waldo's possessiveness over 'Laura' arising from different desires than those motivating Mark. The columnist's reference to a corpse does not refer to the woman but to the portrait that he has accused the detective of dating, just as the deathly discourse brings to mind his description of Jacoby's work as lacking vibrance and warmth. The man's strategy is based on the conception of the portrait as human, a maneuver made possible by the fact that, at this time, Mark's own emotional response to the artwork overrides material considerations. In accord with Vernon Lee's theory of empathy as a transhistorical emotional interaction with the past through art, what Richard Brilliant has called the psychodynamics of portraiture allows Mark to develop an actual bond with a flawless woman.

The danger of this culture of psychodynamic desires is that human beings will always fail to live up to the objects through which they have been idealized. The risk is made painfully apparent when Laura enters her apartment and Mark's reaction seems lukewarm at best. As one critic notes, 'when she returns, the real-life Laura is less adored than her image. ... And for all her sexy beauty, Laura does not project very much heat, except perhaps unintentionally'.[32] The passion between the two never reaches the emotional peaks depicted in Mark's dates with the portrait. In fact, at the moment of the woman's appearance, he first reverts to his cold detective persona and begins interrogating the baffled heroine as if she has intruded. To clarify the mix-up, Laura turns to visual confirmation – a picture of Diane Redfern, a model at Laura's agency who had spent the fateful night in her apartment. Just as Mark's emotional fulfilment is derived from a copy of the actual person, his lament over Laura's demise, it turns out, has arisen from the murder of a different stranger. Diane takes a position somewhere between Laura and 'Laura'; like the former, she was a human being but, like the latter, her primary identity is as a likeness of the heroine.

If we follow Waldo's claim that effective portraiture communicates the artist's desires, then – in a reproduction of the complex aesthetic triangulations of *Dorian Gray* – Mark's passion is not an attraction to Laura but a visceral reaction to the love that Jacoby felt for her. Because the detective and the painter have never seen each other, this depiction of their emotional connection is not to be read as aesthetically mediated homoeroticism. The connection is more precisely one person's recognition of a like sensibility, the pleasure arising from what Sedgwick, in her discussion of camp, refers to as a 'projective fantasy' of shared emotional response. It is the act of desiring that remains under contestation, in part precisely because it lacks corporeality and thereby sustains a risk of undermining the normativization of sex-based desire. Waldo's connection to the artwork similarly attenuates standardized models of desire. By the time the columnist discovers that Laura is not dead and the site of contestation reverts to the bodily, Mark has gained the woman's admiration through a performance of directness and machismo. It is now that we discover that the columnist was the murderer, his killing of Diane being the result of his misidentification of the stranger for the woman he felt he had created and now refused to risk losing to someone else.

If we were to interpret Waldo's actions as being based on a desire rooted in the conventional binary model, then his decision to kill the object of his affections is the illogical conclusion of a crazed fanatic. Such a reading is discouraged, however, by Waldo's complicity in the film's camp stylization of desire. It is in part the wit and banter that positions the relationship between Waldo and Laura within a context of social performance. But Waldo also talks about molding her into someone he could admire, someone who displays taste, class, and refinement. His attraction to Laura never comes across as a physical passion because it is, instead, a combination of an aesthetic appreciation for her beauty and a satisfaction in creating a woman whose tastes and values accord with his own. Waldo therefore can kill Laura without necessarily undermining the source or purpose of his desires because they are invested in a persona that he, Jacoby, Shelby, and the other members of the publicity network have already animated through objectification. If Waldo, in his first attempt, had killed the intended woman and gotten away with it, he could have found another ingenue – Diane Redfern perhaps – through whom to form his paragon. In this sense, Gene Tierney's washed-out performance of Laura seems rather appropriate because a person could never satisfy the range of idealizations that the other characters imposed upon the myth of Laura.

The visualist misfiring that Preminger presents through the de-humanization of the heroine culminates in a portrait of the dead Diane. Her face utterly disfigured by the buckshot, the image encapsulates the objectification of women, the homogenization of the ideally feminine, and the mass commodification of the individual. In Caspary's *Laura*, a character speculates on the impact that a murdered corpse will have on:

> the struggling young painter whose genius goes unrecognized until one of his sitters is violently murdered. And suddenly he, because he had done her portrait, becomes the painter of the year. His name is not only on the lips of collectors, but the public, the public … know him as they know Mickey Rooney. His prices sky-rocket, fashionable women beg to sit for him, he is reproduced in *Life*, *Vogue*, *Town and Country* … [33]

Caspary's extension of consumerist logic here mocks the market system of the art world where sensationalism, no matter how macabre, increases the cultural value of all those who can present themselves as involved in the uncommon events. This drive for recognition and the commodification of the human body has lead, by the end of the twentieth century, to what Nicholas Mirzoeff calls 'global visual culture', in which particular icons or events can attain virtually immediate circulation and significance worldwide. The sensationalized portrait in Caspary's novel is a precursor of this system of media saturation, operating as visual confirmation of, as well as an active agent in the cultural standardization of identities. Thus the central image in the novel's plot is a woman's invisible face or, more precisely, its very invisibility.

At one point, Mark is befuddled by the sense that he has seen Shelby (Vincent Price), a handsome suspect, somewhere before. Eventually it dawns on him that he has not been recollecting the man at all but the marketed masculinity that he embodies – 'a brightly lithographed figure on the gaudy motion-picture poster'.[34] Realizing that Shelby is recognizable not as a person but as a collection of popular products such as Arrow shirts, Chesterfield cigarettes, and Packard cars, Mark concludes that the poseur 'wasn't real' but rather '*the mould of perfection whose flawlessness made no demands*'.[35] The marketed image within which Shelby encases himself makes the man ubiquitous but – as is apparent from Diane's tragedy – this ideal proves dangerous because it threatens to erase individuality, leaving nothing but invisibility and an approximate sense of where one's face should be.

The violence of the domestic in *Blue Gardenia*

Laura offers a grisly commentary on objectifying practices of visualization not only as an individual act but also as a cultural tendency in which cinema itself participates. Despite the challenge of normative streamlining, the critique is undermined by the movie's ending, where the sexually ambiguous murderer is dealt with and the hero and heroine confirm heteronormative closure. As was also standard in Victorian realist novels, the consumer is encouraged to assume a future narrative of marriage and children. In *Laura*, the presence of the commodification process in the domestic or marital space remains unchallenged. Fritz Lang's *Blue Gardenia* (1953), however, which falls more easily than Preminger's film into the category of 'the women's picture', does not only explore the mass market streamlining of domestic identity but also, through *noir* themes of sex and violence and characteristics such as chiaroscuro and camp dialogue, demonstrates its complicity with the more public systems already found in *Laura*. In *Blue Gardenia*, Lang offers a proliferation of portraits that signify characters, diverse ideals of love and attraction, and then ironizes these images through the sexualized combat performed primarily through the dialogue.

While the film's male characters use camp banter flippantly to incorporate sexual innuendo into their public conversations, the women use it primarily either to comment on the prospects of long-term monogamy without sounding too anxious or to deflate and deflect men's advances. Even in these acts of comic self-defense, however, the undertone of abuse typical of *noir* narratives is apparent. As the world-wise Crystal (Ann Sothern) puts it, cigarette dangling from her lips, 'Honey, if a girl killed every man that got fresh with her, how much of the male population do you think there'd be left?' It is this sense that most male–female relations are first defined through desire and violence that leads so many of the characters to magnificent obsessions with impractical ideals.

The oldest of three female roommates and a divorcee, Crystal operates as a conduit between the world-wise, masculine, public space and the more naive, feminine space of the home. Her history also offers her the rare capability of dueling with men in the sexualized battle of wits. In the opening scene, we find Harry Prebble (Raymond Burr) sketching Crystal at her job as a telephone operator while Casey Mayo (Richard Conte), a columnist, asks her questions:

> Crystal: Age? Middle of ... twenties. Nationality: Chicago. My phone number is Granite 1466.
> Casey: I'll check with my numerologist before I call.
> Harry: What is it about you newspaper men? I've been trying to get her phone number for a week. You didn't even have to ask.

Crystal's piece of dialogue suggests a world-wise confidence and an ability to joke with the men. However, it also establishes her concern with aging. Her offer of nationality and phone number pokes fun at Casey's performance of efficiency and authority – a journalist acting like a detective – while maintaining the flirtation. Meanwhile, the columnist jokes back in a way that confirms his reading of Crystal's comment as a mild invitation. The eroticism of Crystal and Casey's transaction is maintained through a banter that, while feeling practiced, still comes across as conscious. However, just as camp competence signals an awareness of everyday sex- and gender-based manipulation and maneuvering, the lack of camp awareness marks a relatively naive view of the construction of society. As Harry demonstrates, such naivete can prove dangerous. A womanizing illustrator who makes his living primarily by drawing pin-up girls, Harry is more than a campless objectifier of other people. Rather than presenting the man's abuse only as sexism, *Blue Gardenia* suggests a broader cultural insidiousness to the system of dehumanization.

Through a complex interconnection among actions, poses, visuals, and text, the film demonstrates the reinforcement of Harry's attitude within the general society, the media, and *film noir* itself. We first see Harry – in the scene quoted above – sketching Crystal while she, an expert at repartee, easily partakes in flirtatious sparring with the columnist Casey. Crystal's willingness to rally with this form of humor risks some people such as Harry interpreting the confidant use of erotic innuendo as encouraging bolder gestures. He takes it as an invitation to call her for a date (even though she had not given her number to him but to Mayo). This slippage reveals the ambiguities in camp that do not simply foster its power of transgression, but also support the potential for dangerous misreadings. Harry's misuse of camp accords with the aggressive approach men take toward satiating their desires within the culture of dating and flirtation but, as *Blue Gardenia* suggests, it also impacts directly on the domestic.

The man's conception of women as first and foremost entities defined in relation to his own interests is echoed by the character Norah's (Anne Baxter) romantic idealization of heteronormative monogamy. Norah, one of Crystal's roommates, pines for her lover who is away in the army. She even enacts her confidence in the purity of their long-distance bond by spending her birthday cooking a roast dinner that she can then share with a photograph of the man. Lighting candles, presenting a bottle of champagne, and looking lovingly into the portrait's eyes, she reads a letter from him that she has been saving for this day. While the head of the man's photograph fills the screen, his voice narrates the letter that informs Norah of his plans to marry somebody else. The discord between the handsome soldier's image gazing fondly out at the viewer and his verbal rejection shatters Norah's romanticism. Having structured her image of gender bonds on idealistic expectations, the crisis of comprehension leads her, in a moment of despair, to go on a date with Harry that ends with her drunk at his studio apartment. The domestic female ideal and the irresponsible masculine one have found each other.

The issue of convergence for Harry and Norah is their victimization through the false narratives reinforced through the cultural reproduction of gendered identities. While the soldier and the artist seem to mark opposing ends of a spectrum of heterosexual male conduct, the man idealized through a portrait and the man who idealizes through portraiture are shown to both be callous and irresponsible. That said, Harry is portrayed as the more inconstant of the two, as signified by the erotic sketches that litter his apartment. The flat also functions as his work space, demonstrating that his professional celebration of women as sexual objects has usurped any possibility of an alternative private identity. Notably, the central text among the drawings that crowd his pad is a painting of a respectable-looking couple cuddling demurely in a romantic setting. An uncharacteristic evocation of a conventional love story, the playboy notes more than once that he has been having trouble finishing the assignment. In contrast to the stability of this image, it is the drunken Norah – who has herself been put off balance by the rupture of her dream – who stumbles against the easel displaying the blissful couple before passing out in the artist's arms. When he drags her to the couch and tries to force her to have sex, their relation becomes a parody of the painting of the man supporting and protecting his love. Norah struggles, later awakens in a drunken stupor, and flees the apartment, losing all recollection of the evening's events. Harry is found the next morning bludgeoned to death with a poker. The culture of objectification proves to be dangerous not only to women.

Through these various relations among people and portraits, Lang establishes a range of images of desire that can be placed on a spectrum that includes the idealistic sketch; Norah's domestic dream; the romantic dinner between a woman and a portrait; Norah's unfulfilling long-distance relationship; Harry's abusive relation with women; and his relation to his erotic art. Arranging these images as a spectrum from the heterosexual ideal to the inhuman suggests greater clarity than actually exists because it erases the possibility of alternate conceptions of affection before they are even considered. The fact that Harry is the murder victim, for example, is easily forgotten in this spectrum because he is such an unpleasant character. One might also forget that the film has Norah choose to go out with Harry, has her choose to drink too much (although he does nothing to stop her), and has her first encourage a sexual encounter by grabbing the man and forcefully kissing him. Of greater importance, such a spectrum maximizes the distance between the romantic vision and the dehumanizing objectification when, in fact, both prove dangerous and both are defined by visual art – through drawings, no less, created by the same individual. This is not to say that the spectrum is not informative, but to demonstrate that Lang's film problematizes the notion of admirable and despicable desires by positioning both images within the context of normativizing visuality. Albeit addressing different notions of attraction, the drawing of the romantic couple and those of the pin-up girls are done in the same sketchy style, emphasizing their mutual aim of standardizing idealistic conceptions of gender and sexuality.

By extending the fantasies into both *noir* literature and sensationalist tabloid journalism, *Blue Gardenia* proffers the danger behind the broader cultural network weaving through these visions of desire. The youngest roommate Sally (Jeff Donnell) comes across as comic when she imitates Crystal's camp dialogue without recognizing the erotic image that she evokes by doing so. Part of the humor arises from hearing such language from the mouth of an innocent, but the juxtaposition also carries a warning to individuals who choose to model themselves on sexual personae. The dangerous glamorization is echoed by the main influence on Sally – the pulp novels that she consumes every chance that she gets. In one scene, we see her asleep on her bed seemingly satiated from an evening's reading of the novel that lay next to her. Entitled *My Knife Is Bloody*, the book depicts a raven-haired beauty with a lascivious expression on her face and a bloody dagger in her upheld hand. In another scene, Sally falls into sheer rapture when the rental library at the drugstore calls to tell her that the latest Mickey Mallet Mystery has arrived. 'It's all about a beautiful, red-haired debutante', bubbles Sally, 'who gets hit in the head, stabbed in the back, shot in the stomach … ', 'How do you know all that?' asks Norah, 'You haven't even read it yet', to which Sally replies, 'That's what they're all about.' 'Lucky girl', muses Crystal, 'living a life of passion and violence.' The humor of Crystal's comment is undermined by the fact that Sally does see reality through the fiction that she reads. When she hears of Harry's murder, she offers the unintentionally camp reflection, 'I never liked Prebble when he was alive, but now that he's been murdered, that always makes a man so romantic'. Sally's glamorization of a corpse echoes Mark's infatuation with the dead Laura; in a sense, having the person out of the way makes the romanticization of the individual easier because the complications of reality and respect no longer impinge on the fabrication.

The danger of *noir* objectification, specifically, is made apparent when Norah – anxious that she may have been Harry's murderer – has to listen to Sally condemn the missing murderer as identical to the tramps in her pulp novels. The slippery slope is made especially clear by the extension of *noir* conventions from Sally's novel to the newspapers. 'Listen to this', Sally exclaims with pleasure while reading Casey's column about Harry's death, 'he's almost as good as Mickey Mallet!' By complementing the journalist for his similarity to a fiction writer, Sally establishes the criterion by which newspapers are sold. Similarly, the first image we have of the victim after his murder is that of a photographer taking a picture of his body fully covered in a blanket and being wheeled out of the studio. 'He ain't very photogenic today', offers a cop nonchalantly. The sardonic quip reminds viewers of the photographer's ultimate intentions – not reporting the facts but getting an entrancing image for the front page.

Before Casey falls for Norah, his main motivation in solving the murder is selling copy. According to him, the first lesson of modern journalism is that 'everybody wants to read about murder, even when an unknown doll kills a guy nobody ever heard of before'. The second lesson, he states, '– add the element of sex', trailing off as he writes his column about the unsolved murder: '… beautiful blonde, defending her virtue …'. When asked how he knows the murderer is attractive, Casey deadpans 'They're always beautiful'. The irony is that Casey is falling in love with Norah, herself a beautiful blonde who had to defend her virtue in her scuffle with Harry. Casey's view is reinforced by the newspapers. 'Painter of Calendar Girls Murdered in Studio Mystery', reads *The Daily Tribune*. 'Casey Mayo Captures Blue Gardenia', offers another front page, tagging on for the sake of emphasis 'Beautiful Murderess Caught by Columnist'. The first headline foregrounds the murder victims interest in calendar girls. The second depicts Casey as a hero while the murder suspect is constructed as an object of desire.

The ease with which crime is reproduced as pulp art and literature has a disturbing impact on individuals' lives. However, rather than depict a woman fulfilling the role of a *femme fatale*, *Blue Gardenia* dissects the image industry itself by portraying Norah as a woman struggling to escape self-identifying with the persona that the papers, novels, and their readers have constructed for the murderer. The difficulties from which Casey eventually saves Norah attain momentum from his own eager production of sexualized criminality, a genre of narrative that readers such as Sally and the *film-noir* audience demand. As Sally makes clear, one's drive to consume is rooted in an expectation of buying something that one has consumed before. Similarly, *Blue Gardenia* depicts actual *noir* conventions directing characters' interpretations of their reality. The original becomes less valued than the reproduced image – that which people feel they know is worthy of attention. *Noir* tends to focus on the masculine, urban space but, as Sally attests, it gained influence through the more private act of consumption. As such, the genre foregrounds the inevitable interconnections between the two and presents the pre-marital, aggressive sexuality idealized most commonly through the objectification of women as reinforced by the naively romantic model of heteronormative marital bliss.

Scarlet Street and the victim of his own desires

Blue Gardenia effectively demonstrates the mutual support and damage caused by the sexual objectification attributed primarily to men, on one hand, and the domestic idealism attributed to women, on the other. The same dichotomy exists in the relationship between the subject and object of the gaze, where individuals who thrive on a self-image of control and containment can ultimately find themselves imprisoned by their fetishization of objectification itself. As in the later *Blue Gardenia*, Fritz Lang's *Scarlet Street* (1942) offers a range of characters whose idealizations hinder any actual fulfillment. Through the film's hero Chris Cross (Edward G. Robinson), however, Lang offers a much harsher extension of the equation by portraying a modern-day painter whose self-image becomes fully gutted and replaced by the *persona noir* of his own violent obsession.

Through its suggestion of casual levity, the dark camp dialogue of *Scarlet Street* functions to normalize the abuse that defines most of the relationships. Considering a move to Hollywood, the physically violent Johnny (Dan Duryea) muses, 'I hear of movie actors getting five, ten thousand a week. For what? For acting tough, for punching girls in the face. What do they do I can't do?' Tired of her roommate's criticism of Johnny, his girlfriend Kitty March (Joan Bennett) shouts 'You wouldn't know love if it hit you in the face', to which Millie (Margaret Lindsay) volleys, 'If that's were it hits you, you outta know!' Kitty's misuse of the naive bank clerk Chris Cross would come across as coy if it were not presented as an extension of the disturbingly flippant attitude toward pain offered elsewhere. When the man finally makes his boldest move – taking hold of the woman's shoulders and kissing her face and neck –

she smiles and languidly offers, 'Chris, you're a caveman', belittling his performance of masculine privilege. Having seen Johnny hit Kitty more than once, the viewer would find the woman's comment ironic.

Lang makes sure to demonstrate that the network of dysfunctional bonds is rooted in a system of fiscal exigency. *Scarlet Street*'s chain of unrequited affection attains emotional intensity by being cross-linked with money-driven abuse. Johnny brow-beats Kitty to get money, so Kitty cons Chris, so he steals from his wife Adele and boss JJ. The critique of the fusion of desire and dollars is most efficiently suggested by the very name of Kitty March, perhaps the cruellest of *film noir*'s *femmes fatale*. 'Kitty' alludes not only to the woman's sexuality and her use of that sexuality in a cat-and-mouse game with men, but also to a kitty of money, the communal pool of funds in this case being the finances that she gets out of the bank clerk for herself and her boyfriend.

Scarlet Street does offer a critique of the over-valuation of money, but the characters' obsession with wealth is not juxtaposed against any image of sincere affection. Even Chris's earnest adoration for Kitty come across as unhealthy because his growing knowledge of her false-hoods, theft, and abuse fail to change his mind until he loses control of his actions. Similarly, for much of *Scarlet Street*, we are lead to inter-pret Adele's first husband, Homer, as a masculine, family paragon. The man, we are told, was a police officer who was rewarded medals of bravery after dying in an attempt to save a drowning woman. Adele has the bonds from his pension squirreled away for her retirement, thus relying on him for financial security just as the portrait of him dressed in full uniform brings her a sense of physical security. In one scene, his likeness stares down at Chris while the berated husband wears an apron and cleans dishes.[36] The unflattering photograph, however, suggests all along that Adele's vision of her dead husband is faulty, a reading confirmed when Homer eventually returns home as a bumbling and impoverished thief who falsified his own death in order to escape his marriage. Homer's portrait now signifies a subversion of the normative notions of marital masculinity that nobody has proven capable of fulfilling.

While Homer's portrait evokes the unrealistic demands of masculine perfection, Chris produces paintings that establish a sincere encapsula-tion of his own complex gender – one that he feels mainstream society would not sanction him to articulate, let alone embody. As an amateur artist, the man's greatest difficulty is 'a little trouble with perspective', suggesting his own unrealistic self-image. His paintings appear flat and

cartoonish, much like the exaggerated actors in *films noir*, and the symbolism of some of his works is so simplified as to confound uneducated
viewers who judge the art only by its realism. 'And the things you
paint!' his wife berates, 'It was bad enough when you copied postcards!
… Getting crazier all the time. Oh yes, I saw what you do – girls,
snakes, next thing you'll be painting women without clothes.' 'I've
never seen a woman without any clothes', Chris says, to which Adele
replies 'I should hope not.' While Chris's comment evokes the sense of
a lament, Adele's appear merely callous. When 'The Happy Household
Hour' radio program comes on, the conversation and its suggestions
regarding their inadequate marriage are pushed to the side in favor of
the popular image offered by the media.

Chris's wife comes across as unbearable, but the man's own ideals are
themselves unrealistic, demonstrating the absence of any site of com-
mensurability for his desires and every day life. When Kitty shows
interest in his art, the bank clerk sees this as an opportunity to establish an alternative domestic space – one in which he is the artist and
she is his beautiful wife and model. Kitty spends her hours in the apartment wearing seductive nightgowns, smoking innumerable cigarettes,
and secretly making love to her abusive boyfriend Johnny, while continuing to coerce money out of Chris. In accord with the conventions
of the *femme fatale*, Kitty's power is depicted as particularly sexual but,
as with Rebecca in du Maurier's novel, it is also manifested in what are
traditionally viewed as masculine qualities such as authority and boldness.[37] At the same time, the woman's laziness, subterfuge, and self-
admiration contradict a reading of Kitty as a masculine ideal. Kitty's
destabilization of identificatory conventions is effectively captured in
the portrait that Chris paints of her. It is the hero's very sincerity that
allows him to transfer his own sex- and gender-ambiguities into his
depiction of the woman.

The first artworks that Kitty permits Chris to produce are far more
sexual than he could ever have expected, embodying the man's
sacrifice of himself to his fetish. 'Could I paint you?' he asks as the
couple relaxes in the studio apartment that the hero hides from his
wife. 'Well I was going to do this myself', the woman coos, 'but …
paint me Chris' and she hands him her nail polish. In an echo of his
subservience to Adele, Chris obligingly kneels before Kitty's out-
stretched leg and begins to paint her toes. In one of the cruellest
camp lines of *film noir*, the woman smiles at his supplication and
growls 'They'll be masterpieces'. For Kitty, the scene is a big joke
that confirms her authority over the man. For Chris, who defines

painting as 'a love affair', it is an act of consummation. Similarly, when he discovers that Kitty has been successfully selling his paintings under her own name, the theft does not disturb him. Rather, in his view, the woman's commodification of his affections contributes to the economic vitality of their living arrangement while reinforcing their mutual dependence. 'Why, it's just like we're married', he chirps, 'only I take your name. Well, that gives me a little authority around here.' Although the woman is in charge of the money, it is the man's labor that produces the objects for sale, thereby establishing the closest thing he has ever felt to the traditional identity of a providing husband.

Chris's self-portraits demonstrate that the monetary factors involved in his own image are ultimately incommensurable with the masculine qualities with which he aims to identify. Despite himself, the hero does manage to capture the dynamism of gender in his two self-portraits. Only one of them is actually titled 'Self-portrait' – the piece that Chris paints of Kitty once he feels he has an authority rooted in the sale of his art. But despite his new-found source of masculinity, his subject retains her own forcefulness. In the picture, the woman appears not as a kittenish female, but as an assertive individual sitting stiff-backed and directing a cold, uninviting stare directly at the viewer. She seems to mock the doll-like, pretty details with which Chris adorns her, such as the hands folded demurely in her lap or the kissing doves painted on the chair back. One might expect her persona as a *femme fatale* would result in an image of her using sexuality to encourage an objectification that she can then turn against her admirers, but instead she offers a sternness that spurns such ogling and defies the authority of the artist. When Chris's love of Kitty turns to hate and he murders her, the picture of the woman becomes even more a self-portrait because it more accurately embodies the emotions of the person who painted it. The artificial stiffness of the woman in the picture echoes the coldness of Chris's emotions as well as the stiffness of the corpse that he has created.

The painting by Chris that I am calling his second self-portrait is never explicitly defined as a likeness of anybody. It is through visual placement and narrative parallels that one is encouraged to read the piece as the artist's vision of himself as a victim of both lucre and his own fetish. Unlike the detailed painting of Kitty, this picture depicts a dark silhouette walking down an empty street at night. The subject's identity is indeterminate, but its outline suggests that the individual is a man wearing a trench coat and fedora like the ones that Chris always wears. The unrealistic image echoes the exaggeration of personae by which all the city's denizens act and define each other. Despite a clear sky sprinkled with stars, the man in the painting carries a black umbrella over his head. Combined with the urban, night setting, the flat figure exudes a sinister, isolated aura appropriate to the film's pessimism. The dark silhouette of a man in a starry night can be read as Chris's attempt to use his aesthetic language to imagine how an object – in this case himself – makes him feel and then 'draw[ ] a line around it'; as such, it is the visualization of melodramatic emotion itself. The blackness of the figure might symbolize a sense of inadequacy or lack of a coherent self-image regarding the envisioned manly ideals that Adele and Kitty worshipped in Homer and Johnny. But it also signifies the emptiness of Chris's life as a middle-aged bank clerk in a loveless marriage who never fulfilled his dream of becoming a famous artist. At the same time, it echoes the emptiness he feels after having allowed himself to become taken over by his quest for a form of domestic bliss that could never exist.

In the final scene of the movie, after Chris has lost his job for stealing to support Kitty, we see the impoverished man shuffling down a winter street, crowds of Christmas shoppers swarming around him in their joyful pursuit of consumer goods. He passes an art gallery where he sees that his 'Self-Portrait' of Kitty has sold for $10,000. As the lone man snuggles further into his baggy coat and hat, the crowd fades from the scene until we see only Chris's figure barely moving through an urban darkness spotted not with stars but with strings of lights from the businesses selling their products. The hero has become his own self-portrait, has morphed into the pre-visualized subject position of his own failure.

In contrast to the implications of *Laura* and *Blue Gardenia*, the more persistently pessimistic *Scarlet Street*'s depiction of image commodification does not end with a plethora of indistinguishable facsimiles marking an erasure of distinctions between humans and their personae. Rather, Lang offers the image of an anonymous individual without any resources at all to participate in the economic exchange of identities. With the advent of mass image production and popular culture's own increased attention to the visual, the search for a means of self-visualization explored so frequently in the Victorian novel seems, with *Scarlet Street* and the rise of mainstream film in general, to have become futile. As *Laura*, *Blue Gardenia*, and *Scarlet Street* all suggest, however, even if cinema's popularity risks facilitating the gutting of identity through homogenization, the medium need not blindly encourage the process. A despondency may underlie *noir*'s references to its own contribution to cultural commodification and stream-lining but, in its turn to the visualist politics of dissident portraiture, it also reveals a self-awareness and a longing to continue envisioning alternative paradigms of sexuality, gender, and desire.

Epilogue

In one scene in *Scarlet Street*, we see Chris Cross kneeling before Kitty March as she has him paint her toenails. The scene is a mockery of his desire to capture her on canvas, and the image represents the bind of those who wish to categorize others. The desire for control results paradoxically in one's reliance on and fetish for that which continues to allude: the unsanctioned, the dissident, the deviant. The same image of the male subject groveling at the toes of his subject can be seen in Caspary's *Laura*. The gum-shoe detective acknowledges, more than once, that the first thing he looks at on a woman is her ankles.[1] 'It was hard', the man comments callously at one point, 'to think of those legs dead and gone forever'.[2] In accord with the empathy described through the portraits in works such as Lee's 'Oke of Okehurst' (1892), Woolf's *Orlando* (1928), and du Maurier's *Rebecca* (1938), the image of the foot-fetishist combines control and authority with an erotically charged dependence that exposes the dominant individual's sense of fallibility and even evokes empathy for his self-doubt. The power dynamics reflect the mutual dependence between an object of desire and its producer or consumer as well as the emotional volatility of the relationship. It also reveals that, as far back as the invention of the photograph, nonvisual contributions to visuality have had a crucial influence because of their relative invisibility, a situation that had been exacerbated in part by the common assumption that sight is unmediated and uninfluenced.

The first person to produce a photograph, Joseph de Nicephore Niepce could not draw. He would turn to his son for the initial illustrations that he would then reproduce as lithographs. But in 1814, Isadore was drafted to serve in the army at Waterloo, and this meant that Joseph had to find a new supplier of visual images. But he never did find anyone efficient or convenient enough with which to replace his son. Indeed, as the story goes, Niepce senior did not appear to have tried to find a person to replace Isadore at all, focusing instead on inventing a form of mechanical reproduction. Decades after his son's initial departure, however, the father was only somewhat closer to a solution and one could still find him hanging pieces of slate outside his window for much of the day in the hopes of capturing an image of something, anything. Cut to an auction in Paris on 21 March 2002, when what is believed to be the world's first photograph re-surfaced. It is an 1825 reproduction by Niepce of a seventeenth-century Dutch pen and ink drawing of a boy and a horse. The historic 'heliograph', as he called his reproductions, is accompanied by a set of letters that he had written to his son detailing the light-sensitive chemicals and techniques he used in creating the permanent image.[3] As this historic pair of items – the photo and the letter – makes clear, the invention of photography, considered by many to be the most influential contribution to nineteenth-century visual culture, came into being with a verbal compendium. Moreover, in the same instant that this written text made its contribution to visuality, it also invested the phenomenon with human affection and mutual dependence by recording a relationship between father and son. Echoing the empathy between the two men, Isadore would eventually go on to take his father's place as the partner of Louis Daguerre.

In my introduction I discussed the psychodynamics of portraiture and the way in which the genre participates in emotional interactions within western society. The story of Joseph Niepce's invention is similarly displayed against a background of human empathy. Losing his son to the needs of the nation, the father directs his attention and most of his savings to inventing a machine that would retain a permanent likeness of loved ones. Why not find somebody else who could draw? Why not hire a professional rather than spend one's money on building a substitute for his previous assistant? Niepce, it seems, felt that nobody could replace his son. Perhaps he had been struggling to create more than just a machine that could fulfill the function of illustrator. This of course is speculation, but it is amazing that this first photograph has for over 175 years remained coupled with letters in which the father tells his son about his still inadequate efforts to replace even this one role in their relationship. The words draw out a poignancy of devotion that the equipment with which he made his sketchy reproduction of a boy and a horse could not yet do on its own. The interaction of the verbal and visual texts brings the emotions of history into the present and gives one, as Lee put it, the sense of 'being companioned by the past, of being in a place warmed for our living by the lives of others'.[4] At this pioneering moment in the invention of photography, verbal texts as well as human emotions were being formulated as inseparable elements of visual technology.

Portraiture and its emotive function had existed before Niepce's heliographs. Likewise, the 1825 artifacts reflect the empathic element of visuality found in earlier historical texts as much as they suggest those that came later such as Braddon's *Lady Audley's Secret* (1862), Lang's *Blue Gardenia* (1953), and others that this study has addressed. What the Niepce piece does not put forward as strongly is the disturbing sense of alienation prevalent in so many of these later works – an alienation characterized by not only an emotional discomfort but also a sense of gendered or sexual instability. It is the combination of emotional sympathy and threat of alienation that is captured so effectively, for example, in the texts by Wilde, Lee, du Maurier, and the *noir* texts that followed. The same earnest excess is even apparent in earlier pieces such as *The Half Sisters* (1848), although it had not attained the stylizations characteristic of later works. Jewsbury's exploration of women's social bonds results in a realistic image of female–female empathy that threatens and yet never fully over-rides the alienating pressures of the 'still-life people' who blindly maintain marital traditions. Even in *The Half Sisters*, in which alternative desires are not explicitly portrayed, the image of gender deviancy is made manifest through a visuality that constructs the unconventional woman as a *sexual* monstrosity 'stalk[ing] through life [with] neither the softness of a woman, nor the firm, well-proportioned principle of a man' – 'a bat in the human species'.[5] From one perspective, Jewsbury's woman artist is seen to threaten transgression. From another, the novel can be read as proposing a sympathetic recognition of desires that find themselves dominated by and alienated through larger social institutions.

One of the aims of this study has been to chart domination and submission as a central defining relationship in nineteenth-century sexual visuality. What has become apparent in the process is not only that Victorian authors were aware of the politics of sexual visuality but that they used their writing to participate in it. Theorists such as W.J.T. Mitchell, Ella Shohat, Robert Stam, and others have noted that sight is not pure but inevitably multi-media, multi-sensory, and culturally inflected. As Jonathan Crary has argued, 'privileging the category of visuality runs the risk of ignoring the forces of specialization and separation that allowed such a notion to become the intellectually available concept that it is today'.[6] While Western society has contributed to this network of influences in various ways, a number of people since at least the early-nineteenth century have been aware of the benefits of nevertheless maintaining a visualist essentialism that offered a subterfugal manoeuverability within the realm of sexual politics.

The hyper-awareness recognized in current Western society's infatuation with visual culture has often been attributed to new scopic technologies. Such innovations have definitely contributed to our veneration of the visual, but Victorian Gothic and sensation authors' intense, sustained exploration of sexual visuality and its extension into popular cinema demonstrates that our sensitivity to the politics of visuality is equally rooted in a nineteenth-century aesthetic tradition of using media hybridization to reformulate the apparently invisible as the unsightly. As literature's dissident portraits make apparent, visuality made a crucial contribution to the formation of those modern sex- and gender-based identities that are more often seen as the product of juridical and scientific discourses with an eye for defining normal sexual identities and excising anomalies. Portraiture provided an emotional space that sanctioned not simply the visualization, but the vivification of the unsightly. It drew readers – like the willing subjects of a portrait painter – to acquiesce to the destabilization of sexuality, economic privilege, and subjective identity. Eventually, Victorian struggles over cultural authority resulted in the formation of a portraiture-based visuality that has circumscribed Western society's conception of sexuality and gender through to the present day.

The scientific, ethical, and commercial streamlining of sexual identity that attained full torque during the nineteenth century operates on a process of visualization, consumption, and replacement that is generally unsympathetic in its attempt to pin down and limit the influence of uncommon desires. Indeed every act of categorization (whether supportive or demonizing) leads not to a state of contentment or security but to the desire to locate other previously unseen or unacknowledged sexualities as an affirmation of the institutions' self-image of perfection. The system's inability to assure even itself of hegemonic fixity fosters not only a greater scrutiny of the social margins but also a sustained anxiety regarding the potential recognition of deviancy within itself. As the character Waldo in

Laura (1942) puts it, 'A man who distrusts his body, my love, seeks weakness and impotence in every other living creature'.[7] Dorian Gray is perhaps the individual whose combat with portraiture most dramatically makes this clear. 'Sin', says Basil (the moral measure of Wilde's novel), 'is a thing that writes itself across a man's face. It cannot be concealed.'[8] The uneasiness arising from an awareness not only of the uniqueness of one's own body and emotions, but also of their mutability foster an impulse to see that which is different as unsightly and dangerous. One result of this sustained discomfort is that it encourages people to construct their own image in accord with the most common of ideals. At the same time, increased self-inspection results in more and more people recognizing themselves as distinct and acknowledging the dissident potential within their differences.

Notes

Introduction

1. Mirzoeff, *Bodyscape: Art, Modernity and the Ideal Figure* (London: Routledge, 1995), p. 3.
2. Desire is of course not limited to an individual's relation to the human body. The interdependence of visuality and sexuality, however, as it relates to the iteration of desires and sexual identities is most apparent in relation to the arousal caused by the human body. Garrett Stewart offers an informative discussion of the body and the verbal evocation of visual art as it relates to textual consumption ('Reading Figures: The Legible Image of Victorian Textuality', *Victorian Literature and the Victorian Visual Imagination* [Berkeley: University of California Press, 1995], pp. 345–67).
3. In *Discipline and Punish*, Foucault uses Bentham's model of the panopticon to argue for the existence of an institutionalized system of surveillance that encourages a self-monitoring even within seemingly private contexts (*Discipline and Punish: The Birth of the Prison* [(London: Allen Lee, 1977)]. John Tagg has demonstrated the applicability of Foucault's model of surveillance to nineteenth-century approaches to photography (*The Burden of Representation: Essays on Photographies and Histories* [Amherst: University of Massachusetts Press, 1988].
4. The ease with which computer rhetoric can be transposed onto a discussion of portraiture reflects both the current reliance on rhetoric as part of the effort by scholars to establish cyberculture as a field warranting independent study, as well as the indebtedness of the field to past visual cultures such as that in which Victorian art took part. Two useful texts among a number that can be cited for a vocabulary reflective of nineteenth-century visuality, despite their focus on a new cybercultural era, are David Bell's *Introduction to Cybercultures* (2001) and Dani Cavallaro's *Cyperpunk and Cyberculture* (2000).
5. Quoted in Audrey Linkman, *The Victorians: Photographic Portraits* (London: Tauris Parke Books, 1993), p. 33.
6. Quoted in Helmut Gernsheim, *Julia Margaret Cameron: Her Life and Photographic Work* (New York: Aperture, 1975), p. 14.
7. Richard C. Sha, *The Visual and Verbal Sketch in British Romanticism* (Philadelphia: University of Pennsylvania Press, 1998), p. 3.
8. Nicholas Mirzoeff, 'What is Visual Culture', *An Introduction to Visual Culture* (London: Routledge, 1999), pp. 3–13: p. 6.
9. Richard Brilliant, *Portraiture* (London: Reaktion Books, 1991), p. 24.
10. Hans-George Gadamer, *Truth and Method* (New York: Crossroads, 1989).
11. The pastime of gallery gazing appears not to have waned even 20 years later, as suggested by William Powell Frith's crowded room in *The Private View of the Royal Academy in 1881* (1881–82). On the subject of art gallery attendance during the Victorian period, see Giles Waterfield's (ed.), *Palaces*

of Art: Art Galleries in Britain, 1790–1990 (1991) and Frances Borzello's *Civilising Caliban. The Misuse of Art 1875–1980* (1987).

12. Linkman, p. 12.
13. For discussions of the political rhetoric imbued within Queen Victoria's numerous portraits, see Ira Nadel's 'Portraits of the Queen' and Margaret Homans's '"To the Queen's Private Apartments": Royal Family Portraiture and the Construction of Victoria's Sovereign Obedience'.
14. Lynda Nead, *Victorian Babylon: People, Streets and Images in Nineteenth-Century London* (New Haven: Yale University Press, 2000), pp. 151–2.
15. The vogue of the *carte-de-visite*, is discussed in William C. Darrah's *Cartes de Visite in Nineteenth Century Photography* (1991).
16. Laurence Senelick, 'Melodramatic Gesture in Carte-de-Visite Photographs', *Theatre* (Spring 1987), pp. 5–13.
17. *Daily Telegraph* (6 April, 1858), p. 5.
18. For a thorough consideration of possible meanings of the recent term 'visual culture', see John A. Walker and Sara Chaplin's *Visual Culture* (1997).
19. W.J.T. Mitchell, *Picture Theory* (Chicago: University of Chicago Press, 1994), p. 356.
20. Norman Bryson, 'The Gaze in the Expanded Field', *Vision and Visuality* (Seattle: Bay View, 1988), pp. 91–4.
21. Geoffrey Batchen, *Burning with Desire: The Conception of Photography* (Cambridge, MA: MIT Press, 1997).
22. Nancy Armstrong, *Fiction in the Art of Photography: The Legacy of British Realism* (Cambridge: Harvard University Press, 1999), p. 9.
23. Kevin Z. Moore, 'Viewing the Victorians: Recent Research on Victorian Visuality', *Victorian Literature and Culture*, 25.2 (1997), pp. 367–85: p. 367.
24. Sheridan Le Fanu, 'Green Tea', *All the Year Round*, London. Nos 47–50 (23 Oct. – 13 Nov. 1869); pp. 501–4, 525–8, 548–52, 572–6, p. 572.
25. John A. Walker and Sarah Chaplin, *Visual Culture: An Introduction* (Manchester: Manchester University Press, 1997), p. 18.
26. Ella Shohat and Robert Stam, 'Narrativizing Visual Culture', *Visual Culture Reader* (ed. Nicholas Mirzeoff, London: Routledge, 1998), pp. 27–49: p. 45.
27. Mitchell, p. 96.
28. Armstrong, p. 7–8.
29. Armstrong, p. 3.
30. Armstrong, p. 5. On the important role of vision in nineteenth-century realism, see also Peter Brooks's *Body Work: Objects of Desire in Modern Narrative* (1993) and Jennifer Green-Lewis's *Framing the Victorians: Photography and the Culture of Realism* (1996).
31. Jonathan Crary, *Suspension of Perception: Attention, Spectacle, and Modern Culture* (Cambridge, MA: MIT Press, 1999), pp. 2–3.
32. Batchen, p. 274.
33. At an auction in Paris on 21 March, 2002, what is believed to be the world's first photograph surfaced. It is a reproduction by Joseph de Nicephore Niepce of a seventeenth-century Dutch pen and ink drawing of a boy and a horse.
34. The panorama precedes the century only slightly, appearing in 1792. On nineteenth-century Britain's turn to visual culture, see Nancy Armstrong's *Fiction in the Age of Photography* (1999), Kate Flint's *Victorians and the Visual Imagination* (2000), Kevin Z. Moore's 'Viewing the Victorians' (1997), and

Carol T. Christ and John O. Jordan's collection *Victorian Literature and the Victorian Visual Imagination* (1995).

35. Martin Heidegger, 'The Age of the World Picture', *The Question Concerning Technology and Other Essays* (New York: Garland, 1977), p. 130.

36. John Ruskin, *The Eagle's Nest, Works*, vol. XXII (1872), p. 194.

37. John Ruskin, *Modern Painters*, vol. 1 (London: George Allen, 1900), pp. 142–3.

38. Moore, p. 371.

39. Moore, p. 368.

40. Jeff Nunokawa formulates a similar model of the way in which social spectacle can control visualization, in this case with regard to homosexuality specifically. While referring to 'the multivalence of this involuntary spectacle,' Nunokawa suggests minimal agency for the subject associated with the visualized sexuality; while those 'who see him are no more able to decide how to receive it than he is how to present it', 'the figure whom it spotlights has no say over its production' and his 'artistic powers of self-expression are paralyzed by the spell of the erotic' (*Tame Passions of Wilde: The Styles of Manageable Desire* [Princeton: Princeton University Press, 2003], p. 23).

41. Michel Foucault, *The History of Sexuality*, vol. 1. (New York: Vintage, 1980), p. 101.

42. Foucault, p. 102.

43. David Bergman 'Introduction', *Camp Grounds: Style and Homosexuality* (Amherst: University of Massachusetts Press, 1993), pp. 3–16; Judith Butler, *Gender Trouble: Feminism and the Subversion of Identity* (New York: Routledge, 1990); Marjorie Garber, *Bisexuality and the Eroticism of Everyday Life* (New York: Routledge, 2000); Eve Kosofsky Sedgwick, *Epistemology of the Closet* (Berkeley: University of California Press, 1990).

1 Lady in Green with Novel

1. Dinah Mulock Craik, *Olive* (Oxford: Oxford University Press, 1999), p. 121.

2. Terry Castle, *The Apparitional Lesbian: Female Homosexuality and Modern Culture* (New York: Columbia University Press, 1993), p. 62.

3. Joan Friedman, 'Every Lady Her Own Drawing Master', *Apollo*, 105 (Apr. 1977), pp. 262–7; Roszika Parker and Griselda Pollock, *Old Mistresses* (London: Routledge, 1981); Jane Kromm, 'Visual Culture and Scopic Custom in *Jane Eyre* and *Villette*', *Victorian Literature and Culture*, 26.2 (1998), pp. 369–94.

4. Whitney Chadwick, *Women, Art, and Society* (London: Thames and Hudson, 1990), p. 164.

5. Mary Hays, *Victim of Prejudice* (Peterborough: Broadview, 1998), p. 138.

6. An exception to this pattern is the heroine of Anne Brontë's *Tenant of Wildfell Hall*. Helen's skill at oil painting is unique, although she does turn to a career in the visual arts only under extreme circumstances and appears likely to end her professional efforts once her fortune has been secured. Brontë herself painted and would have been aware of the economic constrictions involved in a career in the visual arts. Elizabeth

Langland offers a more extensive discussion of Helen as an artist in 'The Voicing of Feminine Desire in Anne Brontë's *The Tenant of Wildfell Hall*', *Gender and Discourse in Victorian Literature and Art*, eds Antony H. Harrison and Beverly Taylor (DeKalb, IL: Northern Illinois University Press, 1992), pp. 111–23.

7. 'Female School of Art', *Illustrated London News* (1868).
8. Craik, *Olive*, p. 121.
9. Quoted in Chadwick, pp. 170–1.
10. Pamela Gerrish Nunn, *Victorian Women Artists* (London: Women's, 1987), p. 42.
11. Elizabeth Ellet, *Artists in All Ages and Countries* (New York: 1859), p. 3.
12. George Du Maurier, 'Female School of Art – (*Useful Occupation for Idle and Ornamental Young Men*)', *Punch* (30 May 1874), p. 232.
13. Dinah Mulock Craik, *About Money and Other Things* (New York, 1887), pp. 184–5.
14. Nunn, p. 22.
15. Lynda Nead, *Victorian Babylon: People, Streets and Images in Nineteenth-Century London* (New Haven: Yale University Press, 2000), p. 160.
16. Laura Mulvey, 'Visual Pleasure and Narrative Cinema', *Visual and Other Pleasures* (Bloomington, IN: Indiana University Press, 1989), pp. 14–26: p. 19.
17. Geraldine Jewsbury, *The Half Sisters* (Oxford: Oxford University Press, 1994), p. 214.
18. Deborah Cherry, *Painting Women: Victorian Women Artists* (London: Routledge, 1993), pp. 80–1.
19. Lillian Faderman, *Surpassing the Love of Men: Romantic Friendship and Love between Women from the Renaissance to the Present* (New York: William Morrow, 1981), p. 152.
20. Geraldine Jewsbury, Untitled Review, *Athenaeum*, 17 (1867), p. 720.
21. Geraldine Jewsbury, 'How Agnes Worral Was Taught to Be Respectable', *Douglas Jerrold's Shilling Magazine*, 5 (1847), pp. 16–24, 246–6: p. 258.
22. Quoted in Faderman, p. 164.
23. Quoted in Virginia Woolf, 'Geraldine and Jane', *Collected Essays*, vol. 4 (London: Hogarth, 1967), pp. 27–39: p. 35.
24. Norma Clarke, *Ambitious Heights: Writing, Friendship, Love – The Jewsbury Sisters, Felicia Hemans, and Jane Welsh Carlyle* (London: Routledge, 1990), p. 198.
25. Quoted in Clarke, p. 71.
26. Clarke, p. 71.
27. Lisa Merrill, *When Romeo Was a Woman: Charlotte Cushman and Her Circle of Female Spectators* (Ann Arbor: University of Michigan Press, 2000).
28. Jewsbury, *The Half Sisters*, p. 33.
29. Ibid., p. 134.
30. Ibid., pp. 216–7.
31. Ibid., p. 218.
32. Ibid., p. 13.
33. Ibid., p. 13.
34. Ibid., p. 15.
35. Ibid., p. 42.

36. Ibid., p. 42.
37. Ibid., pp. 42–3.
38. Ibid., p. 262.
39. Ibid., p. 134; p. 42.
40. Ibid., p. 22.
41. Ibid., p. 42.
42. Ibid., p. 42.
43. Ibid., p. 41.
44. Ibid., p. 275.
45. Ibid., p. 275.
46. Ibid., pp. 278–9.
47. Ibid., p. 329.
48. Ibid., p. 331.
49. Ibid., p. 396.
50. Ibid., p. 132.
51. Ibid., p. 134.
52. Geraldine Jewsbury, *Selection from the Letters of Geraldine Endsor Jewsbury to Jane Welsh Carlyle*, ed. Annie E. Ireland (London: Longmans, Green, 1892), p. 333.
53. Jewsbury, *The Half Sisters*, p. 135.
54. Ibid., p. 136.
55. Ibid., p. 42.
56. Mary Elizabeth Braddon, *Lady Audley's Secret* (Oxford: Oxford University Press, 1998), p. 5.
57. Ibid., p. 11.
58. Ibid., p. 12.
59. Ibid., p. 40.
60. Ibid., p. 310.
61. Ibid., p. 76.
62. Ibid., p. 120.
63. Ibid., p. 158.
64. Ibid., p. 446.
65. Ibid., p. 117.
66. Ibid., p. 70.
67. Ibid., p. 71.
68. Winnifred Hughes, *The Maniac in the Cellar: Sensation Novels in the 1860s* (Princeton: Princeton University Press, 1980), p. 127.
69. Mary Carpenter, 'On the Treatment of Female Convicts', LXVII.CCCXCVII (Jan. 1863), pp. 3–46: p. 31.
70. Carpenter, pp. 33–4.
71. Atavism refers to the state of being in a more primitive or regressive stage of development than humanity in general. The term is perhaps most frequently applied to the image of a colonial ruler regressing to the level of the colonized primitive supposedly being held under control. The most extensive correlation of female women with atavism can be found in Cesare Lombroso and William Ferrero's *The Female Offender* (New York: Philosophical Library, 1958). Their research was intended to establish physiognomic traits by which criminals could be recognized even before they committed any crimes. Their project fits cleanly into a major aim of

Victorian scientific visual culture, that of establishing clear physical signifiers of difference by which people could be categorized and judged. Unfortunately for Lombroso and Ferrero, their research proved inconclusive. They summarized these results by stating that it was difficult to establish which females were most likely to become criminals because they all possessed latent criminality, being atavistically closer to their primitive origins than are males.

72. Lombroso and Ferrero, p. 263.
73. Braddon, p. 237.
74. Lombroso and Ferrero, p. 204.
75. Complicating the more familiar claim that institutional discourses inadvertently affirmed (and thus strengthened the validity of) same-sex desire in their efforts to oppress and criminalize it, Lombroso and Ferrero's description of the latent criminality of strong female friendship implies the potential for criminalizing unsightly desires without having to reify them. Had their physiognomic research produced more definitive conclusions in accord with their misogynistic hypotheses, they could have criminalized female friendship as a sure sign of deviant aggression without envisioning the possible sexuality behind the relations.
76. Braddon, p. 105.
77. Ibid., p. 58.
78. Ibid., p. 58.
79. Ibid., p. 104.
80. Ibid., p. 59.
81. Ibid., p. 110.
82. Ibid., p. 207.
83. Ibid., pp. 331–2.
84. Elaine Showalter, 'Desperate Remedies: Sensation Novels of the 1860s', *The Victorian Newsletter*, 49 (Spring 1976), pp. 1–5.
85. D.A. Miller, *The Novel and the Police* (Berkeley: University of California Press, 1988).
86. Braddon, p. 379.
87. Pamela K. Gilbert, *Disease, Desire, and the Body in Victorian Women's Popular Novels* (Cambridge: Cambridge University Press, 1997), p. 94.
88. Braddon, *Lady Audley's Secret*, p. 363.
89. Craik, *Olive*, p. 8.
90. Ibid., p. 81.
91. Ibid., p. 30.
92. Ibid., p. 50.
93. Ibid., p. 56.
94. Ibid., p. 130.
95. Ibid., p. 85.
96. Ibid., p. 119.
97. Ibid., p. 160.
98. Kate Flint, *The Victorians and the Visual Imagination* (Cambridge: Cambridge University Press, 2000), p. 64.
99. Flint, p. 66.
100. Craik, *Olive*, p. 118.

101. Dinah Mulock Craik, *A Woman's Thoughts about Women* (London, 1858), p. 24.
102. Craik, *About Money*, p. 7.
103. Craik, *Woman's Thoughts*, pp. 50–1.
104. Ibid., p. 58.
105. Cora Kaplan, 'Introduction', *Olive* by Dinah Mulock Craik (Oxford: Oxford University Press, 1999).
106. Sally Mitchell, *Dinah Mulock Craik* (Boston: G.K. Hall, 1983).
107. Craik, *Olive*, p. 126.
108. Ibid., p. 152.
109. Ibid., p. 127.
110. Ibid., p. 123.
111. Ibid., p. 111.
112. Ibid., p. 127.
113. Ibid., p. 249.
114. Ibid., p. 9.
115. Craik, *About Money*, p. 194.
116. Ibid., p. 197.
117. Ibid., p. 194.
118. Craik, *Olive*, pp. 57–8.
119. Ibid., p. 185.

2 Framed and Hung

1. Wilkie Collins, 'A Terribly Strange Bed', *Mad Monkton and Other Tales*, ed. Norman Page (Oxford: Oxford University Press, 1994), pp. 1–20: p. 12.
2. Related uses of portraiture as a visual context for the analysis of gender politics appear in Collins's stories 'Mad Monkton', 'The Lady of Glenwith Grange', and 'The Clergyman's Confession'.
3. Ruskin, John. "Modern Manufacture and Design", *The Two Paths* (London: Cassell, 1907), pp. 73–100.
4. Wilkie Collins, *A Rogue's Life: From His Birth to His Marriage* (New York: AMS, 1970), p. 57.
5. Ibid., pp. 59–61.
6. Robert Vaughan, *The Age of Great Cities: or Modern Society Viewed in Its Relation to Intelligence, Morals and Religion* (Shannon: Irish University Press, 1971), p. 134.
7. Paula Gillet, *Worlds of Art: Painters in Victorian Society* (New Brunswick, NJ: Rutgers University Press, 1990), pp. 3–5.
8. Wilkie Collins, *Hide and Seek* (Oxford: Oxford University Press, 1993), p. 14.
9. Richard Brilliant, *Portraiture* (London: Reaktion Books, 1991), p. 11.
10. Collins, *Hide and Seek*, p. 229.
11. Sophia Andres, 'Pre-Raphaelite Painting and Jungian Images in Wilkie Collins's *The Woman in White*', *Victorian Newsletter*, 88 (Fall 1995), pp. 26–31; Ira B. Nadel, 'Wilkie Collins and His Illustrators', *Wilkie Collins to the Forefront: Some Reassessments*, eds Nelson Smith and R.C. Terry (New York: AMS Press, 1995).
12. Simone Cooke, '"Mistaken for a PRB": Wilkie Collins and the Pre-Raphaelites', *The New Collins Society Newsletter*, 3.1 (Winter 2000), pp.1–6: p. 3.

13. Dianne Sachko Macleod, *Art and the Victorian Middle Class: Money and the Making of Cultural Identity* (Cambridge: Cambridge University Press, 1996).

14. Julie F. Codell, 'The Public Image of the Victorian Artist: Family Biographies', *The Journal of Pre-Raphaelite Studies*, 4 (Fall 1996), pp. 5–34.

15. Samuel Smiles, *Self-Help; with Illustrations of Character, Conduct and Perseverance* (London: John Murray, 1958), p. 350.

16. James Abbot McNeill Whistler's own account of Ruskin's attack on his painting *Nocturne in Black and Gold* and the subsequent trial can be found in his *Gentle Art of Making Enemies* (London: W. Heinemann, 1890). Linda Merrill offers an extensive analysis of the event in *A Pot of Paint: Aesthetics on Trial in Whistler vs. Ruskin* (Washington: Smithsonian Institution, 1992).

17. Joseph A. Kestner, *Masculinities in Victorian Painting* (Aldershot, UK: Scolar, 1995), p. 5.

18. Michael Roper and John Tosh, 'Introduction', *Manful Assertions: Masculinities in Britain since 1800*, eds Michael Roper and John Tosh (London: Routledge, 1991), p. 15. Kestner offers an excellent historical contextualizations of masculinity in relation to visual art and the artist respectively, as does Gillet in *Worlds of Art: Painters in Victorian Society*.

19. Michel Foucault, *The History of Sexuality*, vol. 1 (New York: Vintage, 1980), p. 123.

20. John Ruskin, *Modern Painters*, vol. 1 (London: George Allen, 1900), p. 30.

21. Nuel Pharr Davis, *The Life of Wilkie Collins* (Urbana, IL: University of Illinois Press, 1956), p. 93.

22. Charles Dickens, 'Old Lamps for New Ones', *Household Words* (June 1850), pp. 107–9: p. 108.

23. Ibid., pp. 107–8.

24. Ibid., p. 108.

25. 'Royal Academy: Portraiture', *Victorian Painting: Essays and Reviews*, vol. 2, ed. John Charles Olmsted (New York, Garland, 1983), pp. 14–18: p. 17.

26. Ibid., p. 16.

27. Ibid., p. 15.

28. Emmanuel Cooper, *The Sexual Perspective: Homosexuality and Art in the Last 100 Years in the West* (London: Routledge, 1994).

29. Wilkie Collins, *The Woman in White* (London: Collins, 1952), p. 46.

30. Collins, *Hide and Seek*, p. 54.

31. Lillian Nayder, *Wilkie Collins* (New York: Twayne, 1997), p. 6.

32. Ibid.

33. Wilkie Collins, *Memoirs of the Life of William Collins, Esq. R.A.*, vol. 2 (London, 1848), pp. 311–2.

34. Macleod, p. 33.

35. Collins, *A Rogue's Life*, p. 47.

36. Ibid. p. 40.

37. Tamar Heller, *Dead Secrets: Wilkie Collins and the Female Gothic* (New Haven, CN: Yale University Press, 1992), p. 41.

38. Codell, 'The Public Image of the Victorian Artist'.

39. Collins, *Memoirs*, vol. 1(London, 1848), p. 6.

40. Pierre Bourdieu, *The Rules of Art: Genesis and Structure of the Literary Field* (Stanford: Stanford University, 1996), p. 111.

41. James Eli Adams, *Dandies and Desert Saints: Styles of Victorian Masculinity* (Ithaca: Cornell University Press, 1995), pp. 6–7.
42. William Morris, *Art and Society: Lectures and Essays by William Morris*, ed. Gary Zabel(Boston: George's Hill, 1993), p. 21.
43. Collins, *The Woman in White*, p. 127.
44. Ibid., p. 22.
45. Collin, *Hide and Seek*, p. 64.
46. Ibid., p. 152.
47. Davis, *The Life of Wilkie Collins*.
48. Collins, *Hide and Seek*, p. 33.
49. Ibid., p. 39.
50. Ibid., pp. 39–40.
51. Ibid., pp. 312–3.
52. Ibid., pp. 312.
53. Collins, *The Woman in White*, p. 189.
54. Ibid., p. 374.
55. Ibid., p. 570.
56. Ibid., p. 571.
57. Collins, *Hide and Seek*, p. 314.
58. Collins, *The Woman in White*, p. 37.
59. Ibid., p. 84.
60. Ibid., p. 50.
61. Ibid., p. 53.
62. Ibid., p. 28.
63. Max Nordau, *Degeneration*. (Lincoln: University of Nebraska Press, 1993), pp. 18–19.
64. Nordau, p. 21.
65. Wilkie Collins, *The Law and the Lady* (New York: Harpers, 1873), p. 173.
66. Ibid., p. 214.
67. Ibid., p. 232.
68. Dennis Denisoff, 'The Femininity of Valeria Woodville's Detective Agency', *The New Collins Society Newsletter*, 31 (Winter 2000), pp. 6–11.
69. Collins, *The Law and the Lady*, p. 232.
70. Ibid., p. 235.
71. Ibid., pp. 203–4.
72. Ibid., p. 204.
73. Ibid., pp. 247–8.
74. Ibid., p. 229.
75. Ibid., pp. 229–30.
76. In a review of Tennyson's *Poems, Chiefly Lyrical*, Hallam celebrates poetry of sensation as the best type of poetry because it aims to stimulate the reader's imagination, thus avoiding conventional thought-processes. For Hallam, the imaginative faculties are connected to women, who, he claims, are more attuned to emotion and imaginative play. These arguments are put forward in Arthur Henry Hallam, 'On Some of the Characteristics of Modern Poetry, and on the Lyrical Poems of Alfred Tennyson', *Englishman's Magazine*, 1 (Aug. 1831), pp. 616–28. On the relation of women poets and the feminization of poetry, see Dorothy Mermin, *Godiva's Ride: Women of Letters in England, 1830–1880* (Bloomington: Indiana University Press, 1993).

77. Nordau, p. 22.
78. Collins, *The Law and the Lady*, p. 229.
79. Ibid., p. 203.

3   Posing a Threat

1. Max Nordau, *Degeneration* (Lincoln: University of Nebraska Press, 1993), p. 318.
2. Quoted in Richard Ellmann, *Oscar Wilde* (London: Penguin, 1988), p. 394.
3. Barbara Spackman, 'Interversions', *Perennial Decay: On the Aesthetics and Politics of Decadence* (eds L. Constable, D. Denisoff, and M. Potolsky, Philadelphia: University of Pennsylvania Press, 1999), pp. 35–49: p. 39.
4. Ibid., p. 41. For further discussions of decadence as a shift outside of binary oppositions and the problems arising from such efforts and theorizations, see also Charles Bernheimer, 'Unknowing Decadence', *Perennial Decay: On the Aesthetics and Politics of Decadence* (eds L. Constable, D. Denisoff and M. Potolsky, Philadelphia: University of Pennsylvania Press, 1999), pp. 50–64.
5. Queensberry's anxiety is not especially surprising as the view of trans-generational punishment was not an uncommon one in Victorian England. It was also a mainstay of the literature, and especially that which chose deviance and transgression as its subject. In Horace Walpole's second preface to his *The Castle of Otranto*, considered the first Gothic text, the author suggests that the only apparent moral message of the novel is that the sins of one generation may be paid for by the next. A similar suggestion can be found in Vernon Lee's 'Oke of Okehurst', which I discuss in the following chapter. In all these works, portraits function symbolically as the living influence of dead ancestors.
6. The most popular text addressing this issue is Max Nordau's *Degeneration*, although it focuses more on literature than on visual art. His follow-up study, *On Art and Artists* (1907), tempers somewhat his earlier, notorious position.
7. Heather McPherson, *Fin-de-Siècle Faces: Portraiture in the Age of Proust* (Birmingham: University of Alabama Press, 1988), p. 19.
8. Pierre Bourdieu, *Distinction: A Social Critique of the Judgement of Taste* (Cambridge: Harvard University Press, 1984), pp. 76–7.
9. Kenneth McConkey, *Edwardian Portraits: Images of an Age of Opulence* (Woodbridge, Suffolk: Antique Collectors Club, 1987), p. 16.
10. Kenneth McConkey, '"Well-bred Contortions": 1880–1918', *The British Portrait 1660–1960* (ed. Roy Strong, Woodbridge, Suffolk: Antique Collectors' Club: 1991), p. 353.
11. McPherson, p. 19.
12. Arthur Mayne, *British Profile Miniaturists* (London: Faber and Faber, 1970), p. 93.
13. One notable complication to this general structure regards the numerous painted and photographic portraits of Queen Victoria as ruler, mother, and/or wife. For discussions of portraits of Queen Victoria, see Margaret Homans's '"To the Queen's Private Apartments": Royal Family Portraiture and the Construction of Victoria's Sovereign Obedience', *Victorian Studies*,

37.1 (1993), pp. 1–41; and Ira Nadel's 'Portraits of the Queen', *Victorian Poetry*, 25.3–4 (1987), pp. 169–91.

14. Audrey Linkman, *The Victorians: Photographic Portraits* (London: Tauris Parke Books, 1993), p. 46. See also McConkey's 'Well-bred Contortions', p. 356.

15. Lisa Hamilton, 'Oscar Wilde, New Women, and the Rhetoric of Effeminacy', *Wilde Writings: Contextual Conditions* (ed. J. Bristow, Toronto: University of Toronto Press, 2003), pp. 235–43. On the subject of effeminacy, deviancy, and charicatures of Wilde, see also D. Denisoff's *Aestheticism and Sexual Parody: 1840–1940* (Cambridge: Cambridge University Press, 2001).

16. Ellmann includes these images in his biography of Wilde, between pages 432 and 433.

17. Joseph Bristow, *Effeminate England: Homoerotic Writing after 1885* (Buckingham: Open University Press, 1995).

18. Oscar Wilde, *The Complete Works of Oscar Wilde* (New York: Harper & Row, 1989), p. 118.

19. These images are reproduced between pages 226 and 227 of Ellmann's biography of Wilde.

20. Ellmann, p. 357.

21. Quoted in Michael Holroyd, *Lytton Strachey: The Unknown Years* (London: Heinemann, 1971), p. 357n.

22. Eve Kosofsky Sedgwick, *Tendencies* (Durham, NC: Duke University Press, 1993), p. 58.

23. John Shato Douglas, 8th Marquess of Queensberry, *Marriage and the Relation of the Sexes: An Address to Women* (London: Watts, 1893) p. 5.

24. Queensberry, *Marriage*, p. 12.

25. M. Foucault, *The History of Sexuality*, vol. 1, (New York: Vintage, 1980), p. 118.

26. John Shato Douglas, 8th Marquess of Queensberry, 'The Religion of Secularism and the Perfectibility of Man', *Secular Review* (London. Watts, 188?), pp. 3–16: p. 6.

27. John Shato Douglas, 8th Marquess of Queensberry, 'The Spirit of the Matterhorn' (London: Watts, 1880), p. 27.

28. Mary Cowling, *The Artist as Anthropologist: The Representation of Type and Character in Victorian Art* (Cambridge: Cambridge University Press, 1989); D. Pick, *Faces of Degeneration: A European Disorder, c.1848–c.1918,* (Cambridge: Cambridge University Press, 1989). The fact that Pick's study of correlations between degeneracy and physiognomy addresses almost exclusively works by fin-de-siècle authors – including Arthur Conan Doyle, George Gissing, Bram Stoker, and H.G. Wells – suggests that the equation was reaching a critical stage at the time of Douglas and Wilde's relationship.

29. Quoted in Brian Roberts, *The Mad Bad Line: The Family of Lord Alfred Douglas* (London: Hamish Hamilton, 1981), p. 188.

30. Quoted in Roberts, p. 224.

31. Quoted in Ellmann, p. 394.

32. Quoted in Roberts, p. 216.

33. Judith Butler argues that, although one may not see one's self as socially constructed, one's position as 'I' is the result of repetitions of a performance ('Imitation', p. 311); more specifically, gender is a performance that fosters the 'illusion of an inner sex or essence or psychic gender core ..., the illusion of an inner depth' (p. 317). Butler stresses, however, that gender and other aspects

of one's identity are not a result of *conscious* performance; in *Bodies that Matter* she argues that performance is the generally unrecognized reiteration of norms, and that social and cultural constraints actually sustain performativity (pp. 94–5). She maintains, however, that, while performance is operative whether it is acknowledged or not, it becomes strategic when used to destabilize, and then safeguard against, essentialist notions of identity, converting identity into a site of on-going revision ('Imitation', p. 312).

34. Quoted in Roberts, p. 212.
35. Ibid., p. 229.
36. Ellmann, p. 416.
37. Quoted in Roberts, p. 212.
38. H. Montgomery Hyde, *The Trials of Oscar Wilde* (London: William Hodge, 1948), p. 96.
39. Roberts, p. 219.
40. Quoted in ibid., p. 228.
41. Ibid., p. 255.
42. Quoted from the *Evening Standard*, 3 April 1895, by Ed Cohen, *Talk on the Wilde Side: Toward a Genealogy of a Discourse on Male Sexualities* (Routledge: New York, 1993), p. 151.
43. Quoted from the *Daily Telegraph*, 4 April 1895, by Ed Cohen, p. 162.
44. Hyde, p. 115.
45. W.S. Gilbert and Arthur Sullivan, *Patience; or, Bunthorne's Bride*, *The Complete Plays of Gilbert and Sullivan* (New York: Modern Library, 1936), pp. 184–233: p. 188.
46. Wilde, p. 117.
47. Ibid., p. 117.
48. Ibid., p. 118.
49. Ibid., pp. 112–13.
50. Joris Karl Huysmans, *Against Nature* (London: Penguin, 1959), p. 17.
51. Ibid., p. 18.
52. Wilde, p. 39.
53. Ibid., p. 1152.
54. Ibid., p. 41.
55. Ibid., p. 112.
56. Ibid., p. 113. Wilde may be winking askance at the plethora of texts that influenced *Dorian Gray*. Kerry Powell offers the most extensive catalogue of such works, arguing that 'among the detritus of popular literature a thriving subgenre of fiction in which the props, themes, and even to some degree the dialogue and characterization of *Dorian Gray* are anticipated' ('Tom, Dick, and Dorian Gray: Magic-Picture Mania in Late Victorian Fiction', *Philological Quarterly*, 62.2 [1983], pp. 147–70: pp. 148–9).
57. E. Cohen, pp. 75–7.
58. Wilde, p. 21.
59. Ibid., p. 19.
60. Ibid., p. 21. Christopher Newall argues effectively that, in fact, it was the influence of aestheticism and the Pre-Raphaelites that made portraitists interested in 'the deliberate manipulation of mood as a means of exploring the sitter's inner soul. ... The theory of "art for art's sake" released at least some painters from the dictates of commissions, and portraits came to be

regarded as works of art in their own right rather than mere likenesses of individuals' ('The Victorians: 1830–1880', *The British Portrait 1660–1960*, ed. Roy Strong [Woodbridge, Suffolk: Antique Collectors' Club: 1991], pp. 299–351: p. 335).
61. Wilde, p. 21.
62. Ibid., p. 93.
63. Ibid., p. 41.
64. Ibid., p. 47.
65. Ibid., p. 35.
66. Ibid., p. 24.
67. Ibid., p. 35.
68. McConkey, *Edwardian*, p. 16.
69. Jeff Nunokawa, *Tame Passions of Wilde: The Styles of Manageable Desire* (Princeton: Princeton University Press, 2003), pp. 121–60.
70. Wilde, p. 95.
71. Ibid., p. 94.
72. Ibid., p. 123.

4 The Forest Beyond the Frame

1. Geraldine Jewsbury's *The Half Sisters* and Dinah Mulock Craik's *Olive*, discussed in my first chapter, are both examples of the type of narratives usually read as depicting female-female friendships as ideal and pure. As I argue, however, sexuality quite often rises to the surface of the image through innuendo and alternative discourses such as that of visuality. Notably, cross-sexual desire was also often depicted through suggestion and inference in these texts; the only major difference is that the subterfugal discourse of heterosexual eroticism was a more familiar code and therefore recognized by a broader readership. Important works written on the representations of lesbianism in British literature include Terry Castle, *The Apparitional Lesbian: Female Homosexuality and Modern Culture* (New York: Columbia University Press, 1993); Lillian Faderman, *Surpassing the Love of Men: Romantic Friendship and Love Between Women from the Renaissance to the Present* (New York: William Morrow, 1981); and Lisa L.L. Moore, *Dangerous Intimacies: Toward a Sapphic History of the British Novel* (Durham, NC: Duke University Press, 1997).
2. Peter Gunn, *Vernon Lee/Violet Paget, 1856–1935* (London: Oxford University Press, 1964), pp. 33–4.
3. Virginia Woolf, *Orlando: A Biography* (London: Hogarth, 1928), pp. 156–7.
4. Christa Zorn, *Vernon Lee: Aesthetics, History, and the Victorian Female Intellectual* (Athens: Ohio University Press, 2003), pp. 74–5.
5. Vineta Colby, *Vernon Lee: A Literary Biography* (Charlottesville: University of Virginia, 2003), p. 249.
6. Ibid., p. 348, n. 3.
7. Gunn, p. 229.
8. Like much of the novel *Orlando*, the title of Orlando's poem was no doubt at least partially inspired by the life of Vita Sackville-West. Sackville-West's family estate of Knole is located in Sevenoaks, Kent and, like Orlando's

home, has 'oak trees dotted here and there' (*Orlando*, p. 150). The Okes no doubt likewise derived their family name from the 'oak-dotted park-land' surrounding their manor house ('Oke', p. 187). Of equal importance to my discussion of inheritance, the oak has also appeared in numerous works over the centuries as a symbol of England's own heritage and national vigor.

9. In an explanation of what she calls Lee's 'new historicism', Christa Zorn distinguishes between the references to portraiture in Lee's and Pater's essays. Zorn notes that the difference between their use of portraiture to explain their aesthetics clarifies why Woolf was more critical of Lee than Pater (pp. 55–7).

10. Gunn, p. 98.

11. Catherine Maxwell, 'From Dionysus to "Dionea": Vernon Lee's Portraits', *Word & Image* 13.3 (1997), pp. 253–69: p. 258.

12. Vernon Lee, *The Beautiful: An Introduction to Psychological Aesthetics* (Cambridge: Cambridge University, 1913), p. 59.

13. In her recent biography of Vernon Lee, Vineta Colby has shown that Lee, toward the end of her writings on empathy, doubted her and Kit Astruther-Thompson's earlier claims that the experience of empathy can result in a visible physical response. It is clear, however, that Lee did not see this revision posing any threat to the main arguments of their psychological aesthetics (Colby, pp. 166–7).

14. Lee, p. 65.

15. Quoted in Susan Buck-Morss, *The Dialectics of Seeing: Walter Benjamin and the Arcades Project* (Cambridge, Mass: MIT, 1989), p. 108.

16. Vernon Lee, 'The Sense of the Past', *A Vernon Lee Anthology: Selections from the Earlier Works*, ed. Irene Cooper Willis (London: J. Lane, 1929), pp. 166–74.

17. Ibid., p. 168. Pater offers a similar notion of history's role in aesthetics in various works, including *Studies in the History of the Renaissance* (1873). Lee's debt to Pater is apparent in much of her writing, even in the adaptation of aesthetic rhetoric to the discussion of the human body. However, her focus on the human (female) body as it responds emotionally and physically to beauty adds a dimension to aestheticism that is distinctly her own.

18. Ibid., p. 167.

19. Lee, *Beautiful*, p. 15.

20. Lee, 'Sense', pp. 173–4.

21. Diane Gillespie, *The Sisters' Arts: The Writing and Painting of Virginia Woolf and Vanessa Bell* (Syracuse: Syracuse University Press, 1988), p. 205.

22. Vernon Lee, 'Oke of Okehurst', *Hauntings: Fantastic Stories* (London: John Lane, 1906), pp. 109–91: p. 124.

23. Quoted in Audrey Linkman, *The Victorians: Photographic Portraits* (London: Tauris Parke Books, 1993), p. 33.

24. Quoted in Helmut Gernsheim, *Julia Margaret Cameron: Her Life and Photographic Work* (New York: Aperture, 1975), p. 14.

25. Natasha Aleksiuk, '"A Thousand Angles": Photographic Irony in the Work of Julia Margaret Cameron and Virginia Woolf', *Mosaic*, 33.2 (June 2000), pp. 125–42.

26. Vernon Lee. 'The Blame of Portraits', *Hortus Vitae: Essays on the Gardening of Life* (London: John Lane, 1904), pp. 139–47: p. 140.

27. 'Oke of Okehurst' is not the only text by Lee that uses portraiture to analyze the relation between empathy, aesthetics, and desire. Other works in which the subject is approached include the novel *Miss Brown*; 'Amour Dure', a story about a man who, through portraits, falls in love with a dead woman; and 'Winthrop's Adventure' (first published in 1881 as 'A Wicked Voice'), a story in which a character named Magnus who mocks eighteenth-century music is haunted by the portrait of a famous *castrato*. Foregrounding Lee's interest in exploring gender- and sex-based dissidence, Magnus voices his attraction to the *castrato* as a *femme fatale*: 'That effeminate, fat face of his is almost beautiful. ... I have seen faces like this, if not in real life, at least in my boyish romantic dreams, when I read Swinburne and Baudelaire, the faces of wicked, vindictive women. Oh yes! He is decidedly a beautiful creature' (p. 206).
28. Lee, 'Oke', p. 138.
29. Ibid., p. 153.
30. Zorn, p. 24.
31. Lee, 'Oke', p. 120.
32. Ibid., p. 124.
33. Ibid., p. 110.
34. Ibid., p. 122.
35. Ibid., p. 122.
36. Ibid., p. 127.
37. Same-sex desire has frequently been psychologized in the twentieth century as a dysfunctional Narcissism. Five years after Lee's parody of scientific authority, Havelock Ellis would give 'Narcissism' his stamp of scientific recognition, defining it as an auto-erotic perversion. Ellis's most extensive discussion of Narcissism occurs in *Studies in the Psychology of Sex*, 4 vols (London: University Press, 1897).
38. Lee, 'Oke', p. 128.
39. Ibid., p. 128.
40. Ibid., p. 168.
41. Woolf, *Orlando*, p. 15.
42. Virginia Woolf, 'The Narrow Bridge of Art', *Collected Essays*, vol. 2 (New York: Harcourt, Brace, 1967), p. 223.
43. Woolf, *Orlando*, p. 277.
44. Lee, 'Sense', p. 168.
45. Quoted in J.J. Wilson, 'Why is Orlando Difficult?', *New Feminist Essays on Virginia Woolf*, ed. Jane Marcus (Lincoln: University of Nebraska Press, 1981), pp. 170–84: p. 179.
46. Woolf, *Orlando*, p. 277.
47. Ibid., p. 289.
48. Virginia Woolf, *Diary of Virginia Woolf*, ed. Anne Oliver Bell, vol. 2 (New York: Harcourt Brace Jovanovich, 1978), p. 114.
49. Woolf, *Diary*, p. 156.
50. Virginia Woolf, *Letters of Virginia Woolf*, vol. 6, eds Nigel Nicolson and Joanne Trautmann (New York: Harcourt Brace Jovanovich, 1980), p. 417.
51. Virginia Woolf, 'The Art of Biography', *Collected Essays of Virginia Woolf IV*, ed. Leonard Woolf (London: Hogarth, 1967), pp. 221–8.

52. Virginia Woolf, *To The Lighthouse* (London: Collins, 1987), p. 79.
53. Gillespie, p. 171.
54. Talia Schaffer, 'Posing *Orlando*', *Genders: Sexual Artifice, Images, Politics*, eds Ann Kibbey, Kayann Short, and Abauli Formanfarmaian (New York: New York University Press, 1994), pp. 26–63.
55. Linkman,*The Victorians*.
56. Woolf, *Orlando*, p. 15.
57. Ibid., p. 16.
58. Ibid., p. 17.
59. Ibid., p. 67.
60. Ibid., p. 156.
61. Ibid., p. 287.
62. Ibid., p. 199.
63. Ibid., p. 200.
64. Ibid., p. 197.
65. Faderman, p. 392.
66. Adam Parkes, 'Lesbianism, History, and Censorship: *The Well of Loneliness* and the SUPPRESSED RANDINESS of Virginia Woolf's *Orlando*', *Twentieth Century Literature* 40.4 (1994), pp. 434–60.
67. Sherron E. Knopp, '"If I Saw You Would You Kiss Me?"': Sapphism and the Subversiveness of Virginia Woolf's Orlando', *PMLA* 103.1 (1988), pp. 24–34: p. 33.
68. Merl Storr, 'Editor's Introduction', *Bisexuality: A Critical Reader* (London: Routledge, 1999), p. 8.
69. Marjorie Garber, *Bisexuality and the Eroticism of Everyday Life* (New York: Routledge, 2000), p. 65.
70. R. Colker, *Hybrid: Bisexuals, Multiracials, and Other Misfits under American Law* (New York: New York University Press, 1996).
71. J. Halberstam, *Female Masculinity* (Durham: Duke University Press, 1998), pp. 213–15.
72. Garber, *Bisexuality*, p. 232.
73. Halberstam, p. 52.
74. Garber, *Bisexuality*, p. 233.
75. Woolf, *Orlando*, p. 36.
76. Ibid., p. 127.
77. Ibid., p. 140.
78. Joseph Allen Boone, 'Vacation Cruises; or, The Homoerotics of Orientalism', *PMLA* 110.1 (1995), pp. 89–107.
79. Woolf, *Orlando*, p. 232.
80. Ibid., p. 143.
81. Linkman, p. 137.
82. Certain exceptions to the convention of humility and sexual naïveté demonstrate the artifice of the pose and expression. In John Phillip's *Gypsy Sisters of Seville* (1854), for example, the two (non-British) women direct seductive gazes at the viewer while they stand extremely close together, the fronts of their bodies conceivably touching while their arms and clothing enwrap them. Michael Cohen offers an astute reading of Sir John Everett Millais's *Hearts Are Trump* (1872), a painting of three card-playing sisters in which one gazes at, and exposes her hand to, the viewer (who is the

implied fourth in the card game) while another eyes the more active sister with a look suggesting an understanding of the romantic/erotic play (Michael Cohen, *Sisters: Relation and Rescue in Nineteenth-Century British Novels and Paintings* [Madison, NJ: Farleigh Dickinson University Press, 1995], pp. 30–1).

83. Woolf, *Orlando*, p. 171.
84. Ibid., p. 219.
85. Ibid., p. 220.
86. Ibid., p. 238.
87. Ibid., p. 288.
88. Maria Pramaggiore, 'Extracts from *Epistemologies of the Fence*', *Bisexuality: A Critical Reader*, ed. Merl Storr (London: Routledge, 1999), p. 146.
89. Ibid., p. 147.

5   Where the Boys Are

1. Patricia White, *Uninvited: Classical Hollywood Cinema and Lesbian Representability* (Bloomington, IN: Indiana University Press, 1999), p. xxii.
2. Peter Books, *The Melodramatic Imagination: Balzac, Henry James, and the Mode of Excess* (New York: Columbia University Press, 1985); Simon Shepherd, 'Pauses of Mutual Agitation', *Melodrama: Stage Picture Screen*, eds Jacky Bratton, Jim Cook and Christine Gledhill (London: British Film Institute, 1994), pp. 25–37.
3. M. Meisel, 'Scattered Chiaroscuro: Melodrama as a Matter of Seeing', *Melodrama: Stage Picture Screen*, eds Jacky Bratton, Jim Cook and Christine Gladhill (London: British Film Institute, 1994), pp. 65–81: p. 75.
4. Nina Auerbach, *Daphne du Maurier, Haunted Heiress* (Philadelphia: University of Pennsylvania Press, 2000), p. 135.
5. Daphne du Maurier, *Rebecca* (New York: Avon, 1971), p. 57.
6. Daphne du Maurier, *Rebecca*, p. 118. Avril Horner and Sue Zlosnik offer a useful synopsis of the role of writing – and especially the letter 'R' – in the novel in *Daphne du Maurier: Writing, Identity and the Gothic Imagination* (New York: St. Martins, 1998), pp. 109–11.
7. Daphne du Maurier, *Rebecca*, p. 57.
8. Ibid., p. 182.
9. Mary Ann Doane, *The Desire to Desire: The Woman's Film of the 1940s* (Bloomington, IN: Indiana University Press, 1987), p. 125.
10. Ibid., p. 126.
11. Ibid., pp. 125–6.
12. Diana Fuss observes that in lesbian and gay studies there has been a 'preoccupation with the figure of the homosexual as specter and phantom, as spirit and revenant, as abject and undead': 'Introduction', *Inside/Out: Lesbian Theories, Gay Theories* (New York: Routledge, 1991), p. 3. A catalyst for this, Fuss argues, is that the heterosexual and homosexual are each 'haunted by the other, but here again it is the other who comes to stand in metonymically for the very occurrence of haunting and ghostly visitations'. Terry Castles similarly encourages a reading of texts that allows the 'ghosted' lesbian to materialize (*The Apparitional Lesbian:*

Female Homosexuality and Modern Culture [New York: Columbia University Press, 1993]).

13. Ed Cohen, *Talk on the Wilde Side: Toward a Genealogy of a Discourse on Male Sexualities* (New York: Routledge, 1993), p. 13.
14. William Patrick Day, *In the Circles of Fear and Desire: A Study of Gothic Fantasy* (Chicago: University of Chicago Press, 1948), p. 19.
15. Alison Light, *Forever England: Femininity, Literature and Conservatism Between the Wars* (London: Routledge, 1991).
16. Auerbach, p. 69.
17. Daphne du Maurier, *Gerald: A Portrait* (London: Gollancz, 1934), p. 11.
18. Daphne du Maurier, *Young George du Maurier* (London: Peter Davis, 1951), p. ix.
19. Auerbach, p. 53.
20. du Maurier, *Gerald*, p. 22.
21. Ibid., pp. 233–4.
22. Light, p. 166.
23. du Maurier, *Gerald*, p. 26.
24. Ibid., p. 59.
25. Daphne du Maurier, *Myself When Young – The Shaping of a Writer* (London, Gollancz, 1977), p. 66.
26. Horner and Zlosnick, p. 6.
27. Auerbach, p. 73.
28. Ibid., p. 16.
29. Quoted in Margaret Forster, *Daphne du Maurier* (London: Chatto & Windus, 1993), p. 420.
30. Judith Halberstam, *Female Masculinity* (Durham: Duke University Press, 1998), p. 6.
31. du Maurier, *Rebecca*, p. 294.
32. Ibid., p. 295.
33. Quoted in Forster, p. 222.
34. Auerbach, p. 57.
35. Quoted in Forster, p. 221.
36. Quoted in Forster, p. 222.
37. Daphne du Maurier, *The Infernal World of Branwell Brontë* (Harmondsworth, UK: Penguin, 1960), p. 9.
38. Ibid., p. 10.
39. Daphne du Maurier, *The King's General* (London: Arrow Books, 1992), p. 282.
40. Daphne du Maurier, 'Not after Midnight', *Don't Look Now, and Other Stories* (Harmondsworth: Penguin, 1971), p. 56.
41. Ibid., p. 97.
42. Ibid., p. 100.
43. Auerbach, p. 73.
44. du Maurier, *Rebecca*, p. 27.
45. Ibid., p. 104.
46. du Maurier, *Rebecca*, p. 111.
47. Ibid., p. 53. The novel's wording echoes not only du Maurier's own desire to remain a boy but also her grandfather's articulation of a similar model of male–male affection in *Trilby*. In the Victorian novel, the male characters frequently choose to complement the eponymous heroine by voicing

regrets that she was not of a different sex. As the narrator laments, on behalf of the homosocial network of bohemian artists, 'it was a real pity she wasn't a boy, she would have made such a jolly one' (George Du Maurier, *Trilby* [Oxford: Oxford University Press, 1998], p. 13).

48. du Maurier, *Rebecca*, p. 36.
49. Ibid., p. 265.
50. Ibid., p. 65
51. Ibid., p. 65.
52. Ibid., p. 11.
53. Ibid., p. 15.
54. Ibid., p. 15.
55. Ibid., p. 16.
56. Ibid., p. 19.
57. Ibid., p. 25.
58. Ibid., p. 38.
59. Ibid., p. 301.
60. Ibid., pp. 301–2.
61. Quoted in R.J. Berenstein, 'Adaptation, Censorship, and Audiences of Questionable Type: Lesbian Sightings in *Rebecca* (1940) and *The Uninvited* (1944)', *Cinema Journal* 37.3 (Spring 1998), pp. 16–37: p. 18.
62. White, p. 2.
63. Berenstein, 'Adaptation', p. 17.
64. Rhona J. Berenstein, '"I'm not the sort of person men marry": Monsters, Queers, and Hitchcock's *Rebecca*', *Out In Culture: Gay, Lesbian, and Queer Essays on Popular Culture*, eds Corey K. Creekmur and Alexander Doty (Durham, NC: Duke University Press, 1995), pp. 239–61; p. 239.
65. Ibid., p. 239.
66. Pat Califia, *Sex Changes: The Politics of Transgenderism* (San Francisco: Cleis, 1997), p. 2.
67. du Maurier, *Rebecca*, p. 243.
68. Ibid., pp. 243–4.
69. Ibid., p. 243.
70. Ibid., p. 278.
71. Ibid., p. 279.
72. Ibid., p. 138.
73. Ibid., p. 76.
74. Ibid., p. 275.
75. Ibid., p. 51.
76. Ibid., p. 43.
77. Ibid., p. 136.
78. Ibid., p. 66.
79. Ibid., p. 67.
80. Ibid., p. 272.
81. Ibid., p. 96.
82. Ibid., p. 203.
83. Teresa de Lauretis, *Alice Doesn't: Feminism, Semiotics, Cinema* (Bloomington, IN: Indiana University Press, 1984), pp. 153–4.
84. du Maurier, *Rebecca*, pp. 211–12.
85. Doane, p. 166.

6   The Face in the Crowd

1. Florence Jacobowitz, 'The Man's Melodrama: *Woman in the Window* and *Scarlet Street*', *CineAction!* Summer (1988), pp. 64–73; E. Ann Kaplan, ed., *Women in Film Noir* (London: British Film Institute, 1998), which includes her own frequently cited article 'The Place of Women in Fritz Lang's *The Blue Gardenia*'.; Deborah Thomas, 'How Hollywood Deals with the Deviant Male', *The Movie Book of Film Noir*, ed. Ian Cameron (London: Studio Vista, 1992), pp. 59–69.

2. Frank Krutnik, *In a Lonely Street: Film Noir, Genre, Masculinity* (London: Routledge, 1991), p. 33.

3. Michael Walker, '*Film Noir*: Introduction', *The Movie Book of Film Noir*, ed. Ian Cameron (London: Studio Vista, 1992), pp. 8–58: p. 57.

4. Krutnik, p . 25.

5. Walker has argued for *film noir*'s indebtedness to British crime writers such as Arthur Conan Doyle and Agatha Christie, as well as nineteenth-century French novelists such as Emile Zola and Guy de Maupassant (p. 57). While he notes that the trope of 'city as villain' has roots in nineteenth-century melodrama, which was immensely popular in both literature and theater (p. 30), it is also one of the main features differentiating *fin-de-siécle* Gothic literature such as Wilde's *Picture of Dorian Gray* (1891) and Bram Stoker's *Dracula* (1897) from the Gothic of the eighteenth and early-nineteenth century, with its secluded castles. Despite the urban setting, *film noir*'s tall, harshly shadowed buildings with their ominous doors, dark staircases, and curiously under-populated streets, also evoke the aura of isolated Gothic castles and mansions.

6. The opening chapter of Krutnik's *In a Lonely Street*, which articulates some of the difficulties of generic demarcation, also effectively summarizes stylistic consistencies among films included within the category of *film noir*.

7. Marcia Landy, 'Introduction', *Imitations of Life: A Reader on Film and Television Melodrama*, ed. Marcia Landy (Detroit: Wayne State University, 1991), pp. 14–5.

8. Peter Brooks, *The Melodramatic Imagination: Balzac, Henry James, Melodrama, and the Mode of Excess* (New York: Columbia University Press, 1985).

9. Jacky Bratton, 'The Contending Discourses of Melodrama', *Melodrama: Stage Picture Screen*, eds Jacky Bratton, Jim Cook, and Christine Gledhill; London: British Film Institute, 1994), pp. 38–49: p. 38.

10. J. Redding Ware, *Passing English of the Victorian Era: A Dictionary of Heterodox English, Slang and Phrase* (London: George Routledge, 1909).

11. David Bergman, 'Introduction'. *Camp Grounds: Style and Homosexuality* (ed. David Bergman. Amherst: University of Massachusetts Press, 1993), pp. 3–16: pp. 4–5.

12. Cynthia Morrill, 'Revamping the Gay Sensibility: Queer Camp and *dyke noir*', *The Politics and Poetics of Camp*, ed. M. Meyer (London: Routledge, 1994), pp. 110–29; pp. 112–3.

13. Eve Kosofsky Sedgwick, *Epistemology of the Closet* (Berkeley: University of California Press, 1990), p. 156.

14. Jack Babuscio, 'Camp and the Gay Sensibility', *Camp Grounds: Style and Homosexuality*, ed. D. Bergman (Amherst: University of Massachusetts Press, 1993), pp. 19–38: p. 20.

15. Babuscio, p. 20.
16. Ibid., p. 19.
17. Pamela Robertson, *Guilty Pleasures: Feminist Camp from Mae West to Madonna* (Durham, NC: Duke University Press, 1996).
18. In *Guilty Pleasures*, Pamela Robertson argues effectively that one must also be careful in assuming that certain cultural icons are unaware of their role in the camp experience. She critiques elisions of camp and gay men's culture, arguing that 'most people who have written about camp assume that the exchange between gay men's and women's cultures has been wholly one-sided', implying that 'women are camp but do not knowingly produce themselves as camp and, furthermore, do not even have access to a camp sensibility' (p. 5). As Robertson points out, 'camp has an affinity with feminist discussions of gender construction, performance, and enactment' and therefore would suggest that camp icons can be read as critiques that are feminist or queer (pp. 6, 9). Within the context of *noir* texts, Robertson's comments bring forward a form of camp that is not exclusively gay; at the same time, the ambiguities of intentionality result in such a vague notion of camp that some may argue that it is not camp at all but a broader concept moving toward gallows humor.
19. Ibid., p. 42.
20. Vera Caspary, *Laura* (New York: ibooks, 2000), p. 36.
21. Ibid., p. 201.
22. Ibid., p. 193.
23. Ibid., p. 19.
24. Ibid., p. 8.
25. Eve Kosofsky Sedgwick, *Between Men: English Literature and Male Homosocial Desire* (New York: Columbia University Press, 1985).
26. Caspary, p. 194.
27. Ibid., p. 199.
28. Ibid., p. 17.
29. Ibid., p. 43.
30. Ibid., p. 6.
31. Ibid., p. 32.
32. 'Laura', *Laura*, by Vera Caspary (New York: ibooks, 2000), pp. 235–6: p. 236.
33. Caspary, p. 58.
34. Ibid., p. 23.
35. Ibid., p. 141.
36. Common character types in *noir* texts include masculine women and feminine men, raising additional camp concerns usually discussed within the context of male cross-dressing. In her discussion of men's impersonations of women, Kate Davy argues that 'male drag emphasizes the illusionistic qualities of impersonation in that the actor attempts to simulate that which he is not, the "other." Instead of foregrounding dominant culture's fiercely polarized gender roles, men's Camp tends to reinscribe, rather than undermine, the dominant culture paradigms it appropriates for its parody' (Kate Davy, 'Fe/male Impersonation: The Discourse of Camp', *The Politics and Poetics of Camp* [ed. Moe Meyer, London: Routledge, 1994], pp. 130–48: p. 138). For Davy, male drag emphasizes the difference between men and women. The apparent unnaturalness of a man dressed as a woman does

little more than highlight the impossibility of accepting as normal anything other than manly men and womanly women. Notably, this very argument also appears to reaffirm the binary model that Davy sees in drag because it assumes that the male performers self-identify as men. As Marjorie Garber has argued in *Vested Interests*, using a bipolar model for articulating non-heteronormative sexualities condemns such alternatives to secondary status and disallows their self-articulation. Cross-dressers need not define themselves as men or women at all, or they may define themselves sometimes as one and sometimes as another (Marjorie Garber, *Vested Interested: Cross-Dressing and Cultural Anxiety* [New York: Routledge, 1992]).

37. Walker indirectly suggests the centrality of female masculinity to the *femme fatale* of *film noir* when he associates the persona with the villain of nine-teenth-century melodrama (p. 12). The aggressive female was a popular character in Victorian literature, versions of which can be found in sensa-tion novels such as Mary Braddon's *Lady Audley's Secret* (which was quickly adapted to the stage), Gothic works such as Stoker's *Dracula*, and decadent writing such as Wilde's play *Salome* and the French author Rachilde's *Juggler* (1900). In works of the Gothic, sensational, and decadent, the *femme fatale* leads seemingly admirable male specimens to debase themselves or even to commit crimes such as murder. It is primarily James M. Cain – the author of the novels *The Postman Always Rings Twice*, *Mildred Pierce*, and *Double Indemnity* – who made the *femme fatale* a common personification of the criminal world.

Epilogue

1. Vera Caspary, *Laura* (New York: ibooks, 2000), p. 74.
2. Ibid., p. 140.
3. Historians of photography have been aware that Niepce senior had taken the earliest photographs, but the previous dating of these pieces was around 1826 to 1827. Based on the accompanying letter, the photograph of the drawing of the boy and horse has been dated a year earlier. Despite these early successes in heliography, Niepce's process was both extremely cumber-some and faulty. It took about eight hours of exposure, for example, to capture one, blurry image. The inventor had tried to promote heliography through the Royal Society in England but, in accord with their standard pro-cedure, the institution refused to endorse the discovery because Niepce would not fully disclose its processes. It was soon after, in 1829, that the inventor teamed up with the more famous Louis Daguerre. To Niepce's innovation, Daguerre added the discoveries that the use of heated mercury fumes brought out the latent image, as well as that the use of hot saline bath more readily made the image permanent. This revised process – one that could be much more easily commodified among the broader population – was established in 1837 and is seen as the direct precursor of the modern photograph.
4. Vernon Lee, 'The Sense of the Past', *A Vernon Lee Anthology: Selections from the Earlier Works* (London: J. Lane, 1929), pp. 166–74: p. 168.

5. Geraldine Jewsbury, *The Half Sisters* (Oxford: Oxford University Press, 1994), pp. 216–17.
6. Jonathan Crary, *Suspension of Perception: Attention, Spectacle, and Modern Culture* (Cambridge, MA: MIT Press, 1999), p. 3.
7. Caspary, p. 202.
8. Oscar Wilde, *The Complete Works of Oscar Wilde* (New York: Harper & Row, 1989), p. 117.

References

Adams, James Eli, *Dandies and Desert Saints: Styles of Victorian Masculinity* (Ithaca: Cornell University Press, 1995).

Aleksiuk, Natasha, ' "A Thousand Angles": Photographic Irony in the Work of Julia Margaret Cameron and Virginia Woolf', *Mosaic*, 33.2 (June 2000), 125–42.

Andres, Sophia, 'Pre-Raphaelite Painting and Jungian Images in Wilkie Collins's *The Woman in White*', *Victorian Newsletter*, 88 (Fall 1995), 26–31.

Armstrong, Nancy, *Fiction in the Art of Photography: The Legacy of British Realism* (Cambridge: Harvard University Press, 1999).

'Artful', *Punch* (18 Jan. 1862), 21.

Auerbach, Nina, *Daphne du Maurier, Haunted Heiress* (Philadelphia: University of Pennsylvania Press, 2000).

Babuscio, Jack, 'Camp and the Gay Sensibility', *Camp Grounds: Style and Homosexuality*, ed. David Bergman (Amherst: University of Massachusetts Press, 1993), 19–38.

Batchen, Geoffrey, *Burning with Desire: The Conception of Photography* (Cambridge, MA: MIT Press, 1997).

Bell, David, *An Introduction to Cybercultures* (London: Routledge, 2001).

Benjamin, Walter, 'The Work of Art in the Age of Mechanical Reproduction', *Illuminations*, trans. Harry Zohn (London: Jonathan Cape, 1970).

Berenstein, Rhona J., ' "I'm not the sort of person men marry": Monsters, Queers, and Hitchcock's *Rebecca*', *Out In Culture: Gay, Lesbian, and Queer Essays on Popular Culture*, eds Corey K. Creekmur and Alexander Doty (Durham, NC: Duke University Press, 1995), 239–61.

Berenstein, Rhona J., 'Adaptation, Censorship, and Audiences of Questionable Type: Lesbian Sightings in *Rebecca* (1940) and *The Uninvited* (1944)', *Cinema Journal*, 37.3 (Spring 1998), 16–37.

Bergman, David, 'Introduction', *Camp Grounds: Style and Homosexuality*, ed. David Bergman (Amherst: University of Massachusetts Press, 1993), 3–16.

Bernheimer, Charles, 'Unknowing Decadence', *Perennial Decay: On the Aesthetics and Politics of Decadence*, eds Liz Constable, Matt Potolsky, and Dennis Denisoff (Philadelphia: University of Pennsylvania Press, 1999), 50–64.

Boone, Joseph Allen, 'Vacation Cruises; or, The Homoerotics of Orientalism', *PMLA*, 110.1 (1995), 89–107.

Borzello, Frances, *Civilising Caliban: The Misuse of Art 1875–1980* (London: Routledge, 1987).

Botting, Fred, *Gothic* (London: Routledge, 1996).

Bourdieu, Pierre, *Distinction: A Social Critique of the Judgement of Taste* (Cambridge: Harvard University Press, 1984).

Bourdieu, Pierre, *The Rules of Art: Genesis and Structure of the Literary Field*, trans. Susan Emanuel (Stanford: Stanford University Press, 1996).

Braddon, Mary Elizabeth, *Lady Audley's Secret* (Oxford: Oxford University Press, 1998).

Brantlinger, Patrick, 'What is Sensational about the Sensational?' *Nineteenth Century Fiction*, 37 (1982), 1–28.

Bratton, Jacky, 'The Contending Discourse of Melodrama', *Melodrama: Stage Picture Screen*, eds Jacky Bratton, Jim Cook and Christine Gledhill (London: British Film Institute, 1993), 307–20.

Brilliant, Richard, *Portraiture* (London: Reaktion Books, 1991).

Bristow, Joseph, *Effeminate England: Homoerotic Writing after 1885* (Buckingham: Open University Press, 1995).

Brooks, Peter, *The Melodramatic Imagination: Balzac, Henry James and the Mode of Excess* (New York: Colombia University Press, 1985).

Brooks, Peter, *Body Work: Objects of Desire in Modern Narrative* (Cambridge, MA: Harvard University Press, 1993).

Brontë, Anne, *The Tenant of Wildfell Hall* (Oxford: Oxford University Press, 1992).

Bryson, Norman, 'The Gaze in the Expanded Field', *Vision and Visuality*, ed. Hal Foster (Seattle: Bay View, 1988), 91–4.

Buck-Morss, Susan, *The Dialectics of Seeing: Walter Benjamin and the Arcades Project* (Cambridge, Mass: MIT Press, 1989).

Butler, Judith, *Gender Trouble: Feminism and the Subversion of Identity* (New York: Routledge, 1990).

Butler, Judith, *Bodies That Matter* (New York: Routledge, 1993).

Butler, Judith, 'Imitation and Gender Insubordination', *The Lesbian and Gay Studies Reader*, eds Henry Abelove, Michèle Aina Barale and David M. Halperin (New York: Routledge, 1993), pp. 307–20.

Califia, Pat, *Sex Changes: The Politics of Transgenderism* (San Francisco: Cleis, 1997).

Carpenter, Mary, 'On the Treatment of Female Convicts', LXVII.CCCXCVII (Jan. 1863), 3–46.

Caspary, Vera, *Laura* (New York: ibooks, 2000).

Castle, Terry, *The Apparitional Lesbian: Female Homosexuality and Modern Culture* (New York: Columbia University Press, 1993).

Cavallaro, Dani, *Cyberpunk and Cyberculture: Science Fiction and the Work of William Gibson* (London: The Athlone Press, 2000).

Chadwick, Whitney, *Women, Art, and Society* (London: Thames and Hudson, 1990).

Cherry, Deborah, *Painting Women: Victorian Women Artists* (London: Routledge, 1993).

Christ, Carol T., and John O. Jordan, eds, *Victorian Literature and the Victorian Visual Imagination* (Berkeley: University of California Press, 1995).

Clarke, Norma, *Ambitious Heights: Writing, Friendship, Love – The Jewsbury Sisters, Felicia Hemans, and Jane Welsh Carlyle* (London: Routledge, 1990).

Codell, Julie F., 'The Public Image of the Victorian Artist: Family Biographies', *The Journal of Pre-Raphaelite Studies*, 4 (Fall 1996), 5–34.

Cohen, Ed, *Talk on the Wilde Side: Toward a Genealogy of a Discourse on Male Sexualities* (New York: Routledge, 1993).

Cohen, Michael, *Sisters: Relation and Rescue in Nineteenth-Century British Novels and Paintings* (Madison, NJ: Farleigh Dickinson University Press, 1995).

Colby, Vineta, *Vernon Lee: A Literary Biography* (Charlottesville: University of Virginia Press, 2003).

Colker, R, *Hybrid: Bisexuals, Multiracials, and Other Misfits Under American Law* (New York: New York University Press, 1996).

Collins, Wilkie, *Memoirs of the Life of William Collins, Esq. R.A.* (London: Longman, Brown, Green and Longman, 1848).

Collins, Wilkie, *The Law and the Lady* (New York: Harpers, 1873).

Collins, Wilkie, *The Woman in White* (London: Collins, 1952).

Collins, Wilkie, *A Rogue's Life: From His Birth to His Marriage* (New York: AMS, 1970).

Collins, Wilkie, *Hide and Seek* (Oxford: Oxford University Press, 1993).

Collins, Wilkie, 'A Terribly Strange Bed', *Mad Monkton and Other Tales*, ed. Norman Page (Oxford: Oxford University Press, 1994), 1–20.

Cooke, Simone, ' "Mistaken for a PRB": Wilkie Collins and the Pre-Raphaelites,' *The New Collins Society Newsletter*, 3.1 (Winter 2000), 1–6.

Cooper, Emmanuel, *The Sexual Perspective: Homosexuality and Art in the Last 100 Years in the West* (London: Routledge, 1994).

Cowling, Mary, *The Artist as Anthropologist: The Representation of Type and Character in Victorian Art* (Cambridge: Cambridge University Press, 1989).

Craik, Dinah Mulock, *A Woman's Thoughts about Women* (London: Hurst and Blackett, 1858).

Craik, Dinah Mulock, *About Money and Other Things* (New York, 1887).

Craik, Dinah Mulock, *Olive* (Oxford: Oxford University Press, 1999).

Crary, Jonathan, *Techniques of the Observer: On Vision and Modernity in the Nineteenth Century* (Cambridge, MA: MIT Press, 1990).

Crary, Jonathan, *Suspension of Perception: Attention, Spectacle, and Modern Culture* (Cambridge, MA: MIT Press, 1999).

Darrah, William C., *Cartes de Viste in Nineteenth Century Photography* (Gettysburg, PA: Darrah-Smith Books, 1991).

Davis, Nuel Pharr, *The Life of Wilkie Collins* (Urbana, IL: University of Illinois Press, 1956).

Davy, Kate, 'Fe/male Impersonation: The Discourse of Camp', *The Politics and Poetics of Camp*, ed. Moe Meyer (London: Routledge, 1994), 130–48.

Day, William Patrick, *In the Circles of Fear and Desire: A Study of Gothic Fantasy* (Chicago: University of Chicago Press, 1948).

de Lauretis, Teresa, *Alice Doesn't: Feminism, Semiotics, Cinema* (Bloomington, IN: Indiana University Press, 1984).

Denisoff, Dennis, *Aestheticism and Sexual Parody: 1840–1940* (Cambridge: Cambridge University Press, 2001).

Dickens, Charles, 'Old Lamps for New Ones', *Household Words* (June 1850), 107–9.

Doane, Mary Ann, *The Desire to Desire: The Woman's Film of the 1940s* (Bloomington, IN: Indiana University Press, 1987).

du Maurier, Daphne, *Gerald: A Portrait* (London: Gollancz, 1934).

du Maurier, Daphne, *September Tide* (London: Victor Gollancz, 1949).

du Maurier, Daphne, *Young George du Maurier* (London: Peter Davis, 1951).

du Maurier, Daphne, *The Infernal World of Branwell Brontë* (Harmondsworth, UK: Penguin, 1960).

du Maurier, Daphne, 'Not after Midnight', *Don't Look Now, and Other Stories* (Harmondsworth: Penguin, 1971).

du Maurier, Daphne, *Rebecca* (New York: Avon, 1971).

du Maurier, Daphne, *Myself When Young – The Shaping of a Writer* (London, Gollancz, 1977).

du Maurier, Daphne, *The King's General* (London: Arrow Books, 1992).

Du Maurier, George, 'Female School of Art – (*Useful Occupation for Idle and Ornamental Young Men*)', *Punch* (30 May 1874), 232.

Du Maurier, George, *Trilby* (Oxford: Oxford University, 1998).

Ellet, Elizabeth, *Artists in All Ages and Countries* (New York, 1859).

Ellis, Havelock, *Studies in the Psychology of Sex*, vol. 1 (London: University Press, 1897).

Ellmann, Mary, *Thinking About Women* (London: Virago, 1979).

Ellmann, Richard, *Oscar Wilde* (London: Penguin, 1988).

Faderman, Lillian, *Surpassing the Love of Men: Romantic Friendship and Love Between Women from the Renaissance to the Present* (Oxford: William Morrow, 1981).

'Female School of Art', *Illustrated London News* (London, 1868).

Flint, Kate, *The Victorians and the Visual Imagination* (Cambridge: Cambridge University Press, 2000).

Forster, Margaret, *Daphne du Maurier* (London: Chatto & Windus, 1993).

Foucault, Michel, *Discipline and Punish: The Birth of the Prison*, trans. Alan Sheridan (London: Allen Lee, 1977).

Foucault, Michel, *The History of Sexuality*, vol. 1, Trans. Robert Hurley. (New York: Vintage, 1980).

Friedman, Joan, 'Every Lady Her Own Drawing Master', *Apollo* 105 (Apr. 1977), 262–7.

Fuss, Diana, 'Introduction', *Inside/Out: Lesbian Theories, Gay Theories* (New York: Routledge, 1991).

Gadamer, Hans-George, *Truth and Method*, trans. G. Barden and J. Cumming (New York: Crossroads, 1989).

Garber, Marjorie, *Vested Interested: Cross-Dressing and Cultural Anxiety* (New York: Routledge, 1992).

Garber, Marjorie, *Bisexuality and the Eroticism of Everyday Life* (New York: Routledge, 2000).

Gernsheim, Helmut, *Julia Margaret Cameron: Her Life and Photographic Work* (New York: Aperture, 1975).

Gilbert, Pamela K., *Disease, Desire, and the Body in Victorian Women's Popular Novels* (Cambridge: Cambridge University Press, 1997).

Gilbert, W.S. and Arthur Sullivan, *Patience; or, Bunthorne's Bride, The Complete Plays of Gilbert and Sullivan* (New York: Modern Library, 1936), 184–233.

Gillespie, Diane, *The Sisters' Arts: The Writing and Painting of Virginia Woolf and Vanessa Bell* (Syracuse: Syracuse University Press, 1988).

Gillet, Paula, *Worlds of Art: Painters in Victorian Society* (New Brunswick, NJ: Rutgers University Press, 1990).

Green-Lewis, Jennifer, *Framing the Victorians: Photography and the Culture of Realism* (Ithaca: Cornell University Press, 1996).

Gunn, Peter, *Vernon Lee/Violet Paget, 1856–1935* (London: Oxford University Press, 1964).

Halberstam, Judith, *Skin Shows: Gothic Horror and the Technology of Monsters* (Durham: Duke University Press, 1995).

Halberstam, Judith, *Female Masculinity* (Durham: Duke University Press, 1998).

Hallam, Arthur Henry, 'On Some of the Characteristics of Modern Poetry, and on the Lyrical Poems of Alfred Tennyson', *Englishman's Magazine* 1 (Aug. 1831), 616–28

Hamilton, Lisa, 'Oscar Wilde, New Women, and the Rhetoric of Effeminacy', *Wilde Writings: Contextual Conditions*, ed. Joseph Bristow (Toronto: University of Toronto Press, 2003), 230–53.

Hays, Mary, *Victim of Prejudice* (Peterborough: Broadview, 1998).

Heidegger, Martin, 'The Age of the World Picture', *The Question Concerning Technology and Other Essays*, trans. William Lovitt (New York: Garland, 1977).

Heller, Tamar, *Dead Secrets: Wilkie Collins and the Female Gothic* (New Haven, CN: Yale University Press, 1992).

Hitchcock, Alfred, *Rebecca*, 1940.

Holroyd, Michael, *Lytton Strachey: The Unknown Years* (London: Heinemann, 1971).

Homans, Margaret, ' "To the Queen's Private Apartments": Royal Family Portraiture and the Construction of Victoria's Sovereign Obedience', *Victorian Studies*, 37.1 (1993), 1–41.

Horner, Avril, and Sue Zlosnick, *Daphne du Maurier: Writing, Identity and the Gothic Imagination* (New York: St. Martins, 1998).

Hughes, Winifred, *The Maniac in the Cellar: Sensation Novels in the 1860s* (Princeton: Princeton University Press, 1980).

Huysmans, Joris-Karl, *Against Nature* (London: Penguin, 1959).

Hyde, H. Montgomery, *The Trials of Oscar Wilde* (London: William Hodge, 1948).

Jacobowitz, Florence, 'The Man's Melodrama: *Woman in the Window* and *Scarlet Street*', *CineAction!* (Summer 1988), 64–73.

Jewsbury, Geraldine, 'How Agnes Worral Was Taught to Be Respectable', *Douglas Jerrold's Shilling Magazine* 5 (1847), 16–24, 246–66.

Jewsbury, Geraldine, Untitled Review, *Athenaeum* 17 (1867), 720.

Jewsbury, Geraldine, *Selection from the Letters of Geraldine Endsor Jewsbury to Jane Welsh Carlyle*, ed. Annie E. Ireland (London: Longmans, Green, 1892).

Jewsbury, Geraldine, *The Half Sisters* (Oxford: Oxford University Press, 1994).

Kaplan, Cora, 'Introduction', *Olive* by Dinah Mulock Craik (Oxford: Oxford University Press, 1999).

Kaplan, E. Ann, ed., *Women in Film Noir* (London: British Film Institute, 1998).

Kaufman, Moisés, *Gross Indecency: The Three Trials of Oscar Wilde*, Dir. Moisés Kaufman (Minetta Lane Theatre, New York, 27 Sept. 1997).

Kestner, Joseph A., *Masculinities in Victorian Painting* (Aldershot, UK: Scolar, 1995).

Knopp, Sherron E., ' "If I Saw You Would You Kiss Me?": Sapphism and the Subversiveness of Virginia Woolf's Orlando', *PMLA* 103.1 (1988), 24–34.

Kromm, Jane, 'Visual Culture and Scopic Custom in *Jane Eyre* and *Villete*', *Victorian Literature and Culture*, 26.2 (1998), 369–94.

Krutnik, Frank, *In a Lonely Street: Film Noir, Genre, Masculinity* (London: Routledge, 1991).

Landy, Marcia, 'Introduction', *Imitations of Life: A Reader on Film and Television Melodrama*, ed. Marcia Landy (Detroit: Wayne State University, 1991).

Lang, Fritz, *The Woman in the Window*, 1944.

Lang, Fritz, *Scarlet Street*, 1945.

Lang Fritz, *Blue Gardenia*, 1953.

Langland, Elizabeth, 'The Voicing of Feminine Desire in Anne Brontë's *The Tenant of Wildfell Hall*', *Gender and Discourse in Victorian Literature and Art*, eds Antony H. Harrison and Beverly Taylor (DeKalb, IL: Northern Illinois University Press, 1992), 111–23.

'Laura', *Laura*, Vera Caspary (New York: ibooks, 2000), 235–6.

Lee, Vernon, 'The Blame of Portraits', *Hortus Vitae: Essays on the Gardening of Life* (London: John Lane, 1904), 139–47.

Lee, Vernon, 'Oke of Okehurst', *Hauntings: Fantastic Stories* (London: John Lane, 1906), 109–91.

Lee, Vernon, *The Beautiful: An Introduction to Psychological Aesthetics* (Cambridge: Cambridge University Press, 1913).

Lee, Vernon, 'Winthrop's Adventure', *For Maurice: Five Unlikely Stories* (London: John Lane, 1927), 143–205.

Lee, Vernon, 'The Sense of the Past', *A Vernon Lee Anthology: Selections from the Earlier Works*, ed. Irene Cooper Willis (London: J. Lane, 1929), 166–74.

Le Fanu, Sheridan, 'Green Tea', *All the Year Round*, nos 47–50 (23 Oct.–13 Nov. 1869), 501–4, 525–8, 548–52; 572–6.

Lewin, Albert, *The Picture of Dorian Gray*, 1945.

Light, Alison, *Forever England: Femininity, Literature and Conservatism Between the Wars* (London: Routledge, 1991).

Linkman, Audrey, *The Victorians: Photographic Portraits* (London: Tauris Parke Books, 1993).

Lombroso, Cesare, and William Ferrero, *The Female Offender* (New York: Philosophical Library, 1958).

Macleod, Dianne Sachko, *Art and the Victorian Middle Class: Money and the Making of Cultural Identity* (Cambridge: Cambridge University Press, 1996).

Maxwell, Catherine, 'From Dionysus to "Dionea": Vernon Lee's Portraits', *Word & Image*, 13.3 (July–Sept. 1997), 253–69.

Mayne, Arthur, *British Profile Miniaturists* (London: Faber and Faber, 1970).

McConkey, Kenneth, *Edwardian Portraits: Images of an Age of Opulence* (Woodbridge, Suffolk: Antique Collectors Club, 1987).

McConkey, Kenneth, ' "Well-bred Contortions": 1880–1918', *The British Portrait 1660–1960*, ed. Roy Strong (Woodbridge, Suffolk: Antique Collectors' Club: 1991), 353–86.

McPherson, Heather, *Fin-de-Siècle Faces: Portraiture in the Age of Proust* (Birmingham: University of Alabama Press, 1988).

Meisel, Martin, 'Scattered Chiaroscuro: Melodrama as a Matter of Seeing', *Melodrama: Stage Picture Screen*, eds Jacky Bratton, Jim Cook and Christine Gledhill (London: British Film Institute, 1994), p. 65–81.

Mermin, Dorothy, *Godiva's Ride: Women of Letters in England, 1830–1880* (Bloomington: Indiana University Press, 1993).

Merrill, Linda, *A Pot of Paint: Aesthetics on Trial in Whistler vs. Ruskin* (Washington: Smithsonian Institution, 1992).

Merrill, Lisa, *When Romeo Was a Woman: Charlotte Cushman and Her Circle of Female Spectators* (Ann Arbor: University of Michigan Press, 2000).

Miller, D.A., *The Novel and the Police* (Berkeley: University of California Press, 1988).

Mirzoeff, Nicholas, *Bodyscape: Art, Modernity and the Ideal Figure* (London: Routledge, 1995).

Mirzoeff, Nicholas, 'What is Visual Culture', *An Introduction to Visual Culture* (London: Routledge, 1999), 3–13.

Mitchell, Sally, *Dinah Mulock Craik* (Boston: G.K. Hall, 1983).

Mitchell, W.J.T., *Picture Theory* (Chicago: University of Chicago, 1994).

Moore, Kevin Z., 'Viewing the Victorians: Recent Research on Victorian Visuality', *Victorian Literature and Culture*, 25.2 (1997), 367–85.

Moore, Lisa L., *Dangerous Intimacies: Toward a Sapphic History of the British Novel* (Durham, NC: Duke University Press, 1997).

Morrill, Cynthia, 'Revamping the Gay Sensibility: Queer Camp and *dyke noir*', *The Politics and Poetics of Camp*, ed. Moe Meyer (London: Routledge, 1994), 110–29.

Morris, William, *Art and Society: Lectures and Essays by William Morris*, ed. Gary Zabe (Boston: George's Hill, 1993).

Mulvey, Laura, 'Visual Pleasure and Narrative Cinema', *Visual and Other Pleasures* (Bloomington, IN: Indiana University Press, 1989), 14–26.

Nadel, Ira, 'Portraits of the Queen', *Victorian Poetry*, 25. 3–4 (1987), 169–91.

Nadel, Ira, 'Wilkie Collins and His Illustrators', *Wilkie Collins To the Forefront: Some Reassessments*, eds Nelson Smith and R.C. Terry (New York: AMS, 1995).

Nayder, Lillian, *Wilkie Collins* (New York: Twayne, 1997).

Nead, Lynda, *Victorian Babylon: People, Street and Images in Nineteenth-Century London* (New Haven: Yale University Press, 2000), p. 16.

Newall, Christopher, 'The Victorians: 1830–1880', *The British Portrait 1660–1960*, ed. Roy Strong (Woodbridge, Suffolk: Antique Collectors' Club: 1991), 299–351.

Nordau, Max, *On Art and Artists*, trans. W.F. Harvey (London: T. Fisher Unwin, 1907).

Nordau, Max, *Degeneration* (Lincoln: University of Nebraska Press, 1993).

Nunn, Pamela Gerrish, *Victorian Women Artists* (London: Women's, 1987).

Nunokawa, Jeff, *Tame Passions of Wilde: The Styles of Manageable Desire* (Princeton: Princeton University Press, 2003).

Parker, Roszika and Griselda Pollock, *Old Mistresses* (London: Routledge, 1981).

Parkes, Adam, 'Lesbianism, History, and Censorship: *The Well of Loneliness* and the SUPPRESSED RANDINESS of Virginia Woolf's *Orlando*', *Twentieth Century Literature*, 40.4 (1994), 434–60.

Pick, Daniel, *Faces of Degeneration: A European Disorder, c. 1848–c.1918* (Cambridge: Cambridge University Press, 1989).

Potter, Sally, *Orlando*, 1993.

Powell, Kerry, 'Tom, Dick and Dorian Gray: Magic-Picture Mania in Late Victorian Fiction', *Philological Quarterly*, 62.2 (1983), 147–70.

Pramaggiore, Maria, 'Extracts from *Epistemologies of the Fence*', *Bisexuality: A Critical Reader*, ed. Merl Storr (London: Routledge, 1999).

Preminger, Otto, *Laura*, 1944.

Queensberry, John Sholto Douglas, 8th Marquess of, *The Spirit of the Matterhorn* (London: Watts, 1880).

Queensberry, John Sholto Douglas, 8th Marquess of, *Marriage and the Relation of the Sexes: An Address to Women* (London: Watts, 1893).

Queensberry, John Sholto Douglas, 8th Marquess of, 'The Religion of Secularism and the Perfectibility of Man', *Secular Review* (London. Watts, 188?), 3–16.

Redding Ware, J., *Passing English of the Victorian Era: A Dictionary of Heterodox English, Slang and Phrase* (London: George Routledge, 1909).

Roberts, Brian, *The Mad Bad Line: The Family of Lord Alfred Douglas* (London: Hamish Hamilton, 1981).

Robertson, Pamela, *Guilty Pleasures: Feminist Camp from Mae West to Madonna* (Durham, NC: Duke University Press, 1996).

Roper, Michael, and John Tosh, 'Introduction', *Manful Assertions: Masculinities in Britain since 1800*, eds Michael Roper and John Tosh (London: Routledge, 1991).

'Royal Academy: Portraiture', *Victorian Painting: Essays and Reviews*, ed. John Charles Olmsted, vol. 2 (New York, Garland, 1983), 14–18.

Ruskin, John, *The Eagle's Nest, Works*, v. XXII (London, 1872).

Ruskin, John, *Academy Notes*. 1875.

Ruskin, John, *Modern Painters*, vol. 1 (London: George Allen, 1900).

Ruskin, John, 'Modern Manufacture and Design', *1859. The Two Paths* (London: Cassell, 1907) , pp. 73–100.

Sachko Macleod, Dianne, *Art and the Victorian Middle Class: Money and the Making of Cultural Identity* (Cambridge: Cambridge University Press, 1996).

Schaffer, Talia, 'Posing *Orlando*', *Genders: Sexual Artifice, Images, Politics*, eds Ann Kibbey, Kayann Short, and Abauli Formanfarmaian (New York: New York University Press, 1994), 26–63.

Sedgwick, Eve Kosofsky, *Epistemology of the Closet* (Berkeley: University of California Press, 1990).

Sedgwick, Eve Kosofsky, *Between Men: English Literature and Male Homosocial Desire* (New York: Columbia University Press, 1985).

Sedgwick, Eve Kosofsky, *Tendencies* (Durham, NC: Duke University Press, 1993).

Senelick, Lawrence, 'Melodramatic Gesture in Carte-de-Visite Photographs', *Theatre* (Spring 1987), 5–13.

Sha, Richard C., *The Visual and Verbal Sketch in British Romanticism* (Philadelphia: University of Pennsylvania Press, 1998).

Sheperd, Simon, 'Pauses of Mutual Agitation', *Melodrama: Stage Picture Screen*, eds Jacky Bratton, Jim Cook and Christine Gladhill (London: British Film Institute, 1994).

Shohat, Ella, and Robert Stam, 'Narrativizing Visual Culture', *Visual Culture Reader*, ed. Nicholas Mirzeoff (London: Routledge, 1998), 27–49.

Showalter, Elaine, 'Desperate Remedies: Sensation Novels of the 1860s', *The Victorian Newsletter*, 49 (Spring 1976), 1–5.

Smiles, Samuel, *Self-Help; with Illustrations of Character, Conduct and Perseverence* (London: John Murray, 1958).

Spackman, Barbara, 'Interversions', *Perennial Decay: On the Aesthetics and Politics of Decadence*, eds Liz Constable, Dennis Denisoff, and Matthew Potolsky (Philadelphia: University of Pennsylvania Press, 1999), 35–49.

Stewart, Garrett, 'Reading Figures: The Legible Image of Victorian Textuality', *Victorian Literature and the Victorian Visual Imagination*, eds Carol T. Christ and John O. Jordans (Berkeley: University of California Press, 1995), 345–67.

Storr, Merl, 'Editor's Introduction', *Bisexuality: A Critical Reader* (London: Routledge, 1999).

Tagg, John, *The Burden of Representation: Essays on Photographies and Histories* (Amherst: University of Massachusetts Press, 1988).

Thomas, Deborah, 'How Hollywood Deals with the Deviant Male', *The Movie Book of Film Noir*, ed. Ian Cameron (London: Studio Vista, 1992), 59–69.

Untitled, *Daily Telegraph* (6 April 1958), 5.

Untitled, *Punch* (29 June 1861) 262.

Vaughan, Robert, *The Age of Great Cities: or Modern Society Viewed in Its Relation to Intelligence, Morals and Religion* (Shannon: Irish University Press, 1971).

Walker, John A., and Sarah Chaplin, *Visual Culture: An Introduction* (Manchester: Manchester University Press, 1997).

Walker, Michael, '*Film Noir*: Introduction', *The Movie Book of Film Noir*, ed. Ian Cameron. (London: Studio Vista, 1992), 8–58.

Walpole, Horace, *The Castle of Otranto* (Oxford: Oxford University, 1998).

Waterfield, Giles, ed., *Palaces of Art: Art Galleries in Britain, 1790–1990* (London: Dulwich Picture Gallery and the National Gallery of Scotland, 1991).

Whistler, James Abbot McNeill, *The Gentle Art of Making Enemies* (London: W. Heinemann, 1890).

White, Patricia, *Uninvited: Classical Hollywood Cinema and Lesbian Representability* (Bloomington, IN: Indiana University Press, 1999).

Wilde, Oscar, *The Complete Works of Oscar Wilde* (New York: Harper & Row, 1989).

Wilson, J.J., 'Why is Orlando Difficult?' *New Feminist Essays on Virginia Woolf*, ed. Jane Marcus (Lincoln: University of Nebraska Press, 1981), 170–84.

Woolf, Virginia, *Orlando: A Biography* (London: Hogarth, 1928).

Woolf, Virginia, 'The Art of Biography', *Collected Essays of Virginia Woolf IV*, ed. Leonard Woolf (London: Hogarth, 1967), 221–8.

Woolf, Virginia, 'Geraldine and Jane', *Collected Essays*, vol. 4 (London: Hogarth, 1967), 27–39.

Woolf, Virginia, 'The Narrow Bridge of Art', *Collected Essays*, vol. 2 (New York: Harcourt, Brace, 1967).

Woolf, Virginia, *Letters of Virginia Woolf*, vol. 6: 1936–1941, eds Nigel Nicolson and Joanne Trautmann (New York: Harcourt Brace Jovanovich, 1980).

Woolf, Virginia, *Diary of Virginia Woolf*, ed. Anne Oliver Bell, vol. 2: 1920–1924 (New York: Harcourt Brace Jovanovich, 1978).

Woolf, Virginia, *To The Lighthouse* (London: Collins, 1987).

Zorn, Christa, *Vernon Lee: Aesthetics, History, and the Victorian Female Intellectual* (Athens: Ohio University Press, 2003).

Index